PROMISES KEPT

"Even though you do not love me, you kept your promise."

"Um."

"What? Did you answer?"

"Yes."

He sprang to his feet, was looming over her in one long stride. "Yes, you answered? Or yes, you do not love me?"

Estella glared up at him. She was pulled to his heat, tugged by the ferocious energy crackling from his eyes. She saw the black fringes of his lashes, in startling contrast with the burning sapphire irises. And she caught a hint of his scent, like cut grass and salty wind.

A fluid sensation coiled in her belly, radiated between her legs, down to her toes. She placed both hands on her hips.

"Both. Are you satisfied now?"

Other *Leisure* books by Taylor Jones:
RADIANT

The UNTAMED EARL

TAYLOR JONES

LEISURE BOOKS 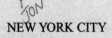 NEW YORK CITY

A LEISURE BOOK®

April 2007

Dorchester Publishing Co., Inc.
200 Madison Avenue
New York, NY 10016

ISBN-10: 0-8439-5845-6
ISBN-13: 978-0-8439-5845-4

Visit us on the web at www.dorchesterpub.com.

The UNTAMED EARL

Prologue

Once a Prankster . . .

Near Brighton, England
August, 1818

For the utmost success in prank-pulling, every possible
kink must be eliminated beforehand. Lying awake at
night, she'd worked out all the sticky details, painstak-
ingly adjusted each step until the prank (her most spec-
tacular to date) promised to tick forward like a well-tuned
clock.

Estella squinted out to the glittering azure sea. Shoving
her straw capote down on her forehead to block the afternoon glare, she peeked around the huge, barnacle-
freckled boulder she was lurking behind.

A long ribbon of pebbly beach curved away, out of
sight. But there was no sign of Godolphin. Nor of her parents, for that matter. A fist of panic gripped her belly, but
she paid no heed.

He would come. He *had* to. Everything depended on
that.

As if taunting her, a seagull shrilled overhead.

Mustering the requisite steely calm, she breathed
deeply of the briny, sluggish wind. The green seaweed

clinging to the base of the rock had an odd stewed-lettuce smell. She wrinkled her nose.

Had the beach been the best place to suggest they meet? Thoughtful, she twisted her lips. In truth, she couldn't picture Godolphin here. His excessively serious manner and inclination to bossiness didn't fit with frothy waves and bathing costumes. He belonged, she decided, at a big desk piled high with papers and oversized, dusty ledgers.

Sighing, she ducked back behind the boulder. Digging her bare toes into the sand, she tried to concentrate on its cool slipperiness, the pink shards of broken shell.

It was no use. Doubt bubbled under her ribs, and a mist of perspiration sprang up on her forehead. Her muslin walking gown suddenly felt itchy and clingy, and the breeze ruffled stray curls into her eyes. Irritated, she swiped them away.

Taking another peek around the boulder, she spied two rounded silhouettes ambling toward her through the haze.

Mama and Papa were right on schedule, but Godolphin should have been here by now.

Nevertheless, she indulged in a satisfied smirk. When her parents saw their estimable Godolphin "Ravishing" their only child (she wasn't exactly sure what this entailed, but, bravely, she was willing to give it a go for the sake of her prank), they'd have an absolute fit.

He'd be caught red-handed and that would be the end of that.

No more aloof, unfathomable Godolphin.

Except—she worried her lower lip between her teeth— he had not yet arrived to play his crucial part.

He wasn't coming. That was it. He'd seen through her plan and was probably chuckling this very second over a glass of brandy. In frustration, she squeezed her eyes shut.

"Waiting for someone?" a low voice the texture of polished mahogany murmured at her shoulder.

"Heavens!" Estella gasped, swinging around. She found

her nose just inches from a row of pewter buttons running down the front of a sturdy chest.

She gulped, then peeked up.

So. He'd come after all.

Godolphin's wide mouth tipped up at the corners. His eyes, an improbable, defiant indigo blue, glimmered like the sea, the pupils contracted to distant pinpoints under the midday sun. The crinkles at their corners tilted down, which made him look sad, even though he smiled. His nose, straight, high bridged, and decidedly patrician, contradicted that sadness with a hint of silent pride. He didn't wear a hat, so the moist wind whipped his long dark hair, teasing it out of the cord at the nape of his sun-browned neck.

For all she knew, she'd been swept out to sea. The radiating blues of his irises made her thirsty. Her gaze was caught on his like a fish on a hook.

The surf seemed to grow louder, each pounding wave vibrating at the base of her skull until there was nothing but that sound. And his eyes.

Without taking a step back, he withdrew a note from inside his jacket. Never taking his eyes from hers, he unfolded it slowly.

With each crackle of the paper, Estella's heart sank lower, her lungs tightening till her ribs ached. The words she had written yesterday morning hummed in her brain: *Let us solidify our acquaintance tomorrow at one o'clock, precisely, by the large rock on the seashore, near the fisherman's—*

"'. . . near the fisherman's hut,'" Godolphin was reading aloud. He used the clear, resonant tone of a bemused barrister. "'I hope, through this rendezvous, to learn the definition of the word Ravishment. Yours, Miss E. Hancock.'"

He folded the note carefully, his expression betraying nothing.

It was all Estella could do not to snatch up her skirts and bolt down the beach.

"Ravishment." He pronounced the word slowly. "Ravishment, with a capital R."

With each savored consonant, Estella understood a bit more the implications of the word. She ripped her eyes away and studied the shoulder seam of his jacket. Perhaps Ravishment did *not* mean, as she had surmised, a simple kiss. Not even with the addition of an embrace. No, there was something else. Something she didn't quite understand, though her body seemed to. Her knees had gone the consistency of jellyfish, the down on her arms stood on end. And something tingled and swooped in her belly as she stared at his firm throat above the white of his cravat.

It *had* to be something she'd eaten.

"Ravishment," he went on, "is not the business of nineteen-year-old debutantes. Or have times changed?"

Estella cocked her chin up a few notches, meeting his eye again. "Am I to believe then, sir, that you have no interest in Ravishing me?"

His eyebrows, straight and black, rose almost imperceptibly. "Whether I have an interest or not is beside the point, Miss Hancock. Your note, and"—his glance flicked down to her bare, sandy toes—"other aspects of your person, have me intrigued. However, I am a gentleman, and as such I am here to escort you back to your parents."

"No." This came out a little too panicked, her voice hoarse and small, carried away by the wind.

Godolphin proffered his arm. "Come," he said, as if trying to coax a pouting child.

Mama and Papa had to be just yards away. At any second they'd round the boulder.

There was no alternative but to initiate the Ravishment herself.

Inexpertly, she threw her arms up around his neck, clasping them tightly behind his head. Standing on her toes, she tilted her head back, pressed her closed lips to his.

What happened next was the first contingency she had not prepared for.

Every nerve trilled to attention, ripped from lassitude by fresh sensations: the grate of his chin against her cheek, the warm solidity of his body, the wild, jarringly intimate newness of his grass-and-leather scent.

And then he clutched her to him with a breath-stealing force, one strong arm wrapped around the circumference of her own slight frame, the other raking long, bare fingers through her tangled curls, leaving her capote dangling at her back by its ribbons.

Even as she felt the pins fall from her hair, she couldn't open her eyes. Her lids were heavy, her feet absurdly light, and she was swept away on a riptide of wonder.

Ravishment, it seemed, *might* be rather nice.

"Oh, goodness me!" a matronly voice squealed.

Godolphin released Estella abruptly. Regaining her footing in the soft sand, dizzy, she turned to face her parents.

"Mama," she panted, breathless. The tip of her tongue slid over her lips. Godolphin's skin had left them salty. "Papa." Why did it feel as though a lunatic grin was affixed to her face? "He—I—"

Then the second contingency she had not anticipated presented itself. Her eyes widened in disbelief. The grin slipped away.

Her parents weren't glaring at Godolphin and rescuing her.

Instead, they stood cozily arm in arm. Beaming.

"I suppose this means she's said yes," Papa boomed, his face flushed magenta with pleasure. He rocked back on his heels. "Knew she would, man, when you asked for her hand yesterday. I saw how she made eyes at you at the Cavendish's musicale." Then he winked—winked!—at Estella.

"I—" she croaked.

The wretched beast had trapped her. She shot Godolphin a sidelong glare. His face was placid, vaguely amused.

Mama clasped her hands in ecstasy. "A wedding!" she cooed, and lunged forward.

Then came the final unforeseen blow. Estella opened her limp arms to receive a comforting embrace. But Mama pushed past her to give *Godolphin* a maternal squeeze.

"Lord Seabrook," Mama gushed, "I can't tell you how overjoyed we will be to have you as our son-in-law."

Chapter One

To Have and to Scold

Castle Seabrook, Sussex
September, 1818

As I write this, dearest Henriette, it is my wedding night. You must cherish this letter, cousin, for it is quite possible that you will never hear from me again.

The beast Godolphin is below stairs, relishing his moment of triumph, imbibing Bermuda rum and American whiskey, and some sort of rot gut French brandy which—do I dare suggest it?—he has probably smuggled across the Channel.

My heart quickens as I anticipate his approach to my poor bridal bower. Mama was unclear on the exact details of Ravishment, as I had feared she would be. I wish that you were here to explain to me what my fate shall be. For the moment, I am thankful that my door is equipped with a stout lock.

I do so wish I had heeded your advice to avoid pulling pranks on gentlemen. After my success with those hapless, spotty young peers in the ton, I had grown too bold, I suppose. And indeed, it turns out Godolphin is no gentleman—

A resounding thud on the bedchamber door made Estella jump on her dainty lacquered chair. Her quill flew from her hand to the carpet, the ink pot wobbled, then toppled over.

She stared as glossy ink flowed across the letter to her cousin, Henriette. "Who's there?" she called. She'd meant to sound airy and nonchalant. Instead, her words came out as a frightened little rasp.

Drat.

There was another thump at the door. The heart-squeezing sound of a big, impatient fist.

Her spotted foxhound, Maggie, woke at last. She hobbled from the foot of the swaybacked four-poster bed, tail wagging drowsily, eyes only half open.

Estella stood, drawing her silk wrapper close. The corner of one ink-dappled page snagged on her sleeve, and black droplets splattered down her front, onto her bare feet.

"I said, who is there?" she repeated, turning to stare at the massive paneled door. In the shifting yellow light of a single candelabra, it took on the quality of a dungeon door. She felt the looming presence outside, could almost taste the electric crackle of anger.

She knew *exactly* who it was.

Her eyes widened as the tarnished brass knob twisted slowly. The door shuddered slightly under the weight of a large body, but held fast. Then the knob wiggled vigorously a few times before falling still.

Several hovering moments of calm were marked by the tick of the clock on the chimney piece.

"I know you're still out there, Godol—whoever you are!" Estella narrowed her eyes at the doorknob, daring it to wiggle even once more.

"*Whoever you are?*" a smoky masculine voice growled. It was muffled by the door, but sarcasm was still evident. "Then it comes as a surprise to you that your husband arrives at your bedchamber on your wedding night?"

"No—I, well yes." Perhaps it would be best to play the innocent. Though she *had* known he'd come. That was why she had locked the door. "Yes, it is indeed a surprise. I believe I bade you good night before I came upstairs. Most of the guests had gone home, and everyone else was too far into their cups to miss me. Including you, it seems."

A rumbling laugh, tinted with bitterness, floated through the keyhole.

"I noticed," Estella pushed on, ignoring a tremor of foreboding, "that you seemed particularly appreciative of the American whiskey Papa supplied for the festivities. No doubt you look forward to more gifts from him. It is a shame my parents embarked on their lengthy journey today. We can expect no more from them for at least six months."

"Estella," the voice said, this time stern as a schoolmaster. *"Unlock this door."*

"I won't." She clutched her arms across her chest. "I—I'm going to sleep."

"Sleep?" He pronounced the word as if it were foreign. Then he assumed a more pompous tone. "It is my right as your husband to gain admittance to your chamber."

Why did the thought of Godolphin in her chamber make her pulse flutter? She screwed her eyes shut, inhaled shakily. The air smelled of stale ticking and mildewy drapes, as though the room had been neglected for centuries. "I was told that husbands and wives, er, grew more acquainted with one another in . . . bedchambers . . . during their wedding trips. But as we shall *have* no wedding trip, I assumed I was exempt from sharing my . . . bed." Her voice trailed off, uncertain. It was definitely better that she deal with the brute in England rather than Paris or Rome. Still, she felt somehow cheated out of her honeymoon. "So, then," she stumbled on, her voice chirpy, "I suppose I'll see you at breakfast."

She waited, holding her breath. There was another leaden silence, and then the floorboards creaked. She didn't breathe again until his footsteps receded to silence.

Returning to the writing desk, Estella glared down at Maggie. "You are no help, dog," she scolded. "Some protectress you are."

Maggie paid her no heed, lazily licking drops of ink from the floor.

The last crate was heavy. As he helped the men hoist it, his shoulder muscles cramped in outrage. This only made him pull all the harder. He wasn't about to forsake his youth for a leather armchair and a glass of brandy simply because of one mishap. Besides, his hand was calloused, the palm tough as shoe leather. He could barely feel the coarse rope or the splintery wood of the crate hovering above the deck. Amid the scraggly crew, the smell of ship's tar, the seaweed and salt tang of the starlit sea, he was at home.

Two other men grabbed the crate and swung it into position next to the others. As the heavy box hit the ship deck, its contents rattling dully, he heaved a sigh of relief.

He bent over the ship's rail. "That is all?" he whispered through the swirling predawn mist. *"C'est tout?"*

Bobbing in the rowboat below, the ship's motley captain glanced up with the jerky motions of a rabbit, nodded twice.

That, at least, was good news. Now and then these fools could do *something* right.

The first hints of sunrise launched lavender streaks across the horizon, over the rippled green-black surface of the sea. A glance over his shoulder revealed the silhouette of Castle Seabrook's tower, just visible over the tree-rimmed cliffs. Haze made its outline indistinct. But as soon as the sun burst over the horizon, any person in the tower might be able to see him, and the ship and rowboat, too.

He swore under his breath, then slid down the rope to the rowboat.

"Go," he hissed to the captain. *"Vite."*

"Must you sigh like that, madam?" Godolphin's fist came down on the tabletop with such an impatient crash that all the silver and breakfast dishes jumped. "It puts me in mind of a spoilt child who hasn't gotten the pony she wanted for her birthday."

Estella, after recovering from her initial shock, drew herself very straight in her high-backed chair. With its lumpy cushion and scratched legs, it had clearly seen better days.

"I did not sigh," she said coldly. She reached for the tarnished coffee pot. It was so heavy, her arm trembled as she lifted it and poured.

Godolphin glowered down the length of the table.

When he was angry—which, Estella was learning, was quite often—his big shoulders hunched, and his dark eyebrows drew down and together. Even in the clear morning sunlight streaming through the windows, his bruise-colored eyes were in shadow. Unreadable, with the dark heat of coals.

"You did sigh," he ground out. "Several times, in fact, and in a way that suggested you desired me to notice."

"Really!" Estella huffed. She smeared butter on a toast triangle so fiercely that the knife poked holes in it. "That is exceedingly unfair, *sir*." She said this with a bite of sarcasm. "I did not sigh, nor did I want you to hear." She took a chomp at the corner of the toast, chewed angrily.

Well, perhaps she *had* sighed. She'd been wallowing in a puddle of misery, trying not to fidget as Godolphin scowled in stony silence. First she'd wondered just how many more nights she could turn the ogre away from her bedchamber. Then she'd reflected at length on why this had to happen to her of all people. A more adult, regal young lady could have handled the predicament with grace. Without dropping crumbs on her lap.

The toast was too dry. She could barely swallow. After a sip of Turkish coffee, she cleared her throat lightly. "However, I must admit that I do know just how a child would feel when promised one thing only to get quite another." She eyed him pointedly, hoping to deflate his overbearing presence. Instead, he seemed to grow larger still, his tanned face enveloped in a fog of annoyance.

"Yes," he admitted, sawing at a bit of bacon so hard the knife screeched against the china, "you would know how a spoilt child feels, since that is exactly what you are. Papa's little princess."

Estella sucked in a sharp breath. His words felt just like a slap. And for the first time, she noticed that his jacket was rumpled, his neck cloth wilted, and there was a shadow of a beard on his square chin. His hair was tied behind his neck. But not neatly. In fact, he had the appearance and temper of a man who hadn't slept a wink.

A tiny twinge of compassion fluttered in her chest, but she ignored it. He was a tortured beast, not an insomniac earl. He had trapped her into marriage, and now she had nowhere to turn.

Feigning calm, she took another sip of coffee. It stung her tongue. She had always drunk chocolate in the morning at home, but she dared not request such a childish beverage at Castle Seabrook.

Godolphin's features had relaxed into gentleness. Perhaps the beast regretted his harsh words. His sad-lidded eyes drifted down from her face, taking in the high, snug bodice of her soft blue morning gown.

And her nearly flat chest. Estella's ears grew warm, and she made an elaborate display of tapping at her boiled egg with a spoon. Anything to make him stop looking *there*.

It seemed to work.

"Estella," he said.

He always said her name differently from anyone else. Lingering on the L's, as if the correct curling of his tongue over the consonants might summon the stars down from heaven. . . .

Which was ridiculous, since he clearly did not care for her.

"Estella," he said again, "as I explained to you during our betrothal—"

"Such as it was," she cut in. "Four weeks is hardly a proper—"

"You know as well as I that your parents had to leave before the Atlantic grew too stormy for a safe passage, and—"

"Then we should have waited until their return in the spring." She knew how pressing Papa's business was, how hard he had to work to compete with other traders like the South China Company.

Godolphin leaned back heavily in his chair. Despite its gigantic proportions, it creaked in protest. "If we had waited that long," he said slowly, "I think we both know you would've found a way to slip out of your commitment."

Estella's jaw locked. He was correct, though she couldn't bring herself to admit it. She stared past him, out the windows, whose gold brocade drapes were speckled with moth holes, to the front lawn, the edge of the sea cliff, and the glimmering ocean beyond.

As he watched her, it seemed as if he were seeking out some sign of truth in her face. She willed it to remain impassive.

He ran a quick palm across his jaw, a habit that made him appear somehow vulnerable. "As I was saying, during our betrothal, brief though it was, I explained to you that I am extremely preoccupied with my work. That is why—" he caught her gaze and held it. His eyes were as deep and dangerous as the sea. "That is why you can't have your wedding trip until the spring."

"*My* wedding trip? Wouldn't it be for both of us?" He managed to make even a honeymoon sound like a child's treat.

He ignored her protest. "My work will keep me busy every day, often into the night."

"Where?"

"In my study. In the tower—but you mustn't go there. I cannot have my work disrupted."

"And what do you do?" Estella felt like laughing bitterly. What a pitiful question to ask of one's own husband.

"Mainly running my estate. Some shipping endeavors. I won't bore you with the particulars."

Shipping endeavors? She knew nothing of this. "Papa is in shipping," she reminded him. "I don't find it boring in the least."

"A young lady like you?" He sipped his coffee.

A frivolous young lady. That was his unspoken meaning. Estella wanted to flounce out of the room, or snap a shrewish retort. Instead, she gave her boiled egg another fierce crack with her spoon.

"It won't do to have you rattling about this big old barn with nothing to occupy you," Godolphin went on. "Mrs. Hobbs will continue to perform most of the house-keeping duties, which leaves very little for you. I'm well aware of your fondness for mischief—" He raised a knowing eyebrow.

Estella shifted in her chair.

"—so I've decided to give you a task to keep you occupied. You shall oversee the redecoration of the castle, as well as the restoration of the formal gardens. Before luncheon, my secretary, Teeters, will show you what needs to be done. You are to meet him in the main foyer at ten o'clock."

Estella gaped at him. Was he absolutely off his head? "This is a . . . the castle is enormous! It's as big as a mountain. It'll take years. No, decades."

Godolphin stirred his coffee. The tiny demitasse spoon made a maddening clinking sound. "Precisely."

Theodore Wilfrid Mimsey-Hubert de Godolphin rode his elderly horse, Thunder, toward the village of Seabrook, his ancestral village. On his way he passed through healthy forests and rolling fields. But the fields lay fallow, instead of full of ripening grain. The thatch-roof cottages were in disrepair. In the yard of one fisherman's cottage, fish nets were draped over a stone wall, full of holes and dead leaves.

Godolphin's tenants turned their backs as he rode by. The few who tipped their hats in greeting did so with hostility in their eyes. They despised him.

Just the way Estella did.

She made his head spin and his heart pound with anger, frustration . . . and desire. There was no point in denying it.

Shaking his head, he leaned forward and patted Thunder on the neck. "Good boy. Good old boy. You've stood by me since I was just a lad. Any advice on how to tame a willful filly?"

The horse just gave his head a toss, snorting gently.

Godolphin's lips twitched into a grimace. "On second thought, old boy, keep your secrets to yourself. I really can't afford the price of success."

He sighed. Any sort of daydreams he once might have indulged in concerning his wedding night had been soundly thrashed by grim reality. The reality was he could never bed his bride. An annulment would be impossible should that occur.

When he reached the village green, his thoughts were still snagged on Estella. How long after he'd first seen that lovely face had he wished he could see it every morning for the rest of his days? One second, perhaps? Maybe two?

Her sweet oval jaw, the curve of cheekbone tinted with an apricot flush, the unruly red-gold of the curls escaping along her hairline. The wide, luminous periwinkle eyes, fringed with thick lashes the color of honey.

And her lithe body, constantly in motion, impossible to pin down. Not a girl's figure exactly—there were lush curves in most of the places where it counted, though her small breasts—

Godolphin swore under his breath, shifted in his saddle. Thoughts of Estella tormented his body with little stabs of desire, poppy red blooms of heat.

"Impossible chit," he snarled into the September sky. In response, a sea-chilled gust of wind sent a handful of yellow leaves spinning from the trees.

Estella had been correct in saying their betrothal had been brief. They hadn't spent even five minutes alone together. During those short weeks, she had seemed shy and skittish, but he'd written her demeanor off as pre-wedding jitters. As they'd said their wedding vows, her eyes had been distant, all but hidden behind the white film of her veil.

And just this morning at breakfast, he'd noticed things about her face he hadn't seen before: the sullen thrust of her lips, a pout that might've been alluring if it weren't so aggravating, the contentious lifting of one delicate eyebrow. The flash in her eyes.

Godolphin's teeth clamped with an aching force. The truth was, he had married a woman he didn't know. She could ruin everything he'd planned for so long.

His plan.

First, he needed to get hold of the key to her father's Brighton warehouse. He knew she had one. Hancock had told him as much.

And in the meantime, he had no other option but to tame the wicked imp.

"Good morning, Your Ladyship." Godolphin's secretary, Teeters, greeted Estella with the most perfunctory of bows. "I trust you are recovered from the wedding festivities?"

Estella, crossing the dim marble expanse of the foyer to meet him, felt her heart plummet to her kid boots. She'd mustered what she hoped was a gracious, countesslike smile, but it fell away because Teeters wore the expression of a man who'd been presented with a box full of writhing caterpillars. His upper lip curling slightly, he shot a glance down at her foxhound Maggie, who trailed after her mistress. Maggie's tail ceased its wagging.

"Good morning," Estella replied at last, bobbing a curtsy. Although Teeters, stocky, balding, and sporting a nose reminiscent of a sea anemone, was no dashing swain, he made her feel inadequate. As though the fawn walking gown and pelisse she'd chosen weren't quite right, the folded parasol under her arm was absurd, and her bonnet had gone out of fashion three seasons ago.

Well. She would *not* let this turnip-nosed little gentleman intimidate her. He was only Godolphin's secretary, after all. As she drew herself very straight, she noticed he was hardly taller than she. "It should be a lovely day for walking," she offered. Perhaps he was just shy.

"Yes. Well." Teeters twisted his hands. "I believe I'm to show you about the castle and gardens, instruct you as to what is to be done regarding the restorations." His drooping eyelids suggested he'd rather ingest a packet of nails.

"I've brought paper and pencil." Estella forced a bright tone and held up her bulging reticule. "I'll be taking notes." The keys to Papa's warehouse and his Brighton house jingled inside. She was in the habit of carrying them with her.

Teeters responded with a quick flare of his nostrils. "Come along then." He began bustling toward the front doors, but then hesitated. "Is the . . . ah, hound to accompany us, Your Ladyship? I do so loathe members of the canine clan."

Maggie yawned widely, revealing a long curl of pink tongue.

"Of course." Estella thrust her chin forward. The topic was not negotiable. "She's miserable if she's left alone."

"And?" Teeters's eyes bulged.

He wasn't shy. He was *loathsome*. "And she chews the furniture when she's miserable."

"I see." He blinked twice, then led the way to the doors. Outside, they were greeted by a swooping rush of brisk air. Estella had to steady her bonnet with her free hand. Maggie lifted her black nose to the wind.

"I do believe the summer has gone," Estella remarked, making a stab at conversation.

"I am glad of it," Teeters replied.

Estella trotted down the huge front steps after him, then tried to keep up as he traversed the front drive and turned round a corner to the rear of the house. "Why?"

"For one thing, the ladies are more decently clothed"— he shot her a look as though she was a tart from ancient Babylon—"and the insects are killed off by the first frost. I despise insects. And there is something rather insidious about warm weather. It boils a man's blood. Makes him do rash things."

Estella frowned. She couldn't tell whether Teeters was speaking of his own rash behavior, or Godolphin's decision to marry her.

"Here we are," Teeters said, wheezing a little from his exertions. He stopped at the foot of the rear terrace and placed a hand on the small of his back.

Castle Seabrook, Estella decided, was of two minds. Stretching in one direction was the modern wing—or the Godolphin clan's notion of modern—constructed with the spires and carved stone molding of the Baroque style. Slumped against this were the ruins of the medieval fortress. There were even the remains of a moat. Estella peered down into it, half expecting some grotesque pond creature to surface. But the water was long gone, and the trench was filled with lush green moss.

"The Godolphins," Teeters said, "have always been advocates of peace—"

Good heavens. Was he going to recite from a six-volume family history?

"—but they were forced to defend themselves in more barbaric times. Hence the moat. And the arrow slits in the ramparts."

Estella craned her neck. Crisp blue sky shone through the upper sections of the ruins where the roof had collapsed. One corner was dominated by a sinister looking tower so tall it rose above the trees, its shadow sprawling across the grounds. Tumbled down building stones ringed the perimeter, the lawn clipped right to their edges.

"His Lordship wishes to retain the appearance of the facade," Teeters told her drily. "It is unusual, of course, but these walls are rich with history." He made it sound as interesting as a bit of crumbling parchment paper. "His Lordship *did* tell you to stay away from the ruins, didn't he?"

Estella ripped her eyes from the tower. "No," she fibbed. "Why would he? As the Countess Seabrook, I shall go wherever I please."

Teeters's eyes bulged. "I'm certain it was merely an oversight. You're not to go in the tower. It's . . . well, clearly, it's just a pile of stones. Uninhabitable. Extremely precarious."

Deciding to keep quiet for the moment, Estella forced herself to nod.

They walked on, across the gently rolling lawns at the back of the castle. Far to the right were walls, encircling an orchard and a kitchen garden. Beyond, the glass roof and finial of an orangerie were visible. Estella made a mental note to pay the orchard a visit. Maggie, since earliest puppyhood, adored apples.

"The formal gardens were designed and planted in 1697," Teeters droned, checking his gold pocket watch for the tenth time. "The Godolphin family enjoyed uncommon prosperity in that period."

If one squinted and tilted one's head at just the right angle, one could see what the formal gardens had once been. They were laid out in a graceful network of white gravel paths, with orderly beds of plants, grand promenades lined with yew trees, fragrant rose bushes. Fountains gurgling crystal waters, flitting birds and Classical statuary. . . .

"It must've been lovely," Estella said sadly. Now everything was choked with tall grass and thicket. The statuary was crumbling, the fountains were dry, the paths obscured by decaying vegetation. The rosebushes looked as though several varieties of creatures made regular breakfasts of them.

"Yes, I suppose it was. I never did see it. It was kept up until His Lordship's mother quit the earth. Since then, it has fallen into shameful disrepair."

Estella glanced up from the cracked urn she'd been studying. She'd known both of Godolphin's parents were dead, but no one had ever bothered to inform her of the details. "When was that?" she quizzed, pencil poised above notebook. Perhaps Teeters could be convinced that the information was crucial to her job.

Teeters turned on his heel, crunching away down the gravel path.

He'd definitely heard her. She marched after him.

"As you can see," he said, coming to a stop near the entrance to an overgrown boxwood maze, "the garden and castle were built with the utmost taste and elegance. No expense was too great for the sake of beauty." His mud-colored eyes flickered for the tiniest moment to Estella. "And *quality.*"

Her ears burned. Was Teeters really insinuating that she wasn't genteel enough to be a countess? She considered the various unladylike uses for her folded parasol.

"I hope that you will attempt to echo these characteristics in your efforts," he went on, bending to yank a weed from the path.

Estella couldn't help noticing the way the seams strained at his trousers. In dire danger of giggling, she looked away.

"I assume," he said, straightening, "you have no prior experience with such things?"

She answered by forming her lips into a grim line.

"I suspected as much." Teeters puffed out his chest. This did nothing for his stature, although it did result in making his melon belly protrude still farther. Then he shrugged. "I did inform His Lordship that the task might be too great for a young lady, and—"

"I can do it," Estella stated. "And I see no reason why it shouldn't be a success."

No reason at all, except that in thwarting Teeters, she just might end up pleasing Godolphin. And *that* wouldn't do at all. The beast needed to be tamed.

"Yes," Teeters agreed drily, as if it had been his idea. "It would be best to clear away the overgrowth and plan the new paths before the winter drives us inside. Perhaps prune the fruit trees—"

"Where's Maggie?" Estella interrupted, glancing about. Not that Teeters cared. He was absorbed in polishing his half-lenses as though they were the crown jewels.

"Maggie?" she called, picking up her skirts and wading through the overgrowth. "Maggie! Come!" She rounded the corner of the maze. Behind it, shaded by the draping limbs of a willow tree, was an open gate. She rushed toward it, whistling and calling. Maggie had always been a London dog. She could get lost in this unfamiliar place.

Estella was about to slip through the gate—the iron was rusty, she saw, and one hinge was broken—when Teeters wheezed after her.

"Your Ladyship! Please, not through there. I believe your animal went toward the castle."

Estella peered through the gate. Behind it was a brambly forest path, the sunlight obscured by overhead branches. She turned, frowning. "I am certain she went this way."

"No, no, no"—Teeters had reached her side, droplets of perspiration hugging his brow—"she most certainly did not. And I am obliged to warn you that this path is not suitable at all for young ladies. It is, in fact, dangerous."

"Dangerous?" Estella stared down the path. "But wouldn't it lead down to the seashore?"

"Ah. Well, yes. But by way of the cliffs. A delicate young lady might fall and twist her ankle. Or worse. It would be advisable to take the path by the rose gardens. The beaches there are ever so much nicer."

Estella narrowed her eyes a fraction. "Mr. Teeters," she said sweetly through clenched teeth. "You really are *too* solicitous. But am I not mistress of this estate now? I am certain Maggie went this way."

Teeters released a snort. "I think not." He made a sweeping gesture with his arm, indicating that she should follow him back toward the castle. "Now, if you would kindly—"

He was interrupted by joyful barking and the crashing of underbrush. Maggie bounded out from the path, tail wagging wildly.

Godolphin emerged from the shadows behind her.

Chapter Two

Beauty and the Beast

Godolphin's hair was wind whipped, his jaw still shadowed, and he wore the same unkempt clothing he had sported at breakfast. He loomed at the mouth of the gate, his large body obscuring the path he'd just climbed. A trace of a frown drifted across his face as he took in Estella and Teeters. Then his features rearranged themselves into mildness.

"Your Lordship," Teeters simpered, "I was giving Her Ladyship a tour of the gardens when she insisted on—"

Godolphin cut him off with a wave of dismissal. "No matter," he murmured. "If I could just have a moment . . ."

"Of course." Teeters bowed deeply and waddled away.

"Maggie," Estella hissed, patting the tops of her thighs. The foxhound snuffled about under a fallen log, pawed the dirt, then sneezed. "Maggie, *come*."

Instead, the dog trotted back to Godolphin and had the audacity to lick his hand.

"No!" Estella yelped. "Maggie, *no!*"

Godolphin chuckled, a rich, warm sound like melting chocolate. "It's aggravating, isn't it?" he said, crouching down to scratch behind Maggie's ears. "She likes the one person in the world you have chosen to detest."

Estella balled her fists. "I do not detest you, sir," she declared. "I merely dislike you. Immensely." Blast. Why had she said that?

After giving Maggie one last caress, Godolphin slowly stood.

Estella felt as if she were shrinking. Her husband was almost a head taller than Papa, and broad chested. Under the charcoal wool of his coat, his arms looked large and capable.

He hadn't the willowy, elegant physique one expected of a blue blood. Instead, he looked like he could hoist a sail alone, or carry barrels over his shoulder up a gangplank.

"If we are to live peacefully under the same roof," he told her, "you will have to change."

"*I* will have to change?" Estella sniffed. "Yes, I suppose that is how it's done. The lady must adapt while the gentleman goes on with business as usual. Business which apparently includes skulking about in the shrubbery."

In a frustrated gesture, he raked long fingers through his hair. "Skulking about? Your vocabulary is colorful, I must admit. However, I'm afraid it can't be considered skulking if one does it on one's own estate."

"No? Even after your—" She glanced over her shoulder. Teeters was nowhere to be seen. Still, she lowered her voice. "Not even after your secretary told me to avoid the very path you came on?"

"Why would he tell you that?"

"You don't believe me? He said the path was dangerous, as a matter of fact."

"Yes. I suppose it is."

"What were you doing down there?" She tried to mask her curiosity with a tone of wifely concern.

Godolphin gave her a long, hard stare before answering. "Nothing in particular. Shall we walk on?" Without waiting for her answer, he encircled her upper arm with a hand and steered her away from the path and the gate, back out into the sunlight.

All her attention was riveted on his hand.

He did not speak as he led her through the gardens. She found herself breathless as she attempted to match his long, easy strides. Maggie gamboled after them, not interested in the least that her mistress was practically being kidnapped.

As they moved, she heard the soft jingling of the keys in his pocket. He seemed to carry his keys on his person at all times. She pressed her lips together. That made two of them, then.

Only when they reached the lawn below the rear terrace did he release her. She felt the imprint his grip had made on her arm, like a hot band. Without him touching her, she felt inconsequential somehow. Almost as though she'd lost something. A surge of irritation swept through her.

"How could you have allowed the gardens to decay like this?" She gestured with a primly gloved hand to the overgrown vista. "Even the slightest bit of maintenance might've—"

"Even the slightest bit of maintenance, as you call it, adds up to a rather large pile of money for an estate of this size. Not to mention the effort and time involved in the upkeep." He folded his arms.

"You needn't speak to me as though I were a child."

He inhaled as if his patience were being taxed and glanced up to the sky. A flock of cawing rooks flew overhead, and his gaze followed them until they disappeared behind the tower. Slowly, he lowered his eyes back to hers. The open gentleness in them surprised her; the downturned crinkles at their corners made her think of a small, sad boy.

"To be honest, Estella—"

Something wavered in her chest. The speaking of her name felt too intimate.

"—my family has been bankrupt for generations."

"Teeters just told me that the gardens had been maintained till your mother—"

He cut her off, his features going dark and stern. "It would be best if you did not speak of things you don't understand." Like a fortress gate slammed shut, his guard was back up. "As I was saying, the Godolphins have been penniless for some time. Only very recently have I acquired the funds to repair the castle and gardens."

His explanation was too convenient, fitting together too neatly. "*How* recently?" she demanded. "As recently as yesterday, perhaps, when our vows were spoken? Or perhaps before then, when you learned the sum of my allowance from Papa, or of his shipping prospects in America?"

"I can't think what you mean, darling." He mounted the terrace steps two at a time.

She didn't *want* to stare. But the way the muscles in his legs shifted beneath his trousers was distracting. And for goodness sake, why did he wear his hair so long, like some ancient barbarian conquerer?

At the top, he paused. "But, contrary to what you'd guess from reading fairy stories, fact is always more interesting than fiction."

> *Things are spiraling into the depths of sheer rottenness faster than I can say, Henriette. For one thing, it has become painfully obvious that Godolphin married me in order to gain access to Papa's money. Poor Papa! If only he knew of the treachery behind Godolphin's handsome smile.*
>
> *Today I was obliged to eat luncheon in solitude. The beast sent word with a servant that he could not join me as his work was too pressing. Imagine snubbing one's new bride in such a fashion! Of course, dining alone is far preferable to a meal in his gloating company.*

Perched at the writing desk in the countess's parlor, Estella gazed out the window to the sea, tapping her quill against her lips.

The lofty chamber was fit for a princess, really. Or it had been once: the robin's egg damask walls, the chandelier dripping with crystals, the blue and white porcelain vases and gilded furniture. The shabbiness wasn't terribly noticeable if one squinted. Even the cobwebs in the corners seemed to evaporate.

Estella examined the stationery. It had once been plush. *The Countess Seabrook,* each yellowed sheet announced at the top, accompanied by tasteful curlicues and the family crest. The crest, along with the usual weaponry and Latin motto, featured two round-eyed, diamond-scaled fish.

Somberness washed over her like cold water. This paper had not been printed for her, but for the previous Countess Seabrook. Godolphin's dead mother.

Maggie, however, was not intimidated by the grand trappings of the peerage nor the possibility of a haunting. She was sprawled on a well-worn cream satin divan, fast asleep.

Estella locked the unfinished letter in the top drawer just as a tentative rap sounded at the door.

"Enter," she called, trying out a gracious-yet-commanding countess voice.

A maid in a starched apron slipped around the door and bobbed a curtsy. She was one of the pair of frightened-looking young women who seemed to be charged with keeping the enormous castle tidy all by themselves. "Your Ladyship. I've been sent to help you sort through your wedding gifts."

Estella sighed. "Very well." It seemed that each minute of her day would be dictated by Godolphin. From afar.

The presents had been piled on a huge oak table at the far end of the parlor. Estella set to work untying the colorful ribbons and removing the pretty cloth and paper wrappings. The maid kept a list of who had sent what. The notes of thanks were going to take days to write.

There were the usual ornamental trinkets, costly and useless: a marble statuette of Pan, a tiny golden mirror, a black-and-red lacquered box with secret compartments lined in silk. Lady Rumplehorn, eccentric to the last, had presented the newlyweds with a rather appalling stuffed parrot under a glass bell. Another guest, some stodgy chum of Godolphin's, had apparently decided that a handsome edition of Samuel Johnson's dictionary was essential to marital bliss.

There were other books, too, an odd assortment of fiction and fact, so when Estella unwrapped Lady Temple's gift, her expectations were not high.

At first glance it appeared to be an old-fashioned lady's book of prayer. It was small and bound in well-fingered white leather, with gilt lettering stamped along its spine, and the pages were edged in gold. It had a delicate lock, too, like a girl's diary.

Estella stared, fascinated.

A tiny key, which was strung with a silver chain, was fitted into the lock. With an almost inaudible click, she twisted it and the covers fell open.

She frowned, confusion mounting, as she leafed through the pages. The text was in French, but it was accompanied by dozens of hand-tinted illustrations of dogs caught in various acts of naughtiness, such as lolling on furniture and stealing food from the table, or else performing tricks. There was even a picture of a small poodle jumping through a flaming hoop. The book was so elegantly crafted, however, that it resembled a medieval book of hours, not a dog training manual.

Lady Temple was the most unimpeachable dowager in the ton, and a close friend of Estella's parents. Estella nibbled her lip, picturing her plump, kind face. Perhaps her mind was growing infirm to send such an odd wedding present.

Then she noticed the envelope, wedged between the pages. Inside, in Lady Temple's flowing script, was a note.

Dearest Estella,
  Though it is somewhat unusual, this is a wedding gift for you only, and not your husband. I am certain that Castle Seabrook contains more than enough knickknacks

and furnishings, so perhaps a more practical sort of gift is called for. Indeed, this volume has proved indispensable to me. I do not exaggerate when I say that within these covers lie the secrets to bliss. That said, you've more use for it than have I. My own pet is fully trained.

Your dear mama told me once that you could never sit still long enough to master your French lessons. Perhaps this book would be just the thing to improve your skills. You might work on refining that beast of yours, too. Indeed, I have found that a pet is much happier if he understands what is expected of him, if it is made perfectly clear how he may please his mistress. Mind, you must wear the key at all times. Keep the book in your reticule by day, and locked safely in your dressing table drawer at night. You never know when you might need it.

And do not, for any reason, allow anyone else to see it. Especially a gentleman. No gentleman whatsoever, be he gardener or vicar. Or husband.

"Your Ladyship?" the maid said.

"Lady Temple sent this," Estella said, stuffing the note back in its envelope. She replaced the envelope between the pages and locked the book. She waited until the maid had risen to retrieve another wrapped gift from the table to put the key around her neck. It was cool, and weighed almost nothing.

Estella unwrapped several more gifts: a preposterously large Chinese vase, more knickknacks, and, from some great aunt, a blank baby book. Estella quickly handed this to the maid with a shudder. There would *never* be any babies. Not with that beast.

Next, she unwrapped a smallish box, made of wood, and lifted the lid. She blinked.

Inside was a pistol. A real one. It was small and rather beautiful, made of silver with an ivory handle inlaid with a gold checkerboard design. Nestled next to it was a little packet of gunpowder, and another of lead shot.

"Your Ladyship?" Quill poised above paper, the maid was looking at her expectantly. She was also craning her neck, trying to see inside the box.

Estella slammed the lid shut, heart thumping. "There was no card with this?" she quizzed, searching the discarded paper and cloth at her feet.

"No, madam. I'll check the table."

They couldn't find a card or tag anywhere. Estella set the pistol, in its box, beneath her chair. "I'll take special care of the thank-you note for this one," she told the maid with a strained smile. "You needn't add it to your list."

From Madame Pettibonne's
Treatise on Canine Behavior, Prepared Especially for the
Lady Handler.
Lesson Ten. On the matter of spilling drinks and strew-
ing articles of clothing about.

Curled on a sofa in her bedchamber, Estella pursed her lips. Now what sort of dog spilled its drinks and strewed articles of clothing about? She reread the sentence, translating slowly in her laborious French.

Yes. She'd read it correctly the first time. She recalled how Maggie sloshed her water on the floor when lapping from her bowl in the kitchen. The foxhound didn't toss clothing about, though. But, upon turning the page, Estella discovered an illustration of a black poodle chewing on a boot. Ah.

The self-indulgent and undisciplined canine, she read on, *is likely to take advantage of the welcome he has been given in his mistress's chamber.*

Well, that made perfect sense. Deciding to give her poor brain a rest from translation, she stretched her legs out on the sofa. A glance at the clock assured her there was still plenty of time to finish dressing for dinner.

She flipped back to the title page. Beneath the flowing script was a tinted engraving of Madame Pettibonne herself, dressed in the costume of the French court in the previous century. Two tiny dogs with lavender bows around their necks posed on her lap. The authoress wore a huge curly wig, and she sported a large black beauty mark on her upper lip. Her waist was corseted, and her display of décolleté was impressive.

Good *heavens.* Estella glanced down at her own nearly flat bosom.

Opposite Madame Pettibonne's picture was a brief preface, in which the authoress mentioned several odd things. These included: *Canines, as well as more complex beasts, will benefit from a strict regimen,* and *The larger beasts can be trained quite as readily as any dog, and with equally satisfactory results.*

Estella chalked up the oddity of these remarks to her poor French. Besides, nearly one hundred years had passed since the book's publication.

At the sound of a sudden rustling and clattering, her head jerked up from the book. Maggie bolted to her feet, growling, and rushed to the ancient carved wardrobe that loomed against the far wall.

Heart thumping, Estella stashed the book under a tasseled roll pillow. It sounded very much as though there was some sort of creature in her wardrobe.

Instantly, she thought of the pistol. But she'd hidden it in the bottom of the wardrobe, so it wouldn't do her a bit of good.

Glancing around for another weapon, she hefted a small, Grecian-style marble bust in her hand. "Come out!" she yelled. "But beware!"

To her horror, the handles twisted and rattled, and then the doors of the wardrobe flew wide.

Maggie barked and lunged.

Abruptly, though, she stopped, tail wagging so wildly that her whole spotted rump shook.

"Godolphin?" Estella's jaw went slack. Then she snapped it shut. "Sir! What do you mean by hiding in my wardrobe and making such a rude entrance? And just how long have you been lurking amongst my garments?" Her voice was severe, but her mind was in a complete muddle about Ravishment, and how one got in—and out of—that sort of pickle.

He came to a halt a few paces before her, ripping a cashmere shawl from his sturdy shoulder and flinging it on the floor.

Madame Pettibonne had mentioned beasts who threw clothing about.

"Wife," Godolphin gritted, "witness with what great restraint I have dealt with you thus far. Did you think you had outwitted me by bolting your chamber door last night?"

"Whatever are you speaking of?" With unsteady hands, Estella replaced the marble bust on the table.

"Just this, my tiresome bride: Our bedchambers are connected through this wardrobe."

Startled, Estella's eyes flew to the wardrobe's gaping doors. Indeed, light shone through the hanging clothes. She gulped.

"Surprised?" Godolphin lowered himself onto the sofa, leaning back casually on the roll pillow.

Oh dear. If the book should wiggle out . . . Estella nibbled her lip.

Lounging on the furniture. Hadn't Madame Pettibonne mentioned something about that, as well?

She glared as he swung an arm along the sofa back, then propped a large black boot atop the opposite knee.

"Oh, please do make yourself comfortable," she said, her tone sticky-sweet as strawberry jam. She crossed her arms, suddenly conscious of her state of partial undress.

Godolphin seemed rather interested in this fact, actually. His eyes were rooted to her throat for some reason or other. Thank goodness she hadn't replaced the key around her neck. It was still lodged in the book's lock.

"You," Estella stammered, "must leave this instant."

Godolphin scratched his temple, as though considering her request, then shrugged. "I won't leave until you have satisfied my curiosity." He gave her entire body a lingering glance, from hairline to bare feet.

Estella reminded herself to breathe.

"Even then," he amended, "I might not leave." He took a big breath. "Why did you marry me?"

The question was so blunt, Estella felt the wind knocked out of her. For a moment her mind was blank. Then it took off running. "Because . . . because I gave you my word that I would."

"Ah." Godolphin leaned his elbows on his knees. "You are an honorable sort of imp, then."

"I am *not* an imp, sir, and I would appreciate not being addressed as such. As far as being honorable, well yes, I am." She straightened her spine, tilted her chin up. "You tricked me into agreeing to marry you, but *I* am true to my word."

"It is surprising that such an accomplished trickster couldn't have found some way to slip out of her betrothal."

"I'm just . . . I like to see things through." She twisted the thin cotton of her sleeve, fingertips moist with anxiety.

"Or perhaps," he suggested, leaning back, both long legs stretched before him, "you did not want to disappoint your parents? Despite your unruly ways, I am impressed by your devotion to Mama and Papa."

She couldn't tell if he was mocking her or not. With Godolphin, it was probably safe to assume he was.

"So, even though you do not love me, you kept your promise."

"Um."

"What? Did you answer?

"Yes."

He sprang to his feet, was looming over her in one long stride. "Yes, you answered? Or yes, you do not love me?"

Estella glared up at him. She was pulled to his heat, tugged by the ferocious energy crackling from his eyes.

She saw the black fringes of his lashes, in startling contrast with the burning sapphire irises. And she caught a hint of his scent, like cut grass and salty wind.

A fluid sensation coiled in her belly, radiated between her legs, down to her toes. She placed both hands on her hips. "Both. Are you satisfied now?"

"Not really."

Instinctively, her fingers wandered to the notch at the base of her throat, where his gaze had come to rest again.

"There is a chink in your otherwise well-laid plans," Godolphin mused.

She looked up in time to see his eyes dart behind her to the bed.

"Although you kept your betrothal promise," he went on, "you have utterly abandoned your wedding vows."

"How so, sir? I agreed to do my best to put your house in order. It isn't my fault that you inform me of nothing and your secretary behaves as if he were my warden."

Godolphin scoffed. "Your role as the housewife, even an ill-used housewife, is of little interest to me. I am speaking of the other, weightier responsibilities you have forsaken."

Again, that crimson heat shimmered between her legs. "I cannot think," she whispered, "what you mean."

"Your marriage vows. Shall I remind you of them?"

"I . . . sir, I need time to change for dinner. And—"

"Love. Honor. Obey. You've neglected each one." He was on his feet again, pacing the length of the carpet.

Estella stole backward, well out of his way. He looked like a barrister pleading his case. A very impassioned barrister, with long dark hair, one lock loose and hanging against his cheekbone. A barrister with unreasonably large shoulders, and lips that moved with a strange, quick grace.

He stopped pacing when he reached her dressing table. "You admit you do not love me. And as far as honoring one's husband, I'm afraid you've failed dismally in that arena, as well." One by one, he picked up Estella's scent bottles, read their labels, and set them back down. As he replaced the third one, his hand bumped into the bottle next to it, and they all went crashing across the tabletop.

"For heaven's sake," Estella said. She rushed to the dressing table. By the time she got there, however, he'd righted all the bottles.

Then he drew out a flask, unscrewed the cap, and drank.

This so completely ruined Estella's image of a barrister—for what sort of legal man would tipple smuggled French brandy while clumsily knocking scent bottles—that she cracked a tiny smile.

Godolphin, wiping his mouth with the back of a hand, stared in disbelief. "You find me amusing?"

"No." Estella forced a frown. "Of course not. *Sir.*"

The hint of flippancy in her tone was clearly not lost on him. His jaw clenched and unclenched. He moved to shove the flask back inside his pocket, but the cap, which hadn't been screwed on properly, snagged on a button and it fell to the floor with a *thunk.* Brandy gurgled out, the amber liquid bleeding onto the carpet, sinking in, making the rich woven colors darker still.

Estella blinked as the last trickle came out, the faint stinging scent of alcohol wafting upward.

Hadn't Madame Pettibonne mentioned something about spilling drinks?

His lips worked in a silent curse, and he bent down to retrieve it. Midway, however, he froze, then straightened.

"That reminds me," he told her, his patrician nostrils flared, "we are left with Obey."

Estella's eyes narrowed. He wouldn't *dare* tell her to clean up that brandy. "While it is painfully obvious," she said primly, "that our holy union was a mistake, our time together has been insufficient to establish whether I am as obedient as a trained monkey or otherwise. Tell me, sir, in what way have I failed to obey your orders?"

"So." His eyes flashed. "You hold that you are an obedient little wife?"

She shrugged in casual agreement. But her breathing was shallow with dread.

"Shall we test your theory, then?" His lips parted slightly, revealing a white gleam of teeth.

The beast looked exactly like a wolf drooling over some plump, hapless lamb in a meadow.

With the lowered lids and dilated pupils of a man studying a priceless painting, he studied the fastenings of her chemise. Estella's belly did at least three quick flips, and she hugged herself tighter still.

"Open your chemise," he commanded.

If she hadn't been so shocked, Estella would've laughed. As it was, all she could manage was a muffled little squeal of indignation. "You detestable brute," she cried, breathless. "I shall never, ever . . . you shan't *ever*—"

In a triumphant gesture he turned his palms up to the ceiling, nodded once. "Thank you, madam. You have proven my point." Bowing elegantly, he stepped through the wardrobe. A moment later he poked his head back through the hanging gowns, pelisses, and shawls. His eyebrow twitched up, and he almost grinned. "We are," he said, "both ensnared in a marriage lacking Love, Honor, *and* Obey. Heaven help us."

As soon as Godolphin disappeared, Estella marched to the wardrobe. Carefully, she transported the pistol to her dressing table, where she locked it in the top drawer. Next, she straightened the scent bottles that he'd knocked over. She worried her lower lip as she did so. Godolphin didn't seem like a man who'd drink to the point of clumsiness. And his speech hadn't been that of an inebriated man.

Next, she opened a crystal box and selected three of her strongest looking hair ribbons. With these, she secured the handles of the wardrobe doors with far more knots than was necessary.

The beast wouldn't be stampeding into her bedchamber through *that* route again.

* * *

Back inside his bedchamber, Godolphin shut the wardrobe doors, then slid the iron bolt shut.

The bolt on Estella's side of the wardrobe had been removed before her arrival at the castle. The nail holes had been filled in with plaster, carefully sanded and stained. Now that she knew about the entrance, of course, she'd probably pile every stick of furniture in her chamber against it.

But it didn't matter. Godolphin had what he needed.

Or had he? He was confused by lust after seeing her half-clothed, and his normally precise, logical mind was nothing short of chaotic. He didn't need this. He'd have to make more of an effort to . . . to what? Not look at her? Because, frankly, one glance was all it took.

His chamber was unlit, and he crossed the carpet through pearly moonlight. His bit of playacting for Estella—the clumsiness, the suggestion of drunkenness—was gone. Now his limbs were steady, his motions purposeful.

Had he overdone it? Would she suspect? Probably not. She didn't know him well enough to discern what was normal behavior on his part. But it would be only a matter of time before she could. Then his options would become more limited, so it was best that he was taking care of this now.

In the brighter moonlight just beside the windows, Godolphin withdrew the two brass keys he'd snatched from Estella's dressing table and slid them in place on his key ring.

He would have liked to have stolen the keys when Estella wasn't around, but he'd quickly learned that she carried them with her at all times.

Suddenly, his belly churned.

What kind of mad mess had he gotten himself into?

He pocketed the key ring.

Chapter Three

. . . Always a Prankster

"I daresay you scarcely remember me, Your Ladyship. Of all the things a bride notices during her wedding, I'm certain the last is the vicar's wife." Mrs. Pansy Lovely settled herself into a lopsided lady's chair in the countess's parlor.

"Oh, but I do," Estella insisted. "I remember you quite clearly." She willed her cheeks not to blush and betray her white lie. Alas, they grew so warm she imagined they must be the exact hue of a boiled beet.

Mrs. Lovely laughed. "Then I must admit you are cleverer than I am. I suspect I wouldn't recognize half of my parents' friends who attended my wedding, should I meet them in the street. Nor my husband's friends, for that matter. Weddings aside, though, I am making an effort to get to know all the parishioners." She pursed her lips, a gesture that was more thoughtful than prim. "Yet, even after sitting in their parlors, if I do see them later, I simply cannot remember their names."

Estella grinned. When the butler Simkin had announced that the vicar's wife had come calling, she'd been a bit apprehensive. At the same time, she'd been relieved, if somewhat guiltily, to have her afternoon thank-you-note writing interrupted.

When Simkin had shown Mrs. Lovely in, Estella had done her best to hide her surprise. The vicar's young wife was as slim and pretty as a London debutante, and she lacked any hint of stodginess. True, her hair was done plainly enough, but one or two bright brown curls had escaped from her bonnet, and they bounced on either side of her heart-shaped face. Though her pelisse was a rather uninspiring chestnut brown, it was beautifully cut. Beneath it, the hem of her walking gown peeked out in the nicest shade of rose.

"I am newly wed, also, Lady Seabrook," Mrs. Lovely said. She reached for a macaroon from the tray on the low table between them.

Estella's glass of orgeat lemonade paused midway to her lips. "Indeed. How long have you been married?"

"Nearly four months." Mrs. Lovely bit into her macaroon and chewed, and her eyes strayed to the carpet.

Estella was sure she had frowned for the briefest of moments.

In an instant, however, her cheerful expression had returned. "As the vicar's wife, I am obliged to call on you and pay my respects, and to welcome you into our community. To inform you of my special projects, to solicit your patronage, spiritual, temporal, and fiscal." She took a deep breath. "But you must know, I am such a rank beginner that I think I am hardly the correct person to be shouldered with such a task."

"That cannot be so." Estella smiled and refilled Mrs. Lovely's glass. "You seem a most intelligent and capable young lady."

"Thank you for the compliment, but . . ."

The doors had swung open with a rush, and Godolphin filled the doorway. Looking like a wild creature with his dark clothing, his windblown hair, and chin shadowed from lack of acquaintance with a good razor, he was absurdly out of place against the cream-colored door frame.

Estella's fingers curled tightly around her glass, and her eyes narrowed a fraction. "Godolphin," she said. Her voice was cold and sweet as a cherry ice.

His eyes, flashing with irritation, swept over Mrs. Lovely. "Pardon me. I did not know you were entertaining." Then he shot Estella a look as dark and angry as a midnight storm.

Her breath snagged, but she forced herself to glare back. Could he not enter a room without melodrama, or even attempt to be polite to a guest?

"The vicar's wife has come to call," she told him. "This is Mrs. Lovely."

Godolphin didn't seem interested in the least. "Is it not early for socializing?"

"Certainly not, sir. It is nearly three o'clock."

He blinked once, then ran a quick, worried hand across his jaw.

So he *could* feel embarrassment, then.

"Please forgive me, ladies." He inclined his head, then left, closing the doors softly behind him.

Estella ignored the sting under her eyelids and sipped lemonade to ease the lump in her throat. Drat. Fat tears were forming in the corners of her eyes. Squeezing her eyes shut, she felt the warmth of a hand on her arm.

"Please tell me if I am too bold," Mrs. Lovely said softly, "but I have heard that the earl can be severe at times. Yet after all that, they say he is fair."

Estella drew her embroidered handkerchief from her sleeve and dabbed at her eyes. "Do they?"

"Oh yes." Pansy's features grew pensive. "Still, that he carries his burdens home for you must make your life difficult at times."

Estella laughed a little. "Well, it *has* been barely two days. A most trying two days." Daintily, she blew her nose. "I don't want him to ever see how much he upsets me."

"Why ever not? Perhaps that is just what he needs."

Tilting her head, Estella considered. "No," she decided finally. "I don't think that would work to my advantage. You see, it's as though we are engaged in some sort of game. Warfare, actually. In such situations, one must never reveal any sign of weakness to one's enemy." She stopped. Such confidences were perhaps too much for a new acquaintance. Yet there was something about the vicar's wife that made her feel at ease, as if they'd been friends for years.

"How horrible," Mrs. Lovely murmured. She shook her head in sympathy, extending her slim fingers toward a chocolate bonbon.

"It is my own fault. I agreed to marry him, and I did."

Mrs. Lovely chewed, thoughtful. "I was acquainted with my husband for four years before we married. I imagine it would be difficult to wed someone you barely know."

Estella's eyebrows shot up, and her stomach sank. "How—how do you know that?"

"The village is full of wagging tongues, Your Ladyship. And I am witness to each and every one in my rounds. Of course, as the vicar's wife, I cannot jump into the fray. But I am aware the general rumor is that the earl took to wife a very young thing whom he scarcely knew."

"People gossip about me? About us?" Estella wrinkled her nose, thoroughly peeved. She had been in the gossip papers in the ton, of course. But she *knew* everyone in London.

"You must keep in mind that the Godolphins are ancient and powerful, and—"

"Yes, yes." Estella fought the urge to roll her eyes. "I know."

"—so it follows that the simple folk will find His Lordship's bride entrancing."

"Oh dear." She wasn't certain if she was ready for this.

"They will look to you for leadership," Mrs. Lovely went on. "They will comment on what you wear, on the upholstery of your barouche. I cannot say that I envy you. But it *is* rather romantic to marry a gentleman in a wager." Her eyes glowed.

Estella gasped. "I wasn't—there was no wager. It was a . . . *is* it romantic?"

Mrs. Lovely nodded enthusiastically. "Exactly like one of those Gothic novels we ladies do love to devour. A princess—that would be you, Your Ladyship—swept away to the castle of the fierce warlord. Not kidnapped, precisely, but carried off as the result of a wager gone awry. Or war booty."

"This particular hero is not the sort to gallop about on white steeds," Estella corrected with a wry smile. "He is a practical man, always working."

"Ah, but he is also an honorable gentleman, a leader who strives only to serve his people."

Was he really so admirable? Estella stared, thoughtful, at the candied violet atop a petit four. "How romantic is it for the hero to live to serve others if he hasn't the faintest notion how to speak civilly to his own wife?"

"I shall think about it," Mrs. Lovely promised. "I have mountains of time to think while I knit woolen socks for the poor farmers' children. I am certain I'll manage to wring some romance from the situation." She smiled brightly.

"And your own romance?" Estella quizzed. "I trust it is happier than mine?"

Mrs. Lovely's face fell, her eyes clouded. "I'm afraid it is no better."

"Oh dear. I'm sorry, I did not mean to pry."

"I presumed to inquire about your marriage, Your Ladyship. It is only fair that you ask after mine."

Estella leaned forward in her chair. "You are not happy?" she whispered. "After four long months, marriage does not improve?"

"It is not . . . what I expected."

The Reverend Edwin Lovely, Estella recalled, was a tall,

slim gentleman with a pleasant, boyishly handsome face, neat dark hair and intelligent brown eyes. His kind face and gentle voice, in fact, had been all that had prevented Estella from bolting down the aisle before she repeated her wedding vows. It already seemed so long ago. A different life.

"He seems most good and thoughtful," Estella assured Mrs. Lovely.

"Oh yes, and well educated, the favorite of my papa, the Bishop of Kent. Papa says my husband will be a bishop someday, too. He is from a fine family. And he used to write me the most beautiful poetry."

Alarmed by the way Mrs. Lovely's voice was choking up, Estella looked about for an extra handkerchief.

"I imagined," Mrs. Lovely continued, "that I would be basking in love and affection for all eternity if I were to wed such a sterling young gentleman. I thought—" Sobs suddenly shook her, and tears streamed down her rosy cheeks.

Estella reached for her arm, patted it. "There, there," she soothed. "Do not cry. It cannot be so bad."

Gradually, Mrs. Lovely's sobs turned to sniffles. She dried her reddened eyes with the lace-edged handkerchief she'd fumbled for in her reticule. "Please forgive me," she said. "I'm terribly ashamed."

"I think," Estella smiled, "we ought to address each other with more intimate names." She smoothed her skirts and sat very tall. "From now on, I am just Estella to you."

"And you," Mrs. Lovely hiccuped, "must call me Pansy."

". . . and then when I returned to th' stable, me horse was gone. No trace o' her, exceptin' th' hoof marks in th' mud leadin' out to th' far pasture." The farmer, wiry and hunched, glared up at Godolphin with watery eyes.

There was a pause. Godolphin, perched high on his magistrate's bench, gazed past the plaintiff, across the village courtroom to the windows. The afternoon sky was clear, he noted. Golden sunbeams slanted through the windows, making geometrical patterns of light and shadow on the rough wooden floor.

All the beauties of nature, however, could not stifle his simmering anger.

"Me lord?" The farmer's voice was edged with concern.

Godolphin started, straightened his cravat. "Pardon me, Mr. Oates. Carry on."

He tried in vain to focus, but his thoughts kept wandering to Estella.

She was, it seemed, no sweet imp, but a little witch. What he'd discovered in his bedchamber that morning had confirmed that her prankster ways had not been abandoned.

"Well," the farmer was saying, "the first place I went lookin' fer her was in Mr. March's barn." Here, he threw a poisonous look in Mr. March's direction. Mr. March snorted his derision. "And sure enough, there she was, eatin' hay like it were her own stall."

Godolphin's thoughts drifted back to his bedchamber. When he had returned home from Brighton last night, it had been nearly dawn. Stumbling about in the dark, he couldn't find a candle or lamp in any of the usual places. After fetching a candelabra from an uninhabited chamber across the corridor, he discovered all his lamps and candles in a neat row, high on the bookshelf.

Then, after he had stripped and washed in his basin, without soap—that, too, had mysteriously vanished— there were no clean clothes in the cupboard. Naked and wet (no towel, either), he'd stumbled to bed. Whereupon he'd discovered that the linens had been arranged in such a fashion as to prevent him from slipping under the covers.

Once a prankster, it seemed, always a prankster.

He sighed. "Mr. March," he said. "Do you have anything to say in your defense?"

* * *

The orange glow of the late afternoon barely penetrated the treetops. Estella squinted, picking her way along the winding forest path. The soles of her kid boots hardly made a sound on the soft loam of the trail, and she was uncomfortably aware of her breath.

Her skin crawled as she imagined the snap of twigs behind her, but when she stopped she heard nothing but the rustle of dry leaves in the breeze, the twitter of birds gathering to migrate south for the coming winter. Pulling up her skirts, she quickened her stride.

She had walked Pansy back to the vicarage, which lay on the outskirts of the village, on the far side. Self-conscious as they'd traversed the green, she'd felt like shrinking back into her bonnet. Not many people had been about, however, and she'd had to endure only a half dozen curious stares. When they'd passed the haberdasher's shop, she was sure the curtains at an upstairs window had whisked aside, revealing a pale smudge of a face behind the glass.

So, upon returning, she had decided to use the hidden pathway the gardener had pointed out to her: "Keep off that path, Countess. It is only for beggars, scullery maids, and wild beasts."

Now, it was a relief to be hidden in the forest. If only she didn't feel so spooked. She wasn't normally a young lady given to fear. She wasn't practical, exactly. But she liked to think of herself as brave.

Still, it would have been nice to have had Maggie along for company.

She rounded a bend that plunged her still deeper into brown-green shadows. Then, with a suddenness that stole her breath, sharp, frigid hands grabbed her from behind. She cried out, instinctively struggling against the clawlike vise around one upper arm, the skeletal arm hooked around her waist.

Out of the corner of her eye, she saw a head move close to her ear. "Didn't nobody warn ye against traipsin' through th' woods all on yer own?" a woman's voice cackled in her ear. "Didn't yer governess ever tell ye the stories about what can happen in th' dark? Monsters and evil spirits abound, pretty countess."

The breath that puffed against Estella's cheek was rancid, hinting at rotten meat and brandy and cheroots. She squirmed to free herself. The bony arms only clasped her more tightly.

"Little London lasses like ye are always weak as kittens," the woman rasped, contempt seeping from every word. "Never had t' work, did ye?" Long fingernails nipped through Estella's sleeve, into her flesh.

"Get *off!*" Estella shrieked. With all her might, she jammed her elbows back, at the same time lunging forward to free herself. The arm around her waist fell away, but the woman held fast to her with one hand. Still, Estella was now able to turn and face her assailant.

She was female, yes, but so grotesque Estella shrank away, and her heart skittered in panic.

The woman's age was unclear, for she was as thin as a broomstick, and completely coated in face powder, rouge, and bloodred lip paint. Her hair—the portion, anyway, that didn't appear to be a moth-eaten wig—was dyed a carroty red. Black roots showed at her hairline.

She was attired in a mauve velvet pelisse that was worn through at one elbow. Her bonnet sported a sagging bunch of silk flowers and what seemed to be a tiny stuffed monkey. Estella gulped back her nausea and forced herself to meet the glittering dark eyes of the woman.

"I—I don't know you, madam. You must be mistaken—"

"I called ye countess, didn't I?" The woman's thin upper lip curled. "I know exactly who ye are. Ain't it a pity that ye can't say th' same?" She tightened her grip.

Estella winced in pain and disgust. Then the woman's necklace, gleaming richly through the gloom, caught her eye. Several large, square-cut diamonds and emeralds were strung on a heavy gold filigree chain.

If nothing else, Estella's years in the ton had taught her to distinguish real gems from paste. And this hag's necklace had to be worth a king's ransom.

"Ha!" the woman smirked. "Fancy me necklace, do ye, love? Fit fer a countess, do ye think?" With her free hand, she cupped a soiled glove protectively over the largest emerald. "A gift from me lover, it is. He's a true gentleman. Knows how t' show his love in all the ways that matter. Which is more than we can say about *some* dogs."

Estella tugged her wrist again. "What do you want?"

The woman hacked out a laugh, pulled Estella so close that her fetid breath nearly made her retch. "Ye tell that man of yers to keep his snout from where it don't belong."

"Madam, I don't know—"

"Th' earl talks big, but he's neglected th' village like any wastrel peer, and some of us know he can't even tame his own wife." She sneered. "He's a harsh one, takin' me little Timmy away jes fer pinchin' some blue blood's purse when he came t' stroll the green and look down his big nose at us. Well, I'll tell ye, little countess, he ain't much of a man at all if he can't mount his bride."

Estella realized she'd gone stock-still, mesmerized by the woman's shocking speech. Recovering, she pulled as hard as she could at her arm, leaning her entire body into the motion. This freed her hand, and the hag was left with only her empty glove.

Running as hard as she could down the dim path, crashing through the twigs and leaves, tearing at her skirts when they snagged in the brambles, Estella did not look back. She didn't stop running until she reached the castle grounds. Only after she'd taken a hot bath and scrubbed her hair and skin vigorously with honeysuckle soap, was the stench of the woman's putrid breath forgotten.

* * *

"The roast pheasant is sublime, darling," Godolphin called down the length of the dinner table.

"Thank you," Estella called back. She didn't meet his eye, but stared straight ahead at the centerpiece of snowy orchids.

Clearly, she sensed his anger. He'd been unable to disguise the abruptness of his motions, tried in vain to relax his clenched jaw. He'd have to confront her about the prank, of course. Such behavior simply could not continue.

"Though," she added airily, "I'm afraid I oughtn't take credit for the food, since I've lived in the castle but two days, while the cook has been in residence for five years. And Mrs. Hobbs is in charge of the household." She took a dainty bite of pheasant.

"Cook has been here for seven years, actually." As he spoke the lie, his voice sounded irritable and hoarse even to his own ears. Blast. Exactly why did he have this incessant urge to bait her? It was bad enough he needed to hold her at arm's length. He kept his face blank as he chewed and swallowed.

Estella dabbed at her lips with her napkin. Hard. "Oh dear," she said, her face angelic. "You are so *terribly* adept at finding all those silly little mistakes I make." Laughing lightly, she tilted her head. Her neck was slim and rounded, ornamented only by a delicate silver chain.

Odd. He didn't recall her wearing that before.

It glimmered in the candlelight, as did the rogue ringlets of tarnished gold that escaped from her satin bandeau. His gaze followed the chain. It was long, and whatever weighted the end was hidden between the modest swell of her breasts.

Moisture sprang to his brow as he willed his body to remain under control.

"I am," she continued, "*so* very grateful. I aim to better myself. Whatever would I do without your help?" Though a smile remained plastered on her face, there was a stubborn glitter in her eyes.

Godolphin wanted to grin, to rush over to her, pull her to her feet and cover her mouth with his. Why? Because, despite having the appearance of some sort of pixie, she could do battle with the best of them?

Or because it was the one thing he could never allow himself to do?

"I beg to differ," he said after another rather large gulp of wine. "I am swiftly finding that my new bride possesses perfections of character beyond all my wildest hopes. Alas, her other, more intimate perfections, I have yet to enjoy."

There was a clatter as Estella's silver fork hit the edge of her plate. In an instant, however, she regained her composure. "Perfection," she rejoined, beaming, "is too strong a word."

"True. Admirable qualities, shall we say?" He speared his haricots verte with a trifle more force than necessary.

She chewed, swallowed. He found himself holding his breath in anticipation of her reply.

Bloody hell. It was almost as if he were *enjoying* this.

"You seem to have taken stock of all my attributes," she finally said, "as though you know me quite well. Remarkable for such a brief acquaintance."

He knew her well enough to believe she would short-sheet a man's bed.

Godolphin remained silent, watched as the lone servant replaced his plate with a helping of lamb cutlets. It was, he mused, alarmingly easy to play the role of bad-tempered husband. As though he'd been doing it for years. Was he turning into some sort of crotchety old codger before his time?

He rubbed a hand across his jaw, then glanced back at Estella. In her pale gold silk evening gown, with her creamy skin radiant beneath all the candles, she smiled prettily and murmured her thanks to the serving man.

In that brief moment, when all her elfin beauty and youthful grace glowed through, something occurred to him.

Perhaps Estella could save him from himself.

Godolphin ran an anxious hand through his hair. He was mad. He'd married her in order to get to the bottom of her papa's nasty little secrets, and to right the wrongs in Village Seabrook. For no other reason.

"I've written for a decorator to come from London," Estella announced, jerking him from his thoughts, "and I've been thinking a great deal about how the rooms ought to look. Downstairs, at least, they should all have a unifying theme, don't you think?"

Ah. Perhaps the brat was becoming tame after all.

"Whatever you wish." He made an effort to smile. However, after a day of incessant scowling, his face was stiff. He was sure the result was some sort of ghoulish grimace.

Estella batted her eyelashes. "Have you ever read about the walled gardens of the Orient?"

He felt his face go as red as the Bordeaux he had just consumed. "*The Orient?*" he ground out.

"All this musty English furniture is dreadfully out of date," she pressed on. "We could do something truly wonderful with indoor fountains, palm trees, parrots in golden cages, silken pillows on the floor. . . ." Up to this point her face had been perfectly earnest. Now it dissolved in giggles.

Irrational anger spiraled, white-hot, in his chest. His hands balled into fists, and he would have dearly loved to slam one, or both, of them on the tabletop. Which, of course, would have been unseemly. Especially in front of the servant.

He contented himself by sawing viciously at his meat. "A joke," he muttered, almost to himself.

"Yes. I have always found humor quite refreshing."

Did he detect a tremor in her voice? A wave of cooling

remorse washed over him. She *had* been only joking, after all.

"The sooner you get started on the redecoration, the better," he said.

She toyed with her fork. "What is the hurry?"

He grinned. "Best to get things underway before any infant Godolphins come along." He could joke, too.

Her face had gone chalky, and her lips were pinched together.

"Time is of the essence," Godolphin blundered on. "One never knows."

"Perhaps." It looked very much as if she would have liked to say something more on this topic. Instead, she fired him a look that would have transformed a lesser man to a chunk of granite.

She *did* have a point. They'd have to share a bed before talk of progeny began.

However, when Love, Honor, and Obey were absent, mightn't one be allowed to Tease?

"I suspect," Estella pronounced, "that I will be so busy with my duties in the castle, there won't be any infants making an appearance for a good while yet." She sipped her wine, adding in a mumble, "Poor hapless little dears."

Calmly, he swallowed. "I beg your pardon?"

"What?" Her expression was innocent.

"I was certain you said something."

"And you are busy, too," she hurried on. "Doing your work." She looked at him pointedly. "Whatever that may be."

"We needn't speak of that."

"No? Am I not the mistress of this household?"

"Indeed, you are. But being mistress of a household doesn't entitle you to meddle in every corner of my private life."

"If you consider that meddling. You work affects me just

as much as it affects you." She paused. "No, it affects me more."

He allowed himself to admire the rather charming effects anger had on her person: the delicate pulse throbbing at the base of her throat, the high color on her cheeks, the fire in her eyes. He speculated on how other activities might have the same effect. Especially *one* activity in particular. "How do you come to the conclusion that my private life affects you?"

"Aside from the fact that, in normal situations, a wife *is* a gentleman's private life, I am absolutely certain that you will work all day tomorrow."

"Probably."

"Which leaves me to my own devices."

"What else?" He shrugged. "Gentlemen's business is a dreadful bore. Nothing but ledgers and books and drawn-out negotiations—"

"Mama helps Papa with all of that. In fact, he says she's better at keeping the books than he is."

"She is, is she? Fascinating. Well, perhaps one day I'll show you what I do," Godolphin conceded. "But I must warn you, it's numbingly dull."

Her eyes were suspicious. "Why must I wait?"

"What is the hurry?"

They glared at each other like duelists facing off at dawn.

Chapter Four

A Wolf Den of One's Own

"Would you like to see the ballroom?" Godolphin asked abruptly.

Estella jumped in her chair. It was the first sentence either of them had spoken since the main course. She swallowed a bite of peach tart. "Um, yes. Yes, of course."

He rose, moved down the length of the dining table. As he approached, she fought a horrid sensation of shrinking. But she would *not* fear her own husband. However beastly he happened to be.

He pulled her chair out, proffering his arm. As she laid her palm over his forearm, she thought she felt him tense. Peeking up at his face through her lashes, she noted the bluish smudges beneath his eyes. Her heart squeezed with pity. "Did you not sleep?" she asked.

Meeting her eye, he released a hard bark of laughter. "No, sweet wife, I did not."

His tone was at once weary and hostile. She decided not to say anything more.

As they quit the dining room, Godolphin muttered something to the manservant. Estella couldn't hear what it was, but the servant nodded, even indulged in a discreet smile.

The ballroom was unlike any Estella had ever seen. Those she'd visited in plush private mansions in London, and even the public assembly rooms in Brighton and Bath, were no match for this strange vaulted space. Moonlight stole, glimmering lavender, through the windows that rose two stories to the arching ceiling. Outside, the night sky was a curtain of sable, studded with diamond stars. Three huge chandeliers dripping with crystal hung, unlit, from the ceiling. She could make out the prim outlines of chairs lining the stone walls.

"This side," Godolphin explained in a hushed tone, gesturing to one end of the huge room, "was part of the original castle. As you can see, it's been added to. The section with the windows was built in my grandfather's time."

Estella walked out onto the darkened floor. Her slippers made a soft scuffle on the expanse of parquet. She tipped her head back. "It's marvelous," she breathed. "The ceiling looks just like a cathedral." Her eyes fell shut, and she could almost hear the long-ago echoes of grand fetes held here. Hundreds of blazing candles, soaring violin music, the swish and rustle of colorful gowns . . .

But now it was so still and dim.

She felt Godolphin move closer. He was inches away, so close she could hear him breathing. "It's yours now," he said. His voice was gruff, almost as though he were ashamed of his tender message. "If you don't like the—"

"Let's leave it just as it is," she whispered. Peering up into his face through the darkness, she saw only shadowed angles, the glitter of his eyes. And she was suddenly, acutely aware of how very alone they were.

Shifting her weight, she found herself a few inches closer. She was inside his atmosphere now. Close enough to touch, to perceive the muffled thud of his heart, sense the charged energy of his presence, almost feel the scruffiness of his cheek.

"Estella," he whispered, his voice pleading and rough.

His neck bent down, and she felt the rush of warm breath—

"You requested music, Your Lordship?" Simkin, Godolphin's ancient butler, glided in through the double doors, balancing a lit candelabra in one hand and a bundle of sheet music in the other.

Estella and Godolphin drew apart. For some odd reason, Estella recalled the time her governess had discovered her stash of sweets hidden in the schoolroom.

Simkin marched to the far corner, where an antique harpsichord stood. After setting the candelabra on top, propping the music in front of the keyboard, and tossing his tails over the bench to sit, he began to play, his back to the dance floor. The notes, delicate, swirling, and complex, drifted up to the vaulted ceiling, echoing about till the whole vast ballroom was filled with Mozart.

"May I?" Godolphin offered a courtly bow.

Grinning, Estella curtsied, extended a gloved hand.

He led her to the center of the floor, his broad palm at the small of her back. Even through his glove, through the layers of her gown and stays, she felt his heat, his vibrant solidity.

Her chest fluttered as he pulled her close, enveloping her hand in his. They began to dance, moving in slow, halting steps.

They were married, for heaven's sake. So why did she feel as if she were doing something naughty? There wasn't a person in the entire world who could tell them what they were doing wasn't allowed.

Which somehow made it all the more frightening.

"Simkin," Godolphin whispered in her ear, "doesn't play dance music. He is descended from a long line of proper butlers who disdain the lower art forms. So I'm afraid we won't be hearing any waltzes tonight."

"Oh, but I love this sonatina," Estella reassured him. She tried not to gloat when his eyebrows lifted in surprise.

Possessing a knowledge of Mozart, she guessed, didn't quite fit his notion of her as a vacuous featherbrain. "Do you realize," she said, mostly to Godolphin's solid shoulder, "that this is the first time we've danced together?"

He pulled back, peered down at her, bemused. "No. It isn't possible."

"It is. In Brighton, I don't believe I saw you dance with *any* lady, though. You'd just stand by the wall, watching. So I can't be jealous."

"You would be . . . jealous? If I danced with another?"

She could have sworn he tightened his grip on her hand ever so slightly, and nudged the small of her back so his hips almost brushed her belly.

"Possibly." She hoped that her airy tone masked the odd sensations she was experiencing.

Again he drew her, almost imperceptibly, closer. "Truth be told, I'm not normally a gentleman given to dancing."

"But you're a splendid dancer."

"Only my wife would think so." His tone was laced with laughter. His cheek brushed her hair.

My wife. The words made her feel hot and cold all over. But she had to get hold of herself. She couldn't let the beast mesmerize her so. It was far too easy for him.

She hated to break the lovely spell he'd cast. It was as though she'd landed in the midst of a fairy story. A castle. By starlight. A dark, handsome stranger . . . Oh, for heaven's sake!

"Why did you burst into my parlor this afternoon?" she demanded. There. She'd done it. All the magic came crashing down, like a beautiful sand castle pulverized by a wave.

His hands flexed.

"I was embarrassed in front of Mrs. Lovely," she complained. Then, for good measure, "And she says the villagers gossip awfully."

She thought he'd stop dancing right then. But he didn't. When he spoke, though, his voice had the gleaming sharpness of a knife edge. "I hope that isn't a petty threat."

Oh dear. Perhaps she'd gone too far. "No, of course it's—but she said—"

"To be perfectly frank, I don't give a tinker's curse what Mrs. Lovely said. Women's prattle is of little interest to me."

A bolt of indignation sliced through Estella. It stung to hear him write off her new friendship as frivolity.

"One would think," he forged ahead, "that the vicar's wife would be a grounding influence on you. But she has already shown herself to be cheeky and self-assured—"

"You speak as though those qualities are undesirable, sir."

There was a pause of several beats. They swirled past the windows. Simkin switched to a Beethoven rondo.

Estella tipped her neck back to get a better look at Godolphin's face. It was a grim mask, his patrician nostrils flared with agitation.

He was *impossible*.

"*I* have been described as cheeky on several occasions," she said. "Even by my own mother. And as far as being self-assured, why, I could not respect a woman who did not strive to be so."

She was a little dizzy from the wine, the dancing, and all the arguing. So when he stopped suddenly, she slammed into his chest. Sucking in a surprised breath, she caught the scent of paper, a hint of tobacco smoke, and the salty tang of the sea. His arms clasped around her to keep her from stumbling.

Simkin played on.

Godolphin's fingers cupped the back of her neck, cradling her like something precious. Her head sank back, instinctively relaxing into his easy strength. How her head knew to do that, she could not say. But she found herself looking up into two liquid dark pools. His sculpted lips were parted; he wore an expression of fierce concentration.

"You *are* cheeky," he murmured. He still sounded put

out, but the corners of his eyes crinkled with amusement. "You are the most cheeky creature I have ever had the privilege of dancing with."

She ought to have come up with some clever retort. But she was paralyzed, dissolving into the inky blue heaven of his gaze.

"Which is why," he went on, his voice barely audible, "I have to kiss you."

Then, without further ado, he touched his lips to hers.

And it was *not* the same as that reckless kiss on the beach in Brighton.

At first he simply brushed his lips against hers. She could not inhale, though she very much would have liked to, since her head felt as light as sea foam, and she was sure her feet, on tiptoe, she noted vaguely, would float up out of her slippers.

She marveled at the softness of his lips. To her confusion, the secret spot between her thighs tingled as his cheek grated against her chin. Strange how she'd never noticed before how thin the skin of her lips was, so exquisitely sensitive, connected in mysterious ways to the nerves in other, distant parts of her body.

Her lashes fluttered shut. Just as soon as she thought she'd got the hang of the lip-touching business, she found he'd managed to work her lips apart. Or perhaps she'd opened them herself. At any rate, she knew she wanted him inside, with a craving more intense than thirst. When his tongue probed, muscular and moist, soft yet demanding, she felt gratified. They were connected as they should be.

Except in seconds, she was hungry for more. *More.* What that meant, exactly, she didn't know. But she was confident that if she succumbed, turned to liquid in Godolphin's arms, he would guide the way, and her body would know the rest.

A small sound, half whimper, half demanding groan, slipped from her throat. She was embarrassed, and her tongue froze in its tentative exploration of the corners of his lips. The sound, however, had the instantaneous effect of making him clutch at her, grab a fistful of her hair, push his hips hard against her.

There was an odd bulge beneath his trousers. She had only the dimmest idea of what it was (visits to cousin Henriette's Yorkshire farm hadn't been *entirely* without edification), but it made her stomach plummet in the most delicious, disturbing way.

She gasped as he pulled his mouth from hers, mindlessly indignant that he'd taken away the source of her pleasure. But when his lips trailed hot, moist kisses down her arched throat, she gasped in discovery. She was trembling, and in a dark corner of her mind she grew aware that she wanted to touch his skin. *Needed* to, really. Without thought, operating solely on instinct, she reached up with one gloved hand, wrapped it around the back of his neck and pressed his face into the base of her own neck.

Simkin played on.

Godolphin was . . . well, he was licking her collar bone, delicately, like a cat. True, she liked it, but it almost tickled, and she was surprised that a gentleman would do such a thing. So she giggled, shattering the bubble of intensity they'd created together. And then she felt a pinching tug at the back of her neck.

"Oh dear," she mumbled, taking a step back. It was too late. He'd straightened, but he held the tiny silver key that hung from the chain around her neck.

He lifted an eyebrow. "I don't remember you wearing this before." His eyes had a frightening luminosity.

"It's nothing. Nothing at all." Deliberately, she took the key from his hand, tucked it back safely beneath the gold silk of her neckline. "It's not . . . I've always worn it." Why did she lie? She looked past his shoulder, ashamed. It was only a silly dog training book.

"Indeed." His tone announced, in no uncertain terms, that he knew she wasn't telling the truth.

With effort she met his eye, then instantly wished she hadn't. Even in the cool moonlight, his eyes burned with anger. He presented her with a stiff bow. "Good evening, dear wife," he said. His voice was as chilly and smooth as marble.

Estella stared at his retreating back. She felt as if she'd been dealt a physical blow. She couldn't quite catch her breath, and her shoulders sagged. The clatter of his boots against the parquet punched holes in the shimmering harpsichord music.

When Estella finally found the will to leave the ballroom several seconds later, Simkin was still playing.

From Madame Pettibonne's
Treatise on Canine Behavior,
Prepared Especially for the Lady Handler.
A Short Explanation of the Personality of the Dog.

. . . Furthermore, as a pack creature, a canine must have his den. There is not a wild dog in Africa nor a wolf in Siberia who does not crave, nay, absolutely require, his own private, sacred spot in which to hole up and wait out the sorrows of life; or to bask in gnawing a bone, when his world is rosy and sweet; or to devise plots against those he preys upon. Into this den, the wild dog will only admit those of his own kind.

Even the most domesticated canine deserves his own little niche, be it a corner of the dampest chamber or an entire suite on the Cote d'Azur. Just remember, Dear Lady Reader, that you MUST NOT intrude upon this private spot.

"What!" you may cry, "let my caniche out of my sight for even a moment?" Indeed, my advice, lovingly administered, is that you do precisely that. You will find that your dog will live longer and be a better companion when he can, from time to time, lap from his golden goblet, chew a stocking or two, then fall on his belly and snore in his darkened cave, alone.

* * *

Estella hadn't decided what she'd do once she got to the top of the tower and found Godolphin. Thinking that far ahead would only ruin the satisfying huff she'd worked herself into. All she knew was that she could not sleep and it was well past midnight, Godolphin wasn't in his bed-chamber, and she, the mistress of the castle, had every right to know what was afoot.

One by one, she mounted the steps. Maggie stayed close behind, her toenails clicking softly on the stone.

Climbing the stairs, Estella turned round and round so many times, she was growing dizzy. She was panting, try-ing to remember exactly how tall the tower appeared from the outside (surely not *this* tall), when the steps came to an abrupt end. She nearly ran into a solid oak door.

Orange light escaped from beneath it. Muffled voices were audible.

She held her breath, straining to hear over her pound-ing heart. The pounding, of course, was a result of the exercise. Not fear. Kneeling, she put an ear against the door, but couldn't make out the words. She hadn't con-sidered the notion that Godolphin would be holed up in his lair with anyone. Who would be with him at such an hour?

Setting the candlestick down, she lowered her cheek to the top step and squinted through the crack.

Ah. Amid the furniture legs and what appeared to be stacks of books and papers on the floor, she could clearly see two sets of men's boots.

The closer boots were slightly shabby, cut low—not a horseman's footwear. The feet were uncommonly stubby. Teeters. A large pair of black boots, worn and muddied, were crossed casually at the ankles nearby. Those, she was certain, were her husband's feet.

She took in a sharp lungful of air, jerking her head away from the door. The stubby boots were walking toward her.

She had just enough time to blow out her candle and

scamper out of sight around the first curve in the stair-well with Maggie hot on her heels, when the door squeaked open.

Teeters's nasal voice echoed down the stairs. "At this point I really wouldn't tend to trust anyone, sir."

There was a rumble from within. Godolphin's voice, but the words were indistinguishable.

Teeters spoke again. "That's true enough. But others could be looking for the ledgers, as well. If what Milton said was true, they are the key to this mystery. Things could easily become dangerous."

Estella frowned. *Milton.* Why was that name so familiar? Milton . . . Papa had purchased the Brighton warehouse in the spring from a gentleman named Milton! It had to be the same person. Papa had grumbled about the exorbitant price of the property, and had hinted that Milton was too fond of wine—

She started at the clap of Godolphin's boots against the floor. Now his voice loomed, large and clear. She could picture him standing at the open doorway at the top of the winding stone stairs. "Things are already dangerous," he said. "Even if others were to search for the ledgers, no one's got the advantage I have in locating them first."

Teeters cleared his throat. "I do see what you mean. An oddly edifying method of trapping your enemy."

"I made up my mind a long time ago to do whatever it takes to destroy Hancock. He is a despicable cur, utterly ruthless."

Despicable cur? Papa, ruthless? Was Godolphin mad?

Estella didn't wait to hear more. Pulling up the hem of her nightgown, she bolted down the steps two at a time. Maggie went so fast that she slithered past her.

Godolphin was Papa's enemy? It couldn't be true. How could he want to destroy the father of his *wife*?

Only when she slammed the bolt home on her bed-chamber door did Estella realize she'd left her candle-stick on the stairs.

* * *

"Whiskey?" Godolphin offered.

Bertie Littlefield lowered himself on a tattered armchair in Castle Seabrook's library. *Pretend to relax.*

"It is the afternoon, I suppose," Bertie said. "Yes. Please." He watched as Godolphin moved in his pompous way to the sideboard and poured out two glasses. It would be whiskey, for the Earl of Seabrook had never been a man to sip brandy, even spurning the rationed rum of their naval days. He'd been captain, after all, keeping the finest spirits in his cabin for private consumption.

"Well, Littlefield," Godolphin said in that annoying way of his, half condescension, half feigned camaraderie. "Thank you for coming. I have a favor to ask of you." He handed Bertie a glass. "But first, I can't tell you how surprised and delighted I am to find you settled in my old stomping grounds, here in Sussex. How long have you been here? Three months?"

"Four." Bertie willed his face to remain composed. "I really couldn't pass up such a ripping opportunity as Hancock offered me. I'm heading the company now, essentially. Hancock has handed over many of his responsibilities to me, especially since the purchase of the new Brighton warehouse. Business possibilities have increased considerably. I'm grateful to the old chap." Bertie permitted himself a sip of whiskey. "After all, though I did attend school with you, I hadn't any ancestral homes to fall back upon once my navy career came down about my ears." He smiled weakly, just as he'd been practicing.

The blood had drained from Godolphin's perfect face, and he shifted in his chair. Oh, he did so hate to be reminded of the accident. Which was probably why he'd avoided Bertie so scrupulously during the summer.

Bertie straightened his back, assuming his best they-can't-knock-me-down-for-long face. "That's all in the past now that Hancock's taken me on. My years in His Majesty's service are paying off. Hancock admires my skill, my knowledge of how to avoid mishaps on the high seas. He lost four ships several years ago, to storms they say, but some whisper of Arab pirates. With my background, he can avoid those disasters from now on. And it'll make me a rich man, to boot."

"You deserve it, Littlefield." Godolphin raised his glass. "Here's to riches and happiness."

Ah. An opening.

"Speaking of happiness," Bertie began, "you must feel fortunate, indeed, to have married Miss Hancock. I must say, I know little of her, but she appears the most—"

Godolphin cut him short. "The most, indeed. In my absence," he went on, abrubtly changing the subject, "certain mysterious events have taken place here at the castle. I was wondering if you would be kind enough to give me your advice. After all, we once led the best crew in the Carib that ever routed out smugglers."

"That we did." Bertie drained his glass, silently cursing his jerky motions. "I'd be happy to help in any way I can."

There was a single rap on the library door.

Both men turned to see Estella slip through. She blinked when she saw Bertie. "I am sorry," she said. "I didn't know you had a visitor."

Bertie watched Godolphin's face. The muscles stiffened, as though he were angered. "Quite all right. If you'd just leave us . . ."

Estella's lips went tight. "Sorry to have bothered you," she said in clipped tones before marching back out.

The door slammed.

Silence. Bertie gazed down into his whiskey, hiding his pleasure. Trouble in paradise. Perfect.

"I knew you'd help me." Godolphin put his unfinished drink on the side table and stood. "I'll show you what I've found."

As they made their way through the dim castle corridors, Bertie's temples began pounding and his right hand, the one that really wasn't even there anymore, began to ache. Phantom pain, but it could have been real.

This was the story of his life, wasn't it? Following Godolphin around, hardly more than his slavey.

From the first day they'd met at school, when Bertie had been merely five years of age, and Godolphin barely older, he had been intrigued by the self-assured aristocrat. Even then, Godolphin had possessed a lively imagination and physical daring that had captivated the spirit of many a boy, several much older. He was a natural leader.

And he, Bertie, was a natural follower. The pain in his right hand shot electric currents of agony up his forearm. Damn it all, *no*. He'd made his way, he had his place, he was doing well. *Very* well. He wouldn't allow Godolphin to destroy his life a second time.

They had passed from the new part of the castle to the old. In a dim antechamber, Godolphin stopped before three doors, and opened the middle one. "Down here."

The grate of the hinges vibrated through Bertie's skull. A blast of icy air hit his face as he peered down a flight of stairs. Candles flickered in rusty wall sconces. The walls and steps shone softly in the feeble light, as though coated with moss.

Godolphin was already heading down, stepping carefully to avoid slipping. His candle sputtered in the dead air. Bertie hurried to catch up. For balance, he was forced to place his left hand on the wall. It was slimy, and cold. There was a soft, persistent dripping sound all around. Instinctively, he moved closer to Godolphin.

Then something rather delicious occurred to him. A person could have an accident down here. A very *bad* accident.

He studied Godolphin's shoulders descending in front of him. For once, the earl appeared almost vulnerable. Just a small push, and he'd go hurtling to a certain death.

Then Bertie could just head back up the stairs and bolt the door. How long before anyone found the corpse?

He struggled to focus. That persistent, keening wail was growing louder inside his skull.

Not now. Think about the money. Think about the power. Think about Estella. The pounding in his head and the pain in his hand and arm evaporated. *Estella.*

"I've had intruders," Godolphin said over his shoulder. "Smugglers. Not in here, but below. In the caves."

"The caves?" Always act dumb. With a man like Godolphin, it was the safest route.

"I imagine you know nothing of them."

Bertie swallowed. "Of the . . . smugglers?"

"Of course not the smugglers. You'd know nothing about the caves, I meant."

They'd reached the foot of the stairs. "The sea is still some distance from here," Godolphin went on, pulling a ring of keys from his pocket. "The tunnels open out on caves that are approachable only at high tide. Even then, ladders would be needed to unload cargo for storage."

"Cargo? Storage? What are you saying?" Bertie had spent years perfecting the modulation of his voice, control of his facial expressions, of his entire body. Hours before a mirror practicing a hundred different expressions. As many hours training his ear to the nuances of the voice: What made one's voice seem concerned? Humble? Afraid?

"What I am saying," Godolphin said as he fit the key in the lock, "is that Castle Seabrook has been used, until very recently, by smugglers."

"As recently as until you decided to return to the castle?" Bertie asked. Inside, he was snickering, but he managed to make his voice sound neutral.

Godolphin's shoulders tensed.

Bullseye.

"They brought their cargo here by sea," Godolphin went on, ignoring Bertie's remark. "Unloaded it into the tunnels, then distributed it. Who knows? Perhaps they even picked up contraband here to sell abroad. It's a perfect place for corrupt enterprise. Quiet. Remote. Naive villagers who won't raise a fuss."

"This is what you want me to help you with? Breaking up a smuggling ring?"

"It's what you do best, Littlefield."

Bertie smiled, and this time he didn't need to pretend. "It is."

Godolphin pushed open the door.

Chapter Five

A Larger, More Complex Beast

"Wretched, bossy bore," Estella seethed. "Pompous, dreary beast." She picked her way around a puddle in the overgrown formal gardens. Raindrops hammered a staccato rhythm on the brim of her bonnet, which had already begun to leak. An icy rivulet trickled down her forehead.

Why had Bertie Littlefield come to call? Was Godolphin attempting to drain information from Littlefield about Papa's business? About Milton and his mysterious ledgers, perhaps? After all, Littlefield was Papa's head overseer, his right hand man.

No matter what Godolphin was doing, here she was, out for a walk in this foul weather, getting drenched to the skin.

In all honesty, she had to admit she took secret, petulant pleasure in the splotches of mud on her boots, in the damp seeping through the shoulders of her pelisse. The dismal weather, and her own physical discomfort, suited her mood just fine. She needed time to think about how she was going to help Papa.

With a bit more force than was absolutely necessary, she batted some jungly iris stalks out of her path with her folded parasol. In retaliation, they snapped back, spraying her with still more water.

"Hang it," she muttered.

Then she had an idea. It was the only obvious step, really. She would have to get into the tower and try to find some clue as to how Godolphin was planning to destroy Papa. In order to do that, she'd have to get hold of Godolphin's key ring, the one he always carried on his person.

How was she going to manage that? Oh, hell.

Maggie did not seem to notice the fuming state her mistress was in. She trailed behind, soggy, tail drooping. Now and then she stopped and cast a wistful glance back toward the castle.

"Yes, I know you want to go back," Estella grumbled. "Curl up by the fire on my sofa, you bad little thing, and steal biscuits off the table. You've got to learn obedience."

Maggie responded by taking a few halfhearted laps from a puddle.

That was exactly the trouble, wasn't it? If you didn't keep some creatures on a tight leash, they'd walk all over you.

Like Maggie. Spoiled since puppyhood, she sat when she felt like it, stayed only when there was roast beef in the immediate vicinity.

Like Godolphin.

Estella stopped in her tracks. Maggie bumped into her legs.

Of course. Madame Pettibonne's book: *Canines, as well as other more complex beasts, will benefit from a strict regimen, and the larger beasts can be trained quite as readily as any canine, and with equally satisfactory results.*

Well, wasn't Godolphin a large, complex beast? Perhaps Lady Temple had given Estella the book with just such a notion in mind. Estella frowned. Lady Temple couldn't have imagined that Godolphin was not simply a stubborn, arrogant man. He did not only want a wife in his bed and a woman to order about, he also wanted to undo his wife's father. Drive him into the poorhouse. Perhaps even into jail.

Still, maybe Lady Temple knew more about the Godolphins than she realized. Perhaps Madame Pettibonne's skills reached further afield than the boudoir. "It's not as though I have many options, dog," she said to her distinctly unhappy hound. "I may as well give it a try. What have I got to lose?"

Suddenly, things didn't feel quite so grim. She'd change into dry clothes and take another peek at Madame Pettibonne's manual. Indulging in a naughty grin, her first in what felt like days, she headed back toward the castle.

Maggie, heartened by this turn of events, trotted close at her heels.

They drew near to the largest fountain, Estella humming under her breath, Maggie snuffling about in the overgrowth. The fountain boasted a statue of Neptune, surrounded by four huge stone fish with bulging eyes and gaping mouths, all covered in grasshopper green lichen.

Estella eyed the statue, and her humming trailed off. She didn't understand why, but fear tensed her neck, slowed her pace. Neptune gazed down at her with empty eyes, moss dripping from the end of his upraised trident.

And then a figure emerged from behind one of the fish. A short, round figure moving briskly toward them.

Estella stifled a cry with a hand pressed to her mouth. Maggie barked, then charged forward, hackles raised, emitting a long howl.

"For God's sake," Teeters sneered, pulling his hands protectively to his chest, "get that confounded cur away from me."

Maggie hunkered in front of him, growling.

"You frightened us," Estella retorted, trying in vain to keep the waver out of her voice. "What do you mean by sneaking up on us like that?"

"Call your dog," Teeters ordered. He made a feeble kicking motion. Maggie snapped at his foot.

"Maggie, come." Estella glared at Teeters, noticing for

the first time that his thinning, mouse-colored hair was soaking wet, for he wore no hat. He wasn't wearing a greatcoat, either, and something bulged beneath the lapel of his jacket.

Reluctantly, Maggie slunk back to her mistress's side. Growls still rumbled in her throat. Estella reached down and gripped her velvet collar.

Teeters gave the foxhound a frosty glance before his eyes darted up to meet Estella's. His expression was pompous. "From the window, I saw you going out for a walk," he began. "Heaven knows why a—why you would go out in such weather. Don't they have scarlet fever in London anymore?"

"My motives are of no concern to you." Estella narrowed her eyes, pondering how much Teeters looked like the river rat she had once spied from a pleasure barge on the Thames. "Is that why you sneaked up on me, then? To rescue me from the elements?"

Teeters snorted.

"No," Estella said. "I thought not."

Teeters took a few steps closer, mincing around a heap of sodden leaves. Maggie strained against her collar, growls intensifying.

"I wanted," he said, "to give you this." From beneath his jacket he pulled a brass candlestick.

Estella's stomach twisted.

"Take it." He thrust the candlestick toward her. Raindrops splashed against it. "It is yours."

Hand shaking, Estella took it.

"I thought it would be best if I gave it to you in private," he went on, "considering the, ahem, *questionable* location where I discovered it."

Estella gulped. "So Godolphin didn't—"

"Your secret is safe. But I must warn you, another oversight of this kind could prove unlucky. I bid you good afternoon, Your Ladyship." Teeters presented her with an exaggerated bow. As he bent, water streamed from his balding pate, splattering onto his small boots. "Perhaps it would be best for all of us if you found a better way to amuse yourself. This isn't London, where a pampered young lady may fill the empty hours with gossip and the theater. It is lamentable that you have taken up spying as your newest pastime."

There was no way she going to get her hands on Godolphin's keys.

"The apple trees still bear fruit," Godolphin told Estella. He gestured with his jaw up at a gnarled, black-branched specimen in the orchard. Late afternoon sun had warmed the wet earth, drying the puddles and the drenched weeds. Godolphin strode about the gardens and spoke to her as though nothing was amiss. As though he hadn't ordered her away from the library earlier.

His ring of keys was in its customary place in the right pocket of his woolen, and very country gentleman, jacket. She heard them jangle softly with every step he took.

"I see." Estella stared up at the rosy apples amid the leaves, so bright against the crisp sky. Smoldering anger clamped her teeth. *He means to frame Papa. My own husband means to frame my father.*

"Although," Godolphin continued, "they'll bear more fruit next year, and the pruning that you'll oversee will ensure that they aren't blighted." He gave her a sharp glance. "Correct?"

Estella nodded curtly. He was intolerably arrogant. He behaved as though she were one of his employees, not his wife. She moved away, sodden twigs bending beneath her kid boots, to the next row of trees. "Pears," she said. Perhaps, if he were to lean over, or reach up, or *something*, the keys would fall from his pocket. What she might do after that, however, was unclear. Grab them and run away? Not likely.

"Pears, yes, and the next row is plums, and then cherries. There are oranges and lemons in the orangerie, too."

Something dark and hard writhed in Estella's chest. She swung to face him, glaring up from under the brim of her white bonnet. "And why now, sir? Why have you neglected the fruit trees until now?"

He gazed down at her coolly. "Because now I have a wife to look after these things for me."

Their gazes locked. His eyes were veiled, his mouth a straight, stubborn line. She wanted to scream. Heat crackled between them, growing more and more intense until she was forced to look away. She called to Maggie, who was chewing a mushy-looking apple that had fallen to the ground.

"Convenient," she muttered. She lifted her chin, meeting his gaze again. "How very convenient."

"Isn't it, though," he bit off. "You're displeased that I sent you away from the library earlier."

"Well, of course! You treated me as though I were an annoying child, not your wife."

"I had important things I needed to discuss with Littlefield."

She narrowed her eyes. "I am certain you did."

"What do you mean by that?"

She couldn't let on that she knew he planned to destroy her father, so she said, "I actually had something rather important to discuss with you, too."

"Which is?"

"We've received an invitation. To a party." She ignored the amusement in his eyes. He made her feel so very petty, somehow. "Hosted by Sir Broderick Shipton and his wife, Penelope. It's in three days' time, at their Brighton house, and we—"

"Absolutely not."

She stared. "It's being given in *our* honor, Godolphin. We *must* go. And besides, they're my parents' dear friends. We can't be rude and—"

"I said"—Godolphin interrupted smoothly—"no."

"Why not?"

He ignored her. "Come. I'll show you the orangerie." He set off toward a gate in the stone wall that enclosed the orchard.

Curse him. He himself was impenetrable as a stone wall. *He* had no gates that she could discern. He meant to destroy her father, and now he meant to isolate her from her friends. But she'd be damned if she was going to sit back and watch. She thought of the keys, one of which had to open the tower. She followed him, with Maggie close behind.

Godolphin pushed the wooden gate open with the heel of his hand. The rusty hinges squawked. Behind him, Estella's footfalls were light even on the orchard's carpet of dead leaves and branches.

What had she meant by challenging him? *Why now?* she'd asked. How much did she know? Or, more importantly, how much might she find out?

"Careful of the nails," he murmured, holding the gate wide so she could step through. She didn't answer or meet his eye. His belly contracted with anxiety. He hadn't considered the possibility that his young, naive wife might be far too observant for her own good. It was imperative that he keep her away from people who might tell her the truth. People like Sir Broderick Shipton and his wife.

"It is lovely." Estella stood, head cocked, examining the orangerie. She seemed to have forgotten her anger. "Truly."

He knew she meant it. The orangerie was long and low, built of local stone, lined with huge paned windows. But the windows were so filthy now, it was difficult to see the foliage of the potted citrus trees inside. The pale green paint on the doors was peeling, and the finial at the top of the terra cotta roof was broken. Fallen roof tiles nested in the weeds that choked the foundation stones.

That familiar knife of guilt twisted beneath his ribs. This place had been neglected for so long. "I'll show you inside, and we'll see what needs to be done. We can bring a glazier from London for all these windows." He strode toward the low, mossy steps that flowed up to three sets of French doors. "The hot water pipes that keep the interior warm are probably sound, but we'll need to have someone check them over just the same." He paused at the top of the steps, turned.

Where the blazes had she gone?

He saw the flash of her white gown, and of the snowy markings on her dog, across the overgrown lawn. She was just beside the high hedge that marked the boundary between the gardens and the sloping wood that led down to the beach.

"No," he called, descending the steps two at a time and loping toward her.

She turned, peering at him strangely. "No?" she called back. She'd been trying to peek through the hedge.

Had he said *no* aloud?

He reached her side, struggling to keep his features placid. "It's—"

"Dangerous." Her voice was tight. "You know, I've not yet been down to the beach, husband. I do love the water, and besides, this is to be my home now. Yet I have been prevented by both you and Teeters from following any of the paths down the cliff. Why? I'm not an invalid, and I don't believe that I've ever given you cause to suppose I am so clumsy that I'll pitch over the edge at the first strong gust of wind." Her eyes narrowed, and they glowed amethyst in the sunlight. "Take me to the beach." She held out her hand, dainty in its white lace glove.

He stared at her proffered hand blankly. He could refuse, but it was clear that her suspicions had been roused. There was no feasible way, short of locking her up, that he could prevent her from venturing down to the beach on her own. It would be best, really, if he escorted her. Then he could control, to some extent, anyway, what she saw down there.

He took her hand. Even though his own hand eclipsed hers, her fingers felt firm, and very strong. He tried to ignore the energy, the shimmering jolt of pure life, that passed between them.

"Fine. Come on, then." He led her to a gap in the hedge, barely detectable due to the overgrowth.

The path wound through shady rose briars, grown over to fairy-story proportions, along the edge of the cliff. The crash of the surf far below could be felt through the ground, and the gusts that whipped upward licked their skin with salty air. The rose thicket swayed, crimson rose hips glossy in the sun.

The path was well-worn, with twisting roots exposed. Estella tripped on one. With a gentleman's instinct that almost surprised him, Godolphin clasped her hand tight to steady her, grabbing her waist with his free hand.

They hesitated. It was just for two seconds, perhaps three. The pounding of the surf throbbed below them, seeming to crescendo. He was exquisitely conscious of her body wound up in his arms, of her delicacy. She raised her eyes. They were huge, and something inside him seemed to shrivel. Because she looked *afraid*. Of *him*.

"I wouldn't have fallen." She moistened her lips, keeping the rest of her body quite still in his arms. "Although I am only the daughter of a merchant," she added in a bitter undertone, "I am not entirely graceless."

"Of course." He released his arm from around her waist. At the mention of her father—which was merely a coincidence, nothing more—he'd gone cold. He kept his grip on her hand, holding perhaps more tightly than necessary. Her fingers were limp in his own. He didn't care.

After a curve, the path pitched steeply down, and to one side a vista opened up. The sea sparkled vastly, just over the rim of the cliff.

Estella sucked in a breath.

Again, that blasted chivalrous instinct kicked in. Who had ever thought it would be a good thing? It was really a damned nuisance. He held her hand tight. "You are afraid of the cliff," he stated.

In response, she yanked her hand from his, sped up to walk a few paces before him. "You will find, husband," she tossed over her shoulder, "that I am afraid of very few things. I gasped because the sea is lovely."

He felt foolish, walking behind her. Her head was high, her shoulders set. For just a moment, he indulged in observing the sway of her hips as she picked her way down the path. The curve of her bottom flashed in and out of sight through the shifting layers of her skirts. From beneath her bonnet, escaped gold-red curls twisted in the wind.

He clenched his jaw, looked out to the sea. Why couldn't Hancock's daughter have been some bland, lumpish girl? Why did she have to be beautiful?

At the base of the path, the beach stretched out on either side of them. To the left, the cliffs gradually sloped down. To the right, in the direction of the castle, the ledges ascended so sharply that much of that section of the beach was shadowed.

Estella, naturally, was walking to the right. She'd gone right up to the edge of the surf, leaving a line of small boot prints in the sand. With one hand she steadied her bonnet, a pose that made her spine arch.

Godolphin's manhood surged in response. His eyes felt hot.

"Down this way," he called over the wind.

She was either ignoring him, or she couldn't hear. She bent, picked up a piece of driftwood, and threw it into the breakers. Maggie crashed into the water after the stick.

It was a peaceful, serene vision, this near stranger and her dog, and he was entranced. Her white gown glowed against the backdrop of indigo ocean, and her motions were liquid.

Then he had the oddest, most inappropriate vision of two tiny children, also in white, playing in the sand beside her.

Panic slapped him. His normally ordered thoughts buzzed like a chaotic hive.

And now she was moving again, toward the cliffs beneath the castle.

Quickly, he went to her side, gripping her upper arm with as much gentleness as he could muster under the circumstances. "Allow me to show you the dunes," he said. "They'll be pretty in this light, and we might see some plovers if we're lucky."

"I'd rather look at the cliffs." She took a lithe sidestep, wriggling out of his grasp. "They're far more unique than some little birds, I dare say. Or can't you trust me down here? Because there's something you don't want me to see?"

His throat was closing. What did she know? "Perhaps," he said easily, "it's simply that I know you can't be trusted on *any* beach. It brings out something rather wild in you."

She immediately blushed at the reference to that day in Brighton. Her gaze leapt past him. "You are suggesting, sir, that you don't want me down here on the beach for fear that I will attempt to Ravish you?"

He *did* like the sound of that. But no. He could not make love to her. It would ruin everything he'd planned.

"I assure you," she said, "I am fully able to control myself in that respect." She marched down the beach.

He watched her slipping away, Maggie following with an oversized piece of driftwood between her teeth. The surge of the blood in his ears was indistinguishable from the crash of the waves. Impossible to distinguish, too, was whether the heat in his blood and the quiver of his nerves was frustration at her disobedience, or sheer lust.

Again, he caught up to her. This time he took both of her shoulders and turned her to face him. He'd had a vague plan of chastising her, of insisting that she return with him to the path. But her sweet face, as she scowled up at him, dealt him a blow.

"You treat me as though I were a domestic animal," she snapped.

"No," he said huskily, looming over her, "I treat you as though you were my wife." His mouth hovered close to hers. He could smell the honeysuckle on her skin, could practically taste her lips.

"Your notions of what wifeliness entails are sadly out of alignment with my own." Her eyes were shadowed by her bonnet brim. "What a pity."

"Perhaps," he said, "I'd be willing to amend my notions for the price of a kiss."

"Ha. A light price that would be."

"Wars have been waged for kisses, my dear."

Her lips parted slightly. By now, he knew this was her mannerism when she was thinking of a clever retort. But he decided to interpret it as an invitation, instead. By her shoulders, he dragged her into his chest and opened her mouth with his.

He'd been prepared for a struggle, or for her to go slack in his arms. Instead, she responded instantly. She yielded, melting against his chest, and he could tell that the memory of their kiss last night in the ballroom was clear in her mind. Throat tipped back, she wound an arm around his waist.

It was exactly the opposite of what he ought to have been doing. One last curse that Hancock's daughter hadn't been born plodding and dour drifted through his mind. Then he gave himself over completely to the moment.

She'd known he was going to kiss her again. She recognized that glow in his eyes. And she really should have dodged his grasp yet again. He was enough of a gentleman not to force himself on her, she knew. But she *wanted* him to kiss her. Inexplicable. Downright alarming, really, when one factored in the knowledge that the utter beast had designs to destroy her own papa.

But what could she possibly do?

Her eyes closed, and the sounds of the surf and her husband's jagged breathing washed over her. When she touched her tongue to his, a growling moan vibrated from his chest. His fingers dug into her flesh like a man clinging for his life.

To surrender to him was sweeter than anything she'd ever known. Sweeter than a goose down pillow when exhausted, sweeter than the richest chocolate, sweeter than spring sunshine. Sweeter, it seemed, than even her own pride and duty to her father.

His tongue was insistent, and his palms rubbed down her sides, pressing into the swells and dips. She was dissolving one moment, and then with the grate of his unshaven skin against her lips, her nerves prickled with vivid life. She was lost in the fascination of his flavor, his moisture, his warmth.

He pressed down on her shoulders, where he'd been holding her so tightly. Again, she yielded, partly curious, partly entranced. Wholly unable to do anything but obey. He was pushing her down. Only when her rump hit the sand did she open her eyes.

He lowered himself over her, obliterating the blue sky with his dark jacket, his broad shoulders, the long black hair that whipped in the wind. He was just a silhouette. Only his eyes burned, like an animal's in the night.

"The sand," she said. Her voice was annoyingly kitten-like. "It's damp."

"Easily remedied." On his knees, he leaned forward, planting a tender kiss on her lips. Her hands trembled. Then he removed his jacket and arranged it on the sand behind her.

Her ears pricked at a soft, teasing jingle.

The keys. How had she forgotten?

He eased her onto her back and lowered himself on top of her.

Then her entire body was shaking, tiny electric quiverings that were much like those from cold. Except she wasn't cold. She was burning, and her pelvis ached. The feel of the hard weight of him frightened her. Yet it also felt oddly safe. A shelter.

And he was kissing her again, harder now. When she peeked through her lashes, she was alarmed to see his face so close to her own, and she saw that his eyes were squeezed shut, his straight eyebrows tilted down in concentration.

Clearly, he took kissing her very, very seriously. Just like everything else in life.

His eyes opened, and he pulled back a little, pushing himself up on his elbows. "I suspect I'm supposed to ask you what's the matter," he whispered. His voice sounded so near against the background of the ocean and the cawing gulls. "But at this point, I'm unable to formulate even one small reason why *anything* could be the matter."

She knew she hated him. But she couldn't help it; she smiled. "There are a thousand things wrong, I think. But I can't remember precisely what they are."

"No?" He tilted his head boyishly. "Splendid." Propping himself on one hand, he used the other to remove her bonnet, flinging it to the side. With a palm, he smoothed her forehead. His hand was warm and calloused. Her lids sank lower.

"Why couldn't you have been homely?" he asked.

Her eyes flew wide. "What?"

"Or at the very least, merely pretty? I'm sure I could've managed that."

"What in heaven are you speaking of?"

The muscles at the outer corners of his eyes tensed. "I can't possibly resist you, Estella. I'm afraid that's becoming patently clear."

She swiped her hair from her eyes. "Is it part of Godolphin tradition to attempt to resist one's new wife?" Nervous laughter came from nowhere. "Some sort of medieval rite?"

A smile curved his lips. "Nothing like that. There'd be no Godolphins left if that were the case." He kissed her forehead, then her nose. Then lower—she thought he was going to kiss her lips, and she parted them mindlessly to receive him, but he kissed her chin instead. "I'm going to have to resist you, my dear, because you don't want me."

She didn't want him? If only that were the case. Despite all that she knew of him, she had somehow found herself pinned on the damp sand with this enormous beast atop her. "Why?" she managed.

He got to his feet, looking down at her. "Why do I think you don't want me? Because we were wed three days ago, and we have yet to share a bed."

Humiliation made her skin clammy. She sat up, began busily brushing sand from her skirts. She felt so foolish. Small and alone, and utterly confused.

Turning, he stalked away from her, to the waterline, and stood looking out at the horizon, his back to her. Wind tossed his hair, rippled his white shirt.

She wanted nothing more than to get away. He seemed to be playing some sort of game with her, but she couldn't fathom what it was. She stood, calling for Maggie, who had wandered far down to the base of the cliffs.

Then she saw the caves.

Three black mouths gaped directly beneath the tumbling form of Castle Seabrook's ancient wing. They were a ways up the cliff, though not too high up to clamber to from the beach. Perhaps at high tide they would be accessible by boat. A rivulet of water trickled down from one cave, evidence of a spring inside. Could these caves be what Godolphin and Teeters hadn't wanted her to see?

Quickly, she scooped up Godolphin's jacket. It wouldn't do if Godolphin saw that she'd noticed the caves.

The ring of keys fell from the pocket, landing in the sand with a clink and a thud.

Her breath caught. A sideways glance told her that

Godolphin's back was still to her. She plucked the keys from the sand and stuffed them down her bodice, feeling fortunate that there was so much room there.

One second later, Godolphin turned.

She held out his jacket with a smile.

He'd behaved like an utter cad.

Self-reproach dogged Godolphin with each step he took up the cliff path.

Estella again walked ahead, avoiding looking at him. Why would she want to? He'd been in the midst of seducing her, of giving in to the glowing spark of attraction between them. And she'd been receptive. For a few moments he was sure he'd been transported straight to heaven, her supple body moving beneath his, her tongue dancing, alive and so sweet in his mouth.

Luckily, he'd regained his self-control. But he hadn't missed the hurt in her eyes.

At the top of the slope, he watched her shoulders brushing through the overgrown rose thicket. Her motions were stiff.

It was better this way. Better that she be hurt, because then she'd stay away from him, and his body wouldn't have the opportunity to lord its power over his intellect again.

He had so much work to do. In a habitual gesture, he touched his hand to his jacket pocket.

His lungs seized. Where were his keys?

"You go ahead," he said to Estella. She stopped, turned. Yes. Her eyes were wide with pain. "I seem to have left something on the beach."

She had ten minutes, no more. After she was sure Godolphin was out of sight along the cliff path, Estella broke into a run. Maggie galloped joyfully beside her, tongue lolling.

"This is no game, dog," Estella muttered. "He's already

missed his keys." If she was going to find a clue as to just how and why Godolphin planned to destroy Papa, it would be in the tower.

When she reached the formal gardens, she slowed to a brisk walk. She didn't want any of the servants—or, heaven forbid, Teeters—to see her running. News could get back to Godolphin.

When she reached the top of the spiraling tower steps, she was so winded she could scarcely breathe. Her fingers shook so badly that she lost precious moments as she tried one key after another in the door.

The third key didn't fit, and when she withdrew it from the lock, she blinked with recognition. Her lungs froze, and she turned the key over.

It was the key to Papa's warehouse. *Her* key to Papa's warehouse. She hadn't even noticed it had been missing. Fingers shaking with fear, she removed the stolen key and slipped it into her bodice.

Maggie nudged her, bored.

Estella snapped back to action. She didn't have time to waste.

The smallest key, of bright brass, fit in the tower door's lock. Heart pounding, she pushed the door inward.

Chapter Six

The Warehouse

What had she been expecting? Skeletons? Mounds of gold doubloons? Shackled prisoners?

Godolphin's tower study looked like just that: a study. True, the room was circular in shape, with several tall, narrow windows filtering the afternoon light. But there were the usual bookcases groaning with dull-looking tomes, and a massive desk piled high with two stacks of ledgers. There was a map table, too. She moved toward this. A maritime map was spread across the top. She saw a dot on the coastline labeled *Brighton*.

Did Godolphin sail?

Not that she knew of. But Papa's ships docked in Brighton to unload. Papa's warehouses in Brighton and other coastal towns were filled with furniture, bolts of cotton and tobacco from America, and silks and porcelain from the Far East. From there, the goods were distributed all over Britain.

Resolving to ask Godolphin about sailing, Estella turned her attention to the desk. The first pile of ledgers turned out to be unintelligible. They were accounts, possibly for the estate, but while the columns of neat numbers were easy to understand (and correctly calculated, she noted), the labels for the columns were all abbreviated: *Stb. Cts.*, one column said. And another, *Mmnt.*

Each ledger, she saw, had a date in the upper right-hand corner. The bottom-most ledger was dated July 1788, and the topmost was marked May 1818. Just months ago. And something caught her eye: Printed neatly at the very top it read *Marblegate House.*

Why did Godolphin have the account books for some house she'd never heard of? He'd been living in Castle Seabrook for the last seven years, hadn't he?

She couldn't very well stand about puzzling over it. She picked up the topmost ledger from the second stack.

When she opened the cover and read the heading atop the first page, her jaw fell open.

It read, *The South China Company, Records August 1818.*

She flipped through the book, and then checked the rest of the ledgers. They were filled with import and export records for the South China Company. Papa's foremost business competitor. She'd heard about this company nearly her entire life, how its owner remained anonymous, shrouded in secrecy. How it had often beat Papa's own Hancock Enterprises to the chase in cornering foreign markets, outpricing Papa for trade deals from Boston to Bombay. The South China Company wasn't unscrupulous, but it was shrewd and quick. Papa had often wondered who headed the company.

Well. She set her lips. He'd soon know.

Hands shaking, she opened the top desk drawer. Inside were extra quills and pencils, a broken watch. And a dagger, unsheathed. Long, lethal looking, with a handle of silver and gold. She picked it up, and it was heavy, icy in her hands. Carved on the handle was the Godolphin family crest, just like on her stationery, with diamond-scaled fish and curlicues.

She replaced the dagger and opened the next drawer. A palm-sized book with a worn leather cover nestled inside. Conscious of the seconds ticking away, she snatched the book up and flipped through it. It was half-filled with ink scribblings, in the same hand as the Marblegate House and the South China Company ledgers. Godolphin's handwriting, presumably. Almost everything was abbreviated.

The man was awfully careful about making certain no one could snoop successfully amongst his things.

That question, which had been humming in her brain all day, rose to a clamor. What was he hiding? Maritime maps, the caves, household accounts from some other estate. And his intention to destroy Papa. There had to be some way it all added up.

The South China Company had to be the link.

She flipped to the last written page in the notebook. *9 Cblr. Whrf.*

Estella blinked. Number nine Cobbler's Wharf was the address of Papa's Brighton warehouse. And next, *J.B. & P.S., 8–7, B., 9–6.*

Joe Brady, Patrick Small. They were the men who worked in the warehouse. The B. must refer to Bertie Littlefield. The numbers had to indicate the hours they worked.

Estella's blood rushed hot and fast as she replaced the book in the drawer. She might not have learned what Godolphin was planning on doing to her father. But at least she had a lead as to *how* and *why*.

She was out of time. She turned toward the door.

"Ah. I thought I'd find you here." Godolphin allowed himself a flicker of gloating, watching his wife freeze in the middle of his study floor. Her skin had gone chalky, and he saw her pulse throbbing at the base of her throat. He didn't know why—the little witch had tricked him and stolen his keys—but he was the one feeling guilty. "Here." He held out his hand. "Give me the keys. It'll save you the bother of having to go back down to the beach again."

"I . . ." The single syllable wavered. She gulped. "I just

wanted to see what was in here. You won't tell me what sort of work you do."

His jaw locked. "And did you find out?"

"No." Her gaze flicked to the stone floor. "I hadn't the time."

Godolphin lounged against the door frame, his arms folded. "I suppose it's best that you satisfied your curiosity early on. Heaven knows what sorts of things you were imagining. It's rather like the fairy story of Bluebeard."

She was glaring, now, all fear transformed to anger. "Bluebeard—you may have trouble recollecting the tale, since it's been ages and ages and *ages* since you were little—"

He suppressed a chuckle.

"—even Bluebeard," she went on, "had the decency to entrust his wife with a key."

"No fairy-story heroine, darling, is so audacious as to steal a key from her husband during a kiss. And you forget that Bluebeard's new wife made a rather horrific discovery upon unlocking the door. Whereas you've found nothing but dusty books and ledgers." Again, that golden heat in his loins. His palms itched with the need to feel her, and his breath grew shallow at the memory of her taste. He threw off the surge of desire. "The keys, madam." He held out his hand and stepped forward.

She took a step back, her bottom bumping the edge of his desk.

Slowly, he advanced toward her. She seemed to be holding her breath, for he heard nothing but the ocean wind shuddering against the window panes, and the pounding of his own blood in his ears.

"The keys." He was so close to her now, he only had to whisper.

She leaned back as far as she could over the desk, craning her neck upward to look at him with those violet-blue eyes. They smoldered with challenge. "*Your* keys?"

The *your* was only slightly inflected. Had she noticed the warehouse key, and the key to her father's Brighton house on the ring? Even if she'd taken them back, though, he'd already made copies.

Very deliberately, he placed his palms flat on the desk, one beside each of her hips. She was ensnared now, and that drenching need to possess sloshed over him. Close was never close enough. He could not kiss her deep enough. He wanted her to be his. But she wasn't.

"You are a bully, sir." She swallowed, but didn't look away.

"I am your husband, madam. You belong to me." God, it sounded like a joke, even to him.

"I belong to no one but myself."

"Then why did you marry me?"

She sniffed. "Certainly not to *belong* to another person."

"No?" He leaned closer, near enough to inhale the pale honeysuckle scent at her golden-downed temple. His eyes closed, and his hips pressed into hers.

She let out a little gasp.

He would allow her to go, he told himself, if she tried to get away.

But she didn't try.

Brushing his lips very lightly down her cheek, he whispered, "The keys, Estella. Give them to me."

A dry cough emanated from behind him.

Blast. That would be Teeters. Willing his manhood to subside, Godolphin turned.

"I'm terribly sorry to interrupt," Teeters said briskly. His eyes were impossible to see through the glare of his spectacles, and he held a bundle of papers against his chest. "You had instructed me to meet you here at three o'clock."

"I did." Godolphin felt like shoving Teeters out the door and slamming it shut. Irrational, yes. But so very tempting.

He heard a metallic clink, and then Estella slipped past him.

"Good afternoon, Teeters," she said, dodging out the door past him.

The keys, Godolphin saw, sat on the desk blotter.

Crouched in a yellow pool of light in the warehouse loft, Bertie Littlefield fumbled with the Oriental puzzle padlock.

"Hang it," he swore softly, and flexed his left hand. It was strong after seven years, but he'd never get used to using it. His right arm and hand tingled. He'd been born right-handed, but one couldn't bleeding well *use* one's right hand if it was gone. He could still feel it, the memory of it, wanting to help. But the bits and pieces of it were long gone, devoured by unthinkable creatures on the bottom of the Caribbean Sea.

He nudged the gas lamp closer to the safe and tried again. The first hundred or so combinations he'd tried hadn't worked. He'd been fooling with the padlock every night for the last three days, since Hancock had sailed for America. All Bertie saw when he closed his eyes and tried to sleep was the padlock.

He was beginning to lose patience. Which meant that the terrible high-pitched wail in his head, always fading in and out, was growing louder. If he didn't calm himself, it'd become a horde of banshees, all screaming at the top of their lungs.

Squeezing his eyes shut, he strained to think above the shrieking. The puzzle padlock had been brought by Hancock from China, and it was masterfully made. It contained five revolving disks, of graduated sizes, one on top of the other, and in order for the hasp to be released, the disks had to be aligned just so. Complicating matters was the fact that the disks didn't have numbers or letters. For God's sake, even Mandarin calligraphy would have been helpful. No, the puzzle padlock had tiny pictures engraved in the metal. Birds, fishes, clouds, what looked like a bowl of rice, a boat, a shoe. Bertie couldn't even tell what many of them were, actually. There was no rhyme or reason to it, and he'd been trying combinations of pictures at random.

Estella would know what the combination was.

He heaved himself to his feet, scooping up his lamp. Estella, her cursed Papa's most priceless treasure, had to know how to crack this safe.

"For you, madam," the footman uttered.

He hovered discreetly over Estella's chair, proffering a note on a tarnished silver tray. The gold embroidery on the cuff of his livery jacket was tattered, she noticed.

"Thank you." Her throat was scratchy from the humiliation of having waited at the dining table for twenty minutes for her husband, who had not appeared. Not that she *wanted* to see him. She didn't know what those Marblegate House ledgers meant, but the meaning of the South China Company records was clear: It was Godolphin's company. He meant to drive Papa out of business through any method necessary, including framing Papa. What was worse, Godolphin had married her in order to do this. It was too sickening to contemplate.

Well, she would *not* show her hand by letting Godolphin know she'd seen those ledgers. It was better for him to think she was a gullible twit.

She took the note. Not until after the footman had disappeared through the huge paneled doors did she unfold it.

Darling, it read. *Please accept my apologies. Urgent business has called me away.—G.*

"Sneaky wretch," she mumbled. She stood suddenly, pushing her chair back. The stolen warehouse key. The hours of the warehouse employees in his blasted little notebook.

It was time, she decided, to wield her powers as mistress of the castle and instruct that one of the carriages be readied for an evening foray into Brighton.

* * *

Even before he'd unlocked the door and stepped into the ink black, musty warehouse, Godolphin knew something was amiss.

He closed the door silently behind him, shutting out the evening drizzle. Standing very still, he strained his ears. A creak. The wind, perhaps, working at a loose shingle. An almost imperceptible scuffling sound. A mouse. A rambling warehouse like this had to have mice.

But clamminess wrapped itself around his neck. He knew, beyond a shadow of a doubt, that he wasn't alone in the darkness.

He'd come here to search for the ledgers that would incriminate Hancock. Milton, the florid, grasping man who'd sold the Brighton property to Hancock, had told Godolphin that there were records of incriminating information. True, Milton had said this just before clearing out of town, and Godolphin had had to give him twenty pounds for that bit of information. But it was, at this point, the only lead.

Yet how could he search for the ledgers if he wasn't alone? He wasn't afraid. That feeling was foreign to him. But he wasn't a fool, either. He'd have to hide and wait for whoever was here to leave. His eyes had adjusted to the darkness, and now he could see indistinct black forms against a lighter gray. There were windows high on the warehouse walls, and these admitted a little light. He saw a staircase that seemed to lead to a high platform or dais, perhaps for the overseer, poor old Bertie.

Godolphin braced himself against the familiar gut wrench of guilt. Could things have been different? Could he have prevented Bertie from losing his arm?

Stop. Now wasn't the time to mull it over.

He moved carefully to the stairs, breathing shallowly, and crept up the twelve steps to the platform. Then he waited.

* * *

"Hullo?" Estella called out from the open warehouse door. As she'd expected, the door had been unlocked. Inside, the warehouse yawned pitch-black, cool as a tomb. Behind her, the wind howled, and a spray of fine drizzle whipped past her from outside. She crouched, set her lamp on the floor, and with freezing fingers managed to light it. The gas hissed. She stood, closed the door, and held the lamp aloft.

The lamp was small, and its light didn't extend far into the dark reaches of the warehouse. But she'd been here a few times with Papa. The main floor was huge, open, with wooden crates stacked around the perimeter and in rows across the floor.

"Hullo?" she called again. She'd come expecting to find Godolphin snooping about, but perhaps she'd misinterpreted the clues. Why had the door been unlocked, though?

Slowly, she walked down an aisle between rows of crates. They were labeled with thick black paint on the splintery wood. SHANGHAI/PORCELAIN. CALCUTTA/SILK. BOSTON/PEWTER.

Everything was just as it should be. What in heaven did Godolphin think he could prove about Papa's business?

She reached the end of the aisle. Then she stopped.

It was peculiar, was it not . . .

No. She couldn't think these thoughts.

But the nagging persisted.

Chinese porcelain and Indian silk were extremely valuable objects. Papa, she knew, was a shrewd and careful businessman. So how could he leave these luxurious goods unprotected? His London warehouses had night watchmen, and the doors were barred with considerably more than a single lock and key.

She hesitated for two seconds, and then went in search of a tool.

It didn't take long for her to find a crowbar on a long workbench below the overseer's dais. She returned to the

Shanghai/porcelain crates, set the lamp on the floor. When she hefted a crate to the floor, she already knew. It was light—far too light—to contain dishes. And it didn't rattle.

Mislabeled. The crate was mislabeled. Or else being reused for something light and soft, like textiles.

She fit the tapered end of the crowbar under the edge of the crate's lid, and leaned down with all her might. The nails screeched as they gave way.

"Miss Hancock," a voice purred behind her.

She screamed. The crowbar clanked on the stone floor. She instinctively moved away from the voice, even as she turned.

"Or, I ought to say," Bertie Littlefield said, "Lady Seabrook. My, but you've gone up in the world."

"Mr. Littlefield." Estella held her breath to slow her sprinting heart. Since the lamp was on the floor, it made Bertie's face look ghoulish. Ordinarily, he was a fair, ginger-haired man of medium build, utterly nondescript except for the fact of his missing right arm. Now, though, his eye sockets were deep in shadow, his mouth feral.

"What are you doing here?" she asked.

He chuckled. "What am I doing here, Her Ladyship asks." He sucked in a spastic breath. "What are *you* doing here? I work here, you may recall. Every day, and often long into the night. Keeping your Papa's business running smoothly so that you may reap the rewards of being a wealthy man's daughter."

Estella inched back another half step. Perhaps he was drunk. He didn't seem drunk, exactly, but his hostility was palpable. He'd never been anything but a gentleman to her before.

Bertie stared down at the crate. The lid was raised slightly, but still attached. "Castle Seabrook hasn't enough porcelain for your tastes?"

"Not the sort I prefer. I wanted some of the blue and white variety, with the pictures of . . . pagodas painted on them." She swallowed. "There doesn't seem to be porcelain in that crate, though. It's too light."

Bertie's upper lip peeled away from his teeth. "Who have you been talking to?"

"No one—what do you mean?"

He ignored her. "That cur Johnson?"

"I am not acquainted with a Johnson, so I can assure you that I've not been speaking with one. I'm here because Papa—my father—said I might help myself to anything in the warehouse."

"In the middle of the night?"

"It's not the middle of the night. It couldn't be even ten o'clock yet."

"I can't think of anything more tiresome than arguing petty points with a nineteen-year-old," Bertie suddenly snarled.

Fear clawed the base of her skull. There was something very wrong with Bertie, and she needed to leave. Immediately. "Good evening, then," she said. She walked deliberately past him in the aisle. "I'll just leave the lamp for you, since you seem to have been working in utter darkness."

She'd almost made it by him when he reached out with an eel-like motion and caught her wrist.

"Unhand me!" she yelled. His fingers were bone cold.

There was a distinct thump from somewhere in the warehouse. Panic ripped through her. There was someone else. Bertie had an accomplice.

She tore her wrist away and ran.

"You have to *tell* me if you want something from the warehouse!" Bertie shrieked after her. "I need to keep track of it in the ledgers! You can't just come and help yourself! *I'm* the overseer! *I'm* the head of this business while your father is away!"

He's utterly mad. He's mad. He's mad. Estella didn't even shut the door, but dashed out into the wet night, jogged down to the end of the wharf where her carriage waited, and scrambled in. She didn't breathe properly until the carriage pulled into the circular drive in front of Castle Seabrook.

Godolphin's young stallion raced down the muddy road. Thunder, safe and warm in his stable, wouldn't have been up to tonight's ride. The drizzle had turned to a steady shower, with winds slicing up from the Channel. The sky was a wet wool blanket.

Godolphin wasn't thinking of Thunder. He was too numb. Watching Bertie's behavior with Estella had told him two important things. First, that there was a side to Bertie he'd never seen before, a hysterical, malicious side. His mention of Johnson, a villager recently jailed for fighting, disturbed him to the core. He needed to think on this, but it would have to wait.

After Estella had left, Bertie had hammered the lid of the crate shut, replaced it on the stack with the others. Then he'd returned up the steps, presumably to the loft from where he'd come. After a few minutes, Godolphin had decided it was safe to creep out.

The second thing he had learned was that he was beginning to care for Estella. It had been all he could do to stay hidden when Bertie had grabbed her. A feeling of absolute outrage and, yes, fear, had gripped him when Bertie had screamed after her.

Godolphin didn't even pause to ponder what affection for his temporary wife could mean for his carefully laid plans. All he wanted was to reach her, to see that she was all right. To hold her, protect her. He'd consider his plans in the morning.

By the time Godolphin had reached the stables, he was soaked through. He roused the stable boy, Timmy, to care for the wet, muddy horse. Then he practically ran all the way to Estella's chamber.

Just outside the door, he stopped. He needed to collect

himself. He couldn't just burst in. Her nerves would be jangling after her encounter with Bertie.

He knocked.

Silence.

Another knock, a little louder.

"Yes?" came the muffled response.

He thought of his behavior earlier that day. The kiss on the beach, then the way he'd retreated. He'd confused her. And then their encounter in the tower, interrupted by Teeters.

"Your husband," he said, too gruffly. "Godolphin."

A padding of feet, growing louder. The door latch being clicked to the side. Then her face, pale and sweet, in the crack of the door.

Tenderness flowed through him like some sweet fluid. He would hold her, protect her tonight, no matter what the cost. It was irrational, as all his thoughts were concerning Estella. But he'd made up his mind.

"What is it?" she asked, cocking her head. "Heavens, you're soaked to the skin."

"Am I?" He couldn't pull his eyes from her face.

"You ought to change. You'll surely catch a chill." Her tone was formal, distant. And why shouldn't it be? He'd treated her badly.

She looked as though she was about to shut the door. For some reason, that was absolutely the last thing he wanted. "How was dinner?" he asked. Perhaps she'd tell him about Bertie and the warehouse.

No such luck.

"Dinner?" Her gaze shot up to his face. "Dinner was delicious. Pity you weren't able to dine with me."

"May I enter?"

She stared.

"Very well." Stepping back, she admitted him.

He followed. Through the near darkness she moved to the mantelpiece. A match sizzled as she struck it, catching the two of them in its yellow flare. Her hair glowed like pale fire as she set the match to a candlewick. She blew out the match, watched the delicate gray curls of smoke twist toward the ceiling.

Anything to avoid looking at him, apparently.

"Were you sleeping?" he asked.

"Trying. Maggie's afraid of the thunder."

Despite himself, Godolphin smiled. "Where is she?"

"Under the bed. You'll hear a whine the next time there's a rumble."

"So she doesn't protect you when there's thunder."

Estella looked him in the eye. "Clearly not."

Godolphin walked toward her, and her eyes rounded. But he stopped short, and lowered himself onto the dainty couch. It groaned softly under his weight. "I suppose I'll ruin it."

"The couch?" She lifted an eyebrow. "It wasn't in very good condition to begin with."

"All the same, I ought to remove these wet clothes." He'd said that to get a reaction from her. It worked.

"*Here?* But you haven't anything to . . . change in to."

"I'll manage." He leaned over and yanked off his wet boots. Leaning back again, he removed his jacket.

She fidgeted.

Next, he unbuttoned his waistcoat, heaped it atop the sodden jacket next to him.

"Is this why you wanted admittance to my chamber?"

He unbuttoned his shirt. Her eyes, he saw, were riveted to the top of his chest. He paused, considering, his gaze tangled in hers. "I'm sorry about how I behaved on the beach this afternoon," he admitted truthfully.

"About . . . kissing me?"

"No. I wouldn't want to take that back for the world."

Her eyes dropped to the floor.

"I want to hold you tonight, Estella."

"What?" she squeaked.

"No Ravishment. I promise. I'm not nineteen years old

anymore. I'm not thirty years old anymore, for that matter." He unbuttoned his cuffs. "I can control myself. So, if you were in bed, please, go back. I'll join you."

Her mouth opened, then shut again. She appeared to be struggling with some objection.

"Go," he said in his most commanding tone.

Miraculously, she did.

Godolphin was abruptly aware of his manhood, hard as steel. He stripped off his shirt. But he would have to leave his trousers on.

When he took the candle and moved to the bed, he found her with blankets up to her chin, and she was on the farthest edge. "You must stay *entirely* on your side of the bed." Her eyes flashed in the candlelight. She seemed to be deliberately avoiding looking at his torso.

"Of course." He grinned. Probably he looked like a ravenous wolf. It was a good thing she'd covered herself from neck to toe.

Frowning, she squeezed even farther to the edge. "Do not cross the center line." With a hand, she indicated an imaginary boundary down the middle of the bed.

As he lowered himself on the edge of the mattress, she rolled a bit in his direction. Gripping the edge of the mattress on her side, she dragged herself uphill.

He leaned forward to blow out the candle. As he did so, she released her hold on the mattress, rolled a few inches in his direction.

He straightened, glancing over his shoulder. "Do not cross the centerline."

Estella glared, and huffily fell back onto the pillows. "Well. Good night, then." She flipped over onto her side so her back was to him.

He lay down on top of the bedclothes, still in his rain-damp trousers. Estella's breathing gradually deepened and slowed. She seemed to relax, and her presence filled the room with a warm heaviness. Despite the bitter storm outside, despite his body next to her, she'd fallen asleep.

He was uncomfortable, and a little chilled. It didn't matter. For the first time, he was in the same bed as his wife.

His wife? Why in blazes was he thinking like this? Yes, they were wed. But only temporarily. With luck, in a few short weeks he'd have gotten to the bottom of Hancock's crimes, and the marriage would be annulled. He'd be a free man.

The only problem was, he was beginning to suspect he didn't *want* to be a free man.

Chapter Seven

Cannot Manage It Any Longer

Godolphin crossed the stable yard in five long strides. The sun was just rising over the sea, the rays lighting up the storm-cleared air, reflecting off the huge puddles on the ground. His heart was conflicted. He was burdened with the sad knowledge that his old friend Bertie was not who he seemed. Yet at the same time, his soul was humming with a quiet happiness from lying beside Estella all night.

Heaving open the huge sliding door of the stable helped clear his head. He planned to ride into the village and visit Johnson, the man Bertie had mentioned last night, in jail. Godolphin also needed time to think, away from the household staff, away from the watchful eyes of Teeters. Far from the temptation of his temporary bride.

Inside, the stable was dim, filled with the sweet smell of hay, the tang of horse sweat and dung. "Thunder," he whispered, afraid of awakening the several horses in the stalls lining the corridor. When he clucked his tongue, he heard a horse snort, and another scrape its hoof on the floor.

But, he knew from long experience, neither horse was Thunder.

Panic soured his stomach. He hurried to Thunder's stall.

Peering through the window above the door, he saw that the stall was empty.

The sound of footsteps made him turn. The stable boy, Timmy, looking sleepy, with his straight yellow hair flattened on one side, came toward him. "Th' old one's out in th' meadow, Yer Lordship." He rubbed his eyes with a grubby fist. "Just as you ordered."

The relief of hearing that Thunder was not dead was swiftly replaced with annoyance. "What are you talking about, lad?" he asked, keeping his voice gentle. Timmy was, after all, only twelve. "You know Thunder is to be stabled every evening. The nights are growing cold and wet, and he is elderly."

Timmy was wide awake now. Confused. "But yer note—"

Godolphin made no reply, but brushed past him, out the rear doors. At the far end of the pasture he saw Thunder grazing on the last green shoots of the year. "He'll catch a chill; he'll be soaking wet," Godolphin muttered. Neatly, he hopped the fence and strode across the pasture. Timmy stumbled along behind. The grass was so thick and wet it felt like wading through a bog. In no time, his trousers were thoroughly soaked above his boots.

Halfway across the pasture, Godolphin squinted in disbelief. "The imp," he spat. "The little witch. What in God's name did she *do* to him?"

Side by side, Godolphin and Timmy gaped, stunned, at the old stallion.

Thunder's tail was neatly plaited, woven with dead weeds and geranium-colored ribbons. His mane had been braided in several little plaits, and his forelock, once long—and, Godolphin had often thought, rather rakish—was crudely hacked away so nothing but a stumpy sprout of hair remained. More pink ribbons, drooping with rainwater, were tied in large bows at his fetlocks. Around his neck still more ribbons were strung, along with a small placard made of Castle Seabrook stationery. In an imbecilic scrawl were the words CANNOT MANAGE IT ANY LONGER. The sloppy lettering, in blue-black ink, was clearly intended to disguise its writer.

Godolphin tore the card from the horse's neck. "Who did this?" he rasped. "Did you see her?"

Timmy could muster only a squeak.

"Who did this?" Godolphin spun around, and Timmy's eyes bugged in terror.

"I was visitin' me mum in the village, Yer Lordship, and I thought I'd wait out the storm. So I didn't get back till just before you returned last night. I'd known th' rain was comin', so I'd put all th' beasts inside before I left. But when I got back, I found someone'd let the old stallion loose. Tacked to his stall door were the note that said he were to stay in th' meadow for th' night." He crossed his knobby arms across his chest, nervously fingering his sleeves. " 'Orders of His Lordship,' it said."

"Show me the note."

But he didn't need to see the note. He knew Estella was behind this prank.

"Do you recognize this?" Godolphin asked, dangling a pink ribbon from his fingers. His voice was too level and smooth, like a man using his last reserves to rein in fury.

Estella bolted upright in bed, where she'd been luxuriating, and crawled back defensively against the pillows. Every fiber in her body tensed as she registered Godolphin's flashing eyes, the faint flush across his cheekbones. His hair had obviously been combed neatly at some point in the morning, and he'd even shaved. But now a straight black lock had come free, giving him the aspect of a pillaging pirate. His clothes, too, were tidier than usual. His pants looked damp at the knees, though, and his boots were mucky.

He stalked to the bedside, dangled the ribbon in front of her face. "Answer me." His voice was still under control. Just barely. "Do you recognize this?"

Estella scowled up at him. He had quite effectively shattered her feeling of happiness. "I suppose it could be one of my hair ribbons." She flashed him what she hoped was a look of defiance, but under the covers her toes curled. Never had she seen him quite so angry.

"You suppose?" Godolphin looked at the ribbon as if it made him physically ill, then stuffed it in his pocket. "Just how many ladies on this estate wear pink hair ribbons, madam? One? Two? All of them?"

So. He wanted to argue petty points, did he? Estella jutted her lower lip. "I imagine one of the women here might choose to wear a pink ribbon, sir."

He laughed, a bitter, choked sound. "Do you fancy Cook wears one in the kitchens when no one is about?"

"One of the maids could easily favor pink ribbons."

"Have you seen a maid wearing one?"

"Well, no." Estella's defiance faltered. "But they can wear what they please in the village on their days off."

This possibility seemed to catch him off guard. He stood there, breathing heavily, before apparently rejecting it. "Enough of this silly banter. You deny this ribbon is yours, then."

"Allow me to look at it more closely." She was certain it wasn't hers, but she thought she'd humor him.

He yanked it from his pocket and tossed it on the coverlet. Ignoring the way her belly had gone hollow, Estella picked it up with shaky fingers, then quickly dropped it. "No," she stated. "It does not belong to me. Mine are of Indian silk, of a softer shade of pink. This is a common ribbon that one might purchase from any haberdasher's shop." Her words rang snobbish in her ears, but it was the simple truth.

Godolphin reared back, his eyes narrowed in disbelief. "By God, woman, but you are a piece of work." He patted his pockets, almost frantically, as if searching for some-thing else.

In fact, he appeared to have gone quite mad. Slowly, so he wouldn't notice, she inched farther back against the headboard, clasping her arms across her chest. She'd heard about this sort of thing. These ancient families were inbred, often quite batty, shut up in their moldering estates with ghosts and delusions of grandeur. Even the King was cracked, everyone said—

"This," Godolphin hissed, tearing what appeared to be a hank of horse hair from inside his jacket. "This, madam." He held it aloft.

Involuntarily, Estella wrinkled her nose. It smelled like a barn.

"What is this?" he demanded.

"Perhaps a bit of stuffing from an old settee?" she shot back.

Next, he pulled out a note card and flung it onto her lap. She looked down at it, then picked it up delicately be-tween two fingers. It was one of her own, from the supply in the writing desk in the countess's parlor, with the Godolphin coat of arms at the top. In mounting alarm, she read the childish scrawl, then raised her eyes to meet her husband's.

"What does this mean, 'Cannot manage it any longer'?"

"You tell me." His eyes were suddenly as cold as flint.

"All I know"—from somewhere, she found an offended voice—"is that you have come crashing into my bedcham-ber like a—a rabid beast, and are in the process of insinu-ating that I am responsible for some sort of prank. A prank that sounds rather intriguing, actually, given the as-sortment of clues you have presented thus far."

"A prank? To slander your husband's reputation? To maim my horse—"

"Maim?" Estella cried in genuine alarm. "Thunder has been hurt?"

Godolphin shifted, scratched his eyebrow. "Not . . . not

maimed in the typical sense. But his forelock and mane appear to have been hacked with dull scissors." He frowned, remembering himself. "But you already know all the details, don't you, since you are the mastermind."

"I didn't—"

"Listen, imp. I admit that I have been reluctant to strong-arm you into submission. Out of respect."

She couldn't speak. Her jaw seemed to be frozen, slightly ajar, and the cords in her neck clenched so hard her head ached.

"You have no answer?" he scoffed. "In light of this prank, and the one in which you hid my soap and lamps, and short-sheeted my bed—"

"I did no such thing!"

"—I have come to a decision." Crossing his arms, he waited for her reply.

Using all her energy, she wetted her lips. "Oh?"

"I will release you."

Estella blinked three times. "Release me?"

"It is plain you will never make a suitable wife. You are free to go."

Ruby red anger pooled before Estella's eyes.

"That's what you want, isn't it?" he said. "Release from your marriage vows?"

"Who will have me, now that you've cast me off?" She allowed self-pity to trickle in. "My parents won't return from America for months—"

"You will find another husband. One you are capable of loving. As for your parents, I'm certain Lady Temple would be happy to take you in until they—"

"There will be no other husband." The utterance, pitched low, flowed from her lips almost before it had registered as a thought. She didn't know if it was the truth. Maybe she was simply afraid of what her future might hold after a failed, and scandalously brief, marriage.

He seemed to detect the terror in her voice. "Don't be

afraid. We will file a petition for an annulment. There shouldn't be any difficulty, as we have never . . . never known each other as man and wife. Our entire union was predicated on a lie."

Estella crawled onto her knees, raising herself up to see straight into his face. Only vaguely conscious of her flimsy, rumpled nightshift, she looked him squarely in the eye. "No." The single syllable was flat, resolute. And she meant it. If she left Castle Seabrook, she wouldn't be able to save Papa. *"No."*

At last, he was at a loss for words. Confusion floated over his face. "Very well," he said finally. His voice held wonder, mixed with a dash of trepidation. "You do realize that things will have to change in this household," he told her before he left.

"Indeed," Estella muttered to herself, flopping back against the pillows. "They certainly will."

From Madame Pettibonne's
Treatise on Canine Behavior, Prepared Especially for the
Lady Handler.
Varying Personalities of the Domesticated Breeds.
Hounds. There is a sort of Hound whose plight is to never know how to please his mistress, though he may try mightily to do so. Hounds have the best of intentions, but through reticence or a misplaced feeling of fear (they are sensitive beasts, with uncanny senses of smell and hearing, leaving them rather skittish), they are loath to do the very duty their mistresses acquired them to accomplish. Furthermore, this type of canine is difficult to retrain, for his natural shyness, combined at times with a history of unsavory experiences with previous mistresses, has left him utterly without courage.

Mrs. Pansy Lovely furrowed her alabaster brow, bit into a bonbon, and reread the passage aloud. Her French was excellent, and she translated the passage seamlessly. When she was done, she fixed her brown eyes on Estella. "I do see what you mean," she said.

"I *know*," Estella blurted. It had been difficult to sit still in Pansy's airy parlor in the vicarage, despite the staid comfort of her chintz-covered sofa before the fire. Golden afternoon sunshine poured through the arched windows, bathing the small, tastefully appointed chamber in light.

Pansy chewed her sweet, studying the illustration. Estella peeked around her shoulder. A guilty-looking hound hid beneath a canopied bed, with a likeness of Madame Pettibonne searching her boudoir for her dog. "The authoress is certainly possessed of . . . all the fruits of nature," Pansy marveled.

Subconsciously, Estella folded her arms below her chest. All her London modiste's artful tucks and ruffles at her peach-colored bodice could not make up for her own bosom's near flatness. "Indeed," she agreed. "Well, she's Parisian, you know."

Pansy nodded thoughtfully.

"But," Estella hurried on, "you do understand what I mean, then?"

"Yes. It would seem that Madame Pettibonne's advice is in truth intended to assist ladies in taming not dogs, but their husbands."

"Not *only* their husbands," Estella ventured.

"True." Pansy took another good look at the picture of Madame Pettibonne. "Gentlemen, then. Taming gentlemen. It's odd. The description of the hound reminded me ever so much of my dear Edwin."

Estella emitted an unladylike snort of laughter. Swiftly, she attempted to disguise it as a sneeze by whipping out a lace handkerchief.

"Truly," Pansy insisted. "He is shy, and sensitive. And he does try to please me. It's just that—"

"He doesn't have the faintest notion how?"

Sighing, Pansy selected a clove biscuit from the tray on the table before them. "No. He doesn't. Which doesn't make sense at all." Her eyes darted to the door. Seemingly satisfied that it was shut firmly, she leaned closer, lowering her voice to a top-secret whisper. "I have always found him marvelously romantic, and he has the sensibilities of a poet, and the graceful white hands of a pianist. It is fitting that he became a man of the cloth, for in truth he was not made for this world."

Estella tried desperately to match up Pansy's description with the slightly frail vicar who'd presided over her wedding. She could just see this ethereal man hiking in the mountains, rhapsodizing in rhyme on the beauties of nature.

Clearly, Pansy was desperately in love with her husband.

"Let me see." Estella took the book from her friend's lap and studied the passage on hounds. "Ah. Did he ever have an unsavory experience with a previous mistress?"

Pansy giggled nervously, spilling biscuit crumbs onto her lap. "Oh dear. Well, when he went up to Oxford there was—his sister told me this, and she is a bit of a gossip, and not entirely trustworthy—but she did say there was a young lady there who broke his heart."

Estella beamed, victorious. "Madame Pettibonne is the foremost expert on gentlemen, it seems. Now listen:

" 'If you discover yourself in possession of a Hound, what follows are several instructions to aid you in your training.

" 'A cautionary note for our Lady Reader: Behaving in a forward fashion, or being excessively strict, will only push your Hound further into retreat. The Lady must work in careful increments, thus:

" 'One. Praise must be administered. At first, once or twice daily, then increasing in frequency until the Hound can withstand consistent praise without cringing or slinking away. This stage may take a few days, or even a matter of months, depending on your particular Hound's sense of inadequacy.' "

Estella gave Pansy a frank look. "Do you think you can praise him?"

"Yes, of course. But I didn't think he needed it."

"He is a hound. He needs it."

"Forgive me for being bold—"

Estella waved a dismissive hand. "We are two young wives caught in less than ideal circumstances. If we are to better our marriages, we must help each other. We are equals. Feel free to say anything."

Smiling, Pansy refilled Estella's tiny crystal glass with cherry cordial. Sunlight glinted off the crimson liquid, and a faint whiff of alcohol and fruit kissed Estella's nostrils. Mama had never served cordial unless someone's nerves were in need of steadying. Unless Pansy's nerves were as jangled as a drawer full of cutlery, which did not seem to be the case, her criteria for serving cordial were somewhat less stringent.

"Well, then, what about the earl?" Pansy pressed. "Is he a hound?"

"I'm not certain." Estella considered. Godolphin wasn't shy, and he didn't seem sensitive in the least. He had courage to spare. But he most certainly did *not* know how to please his mistress. Announcing, after just six days of horrid marriage, that he wanted an annulment wasn't conducive to pleasure. "Pansy," she said slowly, "if we are to assist each other in, um, training our pets, there is something you must know."

"Go on. Why, you look quite pale."

"This morning, my husband suggested an annulment."

Very carefully, Pansy set her cordial glass down on the table. In her distress, a few bright drops still sloshed over the side. "He *didn't,*" she whispered.

"He did. But I flatly refused to agree to such a notion."

"And rightly so." Pansy had gone from thunderstruck to indignant. "How cruel—but why?"

"It seems someone has pulled pranks on him. He believes it was I. Admittedly—" here, Estella prodded the blue wool carpet with the toe of her slipper "—admittedly, I have been a bit of a prankster in the past. But this time it wasn't me."

"Playing a few pranks hardly seems grounds for annulment." Pansy frowned.

"It wasn't only the pranks . . . he was also quite put out about my not—about the thing that wives must do, I mean. In the bedchamber. Which I—I haven't done. Yet." Drat. Her ears were hot as cinders now, and she was sure her cheeks were as red as the cherry cordial she'd imbibed. She pressed a cooling palm to her forehead. Perhaps too much cherry cordial.

But Pansy was not flustered. "Ah. I see. That *would* make a gentleman put out, pranks or no."

"But I don't want to, er, do *that*—"

"What?"

"Ravishment." Estella coughed lightly into her handkerchief. "I don't want to until he's tamed."

"That makes perfect sense." Pansy's cupid lips formed a resolute line. "I stand by your decision completely."

As much as Estella liked Pansy, she decided the topic must be changed, and quickly. Ravishment was not something she felt comfortable discussing over a plate of bonbons and biscuits. She refused to acknowledge the persistent little voice in the back of her mind, which suggested that she didn't like the topic because she didn't know what it *was*.

Even Pansy probably knew. It was too embarrassing.

Estella munched the crispy biscuit, swallowed, and then asked, "Do you know anyone in the village by the name of Timmy?"

Carefully, Pansy closed the book, laying a palm on its worn leather cover. "I should think *you* would be acquainted with Timmy."

"Should I?"

"He is the stable boy at Castle Seabrook, dear. At least, he has been for the past three months."

Estella thought hard. What else had the strange woman said? Ah yes. That the earl had punished Timmy severely.

"The earl," Pansy clarified, "apprenticed Timmy to his groom. I remember hearing talk—I *always* hear talk—that Timmy committed some crime, and—"

"What was his crime?" Estella interrupted. The thought of a hardened criminal on her estate was unnerving. Especially if his mama decided to come calling.

"Oh, I don't know. Timmy's just a youth, and small for his age. I'm sure it was but a boyish prank gone awry."

Estella suddenly felt a kinship with the boy. She knew all about pranks turned bad.

"The earl is the magistrate, of course, so—"

"The magistrate?" Suddenly, it felt terribly stuffy in the little parlor. She tugged at the neckline of her gown. "I didn't know Godolphin is the magistrate."

"Oh dear." Pansy gave her a soulful, commiserating look. "Things are worse than I'd thought. Here. Have some more cordial." She refilled Estella's glass. "Instead of sending Timmy to the workhouse, your husband decided it would be best if the boy learned a useful trade. So he apprenticed him to the groom. Heaven knows if it will work out in the end. The poor child had a rather . . . disadvantageous upbringing. His mother, Violet Plympton, is the proprietress of the village haberdasher's shop. His father . . . I've no notion who his father is."

Estella sensed her friend didn't want to discuss the particulars of Timmy's upbringing. From the way she pursed her lips and shook her head, Estella presumed it was on the sordid side.

Which, of course, would be what one would expect with a mama who wore such garish face paint, and had a stuffed monkey attached to her bonnet.

"Now," Pansy said with a grin, cracking open the book again, "back to Madame Pettibonne's advice. Is the earl a hound, or is he not?"

"Quite possibly. He most definitely doesn't know how to please me."

"Then let us both try step one in the training manual."

Estella mustered a weak smile of acquiescence. This morning she'd made the rash decision to see her marriage through, no matter what. For Papa.

Now, Madame Pettibonne's advice danced tantalizingly before her, like a display of cakes and ices in a confectioner's window. The training manual seemed to be her only hope.

"Good," Pansy said. "We will employ the praise technique, and meet tomorrow to compare results."

In contrast to the brigs Godolphin had seen in the navy, Village Seabrook's jail seemed almost cozy. It was a small stone building, with slate shingles and a domestic-looking hedge separating it from the lane. Although it was just next door to the courthouse, Godolphin had not yet been in it.

With what had become a mental habit in the past few months, he pushed the squirming guilt to the back of his mind.

"Your Lordship," the guard said as Godolphin ducked through the low doorway. "This is indeed an unexpected— and pleasant—surprise." He stood behind his worn desk.

Godolphin nodded. He noted the chill in the squat, middle-aged guard's eyes. The word *pleasant* had been merely a formality. "I need to speak to Johnson," he said. "He's still here, I take it."

The guard's eyes narrowed almost imperceptibly. "He's still here, Your Lordship. You yourself sentenced him to nine days in jail—"

Godolphin's jaw locked. The guard's behavior was too impertinent for addressing an earl. Yet, did Godolphin deserve any better after he'd neglected the village for so long?

"This way." The guard unlocked the iron door at the back of the anteroom. Beyond was a cool corridor that smelled of damp and minerals. Cells lined either side, but they were all unoccupied, except for one.

Johnson sat on the wooden bench in his cell, rubbing his eyes. He'd clearly been woken from a nap.

"Unlock the cell," Godolphin directed the guard.

"Very well." The guard's tone held a hint of resentment. Godolphin ignored it.

"Had second thoughts, Lordship?" Johnson asked mockingly. His simple fisherman's clothes were wrinkled. His eyes were watery, and one of them was purple and swollen with a black eye. Godolphin had sentenced him for fighting and drunkenness. "Come t' set me free?"

Godolphin gave Johnson a sharp, silencing glance. Johnson sniffed defiantly, but fell silent. Godolphin then turned to the guard. "Leave us."

"He oughtn't to be unlocked."

"I'll deal with it." Godolphin's tone was final.

The guard shuffled away.

Inside the cell, Godolphin seated himself on a three-legged stool. Johnson's unemptied chamber pot gave the cramped space a rank stench.

"Ooh, a tea party with the earl," Johnson cooed.

"They don't bring you anything to read?" Godolphin asked. "No newspapers? Books?"

Johnson snorted. "I canna read, Lordship. Yer father didn't pay for a school in this village. My children canna read, neither."

At the mention of his father, something shut down, locked for Godolphin. "I've come to ask you about your relationship to Bertram Littlefield," he said, opting for bluntness.

"Littlefield. Little *somethin'*, I fancy." Johnson's contempt was unmasked. "What do ye want to know? I've got lots and lots t' tell."

"Regarding what?"

"Why, regardin' what's become of th' village since you an' yer blessed pa decided to let th' place go t' hell."

Why the persistence about his father? Godolphin's temples gave a pang. "What are you suggesting? Littlefield has been in the neighborhood for only a few months, has he not?"

"Years, more like."

"But that doesn't make a bit of sense. Hancock only bought the Brighton property this year."

Johnson shrugged. "Littlefield's been around here fer years. We never see Hancock down here. Jest Littlefield."

Godolphin forced his face to remain immobile. He'd believed Bertie had been innocently overseeing Hancock's warehouse. But if Bertie had been in the village on a regular basis, it could only mean that he was also overseeing Hancock's smuggling through the village. It also seemed to mean that Hancock had been smuggling in the area long before he'd bought a legitimate property.

"And," Johnson went on, leaning forward on his bench, "I don't mind sayin' that Littlefield has become a right nuisance. His smugglin's destroyin' th' village. Oh, when it all started, three or four years back, we were happy for th' extra income it brought. Paid handsomely, we were."

"Paid for what?"

"Unloadin' th' ships. Cartin' th' stuff into Brighton. And the rest of us, jest keepin' mum. Easy silver for every man, woman and child."

His darkest suspicions confirmed, Godolphin's head was now pounding in earnest. "Why, Mr. Johnson, are you no longer keeping mum?"

At this, Johnson spat into the chamber pot.

Godolphin averted his eyes.

"Littlefield fancies hisself some kind of king, that's why. I'm tired of it. Why, that's th' reason I got this." Johnson pointed to his black eye. "The village is startin' t' take sides."

"Why did no one come to me about this?" Godolphin asked sharply. But he already knew the answer.

"Why would we come t' *you*? Most of us figure *you're* th' reason the village is rotten to th' core. Ye neglected us." He snorted. "An' then ye come prancin' in and call yerself magistrate an' lock us up! Like we take ye seriously after what happened with yer pa—"

"Silence!" Godolphin snapped. He heaved himself to his feet, towering over Johnson.

Johnson shrank back against the wall.

"What does Littlefield have planned?" Godolphin demanded.

"Control. The business. All th' profits. With th' old man gone—"

"Hancock?"

"Aye. He's gone, so Littlefield's seizin' his chance. He wants it all." Johnson's eyes flicked up and down Godolphin's frame. "Wants yer missus in th' bargain, some say. By th' sound of it, he's going t' get her. Canna manage it any longer, eh?"

Reflexively, Godolphin curled his fists. He didn't know how word of Estella's prank had spread so quickly, and he didn't want to ask. If he heard anything more about a link between Bertie and Estella (and it would be unfounded, of course, mere revolting gossip), he was in danger of losing control.

"Thank you for your help," Godolphin said. "I'll tell the guard you are free to go."

As he left the jail, his head throbbed as though it were being squeezed in a vise.

Chapter Eight

Come, Sit, Stay

"Good girl, Maggie. You are *such* a good dog!"

Groggy, Maggie opened one eye, gave her tail a feeble wag, then shut her eye again.

Estella straightened, propping her hands on her hips. The problem was that Madame Pettibonne hadn't gone into specifics. When did one administer praise? At any given time?

The fact that Maggie was lolling on a velvet sofa in the countess's parlor should be taken into consideration, too. Having free reign over the upholstered furniture had always been a point of contention between dog and mistress. Thus far, however, Maggie had won the battle.

"Come," Estella commanded, walking backward while patting the tops of her thighs. "Maggie, you bad thing, *come*." Oh dear. That wasn't exactly praise, was it?

Maggie had lifted her head, however, and her ears pricked up.

"That's it."

The foxhound seemed curious more than anything, but she willed her spotted limbs to disembark from the sofa and pad over to her mistress.

Estella threw her arms around the dog's neck, kissing

the top of her silky head. "Good girl! The dearest, sweetest little pet in all of England."

Maggie swiped her pink tongue over Estella's cheek.

Success. Tonight, she would be ready to try the praise technique on a larger, more complex beast.

There was a knock at the door.

"Enter," Estella called.

One of the maids peeked her head around the door. "There is a Mr. Littlefield here to see you, Your Ladyship."

Estella's belly knotted. "What does he want?"

The maid looked confused. "I cannot say, Your Ladyship."

"Very well." Estella stroked Maggie, this time to calm herself. "Send him in."

When Bertie Littlefield was shown into the parlor a few minutes later, Estella was standing by the windows. She wanted to keep as much distance between him and herself as possible. Last night in the warehouse, he'd been downright scary.

"Good afternoon, Mr. Littlefield," she said.

"Good afternoon, Miss Hancock." Deliberately, he met her eyes.

Maggie growled softly. Which was odd, because she liked almost everyone.

Estella ignored the incorrect way Bertie had addressed her. "Were you hoping to speak to my husband?" Bertie's ginger hair, she noted, was neatly combed, and he wore a black suit of clothes. He carried a small box in his left hand. His right sleeve hung slack at his side, like the ghost of an arm.

One corner of his mouth twitched. "No, no. I came here to see you. To apologize for how I behaved last night. I've been overworked lately, and my nerves aren't as steady as they once were. I'm normally steady as a rock. Why, you know that. We have, after all, been acquainted for years."

For some reason, Estella's heart was thudding. "Won't you please have a seat?" She gestured to a chair.

"Of course, of course. Thank you for asking. You were always so very thoughtful. People said you were spoiled—"

She frowned.

"—but I always knew that wasn't so." He was hovering next to the chair, waiting for her to sit.

Reluctant, she crossed the room and sat in a chair three yards away.

He sat. "You are a perfect angel, if I may be so bold."

"You may not," Estella replied softly. Fear prickled up her spine. He was rambling and behaving as though they had a far more intimate acquaintance than they really did. He was merely her father's employee.

"I am sorry." Bertie *sounded* genuine. But his eyes were cold. Abruptly, he stood, and moved toward her.

She shrank back into her chair. Her pulse sped. But he only passed her the small box he'd brought, then returned to his own seat.

She glanced down at the box. It was wooden, lacquered, painted with an intricate, colorful design of flowers and peacocks. "What is this?"

"A wedding gift. For you. And a token of my sincerest apologies for being so impolite to you last night."

The box grew heavy in her hands. Her fingers were numb.

"Go on. Open it."

Slowly, she lifted the hinged lid. The box was lined with black velvet, and there was a matching pouch nestled inside.

"It's a gift fitting for a countess." His voice was suddenly harsher, higher in pitch.

Dread made her nauseous. But she untied the pouch, and poured a heavy gold necklace into her hand. She gasped.

"Do you like it?" Bertie demanded.

"I can't accept this. It's too much." She stared down at the necklace. Several large, square-cut diamonds and emeralds set on a filigree chain . . .

The very same necklace that that horrible woman in the woods—Timmy's mother, Violet Plympton—had been wearing the day she'd accosted her.

"I say that you're perfect," Bertie snapped, "and you turn right round and refuse to accept my gift?"

Steadily, she met his eyes. "What is the meaning of this?" The necklace felt like ice in her palm. "This gift is far too valuable for me to accept. And I'm—my husband—"

"Your *husband*," Bertie said frostily. "You say that so easily for a new bride of only, what, five days? Six?" He hacked out a laugh. "If only you knew the sort of secrets your *husband* is keeping from you!"

Her throat had gone dry. Was he referring to the South China Company?

"He beat me to it, Miss Hancock. That's all. The way he beat me to everything. Things might've been different. I asked for your father's permission to begin courting you, and no sooner had I done that than your *husband*"—again, he said this with a sneer—"appeared from nowhere and beat me to the chase."

Appeared from nowhere? "Mr. Littlefield, I am sure I don't know what you are speaking of. I think it would be best if you came back to visit some other time." Estella quickly replaced the necklace in its pouch and box. She rose, moved to Bertie, and placed the box in his hand. Then she rang the bell for the maid. "It was, of course, lovely to see you."

Bertie said nothing else, even when the maid came and escorted him away. He was white-lipped with rage. His right shoulder, just above where his arm had been severed, trembled.

And he had left the necklace on the chair.

* * *

Estella dressed for dinner with extra care. She was sure it wasn't the memory of the kisses she'd shared with her reluctant husband that made her worry about her appearance. She was normally an honest young lady. But tonight she was left with no choice but to be less than honest on two points.

Dishonest Point One: she'd decided not to tell Godolphin about Bertie's gift of the necklace. She'd hidden it behind a row of books beneath the window seat in her bedchamber. And there it would remain, until she figured out a more permanent way to dispose of it. There was no point in telling Godolphin about it. It would only upset him, and perhaps even result in a scene between the two men.

Further, it was likely that Godolphin wouldn't even believe how she'd acquired the necklace, since just this morning he'd accused her of some silly prank involving his horse.

Sighing, Estella fastened her bandeau. That reminded her of the Shipton's party invitation. How could she tell them they weren't coming, that Godolphin refused?

Dishonest Point Two: tonight she would begin her experiment with Madame Pettibonne's manual, beginning with the praise technique. Well, this wasn't dishonest, exactly. But it wasn't particularly straightforward, either.

She dabbed a little violet water on her throat, and stood. Maggie led the way to the bedchamber door.

Desperate situations called for desperate measures. This sham of a marriage was most assuredly a desperate situation.

"The gardener said we ought to decide what's to be done with the orangerie," Estella told Godolphin. "As soon as possible." One of her golden eyebrows arched upward. "If, that is, you can be distracted from your work."

Godolphin stared down the dining table at his wife. The candlelight picked out the gilt threads in her upswept waves, and gleamed subtly off her pale lavender gown. Under cap sleeves, her upper arms were slim, vulnerable. Her bodice was low, exposing the creamy purity of her modest décolleté.

Her face, on the other hand, glowed with contentious, elfin naughtiness.

"I know," he answered finally. Conversation had been strained since the watercress soup, and it showed no sign of improving.

There was a pause. He could almost hear her thinking.

"Oh good," she said suddenly, tossing him a grin. "How thoughtful of you to, um, to know. About deciding what to do with the orangerie, I mean."

Godolphin narrowed his eyes. What was the brat up to now? "It's not thoughtful of me, actually," he replied blandly. "The gardener told me this afternoon."

This did not deflate Estella in the least. "But you *remembered.*"

"I may be several years older than you, darling, but my memory is not all that bad. I still am able to remember what someone told me three hours ago."

Estella gave her shoulders a graceful shrug, took a bite of buttered carrots.

"I will be busy with my work tomorrow—"

"Of course." She frowned down into her plate.

Godolphin felt a twinge of remorse. If only this business could be finally over and done with. He turned his glass of claret round and round by its stem, studying the circular dents the base made on the tablecloth. "I've arranged for the orangerie to be opened up tonight," he told her. "I thought we could take a stroll through it after dinner. Together."

To his relief, her brow seemed to smooth and her shoulders relaxed. "A splendid idea." She smiled brilliantly, revealing small, even teeth.

Inexplicably, apprehension prickled the back of his neck.

Over the dessert of custard, they exchanged few words, and after she'd run to fetch her shawl, they met in the foyer. Godolphin proffered his arm.

As she laid her hand, light as a leaf, on his arm, he felt his chest expand. He'd always been a man with the utmost assurance in himself. But around Estella, this quality took on mythic proportions, as though she made him bigger, stronger. When she smiled up at him, the glitter in her eye lit a match to the kindling of his desire.

Good God. They needed to keep moving.

In silence, they exited through the glass terrace doors. The night air, fragrant with fallen leaves, had a decided nip. Instinctively he drew her closer, clenching his jaw as her hip grazed his thigh. As they descended the terrace steps and set off across the lawn, Estella tipped her head back. "Look at the stars. You can't see the stars very well in London, you know. Because of all the gas lamps and Thames fog."

Instead of looking up, he looked down at her upraised eyes. "Indeed. The stars are lovely tonight."

Then he heard his words, as if mimicked back to him by a jeering parrot. Was he dissolving into an utter lovesstruck puddle then? The stars were in *his* eyes.

"Come on," he said gruffly. He gave her arm a gentle tug, and they were off again.

The orangerie had been lit up inside. The rows and rows of tall, arched windows glowed amber. The last moths of the year, attracted by the light, flitted inside like tiny ghosts.

He heard Estella suck in a breath, and for a moment he envied her sense of wonder and beauty.

He escorted her inside.

Estella released his arm and walked down the center path, which was paved with blue Spanish tiles. Her small feet made a scuffing sound as she walked.

He paused, watching her back longingly. Why did he always seem to be seeing her from this perspective, as she retreated?

The central path was lined with miniature orange and lemon trees in huge clay pots. The structure had been erected by Godolphin's great-grandfather nearly a century before, and many of the citrus trees were that old, stunted by the pots, gnarled with neglect.

Still, like an omen of hope, Godolphin spied a few snowy blossoms clinging to one tree. He inhaled deeply of the sweetened air.

She'd disappeared around the corner. He felt a tug, standing there alone, as if he'd been robbed of a cloak in winter. Then he set off after her, brushing past dusty, emerald green leaves.

When he rounded the corner, she wasn't there. The tile-floored clearing, with a dried-up stone fountain in the middle, was empty. But a flicker of motion caught his eye, and he saw a fluttering skirt hem disappear around a terra-cotta pot.

He stopped in his tracks. Hot annoyance clouded his thoughts, and he ran a finger under his cravat. What in Hades was she up to now?

Her face, cheeks pink and eyes aglow, peeked around an orange tree. "Come," she said, and then laughed nervously. Almost as though in awe of her own audacity.

"You act as though you want to be chased," he grumbled.

"Perhaps," she retorted lightly. "Or perhaps I want only to be obeyed." She crooked a gloved finger, then disappeared again with a whispering rustle of petticoats and gown.

He didn't know what made him follow her, and he half hated himself for doing so, though he could not have said why. Part of him wanted to stalk off in the other direction and disappear until tomorrow or the next day. Instead, as if possessed, he followed.

"Like a damned pitiful dog," he grumbled to himself. "Chasing the girl about—"

He rounded yet another corner. There she was, perched on a carved stone bench, hothouse vines climbing in an unruly, luxuriant arc over her. Her cashmere shawl had slipped down from one shoulder, giving her a vaguely wanton appearance.

Liquid heat pulsed through him, reminding him of his fingertips and toes. Of all of his extremities, in fact.

"Sit." She gave him a mysterious half smile, slowly lowering a hand to tap the bench beside her. "Please."

Each beat of his heart was pronounced in every vein, throbbing with life. With hope.

But he had to remember himself. *He* was the master of this situation; he mustn't crumble like a swooning fool.

"Please, sit," she repeated, softer this time. There wasn't much light in this corner, and her lashes cast absurdly long shadows across her cheeks. Her eyes themselves were in shadow.

Intrigued, wondering just where this little farce was leading, he joined her in two long strides, lowered himself on the bench. It wasn't really constructed for a man of his proportions, and he felt a bit ridiculous perched on it. Like a bloody gnome on a mushroom.

Fitting, considering he was in the company of a flighty nymph.

They sat in silence for nearly a minute. They weren't touching, but he felt her. Not heat, exactly, but a vibrating energy by his side. He studied his own black, wool-clad thigh next to her silken lap. As if he'd conjured the ability to see through matter, the lush outline of her thigh beneath the fine fabric became visible.

He had to look away, study the neutral shapes of the potted orange trees before them.

"They still bear fruit," he remarked. "Some of them, anyway. In winter. Those pipes there"—he gestured to pipes along the walls—"are pumped full of hot water during the coldest months. It's as warm as Italy in here."

She shifted. "I have never been to Italy. I hear it is quite nice. My cousin Henriette—you didn't meet her, did you?—journeyed there." She tilted her head up to regard him. "On her wedding trip."

Godolphin suppressed a groan. "You're not still miffed about that, are you?"

"*Still*, sir?" She adopted a tone of incredulity. "We have been married not yet a week. At this point, we'd be skirting the Alps in our coach."

"Estella." He swiveled to face her, gripped her shoulders. They felt more solid than they looked. "We will go to Italy. I promise. When I—just as soon as I finish some business."

She wiggled her shoulders, freeing herself. "Business," she huffed. "Whatever it is, I know it takes precedence over me."

The horrid little princess. He recoiled, felt the opening in his soul slam shut. "Does it come as a surprise that human lives are of more import than your whims and pleasures? I was told you were coddled by your parents, but I was unaware of the extent of it."

Instantly, the color drained from her cheeks, and she curled back, too, as though he'd struck her. "You never said . . . What do you mean, human lives?"

He'd revealed too much. That was the danger of being in her company. Skimming his palm over his jaw, he sighed. "I'm sorry. Of course you didn't know."

Several long beats of silence passed. Each moment was ponderous, weighted with unspoken words.

"Does it have something to do with . . ." Her voice trailed away, uncertain. She took a deep breath. "Why did you not tell me you are a magistrate?"

"I didn't think you needed to know."

"But I'm your *wife*."

"Correct. Meaning I will give you all the information

you'll require to run the household, to properly raise our children, uphold the Godolphin name." He couldn't bear to look at her. He knew he was being cruel and dishonest, and he heard her draw in a small gasp at his words.

Why did she make him behave like this?

His body throbbed the answer.

"What do you think?" he asked abruptly, cursing the gruffness in his tone. "Shall we tear the whole thing down and build a folly? They're all the rage, I'm told. I don't even like oranges."

She gazed at him as if he'd gone completely batty. "I think the orangerie is lovely," she replied breezily, "and I happen to be fond of oranges. Maggie likes them, too."

He couldn't help it. He laughed.

"But," she continued, "otherwise, a folly would be a wonderful idea. How clever of you to think of it."

Quite unreasonably, he puffed up a little at her praise. Shrugging modestly, he said, "Not really all that clever, I'm afraid. Our neighbor, Lord Piltonshire, is having one built at Thrandymede."

"I still think you're clever."

Was she submitting so readily? It almost seemed too easy. She must have taken his warning about her needing to behave better seriously. "Do what you like to the orangerie," he said, feeling suddenly expansive.

"I don't want to change a thing. I'll just have it cleaned, repair the broken windows, a fresh coat of paint—"

"And the Shiptons' party. We will go. I'm sorry I was such a brute about it before. I suppose the invitation took me off guard."

He meant it. Although it would be difficult to make certain she didn't hear anything she shouldn't at the party, he suddenly wanted to make her happy.

"Thank you," was all she said. Then, *"Oh."*

Because he couldn't control himself, he'd gripped her by the shoulders again, drawn her close. The fact that she didn't struggle, but stared up at him, breathing hard and fast, eyes round, lips parted, made every fiber in his body sing.

"Sir, I—"

"Kiss me."

Her gasp was cut off by his mouth, and as he joined his opened lips to hers, he tasted the rest of her exhalation, a warm, claret-scented breeze. When his tongue delved deeper, meeting the soft wet tip of hers, he felt her hold her breath. But at the same time, her neck relaxed, tipping her head farther back. She was opening herself to him.

This simple motion made him frantic. He felt hot and featherlight. He wanted to taste her and feel her. Fast. More. At once. For who knew when she'd ever let him kiss her again.

But God. Oh God. She was kissing him back, twining her tongue around his, filling his mouth with her ripe fruit taste, her moist fullness, her trilling energy. He became ferocious, like a starving beast, and he tugged at her hair, his teeth hitting hers like a wolf's fang to bone.

She jerked back away, and looked at the floor, tugging her shawl close around her.

It took several seconds for the beast to recede and the gentleman to return. "I'm sorry." He wanted to pound his forehead against a wall. "I frightened you."

"No . . . no, it's all right." She gave a smile, but its brightness was like brittle glass.

Hell. He'd made a mess of things. Again. Not knowing what else to do (or how else to save face, though he could scarcely admit *that* to himself), he drew his gold watch from his waistcoat, pretended to check it. In truth, behind his eyelids there was such a magenta haze of desire that he could barely see. "I've got to . . ." His throat was tight. He stood. "I've got to go," he told her, more clearly this time.

"Stay," she implored. "You are such a good—we've only just . . ."

He leaned down, despising himself, and kissed the golden down at her temple. "If only I could."

"No, no, please. Don't remove your bonnet," Pansy told Estella in the foyer of the vicarage. "We'll take a stroll through the village."

They linked elbows and walked out into the garden. Late-blooming flowers lined the paths. Yellow-and-rust-colored foliage partially obscured the pretty gray stone church next door, and fallen leaves blanketed the head-stones in the cemetery. At the end of the path, they turned onto the lane that meandered into the village center.

"Well, you know," Pansy began, "I could scarcely believe it. Who would have ever thought that a gentle word of praise now and then would work such wonders?" She was breathless with excitement, her cheeks pink. "I tried it first not an hour after you departed yesterday. I was sitting in the parlor, and had taken out my knitting—more socks for the Smyth children, poor dears, I don't know *how* they wear them out so quickly—and Edwin came in. In truth, he appeared rather dejected, and I asked him what was the matter." She paused to gasp for breath, and to straighten her bonnet, which was askew from all her gesturing.

"Go on," Estella prompted. They were making very slow progress down the lane, which was lined with hedges and snug thatch-roofed cottages.

"He said he was having an awful time writing his sermon for this week. At that point, with Madame Petti-bonne's excellent advice in mind, I told him he was the cleverest gentleman I knew and if anyone could write an inspiring sermon, it would be he."

"And did he believe you?"

"Well, of course he did, because I meant every word. It's just that I wouldn't ever have thought of telling him that all on my own. Until reading about hound behavior, I was

certain Edwin would be somehow insulted if I compli-
mented him."

"But he wasn't."

"Not at all. Oh, Estella, I am so happy, and ever so encouraged to move on to step two." They'd stopped in the
middle of the lane, and Pansy was peering into her face.
Her expression was suddenly grave. "You don't seem . . .
did the praise technique not work on the earl?"

Nervous, Estella swung her reticule on its braided cord
handles. The bag was heavy with Madame Pettibonne's
book, and a corner bumped into her shin. "Ouch." She
winced. "Um, not as well as . . . well, it did work. At first.
Last night. For a minute or two. He seemed flattered
when I praised him, and I did mean every word. I think."

"You think?"

Estella bit her lower lip. How could she explain? Godolphin wasn't an ordinary man. Somehow, she sensed he
was impervious to tricks. He wouldn't respond to praise
in the same manner as the vicar. "Perhaps the book wasn't
meant for every gentleman," she suggested at last.

"But it worked so well on Edwin," Pansy muttered, almost to herself. She gazed past Estella's shoulder, thinking. Then her eyebrows shot up. "Perhaps only step one
didn't work. What is step two? Perhaps, if you try it, you'll
be met with more success."

"Step two?"

"You have the book with you, don't you? Though the
people who live in these cottages are known to spy on the
lane from behind their curtains, they'll assume we're consulting the Psalms." Her grin was cheeky.

Estella couldn't resist a guilty look around. The lane
was empty, however, and no motion came from any of the
cottages. Something caught her eye, but it was only sunlight dancing off a mullioned window. The last finches of
the year twittered inside a hedge, and a chilly breeze ruffled the hem of her merino pelisse.

"Yes—" she fumbled with her reticule, drawing out the

little white leather book. She hadn't bothered to lock it, and a vague sense of panic rippled over her. Anyone could have read it while she left it unattended in her bedchamber. A maid. Or Godolphin. She swallowed, flipping to the page on hounds. "Here," she passed the book to Pansy, "your French is far better than mine."

With an expression as serious as if she were pronouncing a sentence of death, Pansy began.

" 'Two. Next, the Lady Handler must combine, with the Praise, Little Endearments. In the beginning your Hound will be suspicious. It is extremely likely that, in his past, endearments from negligent mistresses were fraught with peril. Yet kind consideration and restraint will eventually calm his fears. Soon, he will crave, even beg for, his mistress's Little Endearments.' "

"That is all?" Estella quizzed. It was impossible to imagine such a simple ploy succeeding with Godolphin. It would be like addressing a werewolf as "sweetheart."

Linking arms again, they resumed their stroll into the village center. Leaves crackled under their walking boots, and the crisp air was spicy with wood smoke.

"I wonder," Pansy said after a minute, "if I might ask you a favor."

"Of course."

"In several days' time, the Sunday school children will be putting on their Michaelmas pantomime. As the new vicar's wife, I've inherited the responsibility of overseeing the whole thing, and I admit that I'm inspired—rather vainly, I do realize—to make it the best Michaelmas pantomime Seabrook has ever seen."

"I know just how you feel." Estella gave her arm a reassuring squeeze. "I, too, want to excel in my role as the new Lady Seabrook, but I do not feel quite up to that task."

"You'll be wonderful. Just give yourself some time."

Estella sighed. "I wouldn't be so certain. But tell me, what is the favor?"

Pansy laughed, a breathy sound touched with a note of

anxiety. "I'm afraid I've taken on a bit more than I can handle. I went about recruiting children for the chorus, and I did *too* good a job of making it sound like a jolly time. Now every child in the village out of diapers—and, I fear, at least one still in them—has signed on. Our little church simply isn't big enough for the production."

"The castle ballroom will be perfect," Estella informed her with a grin. "It's fitting that we mark my arrival as the new countess with a celebration. And it's high time the earl invited the village folk into the castle."

"Thank you." Pansy was beaming.

Estella's belly squeezed. Would Godolphin be angry that she'd agreed to such a notion without consulting him first?

They'd reached the village green. Someone's dirty white goat was staked out to graze, keeping the grass smooth as felt. The sound of chatter and laughter emanated from the inn, where people would be consuming their midday meal. A faded sign announced THE WICKED MERMAID. A stagecoach was stopped in front, pausing on its way farther up the coast. A servant girl, basket slung over her arm, emerged from the chemist's shop. She paused, catching sight of Estella and Pansy, then hurried away.

"They dare not stare for too long," Pansy remarked with a giggle. "That is Mrs. Hadley's confectioner's shop"— she pointed to a storefront boasting pretty bow windows—"where they make the most scrumptious cream buns. And that is the haberdasher's shop. Now, I'm in desperate need of new laces for my walking boots, but I'm so dreadfully afraid of Violet Plympton."

Estella took a deep breath. "Why?" Perhaps now she'd learn more about why Violet had accosted her in the wood.

"Don't stare!" Pansy dragged Estella behind a stout oak tree at the edge of the green. The goat, chewing slowly, stared at them with yellow eyes.

Estella peeked around the tree, feeling bold. "Let's go in."

"I don't know. The last time I ventured in there—with the maid, for protection—she implied that Edwin was trying to drive her out of business because she doesn't attend Sunday service. And"— she wrinkled her nose— "did you *see* that horrible monkey she wears on her bonnet? I vow, its little glass eyes follow you about the room."

Estella braced her shoulders against a shudder of disgust. "I need to ask her something," she said slowly.

Pansy shot her an inquisitive glance.

"Nothing important," Estella rushed on. "Just a question about, um, buttons."

As they entered, even the tinkle of the door's bell was ominous. Estella crept in first, with Pansy on her heels. No one was behind the long wooden counter. A green velvet curtain at the back concealed the rear room.

Estella jumped as the door slammed shut behind them. Pansy cleared her throat. Still, nobody emerged from behind the curtain.

Standing very close together, they examined the goods in silence, feigning interest, their eyes darting over to the curtain at regular intervals. The shop was dim, musty smelling, and dust motes spun in the shaft of light coming through the window.

Estella moved to the glass-topped display case, and peered in. Lengths of lace, hairpins, buttons, and spools of ribbon were jumbled together, much of the merchandise looking rather worn.

"Let's go," Pansy whispered.

Estella nodded. Just before she turned to leave, however, something in the display case caught her eye. Her breath hitched. There, leaning against a stack of folded handkerchiefs, was a half-spent spool of geranium-colored satin ribbon.

The exact same ribbon the prankster had used on Godolphin's horse.

Chapter Nine

The Puzzle Padlock

"Let's not dawdle, darling," Godolphin breathed in Estella's ear.

"Oh, I wouldn't dream of dawdling," she retorted.

Arm in arm, they mounted the broad steps leading to Sir Broderick and Lady Penelope's front door.

"You did agree to attend this party," Estella reminded Godolphin.

"Mmm. That I did."

"Grudgingly, of course." She frowned. "Although it is being given in our honor."

"Indeed. A celebration of the earthly paradise that is marriage." He rapped on the door.

"You are sarcastic," she mumbled.

He flashed her a grin. "Not at all. And do stop scowling and play your part. Try to look happy. We're newlyweds. Remember?"

She grit her teeth. "How could I forget?"

The door swung open, and they were sucked into the glitter and hum of the Shipton house. They were greeted by their hosts and dozens of guests, most of whom Estella knew. Godolphin never left her side as they circulated.

Once they'd said hello to almost everyone, Godolphin's

grip on her arm relaxed and his hand rested, in mockery of a loving gesture, on her back. "Come, Estella. Let's step out onto the terrace." He swiped two glasses of champagne from a passing silver tray. "It is stuffy, don't you think?"

Estella stared up at him. Did he have to persist in being so rude? "We have only just arrived. Perhaps we should circulate some more. Converse with people. You could introduce me to your friends. We could act as though—"

"—as though we were in love?" His eyes flashed so coldly, a chill flowed through Estella's veins. "It's exhausting, is it not?"

Before she could formulate a reply, they were waylaid by a black-whiskered gentleman.

"I do say, old chum," the man said to Godolphin, "it is grand to see you're back—"

"Yes," Godolphin interrupted. "Too many years in the navy, I think."

"Not the navy, Seabrook. I meant—"

"Oh, I know what you mean, Lovelace. Have you made the acquaintance of my wife?"

Godolphin looked distinctly uneasy. Estella's eyes narrowed as she curtsied prettily for Lovelace.

"How is it, being back in your old haunts?" Lovelace asked, after a round of hearty congratulations. Without waiting for Godolphin to answer, he continued, now addressing Estella. "Godolphin and I went to university together, but afterward he went his way and I went mine. But now, here we are, together again. Smashing." He downed his glass of champagne in one gulp and looked about for a serving man.

"Where did you live, Mr. Lovelace?" Estella asked.

"Where did *I* live?" Lovelace's broad forehead furrowed. "Why, here. Cushing Manor. Four miles inland."

Confusion rippled dimly, but Estella decided the gentleman had simply had too much champagne. Because, if he'd been living in the neighborhood all this time, and so had Godolphin, why hadn't they met in so many years? A feud, perhaps? Godolphin did not seem like the feuding sort, though. He was too rational.

"Speaking of school, Godolphin," Lovelace went on, "there's old Bertie Littlefield." He gestured with his chin. "Dreary chap. His presence is rather like a permanent thundercloud, eh?"

Godolphin's gaze followed. "Odd he'd be here." He fumbled with his own empty glass, then laughed.

False laughter, Estella noted. She watched as Bertie Littlefield glanced over his shoulder before slinking through a doorway and out of sight.

"Too many people, not enough champagne," Godolphin quipped. "Please excuse us, Lovelace, while we go in search of the drinks table." He took Estella's arm.

As Godolphin pulled Estella after him, he heard Lovelace call out, "Do send word when you've discovered the mother lode of champagne, won't you? I'm parched."

Sweat misted Godolphin's forehead.

Estella struggled to pull free of his grip. He felt like a first-rate cad for handling her so roughly, but it had to be. If she spent any time talking to the local gentry here, his carefully laid plans were at risk of shattering. Within twenty minutes she would know all about his life, about Marblegate, his father, everything. He marched her toward the terrace doors.

"*Sir*," Estella hissed, tugging her arm, "what is the matter with you? Unhand me at once."

"I'm afraid," he drawled, "that's simply not possible at present."

Outside, the hum of the party was muted by the faint sound of the ocean. The sky hung heavy and black, and not a star was to be seen.

"Why are we out here?" Estella jerked her arm from his. "I don't want to be outside; it's too cold."

It was difficult to see her eyes in the half-light. But for

all her scolding speech, there was a waver of fear in her voice.

Fear. He had never loathed himself more.

"You'll stay here till I return," he answered, too harshly. "Don't even argue the point."

"This is madness! What in heaven has gotten into you?"

Godolphin turned abruptly and glared at her. "Do as I say." He disappeared through the terrace doors.

Estella's heart throbbed. Why was Godolphin doing this? Did he really hate all those people so much, or was he just trying to spite her?

Or something else. Again, doubt rippled.

She placed her hand on the terrace door handle, but stopped short. Inside, it was a blur of light and activity, but she saw Godolphin's broad back slip through the very doorway through which Littlefield had exited.

He was following Littlefield.

Lady Penelope appeared on the other side of the glass, and opened the door. "Come in, come in, Countess," she chirped. "You ought not be outside this time of year in only a flimsy shawl! I know this must be overwhelming for you, but ever so many people haven't said hello yet."

"No." Estella smiled through her shame and confusion. "I suppose I oughtn't."

Lady Penelope's sister-in-law, Sir Broderick's elder sister, Lady Lucy, inspected Estella from beneath her lace cap. "So you went and married that wild young Seabrook, did you?" Her skin was sagging with age, dusted with powder, but her sable eyes were as alert as a bird's.

"I did, madam."

"Well, any woman worth her salt could see he's got—"

Lady Penelope giggled. "Now, now, Lucy. None of your observations." She cast her friendly gray eyes on Estella. "Lucy's observations are best when administered with vinaigrettes and brandy."

"Still," Lady Lucy insisted, "he is enigmatic."

Estella arched her eyebrows. "Indeed, I am discovering that to be true."

"Gone away all those years."

Why was it painful to swallow? "In the navy, do you mean?"

"Yes, of course, and all those years in the North, at Marblegate House. His return was unexpected, but of course we were delighted to see him again after so long."

Marblegate House. The ledgers in Godolphin's tower study.

"He owns many estates," Estella said slowly, "does he not?"

Lady Lucy laughed. "In my day a young woman would know these details *before* the nuptials, but we weren't much for love matches back then."

"Now he's home," Lady Penelope said, "where he belongs, and high time, too. Village Seabrook is in a sorry state these days, although the new vicar and his wife are most certainly a blessing. Godolphin's arrival this summer was sorely needed. Of course"—she cast her sweet gaze on Estella—"you know all of this."

Estella's pulse hammered against her eardrums. The orchestra was playing a waltz that she used to love. Now the notes sounded sour. All the smiling faces around her looked like wax dolls with blank glass eyes.

Godolphin had deceived her. He'd lied about how long he'd lived in Seabrook. *Lied.* No wonder the castle was in a shambles, and pitifully understaffed. No wonder the servants acted so oddly.

Then a question screamed though her head, thawing her numbness: Why?

Somehow, Estella managed to smile, like yet another wax doll, and stumble her way through polite conversation with the two elderly ladies. She recovered from her shock, though, and her brain clicked frantically forward.

She knew Godolphin had suspicions about Papa, about his business, and designs to implicate him in something.

Now she knew Godolphin had also concocted an elaborate charade about Castle Seabrook, his ancestral home, when in fact he hadn't lived there since he was a youth. Were the two plots linked? Were they tied to The South China Company?

Face stiff from smiling, she excused herself from her hostess and Lady Lucy, ostensibly in search of the retiring room.

The downstairs corridors were well lit with sconces. Yellow light reflected off fine oil paintings, glittered on crystal vases of hothouse flowers, shone on gilded mirrors. But no Godolphin.

With a furtive backward glance, Estella ascended the carpeted staircase. At the top, darkness yawned. The Shiptons had expected no guests to venture upstairs. With a mental apology to her hosts, she stole down the dim hall. At the end, where the corridor intersected another, she heard voices. Her breath caught, and she crept close to the wall.

"The smoking room," a breathless masculine voice said, "is on the first floor, old trout."

Littlefield.

Silent as a moth, Estella peeked around the corner. She saw the empty sleeve of Bertie's dark evening coat tucked up into itself. She ducked her head back, held her breath.

"Why, thank you for the advice," Godolphin said smoothly. "Can't imagine why I didn't know that."

Bertie laughed shrilly. "If you're looking for the old duffer's private lair, it's two doors down, on the right. The ledgers, you know, could be anywhere. Shipton's study is as good a place as any to begin your search. Or have you already begun?"

"The ledgers." Godolphin's voice was flat.

"Although I am aware that it's your aristocratic privilege," Bertie snapped, "I'd rather prefer it if you didn't condescend to me. The ledgers. I know you want them."

"So now you're a regular mind reader, eh?"

"Getting better. Wish I'd been this good before you blew my arm off."

Godolphin's voice lowered. "You know I didn't do that."

"Might as well have, Captain. What does my arm matter? No damage was done to *you*. Same as always, aren't you? Unscathed physique, unmarred face, unblighted conscience. Remember Private Jordan? He has one eye missing, and a bit of nose as well. What've you got to show you've been in harm's way?"

There was a heavy silence. Then, "A lifetime of guilt, Littlefield. I've wished every day that it had been me who took that shot. Good evening."

Estella and Godolphin did not exchange a single word on the way back to the castle. She would never think of it as "home," especially now. Her breathing was shallow, and she held herself stiffly in a corner of the dark carriage. Now and then the moonlight caught the side of Godolphin's face. His cheekbones looked sharp, his eye sockets were tar pits.

She had never felt so intimidated in her entire life, and she struggled to overcome the foreign emotion. But she wouldn't be afraid any longer. *No fear.*

She didn't say a word as the carriage pulled to a stop in the castle drive. She opened the door herself, jumped out, and walked as fast as she could without breaking into a run. She didn't stop until she was in her bedchamber, with the door bolted shut behind her.

By the orange light of the fire in the grate, she checked to make certain the ribbons she'd used to tie the wardrobe doors were secure. She'd allow herself to be cautious. Being careful was one thing, being fearful quite another.

"Maggie?" she called. Her voice shook. Drat. "Maggie, come here!"

Maggie was gone, probably lolling on the kitchen hearth. She knew where her bread was buttered.

It was just as well, because Estella would be going out again tonight. After what Bertie had revealed, she now knew what she had to do to save Papa. She needed those ledgers. And she knew exactly where they were.

The flame of Estella's candle choked in the stuffy warehouse air. Sheltering it with a cupped palm, she searched until she found a hurricane lamp on a shelf. She lit this, and blew out the smaller candle.

In the pulsing flare of the lamp, the warehouse loft suddenly seemed cavernous, filled with eerie throbbing shadows and looming shapes.

They were just crates, she reminded herself. And the animal pelts hanging from the rafters were quite dead. Her ears strained as she moved with the lamp toward the safe. Bertie could be here. So could Godolphin. A chill breathed down her spine.

She placed the lamp on the wooden floor beside the safe. It clattered coldly. Kneeling, she touched the padlock. It was of Oriental origin. She knew enough about foreign imports to discern that. The metalwork on the padlock had a Chinese design, which contrasted sharply with the boxy English safe. She'd seen this same puzzle padlock before. Papa had showed it to her and Mama when he'd brought it home from a trip to the East a few years ago. He'd explained how it worked, boasting that he'd had it crafted specially for himself.

Estella inched the light closer. The base of the lamp scraped harshly across the floor. On the puzzle padlock were dozens of pictures on five revolving disks. She knew she had to arrange the correct picture on each disk so it was aligned with the star at the top of the padlock, and it would open. She'd have those ledgers. Papa would be safe from the men who wanted to destroy him.

A star.

She hadn't realized the significance of this before, but Papa had had the padlock custom-made. The star had to be related to her own name, which meant star.

She studied the disks. The innermost one was also the smallest one. Tiny pictures carved around its circumference depicted a bowl, a dog, a little person that looked like a girl or woman, a kite, and several others. The next disk had more pictures, none of them making any sense. The other disks were equally cryptic.

Estella rocked back on her heels, rubbing her forehead. She was certain she could figure the puzzle. She took a deep breath, then tried to look at the padlock with fresh eyes. She stared at the star. Five points, nothing unusual. Except—she peered closer—there was a tiny candle carved in the center of the star.

At first she thought it looked rather mystical. Except Papa wasn't the mystical sort. And the candle looked an awful lot like a candle on a birthday cake.

Estella smiled. Birthday presents. Papa had always made an enormous to-do about her birthday presents. A picture on the middle disk caught her eye. A little horse. Or, more specifically, a pony. Papa had gifted her with a pony on her seventh birthday. She slid the disk so the pony was on top, below the star.

Now. What had she received on her eighth birthday? She worried her lower lip, straining to remember. She couldn't. And her sixth birthday? She smiled. A dollhouse.

Sure enough, there was a picture of a little house on the second disk. She swiveled it into position. The innermost disk came next. Her fifth birthday present had been a gorgeous, enormous china doll with real red-gold hair and eyelashes, and lovely glass eyes. Estella had named her Posy. Posy still sat on a shelf in the old nursery in London. The little picture of the girl had to represent Posy.

Now. She still couldn't remember what she'd received on her eighth birthday. But her ninth birthday present had been a beautiful jewelry box from Russia. There wasn't a picture of a box on the outermost disk, but there was a picture of a faceted gem. When she slid this disk into place, she felt the padlock beginning to give. She'd been right.

Just one disk to go.

Anxiety gnawed at her. She knew she was close to opening the safe. She felt so vulnerable, though, crouched there in the pool of gaslight, with her back to all those crates. And to the staircase.

Think.

Estella's birthday was in July. The Hancocks were always in London then. What had Papa given her when she'd turned eight?

Oh yes. That had been the year that Mama had fallen ill with typhus. Fortunately, she had recovered, but Papa had taken her up to his brother's home in Scotland to convalesce in cleaner, cooler air than that in London. They had left Estella behind with her cousin Henriette's family. Papa had forgotten Estella's birthday that year.

Estella felt a pang of embarrassment, thinking of what a spoiled fuss she'd raised.

She stared at the second-to-last disk. A turtle, a shoe, a sunburst. And a thistle. Estella had never been to Scotland, but she knew thistles abounded on the moors there.

She slid the thistle picture beneath the star. There was a tiny click, and then the puzzle padlock fell smoothly open.

Her heart thumped in her throat. With trembling fingers, she removed the padlock and opened the safe. A stack of three ledgers sat inside. She placed them as carefully as she could on the floor.

No sooner had she shut the safe and replaced the padlock, than she heard footsteps coming up the stairs.

When Godolphin opened the door at the bottom of the warehouse loft and saw light from above, his breath went shallow. Instinctively, he touched his fingertips to his pistol. Then he crept up the stairs, hugging one side of the wall with his shoulder. He heard a metallic bang, then rustling and quick footsteps.

He reached the top of the stairs. But instead of Bertie, he saw—

"Estella?" he said.

"Godolphin." She stood in the middle of the floor in a defensive posture, arms crossed, cupping her elbows with shaking palms.

He was certain he saw relief sweep across her features. But her eyes were bright and wary. She was still afraid of him, and with good reason. But not as much as she was afraid of Bertie.

Was he a fool to take that as a good sign?

"What," he said, "in God's name are you doing—ah." His eyes fell on the lamp beside the safe. He looked back at her.

She swallowed. "I know what you're trying to do. I know what you want—that you want the ledgers."

"How do you know that?"

Her lips twitched, her chin cocked up a notch. "Powers of deduction, dear husband."

"You overheard what Bertie said earlier. You were spying."

"I'm not a complete twit, you know. You may have tricked me into marriage—"

"You tricked *me* into marriage."

She sniffed. "—and you may have tricked me into thinking that you've been living at Castle Seabrook for years, not weeks—"

"Months."

She glared. "That doesn't make a bit of difference. At any rate, you've underestimated me."

"Have I? Did you manage to open the safe?" He scanned the warehouse, looking for the ledgers. Nothing.

She swallowed. Her cheeks were glowing, and her eyes

sparkled. "I'm afraid I was interrupted. But I'm certain I could figure it out if given enough time."

"The star on the dial. Your father had the padlock made specially, I know that much. That star can't be insignificant." His eyes swept her figure. He didn't know why. She was his adversary, plain and simple, but her artless allure distracted him. His body was too warm, every nerve trilling. He tried to force himself into submission, calling upon the cold rationality he always used in difficult situations. He'd almost managed it when she began to move toward him.

His pulse lunged forward, as if to meet her.

"I could open the safe for you," she said. Her arms were hanging gracefully at her sides, now. She no longer appeared afraid.

"Why would you want to do that?"

"Because I'd rather you had the ledgers than Bertie."

"Your powers of reason are failing you, my dear." His own powers of reason were failing *him*. With each step that took her closer to him, his nerves wound tighter. He itched to touch her. "Wouldn't it be best if neither Bertie nor I had the ledgers?"

She stopped three paces away. The light was behind her, so it was difficult to make out her eyes. Her hair glowed, a halo of rusty gold. "Bertie frightens me," she whispered. "He's unbalanced. I'm afraid he'll do something mad."

Godolphin stiffened. "I won't allow him to harm you." The huskiness in his own voice startled him.

"Whereas *you*," she went on, her tone now arch, "will merely do anything, no matter how manipulative, to frame my father. But I'm not worried, because I know he is innocent. So go ahead, do whatever you want. You'll never incriminate him. Although perhaps, in the process, you do run the risk of incriminating yourself."

"How so?" he growled, suddenly angered.

She met his eyes. "You know."

"No, I don't. Tell me."

"Unfortunately, I have gathered that your Papa was not nearly as scrupulous as my own, and—"

"Enough!" Finally, he felt that chilly rationality. It was a relief.

She swallowed, seeming to shrink away from him.

Guilt taunted him. "I'm sorry," he said. "My father—"

"It's fine," she whispered, eyes cast down.

"Then you'll open the safe for me?"

She looked up. "I'll try."

She had to help Godolphin open the safe. It was the only way she could put him off the scent, since he'd made the correct deduction about the star. If he saw that the safe was empty, he would look for the ledgers elsewhere. That would give her a chance to remove them from the warehouse.

She only hoped that he wouldn't go near the smelly heap of Canadian beaver pelts she'd stuffed the ledgers under.

He followed her to the safe.

Her breath was still shallow from his sudden arrival. Her fingertips were jittery, and as she knelt before the safe again, her knees felt like pudding. She wasn't exactly *afraid*. She did not trust Godolphin—heaven knew he was deceptive beyond belief. But she instinctively knew that he would never hurt her.

"I think," she said, touching the star, "that the pictures are meant to be aligned beneath the star in a certain way."

He crouched down beside her, disturbingly close. She caught the clean scent of his shaving soap.

She licked her lips.

"Have you any idea what the candle means?" His voice was hushed now, and therefore too intimate.

For some reason, it was an effort to breathe evenly. "I

suspect it's some sort of mystical symbol," she lied. "It looks Egyptian or something."

"As a symbol, candles represent the warding off of evil spirits. Or hope. Or, when someone has died, the life of the next world."

Estella tipped her head to face him. "You are a regular encyclopedia, husband. Why did you ask me what it means if you already know so much?"

"Because I doubt your father had any of those meanings in mind when he had the padlock made in China. I'm certain the candle is more personal than that. Did he have pet names for you when you were small?"

"Oh." Estella smiled. "Dozens."

"Did any of them relate to your being a candle? A light, I mean."

Estella pivoted a bit to face him. Life streaked through her when she found herself face to face with him, close enough to touch. More than close enough to touch. Close enough to embrace. To kiss.

His eyes glowed in the lamplight. "You are like a flame," he said in the lowest, roughest whisper. "Bright. Golden. Always shifting."

"And I suppose," she replied in a tone that was meant to sound tart, but came out breathy, "I burn everything in sight?"

His lids drooped slightly. "You scorch me."

"With my words?"

"Yes, your sharp words. Your eyes are scorching, too. And your skin."

"My skin," she exhaled. He was leaning closer. The knowledge that she yearned to touch *his* skin, feel his heat, his solidity, crept over her.

"Your skin." Slowly, he raised an arm, and touched one fingertip to her cheekbone.

Their eyes were locked, and she gasped a little at his touch, but then she felt as though her whole body was melting into that tiny spot where their bodies met. His skin was scorching. It felt like a rivulet of warm wax when he traced it down her cheek, slowly, slowly, to the edge of her jaw. Then he pushed his finger gently, firmly, forcing her to tip her head to the side. She ought to have been incensed. But she really had no choice but to obey, because she couldn't bear the thought of his taking his finger away. It was delicious to obey.

His fingertip continued its way down the side of her neck, stopping at the high-buttoned collar of her pelisse.

He was her enemy. What was she doing?

"No," she gasped, jerking away from his touch, ripping her gaze from his. "The padlock." She swiveled back to face the safe, afraid of what his expression might be if she dared to look.

"The padlock." His voice was level and dangerous.

"It's a birthday candle," Estella blurted in an attempt to smooth over what had just happened. "A candle on a birthday cake." She paused. He was holding his breath, she could tell. "Papa always made such a fuss about my birthdays, and I'm certain that's what the candle means." She thought of Godolphin's plan to frame Papa as a criminal. The deliciousness of his finger on her skin was forgotten in a flash. She swung her head to look at him. "I know your opinion of my father is low—and incorrect, actually—but he is the kindest man in the world. It is shameful what you are trying to do. *Trying*, mind you. You'll never manage it."

Godolphin's jaw was locked, his eyes unreadable. "You agreed to help me open the padlock."

Estella huffed and turned back to the safe. The force of Godolphin's will was palpable, as though if she scratched at his surface she would find hard, shiny steel beneath. She had no choice but to go forward, pretending to help him, so he wouldn't realize she'd already got the ledgers. And she would *not* allow him to touch her again.

"The pictures," Godolphin said, "must be birthday gifts, then. The correct pictures, I mean."

Estella gritted her teeth. It had taken her several minutes to come to that conclusion! "Indeed. That would make sense."

"So you need only remember what your father gave you on five different birthdays."

"But which five?" Estella played dumb. She did not feel at all agreeable.

"Zero, five, ten, fifteen, twenty?"

"Zero?"

"Perhaps he gave your mother a gift upon your birth. That is a traditional gesture. Although, in your case, you would be gift enough. Imagine your mother's delight when the nursemaid handed her a tiny red-haired devil in swaddling clothes."

"You're insolent," Estella gasped, scrambling to her feet. "I shall not assist you after all." She moved to flounce past Godolphin's crouching form, toward the stairs. But he grabbed her by the waist and pulled her on top of him.

"Stop," she squealed. He had somehow gotten her into a half-sitting, half-reclining position across his knees. His thighs felt dense and strappy beneath her bottom. "How dare you!"

"How dare I?" He tightened his arms around her and dumped her gently onto the wooden floor, on her back. He crawled over her, placing a hand on either side of her shoulders. "How dare I call a little devil a little devil?"

She was fuming now. "I am not a devil, and I am not a rag doll that you may toss about according to your whims." A chill from the floor crept through her clothes. Above her, Godolphin hovered in shadow, but she felt his heat. He was breathless.

She pushed at his chest. "Move, you beast."

"A devil and a beast."

"Mmm. Fitting that we are cavorting together, is it not?"

She pushed at his chest again, then drew her hand quickly back. His heart was pounding as though he had a fever. "I would like to leave."

Was it her imagination, or was he leaning closer and closer over her?

"You will not leave," he said mildly. "You said you would assist me in opening the padlock."

"As a devil, I reserve the right to change my mind."

"At the drop of a hat, it seems." He *was* leaning closer, lowering his face so near that she felt the waft of his breath on her cheeks. "So change your mind back."

"You cannot make me."

"Yes. I can."

He bent his elbows, lowering himself, closing the distance between their chests, between their mouths. His lips hovered over hers, barely touching. Her feet flexed. He inhaled deeply. In the wavering lamplight, his face was a puzzle of glowing yellow and deep shadow. She could only see a glitter in his shadowed eye sockets.

Her heart was thumping, and every nerve in her body was riveted on his presence. Thinking was something she was no longer capable of. All she wanted to do was *feel.* She arched her neck a little, closing the distance between their mouths. Their lips parted simultaneously. The taste of him, the feel of his wet tongue, the heat from his lungs, was a kind of relief. As though she'd been holding her breath and waiting, life suspended, ever since the last time they'd kissed.

"No flavor of brimstone or charcoal," he muttered, kissing her throat. "Perhaps you aren't a devil at all, but an angel."

"Haven't you heard? Devils *are* angels. Fallen ones." She wrapped a hand around the back of his neck, and pulled his mouth back to hers.

Chapter Ten

Ravishment with a Capital "R"

This *wasn't* what he had planned.

Devil take it, and how appropriate that expression was. This, kissing Estella, feeling her body rise to meet his, was far better than what he'd planned.

In fact, he couldn't precisely remember what his plan had been. Something to do with ledgers, he dimly remembered. Anything that did not involve Estella's tongue, the pressure of her little hand at his neck, the rush of her excited breath, was dull beyond words. This musty loft, this woman lying in a pool of lamplight, was the exact center of the universe.

He'd pulled up her skirts, was placing a knee between her legs, when she seemed to become aware of just what he was about to do. She burst upright, coppery curls streaming around her shoulders.

"You wanted the padlock open," she blurted.

He rocked back, sitting on his heels. "I can think of more pressing agendas at present, actually."

Her cheeks were aflame. "You've been—how can I—? You're not—you want to frame my father—"

"And *you* said you'd help me open the safe, therefore facilitating this plan of mine."

Confusion swept over her face for a moment, but then her eyes were crackling again. "You tricked me about the castle, about how long you've been living there. Tricked me horribly! Can you imagine how I felt when I learned about that? With all those people at the party who knew something I didn't? Watching me?"

"Estella." His chest felt like lead. "Estella, please listen to me. This has all gotten out of hand, more so than I can begin to describe. I had no intention of sending your father to prison—"

"You *thought* about that? That you could even think of that is—"

"Listen, please. I didn't know about Bertie's involvement. It's quite possible he is more at fault than your father."

"How about *entirely* at fault?" she snapped.

He paused to admire the beautiful ferocity of her loyalty to her father. She was like a tiger. "I never could've foreseen this."

She narrowed her eyes, yanking her skirts down to her shins. *"This?"*

"You being so . . . you making me feel like this. Me wanting you so badly. I never dreamed." *Oh, but you have dreamed,* a tiny voice whispered at the back of his mind. *You've been dreaming ever since you first laid eyes on the girl.* Godolphin ignored the voice. If he admitted that to himself, then all his behavior was too, too unconscionable. How could he live with himself if he'd willingly tricked someone he was half in love with? "Please, Estella, don't torture me because I desire you. Don't torture yourself. We are wed. No court in the world could keep us apart." Were these words really coming from him? Begging, almost? He watched the way her dainty bosom rose and fell. The silver chain around her neck sparkled.

"I'm quite certain," Estella retorted, "that I am not torturing myself in any way."

"But you are," he growled. He leaned on his hands, so

he was on all fours, beastlike, over her. He prowled forward. "Denial is torture."

"Denial?" She tried to keep up her hauteur, but her eyes were hazy with desire.

"Denial." His face was inches from hers.

"And how"—she moistened her lips—"and how might this torture be abated?"

"Oh, easily, my love. Surrender. All you need to do is lean back and surrender to me, and I assure you that every drop of denial will leave your beautiful body." He leaned an inch closer, listening to her panting. His shaft was stiff and ready. "No more torture, Estella. Allow me to help you."

A long pause. Her eyes glowed.

Finally, in response, she kissed him.

All traces of uncertainty were gone from her kiss. He sensed that a veil had lifted, a barrier had been demolished. She would be his. Totally his. He eased her onto her back, cupping her head against the floor. "Is the floor too hard?" he asked.

She shifted. "A little."

He pulled himself to his feet. "I'll get some furs." He began moving to the pelts he'd noticed stacked on some crates.

"No!" she cried.

He stopped, turned. She sat up, and her cheeks were pale in the lamplight.

"They smell," she explained. "Those furs always smell awfully. I honestly don't know how people wear hats made from them. Come." She extended a hand. "It's all right."

With her hand stretched out in invitation, and the wanton, warm smile she gave him, he had no choice but to return to her.

Blood wheezed past her eardrums. The ledgers. He'd come so close to finding the ledgers hidden beneath the beaver pelts.

But he was at her side again, lowering himself on top of her. Then, he caught her around the waist. In a motion that could have been cumbersome, but was in fact graceful, he dragged her to him, then settled himself on his back.

She found herself astride her husband. Her skirts were bunched around her knees. Her kneecaps were against the cold floor, but between her thighs, Godolphin's legs were warm. And there was something very large, very hard, against her pelvis. His hands, spanning her waist, seemed to be pressing her against this hard thing.

He smiled up at her. "Is it the angel in you, darling, or the devil, that makes me respond to you thus?"

She placed her palms on his chest, where his jacket had fallen open. Through the fine linen of his shirt she felt rounded muscle, hard ribs, a thudding heart. She smiled. "I suspect it is a combination of the two. And you? How do you make me forget what a beast you've been?"

"It's probably," he said, tracing her waist with his palms, "the very fact that I *am* a beast."

She tipped her head. He looked so handsome, so powerful, but something about the fact that she was sitting atop him gave *her* a little more power. Which was why, perhaps, she was acting so brazen. He *was* her husband. She could technically be as much of a tart as she wanted. After a lifetime of having to be prim and proper, this was freeing. Exhilarating. "I'm going to tame you, you know," she told him.

He burst out laughing. "Are you now? I won't even ask how you intend to do that." He took her by the elbows and drew her down to him. "And I certainly won't dampen your optimism by telling you that it cannot be done."

"No?" She stared into his eyes. They shone like dark stars. "How are you so certain?"

"Because"—he took a gentle fistful of her hair and pulled her to his mouth—"it has been attempted before, without success." He kissed her, urgently, aggressively, as if to prove just how untamable he was.

But she responded in kind, a wild animal feeling rising from somewhere deep inside of her. *She* was untamable, too, and perhaps more wild and free than he ever was. She met his tongue, danced with him. As the stroking of his hands on her sides, her shoulders, her back, became more insistent, a hot, liquid feeling blossomed between her thighs. It was painful: a sweet, heavy ache that would not be ignored. She kissed his throat. The skin was surprisingly silky beneath her lips. His scent filled her, that warm, spicy, delicious man scent. She licked him, feeling the stubble where his neck met his jaw.

He moaned, and clapped both his hands firmly around her buttocks, began rocking her rhythmically into his hardness.

For a few seconds, this appeased the ache between her legs. Then she needed more. She needed him to touch, to . . . she didn't know. Ravish her. She suddenly had quite a clear idea of what this entailed. It was so obvious, like a knowledge inside her bones. Silly, how she'd thought she didn't know, that she needed someone to tell her about it. She already knew.

Pulling her mouth from his throat, she sat up and fumbled with the buttons of his shirt. She wanted, *needed*, his skin, his heat.

His eyes were open, gazing up at her with an expression that was half-amused, but half deadly serious. "You would unclothe me? Like a youth debauching a dairy maid?"

"Like a devil unclothing a beast," she said. The words were low, sultry. She laughed. "If a beast would wear clothes."

"I believe the wolf in some fairy story did."

"Mmm." Finishing the last button, she peeled his shirt open, exposing his chest. "He dressed like a grandmother." Godolphin's chest was dark gold in the low light. His belly was flat, his rib cage hard, and the muscles span-

ning his upper chest were sculpted. "Not a pirate." Dark
hair made a T shape, trailing down to the waistband of his
trousers. She traced his collarbones, stroked an open-
fingered palm through his chest hair, feeling it all. His
body felt so unlike her own. Hotter, harder.

"I think it's only fair," he said, fumbling with her skirts,
"that I be allowed to return the favor and unclothe you."

Why wasn't she afraid? Well, her thoughts were smudged
together like a ruined oil painting. Nothing was distinct,
but everything was so beautiful, so colorful. Her eyes fell
shut in pleasure as his hands held her ankles. Firmly,
slowly, his gripping hands traveled up her legs. His skin
was a little rough, and it snagged on her silk stockings.
He navigated the bends of her knees, behind which she
felt sweaty, and up to her thighs. Past her garters, to bare
skin.

A shudder convulsed through her entire body at the
shock of his touch there. *No one* had ever touched her
there. The skin was exquisitely sensitive. His fingers felt so
good that it almost hurt. She nudged herself harder
against his member.

"Impatient angel," he muttered.

She merely sighed in response.

It suddenly felt as though there was far too much material between them. Pantalettes, trousers. Too much. Without really thinking, she began undoing his belt buckle,
then the buttons at his waist.

"*Very* impatient devil," he growled. Then his hands
were moving quickly, grabbing at the material of her
pantalettes.

She'd just gotten his trousers unbuttoned when he
ripped her pantalettes at the seam.

She started at the slicing sound, muffled a little by her
skirts. It seemed more real than the subtle shuffling, hard
breathing, the sighs.

What was she doing? This was serious business, Ravishment. It led to serious things. They would be bound. There could be a baby. . . .

These thoughts were forgotten as soon as he touched her in the precise spot where she ached so badly. "Oh," she breathed.

"Yes?" he muttered. He rubbed his thumb in little circular motions.

Something spiraled through her body, thick flames of pleasure, ruby red. She threw her head back, abandoned herself. She no longer possessed a mind. Only a body. There was nothing but this pleasure, his quickening touch, and he was arching into her. She tugged his trousers wide open, but was distracted again by the sweet intensity between her legs.

So, with his other hand he freed himself.

She stared down, through vision hazy red with desire, at his huge, beautiful manhood, standing erect and slightly comical between them.

"Touch me," he instructed softly. "Please."

She wrapped her fingers around him. Steel, sheathed in silk, and so vibrantly alive.

He groaned. "Oh God. Estella. Oh God, *yes.*"

She felt power, touching him. This, she thought confusedly, was assuredly *one* way to tame a beast. But at the same time, she was submitting to him, dissolving into fluid abandon under his touch.

But abruptly, he stopped.

Her eyes flew open. She felt almost accusing, looking down at him.

He smiled. His eyes were soft, but his lips curled rakishly. "Don't look at me like that. You'll like what comes next even more."

She felt bratty. "Oh?"

"Indeed." He set his jaw, took her by the hips, and lifted her.

She felt disconcerted, suddenly powerless, as he drew

her a few inches forward, and positioned her over his manhood.

"Ravishment," he said, almost whispering. "Did you understand, that day on the beach in Brighton? The note?"

Mute, she shook her head. But she understood now. Embarrassment flickered in the back of her mind. A silly little fool she'd been.

Godolphin, however, didn't seem to mind. "It might hurt. Only for a moment—"

"Hurt?" Her mouth went dry. "Ravishment hurts?"

"Just relax, all right, my love?"

It couldn't possibly hurt more than the raging need she felt to be touched again, to feel him, have him fill her. She didn't wait for him, but settled herself over his crest.

"*Oh God,*" he ground out, this time to himself. "Slowly, love." His fingers were digging savagely into her buttocks. "Slowly, or I won't last."

She lowered herself, slowly as she could, and he stretched her and filled her. Then she could go no further. "I—it—"

"Relax." He pushed her down.

Oh dear merciful heavens. Oh crikey, curses, bloody hell. It *hurt.* Hot tears squeezed from her screwed-tight eyes, and she let her hands fall heavily on his shoulders, ready to pull herself away from him.

He stopped her with hands around her waist. "Breathe," he said. "It'll pass."

She paused, resting against his shoulders, and gradually the pain subsided until she only felt completely *filled.* And he was touching her *there* again. The beautiful feeling licked up like velvety flames. She began to rock atop him.

He rocked with her, holding her by the waist, whispering her name, never taking his eyes from hers. The way their eyes were locked was somehow the same as the way their bodies were interlocked below. It was as though the union of their eyes completed a circle, so that something . . . what was it? She couldn't think clearly enough to decide. Something spun around and around as they moved together on the hard floor.

The motions of his thumb between her legs grew quicker, fluttered, and she felt like a dam about to burst. She was losing her head, and his eyes were so dark, so blue, so lustrous, and he felt so big inside her, rubbing her inside, pressing on some mysterious spot deep inside that was both sweetness and pain. She felt powerful—she was taming her beast. But she felt oddly helpless, too, because *he* was also the master of *her*.

This was somehow perfect: they were both the master, both the slave.

And she exploded beneath his touch, crying out. Her call echoed off the rafters. She was shuddering, and her mind was utterly gone. Gone. Only pleasure remained, coursing through her and sustained by his thrusts. These grew harder, till her mouth opened, and he froze with a groan, and she knew he was spilling his seed inside her. She crumpled against his chest. He wrapped his arms around her, holding her tight.

Estella moved before he did. She sat up, eyes hazy, hair a beautiful mess.

He noted that he was holding his breath.

But she smiled. "Ravishment," she said softly, "is rather nice, husband."

He smiled back.

She stood, arranged her skirts and hair, and he sat up and watched. She returned to the safe and knelt down in front of it.

Reality slapped him. The safe. The ledgers. His plan of annulling this sham of a marriage . . . Bloody hell. "All business," he called, trying to sound nonchalant.

"I said I'd open this for you, and so I will." She was frowning, sliding the dials of the puzzle padlock. "I'm certain that I've got the middle disk right. It's a pony."

His mind snapped to attention, and he rose and moved

toward her, buttoning his trousers as he walked. "Which birthday was that?"

"When I turned seven."

"What about when you turned eight?"

"Don't remember." She had yet to look at him. Also, she seemed to be blushing. The wanton devil-angel had disappeared, replaced with an uncertain young woman.

He wrapped an arm around her shoulder. She stiffened under his touch, but didn't pull away. "And your sixth birthday?"

She'd already slid that next dial in place, with a tiny picture of what looked like some sort of building under the star. "A dollhouse."

"Fifth?"

"A doll." She slid the innermost disk into place. "Here. Give it a wiggle. I know this is correct, because it feels loose."

He obliged. The padlock felt about to give way. "Your eighth birthday," he said. "Think."

"I *am*." She tossed him a sidelong scowl. Then she traced an oval fingernail around the dial, the nail clicking minutely against the metal.

She had, he noted, lovely hands.

"Scotland," she said suddenly.

"I gathered that your papa was indulgent," Godolphin said wryly, "but I never heard of an eight-year-old being gifted with an entire country for her birthday."

Another scowl. "That was the year my parents went to Scotland. Without me. Mama had been sick, and they forgot my birthday."

Swiftly, Godolphin scanned the dial. "Is that a thistle?" He touched one of the tiny engraved pictures on the last dial. Then he slid it into position. The padlock fell open.

The safe was empty.

"Littlefield must've got the ledgers," Estella said.

Godolphin gazed at her across the darkened carriage.

This was the first either of them had spoken since they'd left the warehouse together. Godolphin's horse had been tied next to the pair of mares pulling the carriage. They were now bumping along the road, back to the castle for the second time that night.

He glanced out the window. Dawn was a glowing strip above the horizon. "Indeed. I suspect he's been trying to crack that padlock night and day."

"He has. That night I went to the warehouse and he surprised me, I'm certain he came down from the loft."

"How do you suppose he figured what your childhood birthday gifts were, though? Did he ask you?"

"No! I would never . . ." Godolphin heard her swallow. "He probably chanced upon the correct arrangement of the dials by mistake. You can feel when you've got a few right because the padlock starts to give. You noticed that, didn't you? And there aren't that many possible combinations."

"Yes. An imperfect design." The carriage slowed to a halt at the castle steps.

It was so late, there were no footmen to greet them in the castle foyer. Two wall sconces dimly lit the vaulted stone chamber. The echoes of their footsteps seemed deafening.

Why did she feel like an intruder in what was supposed to be her home?

Perhaps—she glanced at Godolphin, who was bolting the front doors—because the entire household was a farce. The servants were like actors in a play; her husband had instructed them to deceive her. Panic began to simmer in her belly. She had given herself to him. So stupid, so thoughtless . . .

He moved to her side, took her hand. "May I have the honor of sharing your bed, wife?" he asked, smiling down at her her.

His face was so handsome, so friendly, but she couldn't shake the dread that was snaking itself around her. She pulled her hand away. "I think—"

Footsteps were approaching from one of the several corridors that led off the foyer.

"Your Lordship." Teeters appeared, short and squat, beneath an arched doorway. "Your Ladyship."

"Teeters," Godolphin said, sounding terse. "Still awake?"

"Just awake, actually. It is dawn, sir. I always rise at dawn." His eyes took in Estella's disheveled hair, her rumpled gown.

She knew that he knew. Her cheeks flamed.

"I was just on my way outside," Teeters said. His facial expression was apologetic, but his tone oozed sarcasm. "A brisk walk at dawn is my daily habit."

"Good night," Estella said loudly. Before Godolphin could protest, she'd slipped her hand from his grasp, heading to her bedchamber to sleep alone.

Estella slept until luncheon. When she woke, she was confused. She'd been dreaming about Godolphin, about his body, about him touching her.

She sat up in bed. Oh dear. That had been rather more than a dream, and now things were complicated one thousandfold. She could not dwell on this latest mishap of hers, however. She needed to get back to the warehouse before someone found the hidden ledgers.

When she returned to the warehouse, no one was about. It was Saturday, and Papa always gave his employees the day off.

And, she soon discovered, the ledgers were no longer beneath the beaver pelts in the loft. Someone had taken them.

"I suggested a Babylonian theme to my husband," Estella told Mr. Pepys, the foppish London decorator, that afternoon. She planned to carry on with the redecoration of the castle, if only for something amusing to do. Besides, it'd be a shame to let Pepys go so soon after he'd arrived. "Fountains, tasseled pillows, beaded curtains. Perhaps a parrot or two. But he didn't seem very keen on the notion." She smiled.

Slowly, Mr. Pepys rose from the trunk of upholstery swatches in the corner of the breakfast room. When his eyes met Estella's, they were bright. "What a splendid idea, Your Ladyship," he replied, voice muted with awe. "I say, in a past life you might've been a decorator."

Laughing, Estella fluttered a dismissive hand. "You flatter me awfully, Mr. Pepys." Crossing her arms, she considered the ceiling. The white plaster was crackled with age, and several yellowish water stains bloomed across it.

Pepys followed her gaze. "The chandelier is stupendous, but we've got to do something about all that dreary white plaster. It looks like a convent, not a castle. Now. What would you think about a trompe l'oeil scene? Cherubs with lavender feathered wings, perhaps, sheer swags, bunches of roses in the corners . . ."

Estella wasn't sure if he was serious or not. The wide gestures he made with his arms, the excited flourishes of his voice, made him seem dramatic. Not to mention the striking cut of his clothes, and the lemony silk of his neck cloth. Cherubs? Could he really be serious? She decided to play along. "There could be an enormous gold-leaf sun radiating from around the chandeliers, and stars, and doves—"

"I do hope we are discussing the ceiling of the Sistine Chapel."

Estella spun around to face the door. "Oh—hello, Godolphin." He would be put out by her escape last night, after he'd asked to sleep with her.

"Good afternoon," was Godolphin's terse reply. He was in his shirtsleeves, and his hair was slightly disheveled.

Pepys, clearly embarrassed by the tension between husband and wife, busied himself by folding a long length of royal blue satin.

"We're just finishing," Estella fumbled on. "Did you have a . . . ?"

"A reason for entering a room in my own home? No. I didn't think I needed one."

Though his arms were piled high with fabric, Pepys managed to present them both with an elegant bow. "I'll just go put these away," he whispered.

Estella thought he tilted his fair eyebrows up a little in sympathy before he left. Godolphin didn't see, as he was glowering out the windows.

Well. She had been feeling oddly soft toward Godolphin, despite everything. But if he was going to make grumpy comments, utterly unprovoked, well, then she would, too. She assumed a haughty expression. "*I* practically have to get a sealed letter of permission from the Archbishop of Canterbury to go in certain parts of my home."

Almost lazily, his indigo gaze drifted away from the windows and fixed on her. "That *was* the idea. Although I don't know how well you've adhered to it."

Her eyes dropped to the floor. Had Teeters told him about the candlestick in the tower after all?

Panicked, she moved over to the table, snatched up a piece of paper from a messy pile. "Do you like this?" she asked, holding up a charcoal sketch of window trimmings Pepys had made. "I rather like the swags on top, and in a nice silvery blue, it would look lovely." Her tone was a bit too brittle, however, her smile forced.

He remained rooted to his spot, face expressionless.

For a mad second, she felt like screaming, pummeling her fists on his lapels like a Gothic heroine. How could he remain so distant, so cold? If he knew about the candlestick, then, for heaven's sake, why didn't he just say so?

"You decide," he said blandly, then briefly pressed the heel of his palm to his brow bone, as though he had a headache. "I won't retract what I said about trusting your taste. However, I am beginning to question your choice of Pepys."

Irritation flared her nostrils. "He comes highly recommended by a dear friend, so—" She stopped. Teeters had just shuffled in, looking like a dung beetle in a black jacket and glossy brown waistcoat. He clasped a stack of ledgers against his round belly, and his expression was harried.

Estella stared hard at the ledgers. They weren't the same ones that had gone missing from the the warehouse. But still . . . She glanced up at Godolphin. Had *Godolphin* taken the ledgers?

Chapter Eleven

The Benefits of a Probable Bosom

"Here you are, Your Lordship," Teeters panted. Then he shot Estella a look of pure disdain. "I was not aware that you were . . . otherwise occupied."

"Just passing by," Godolphin replied mildly. He eyed the ledgers. "Did you find the 1813 records, then?"

"Yes. They were in the library. Unlocked. Anyone could've read them." He looked at Estella pointedly, then turned back to his employer. "Are you certain, Your Lordship, that we should discuss the records in the, ahem, presence of . . . ?" His muddy eyes slid back to Estella.

The horrible little man. Flinging good grace to the winds, Estella drew herself up as tall as she could. Which put her at eye level with Teeters. "If you don't mind, Teeters, I'd like to have a word with my husband. In private."

Teeters's upper lip twitched. "We were in the midst of something quite important. I don't think His Lordship has the time to be bothered with trifles today. Or any day, for that matter."

She knew he was thinking of the disreputable state she'd been in early that morning. But for heaven's sake! She had every right to be Ravished by her own husband.

"I'll speak for myself," Godolphin cut in smoothly. "Thank you." He caught Estella's eye. "Darling—"

Darling? Was he completely batty?

"—I've work to do. I'll see you at dinner." He took a few steps toward the door.

No. She couldn't allow Teeters to win. Luckily, Godolphin's incongruous endearment had reminded her of Madame Pettibonne's second technique on bringing a hound to heel.

She moistened her lips, lowered her lashes in what she fervently hoped passed for a sultry look. The trick, she suspected, was to avoid being whiny. "Godolphin—" she caught up to him, touched his arm "—sweetheart. Please do stay for a few minutes longer."

Godolphin blinked, looked down at her hand resting lightly on his arm. Then he seemed to melt like wax under a flame. "I can spare a few minutes. Of course."

"Thank you." She withdrew her arm. Next, for it was too irresistible, she sneaked a peek at Teeters. She suspected her grin was a trifle victorious, because Teeters went blotchy.

"Your Lordship," he spluttered, "these ledgers can't wait all day. Once we finish with them, there are—"

"Enough." Instead of raising his voice, Godolphin brought it down to a bone-chilling hush.

Teeters's plump neck shifted under his cravat as he swallowed. Shooting Estella one last look of death, he spun on his heel and huffed out.

Godolphin sighed, like a man grown weary of an impetuous child.

Estella winced. The sound was all too familiar.

Lowering himself into a chair by the breakfast table, Godolphin studied her in silence. His eyes skimmed her form and rest at the base of her throat. Rather girlishly, she was relieved she'd chosen her favorite morning gown of pale embroidered muslin. A wash of goose bumps shimmered over her, and she crossed her arms beneath her bodice. How she wished he wouldn't look *there*.

"You are . . ." He seemed to speak with effort, his tone laced with roughness. "You look lovely today, Estella."

She swallowed. "Thank you."

"You wanted to speak to me in private?"

"Yes. Um. No . . . duckie." She would *not* acknowledge the amused grin that had just spread across his face. Perhaps duckie wasn't the most appropriate endearment. "It's just that we've been married for eight days, and we've barely spent eight hours in each other's company." Though she'd been hard-pressed to think of a specific reason she'd wanted him to stay—besides, of course, getting Teeters's goat—a hundred reasons suddenly chorused inside her.

Oh hell. Hot, fat tears were welling in the corners of her eyes. Impatient, she swiped them away with her fingertips, too distressed to bother with a handkerchief like a proper countess.

"Come here," he said, genuine concern coloring his voice. He extended his arm. "Is this about last night? I thought you enjoyed it. Are you . . . are you in pain?"

"Pain? No." Only a little soreness, which she knew would pass. Still wiping the tears, some of which had spilled onto her cheeks, she did as he bade. Coming to a stop a few feet before him, she looked down into his eyes.

And *oh*. She saw such tenderness there. Instead of being remote, his eyes were focused, so very *present*. Concern tightened the muscles around his eyes, turning the crinkles at the corners down so he looked sad. His expression startled and touched her so deeply that still more tears prickled her eyelids.

"I don't know what's wrong with me," she laughed through her tears. "I must be overtired."

Making no response, he curled his arms round her lower back, drew her close.

She sucked in one quick inhalation, then stopped breathing altogether. His forehead, hard and warm, pressed against her small breasts. And his hands . . . well, they were rather low on her back. All right, they were actually cupping her bottom. She could feel the broad, warm span of his palms through her petticoats, almost as if she were stripped naked before him.

What did one do in this situation? For one thing, the doors were wide open. If anyone should happen to walk past . . . And there was no way he could miss the flatness of her chest at this juncture. Not with his nose pressed where it was . . . and she wasn't sure what to do with her arms, so she left them dangling . . . but she couldn't pull away. That would be rude.

Besides, she rather liked it. Her body was responding eagerly, just as it had done last night.

He pulled his head away, looked up into her face. Though he appeared weary and drawn, a wide grin had split his face.

Why had she never noticed how white his teeth were against his stubble-shadowed skin, how his eyes glowed like blue glass?

"Duckie," he mused. "How on earth did you come up with that one?"

"Um—" It was awfully hard to think straight with his hands cupping her bottom like that. "I suppose it doesn't suit you all that well—*oh. Sir.*" He'd given her rump a playful squeeze, drew her closer still, so that she was trapped between his thighs.

Good heavens. He was staring directly at her Lack of a Real Bosom. Unwaveringly.

"So." She coughed delicately. "Did you take the ledgers?"

There. That made him look back up into her face.

"Ledgers?" His voice was pure blandness. "Do you mean those that Teeters had?"

She frowned. "The ledgers that were in the safe. In the warehouse."

"So you already went back for them, then? I wondered where you'd gone this morning."

"How did you know where they were?" she squealed. Why did it seem he was always one step ahead of her?

"I'd thought it odd how you were so alarmed when I went toward those smelly pelts in the warehouse last night. They do reek, by the way. You weren't lying about that." His hands were still planted firmly on her bottom.

"I've a right to those ledgers," Estella said coolly. "I'm the only one who was clever enough to crack the safe. They're mine."

"Ah, but I was clever, too, since I managed to get them without even opening the safe myself."

She frowned. "How did you know that *I'd* got them? Littlefield could've taken them, before."

"Because, duckie, I heard the door of the safe slam shut when I was coming up the stairs."

"You knew the whole time? From the very beginning?" Last night's events took on a whole new light. An embarrassing one. "Nonetheless, the ledgers are still mine," she repeated firmly.

"If you can get them, they're all yours." His eyes twinkled.

"This isn't a game!"

"Then why does it feel like one?" He was staring at her Lack of a Real Bosom again.

Casually, she drew an arm across her chest.

He held her gaze, spoke very low. "You needn't keep trying to hide yourself from me."

Molten heat crept up her neck, heading straight for her cheeks. "I can't think what you mean." The tremor in her voice probably ruined her credibility.

"I adore your body. Every inch of it. Or," he amended with a lopsided smile, "every inch that I've seen."

Oh dear. They were about to broach the treacherous topic of last night. She wasn't sure she was ready for this.

She shifted her weight, nervous, causing him to hold her tighter still.

One hand let go of her bottom, reached around to the front, pulled her arm slowly, gently away. "You are beautiful. Don't be ashamed that you don't possess the improbable proportions of a drawing on a fashion plate."

There was absolutely no way she could choke out a reply around the lump in her throat. But she wanted to thank him for lifting what had felt like a sack of boulders off her back. She took a deep breath. "Mama says when I . . . if I have a baby, then perhaps they will fill out. . . ." Drat. Had she really said that?

He simply shrugged. Then, as she cried out in surprise, he dragged her onto his lap.

"Good heavens, Godolphin," she gasped. His sudden movement had, inexplicably, brought a grin to her face. She was balanced on his knee, the toes of her slippers dangling inches from the floor. To keep her balance, she had no choice but to crook an elbow round his neck.

Because he clearly had no intention of releasing her.

"I've caught you, little devil," he whispered in her ear. "Before you know it, I'll have you completely tamed."

Her breath caught. But no. He couldn't know about Madame Pettibonne's book. Still, her heart was skittering. She wanted to be near him, but was it proper for an earl and his countess to cavort in this manner in their breakfast room? Not once had she ever spied Mama and Papa behaving with such impropriety.

Besides, if more Ravishment was what he had in mind . . .

"Godolphin," she pleaded. "Poppet." Only too late did it occur to her that she was most familiar with endearments of the nursery variety.

He craned his neck in order to peer at her closely. "Now I'm your poppet? My dear, what exactly are you attempting with these odd endearments?"

Suspicion had lowered a veil over his features. She had to remedy this, and quickly.

There was nothing for it. As an emergency measure she would press on to Step Three, the Petting Technique. Hopefully Pansy wouldn't mind.

"I don't mean to use such silly names on you, I assure you." It was the honest truth, too. "They just slipped out— my nanny and governess were exceptionally affectionate ladies." Then, bracing herself, she lifted her free hand and brushed his cheek with the back of it.

She didn't know what she'd expected him to do. Recoil, perhaps, or laugh. Instead, he went quite still, and his eyes fell shut.

As if her petting felt good.

Madame Pettibonne was brilliant!

Encouraged, Estella ran the back of her hand up the square line of his cheek. Turning her wrist, she traced the upper arch of his ear with a tentative fingertip, then smoothed his hair back with the flat of her palm. His hair was soft and fine. Embarrassed, she allowed her hand to fall back into her lap.

He opened his eyes. With the languid precision of a born artist, he reached up and began peeling the top of her sleeve away from her shoulder.

Only vaguely was she was aware of the tiny pop of ripping threads. That seemed so inconsequential, so dull, compared to the intent, hungry expression on her husband's face.

When he'd completely exposed her shoulder, he bent his neck, leaned in.

A shudder shook her. Every nerve in her shoulder ached for his warmth, yearned toward him like a magnet.

He moved the silver chain around her neck to the side. As his mouth met with the shallow notch just below where her collarbone met her shoulder, her lungs pressed out a sigh. Skimming with torturous lightness, his parted lips moved up the side of her neck, wrapped themselves around her earlobe, and he delicately bit. She squeaked with surprise, but permitted her head to tip back as his kisses returned to her throat.

It was true, then. Some beasts *did* bite.

He'd just worked his fingers beneath her chignon, preparing, no doubt, to expedite the Ravishing with a kiss on the mouth, when there was a dry little "ahem" from the doorway.

Estella's eyes flew open (she hadn't really been aware of closing them), and she leapt to her feet, pulling her sleeve back over her shoulder. Teeters posed in the doorway, his expression a picture of pompous disgust.

"Your Lordship—"

"Not now, Teeters," Godolphin ground out. His hands were clutching the arms of the chair so hard, Estella feared the wood might snap.

"I'm terribly sorry, Your Lordship, to interrupt you at such an, er ... inopportune moment." His eyes roved over Estella as if she were a slattern in a public house. Then he turned his attention back to his employer. "It's your mother's bedchamber, sir."

A flood of confusion washed over Godolphin's brow. "Her bedchamber?" He was already on his feet, headed for the door.

"Yes. It's—well, you'd best see for yourself."

"It must've been done some time this morning," Teeters puffed over his shoulder. "I happened to notice that the door was ajar, so I looked inside." He pulled open the door to the former Countess of Seabrook's bedchamber.

The room was dark, the air fusty with mold. There was another smell, too, like turpentine.

"It's difficult to see in the dark, Your Lordship." Teeters threw open a velvet curtain, sending dust swirling. Light flooded the chamber.

Godolphin looked around. He hadn't been in this room for more than ten years. Cobwebs dangled from

every corner and the furniture was coated with grime.
The bedclothes, once pink and ivory, were muted to
splotchy peach and yellow.

"Look." Teeters pointed at the dressing table.

Moist-looking moss was heaped on the tabletop, a
stunned-looking toad peering out from its center. Scent
bottles and cosmetic jars were scattered beneath the table,
lids off, contents spilled, glass shards everywhere.

"Is this just random meanness, or is there a message in
this moss and in this poor creature?" Godolphin muttered, gazing down at the blinking toad.

"It is like something from a crypt, sir."

"Indeed."

"Observe the bed, Your Lordship."

Godolphin's eyes traveled to his mother's four-poster
bed. Behind the gauze curtains he saw a large hump beneath the coverlet. He approached and parted the bed
curtains, yanked back the covers.

His breath stopped in his throat. Three or four long
bones were laid side by side, topped with the skull of a
young horse.

"The neighbors lost a foal last spring," Teeters told him.
"Undoubtedly these are the creature's remains. The effect
is most ghoulish. Did you see the portrait?"

Godolphin's jaw clamped. Dropping the bed curtains,
he swiveled to face the wall where his own childhood portrait hung. His mother had commissioned it when he was
six years old.

He winced. His likeness had been tampered with. His
boyish curls were adorned with a pair of devil's horns, and
a barbed tail protruded from the rump of his short pants.
The paint was oily black, of the sort used in the stables for
the window frames and doors.

Touching a fingertip to the canvas, Godolphin found
the paint was still sticky.

The little witch bride he'd brought into his house

seemed determined to torment him, all the while feigning sweetness like she'd done just moments ago. He spun toward the doorway, intent on finding her and punishing her.

He froze.

Estella hovered in the doorway, a look of dismay upon her all-too-innocent face.

What a splendid little actress.

Her lips parted.

"Don't even try to explain yourself," Godolphin snarled. "I regret bringing you into my home." How he regretted, too, allowing himself to sink into her touch in the breakfast room, allowing himself to believe for a moment that she could love him someday. A sneer stretched his lips. "I was a fool."

He dodged past without looking at her.

"Good evening, Timmy," Estella said.

The youth had been bent over his shovel, scraping manure from the wooden floor of a stall. He paused, then looked up.

"Yer Ladyship," he muttered moodily. His freckled face was scrunched up, and dirt streaked his brow. "Would ye like me to saddle up a mare fer ye, Ladyship?" The sarcastic lilt in his voice told Estella he'd rather have his face scrubbed with ice water and a bristle brush.

Ignoring the hostility radiating from his wiry frame, Estella moved a few steps closer. It was a cool, bright evening, but the stables were dim, warm with sweet hay and pungent horses. Yet her fingers still trembled at her chest, where she clutched her shawl.

"No, thank you, Timmy. I was just—I'm going for a walk. I thought I'd say hello." She swallowed. That hadn't sounded very convincing.

Leaning on his shovel, Timmy narrowed his eyes. He looked as skeptical and world-weary as a man four times his age. "A walk, Ladyship? It's a chilly day fer that, I warrant." His eyes flicked over her flimsy shawl, down to her embroidered slippers.

"Yes, well"—she laughed nervously—"that's why I stepped in here, actually." She arranged her features into what she hoped was aristocratic privilege. The fact that she was no more than six or seven years older than the stable boy made her arrogance seem all the more false. "Tell me," she said, "have you been working all day?"

Timmy shrugged, began shoveling again. The grate of steel against planks set Estella's teeth on edge.

"Since sunrise," he muttered as a shovelful of dung went flying over his shoulder.

Estella did a quick sidestep to avoid being splattered. What a rotten boy. To think she'd felt sorry for him. "So," she hazarded, "you didn't go into the castle at any point today? Or yesterday?"

He froze again, peering over his shoulder at her.

"You didn't," she said, "play any pranks on the earl?"

"I take me meals in the kitchens. Just like everyone else. But I don't know nothin' about any pranks." He rubbed his nose with a fist.

Was he attempting to conceal a smile?

"Someone pulled another prank on th' earl?" he asked.

Ah. There was definitely a waver of mirth in his tone.

Despite herself, Estella's lips twitched upward. "Yes. One of a series, actually. He isn't taking it well."

"I imagine he'd be fumin'," Timmy responded, snorting in a poor effort to rein in a laugh.

Estella forced her lips into a stern line. Timmy's amusement was a clear indication of his guilt. And, though she didn't think the pranks were all *that* bad, she was tired of taking the blame. "They have to stop," she said firmly.

"Yes, Ladyship." His eyes were still twinkling.

Was he admitting to the pranks? Or was he simply acquiescing to his mistress, as any servant would?

"Good. Now that we've taken care of that, I've another question for you."

Timmy's expression had reverted back to adolescent sullenness. "That cheese was goin' to go rotten," he sniffed.

"Cheese?" Estella blinked. "No. About your mama."

Swiftly, Timmy looked away, down to his mucky boots. They had holes in them. One of his toes was visible, hanging an inch over the sole.

Estella swallowed. "Does she . . . who is her . . ." How could she ask this poor lad who his mother's gentleman friend was? He probably wouldn't know, anyway. "Nevermind. It's not important. Good evening."

Estella woke early. Sleep had visited her only in fits and starts, and when it had, she'd been tormented by nightmares of a long, bony woman with a face like a horse sitting to tea in the countess's parlor. Upon waking, Estella could only remember the woman softly neighing and snorting, weeping for her son.

She dressed quickly. She had work to do. The ledgers were missing, and they had to be somewhere in the castle.

First, she let Maggie outside onto the dewy lawns. Then, with Maggie shuffling sleepily behind her, she went to the countess's parlor. She'd decided to sit down and make a list of every place the ledgers might be hidden, then search in a systematic fashion. That's what Papa would do. For that matter, that's what Godolphin would do.

She chewed her lip. She hadn't seen Godolphin since he'd stormed out of his mother's ransacked bedchamber yesterday afternoon. Not only was he undomesticated, he wasn't even fair. She hadn't had a chance to defend herself yet.

The parlor was dark, the moth-eaten draperies still drawn against the night. She crossed the room and threw them wide.

Then she gasped.

Books and papers were strewn across the carpet. The drawers of the writing desk had been pulled out and tossed on the floor, their contents scattered. The uphol-stered furniture had been slashed open, the stuffing spilling out. Porcelain figurines from the mantel had all been smashed on the hearth.

Estella stood, rooted to the spot, and stared. Surely Godolphin hadn't done this, even as revenge for that last prank. He wasn't that sort of man. He was too controlled, too measured.

It must have been Bertie Littlefield. In search of the necklace, or the ledgers. Or both.

Maggie caught Estella's attention. She sniffed the floor, the upturned furniture, her hackles up, every muscle tense. Growling, she slunk to the doorway that led out to the cor-ridor. Looking back, she gave her mistress a pleading look.

"What is it, Maggie?"

The few words of encouragement were all the fox-hound needed. She nosed the door open and passed through, tail high, nose to the floor, snorting and sniffing.

Estella gathered up her skirts and followed at a trot.

Maggie never faltered, leading the way through the new half of Castle Seabrook into the old.

They passed through the Great Hall. Maggie stopped in the little anteroom with the three doors, one of which led to the tower. She whined. Then she seemed to make a de-cision and bolted up the narrow stone stairs, running round and round. Estella had no choice but to follow. Out of breath, they reached the final turn in the stairs. At the top, the door was thrown wide. Both mistress and dog stumbled through.

Godolphin's study was in ruin. Books were strewn, fur-niture smashed. The maritime map was shredded, the map table upturned, two of its legs broken. The desk was swiped clear of ledgers and books. One ledger was ripped to pieces. Estella stooped to retrieve pages. Marblegate House. She sighed and dropped them.

If Godolphin had hidden the ledgers here, they were long gone.

Maggie gave a sharp bark and bolted back down the stairs. Estella followed as quickly as she dared down the steep spiral. At the bottom, Maggie went to the right-hand door and whined.

Estella hesitated. "Down there?"

Maggie pawed the door, so Estella opened it. Stale air gusted up, and the stairwell yawned pitch-black.

Maggie plunged downward.

"Maggie, come!" Estella rushed into the Great Hall, found a candelabra on a side table, and some matches beside the huge fireplace. She lit the tapers and returned to the basement stairs. Maggie was already halfway down the steps. Estella picked her way down, touching the slimy wall with her free hand for balance.

This is madness.

She shoved the thought away.

At the bottom, Estella held the candelabra aloft. They were in a cavernous space of arching stone, filled with wooden racks of dusty wine barrels and bottles. Maggie had disappeared down an aisle between two rows of wine racks.

"Maggie!" Estella hissed. For some reason, she couldn't raise her voice.

Maggie made a sound. It wasn't a whine, a bark, or a growl. It was a weird, warbling howl.

Estella rushed down the aisle, cobwebs sticking to her face and hands, following the howling. Finally, beneath a low arching doorway, she found her dog.

Maggie was lying close to . . . what? Icy dread stabbed Estella, and she could not breathe, could not move, could not think.

A human form lay on the stone floor: a woman, her mauve velvet pelisse askew, one bare leg exposed.

The form moved slightly, then moaned. Estella forced herself forward. She knelt, placing the candelabra on the floor. The woman's hair was in her face, her bonnet tipped sideways. Candlelight bounced off the glass eyes of a tiny stuffed monkey.

It was Violet Plympton, Timmy's mama.

"I must get help," Estella whispered, pushing the hair from Violet's eyes. "My dog will stay and guard you. Don't be afraid."

But no. *No.* Another wash of nausea, for she realized that Violet's chest oozed blood. Deep reddish black blossomed across her bodice, and protruding from the center of the pool was the handle of a dagger.

Godolphin's dagger, his family crest emblazoned on the handle.

Clammy fingers coiled around her wrist. "Don't go nowhere, Countess," Violet pleaded. Her voice was like a shadow. "I'm nearly spent, I do know that, and I don't want t' go alone. 'Tis of no account 'cept my Timmy won't have neither ma nor pa once I'm gone."

Estella forced herself to look away from the dagger and all that blood. She met Violet's eyes. They were growing dim. "Do not worry about Timmy. Godolphin and I will see to his care."

"Aye. Thank you."

Estella fought against a lump in her throat. "Who did this to you?"

Violet began to whimper. "I only wanted what's mine by rights. Me necklace. Me man gave it to me. Tweren't no one's business to take it away."

"Your man? Who is he, Violet?"

"Langlois. The sea captain."

"Did he . . . do this to you?"

Violet coughed. Blood trickled from the corner of her lips. "He *loved* me. He never did harm me, no matter what th' others might've said. He's away now, in France. Tell 'im I love him, please Yer Ladyship, when he gits back."

"I will. Tell me, who did this to you?" Even though she felt ill, Estella stroked Violet's coarse orange hair, trying to comfort her. Violet's eyes were almost empty. *"Who?"*

Violet's grasp loosened. "'Tweren't yer husband, Countess. He's a good man. 'Twere the other. That one-armed monster." Violet's throat rattled, and her hand dropped silently to the floor.

Estella's mind went blank and calm. Somewhere deep inside, she wanted to cry, but this wasn't about her. She needed to be an adult, not a spoiled girl. So she closed Violet's eyelids, and then she went in search of Godolphin.

Chapter Twelve

A Quarrel at the Quill
and Parchment and
Methods of Pet Grooming

He was dreaming. Hot fingers caressed his cheek, plump lips swept his own. The air was infused with the scent of honeysuckle. Whenever he opened his eyes, though, his devil-angel had fled. He closed his eyes and pursued her. Each glimpse of her coppery hair, each sway of her rounded bottom, made him want to sob with frustration.

So when his bedchamber door slammed open, and he heard his name called, when small hands gripped his shoulder and shook him, he gasped, and surfaced from his dream like a swimmer caught too long underwater.

"You've got to come! Oh, please, Godolphin. Something awful has happened!"

He bolted upright in his bed. "For God's sake, Estella, what is the matter?"

Her face was bleached, her voice tremulous. She was perched on the side of his bed, her fingers entwined in his. She was clearly upset, but just as plainly trying to gain mastery of her emotions.

She needed him.

His anger with her over the prank melted.

"In the cellar," she said. "Mrs. Plympton. She's dead." There was a slight pause, and then she added, "Murdered."

As was always the case when faced with disaster, Godolphin's mind clicked into a highly rational, unemotional gear. Naked, he jumped from his bed and dressed.

Estella averted her eyes, and a blush brought a little life back into her face.

"Where in the cellar?" he asked, buttoning his trousers.

"Under an arch, just beyond the wine racks."

"How do you know she was murdered?" He pulled on a boot.

"The blood." Her voice shook. "There was blood." For the first time he noticed the vivid smears on her skirts.

He pulled on his second boot and strode to his wife. He gathered her into his arms. She leaned into him. Tipping her chin up gently, he looked into her eyes. "Take me to her and as we go, tell me how you came to discover her."

They made their way to the cellar, Maggie in the lead, Estella explaining the events of the morning as best she could. "Both your study in the tower and the countess's parlor have been ransacked."

"I sleep past six for once," he said grimly, "and look what goes on."

Violet Plympton lay beyond the wine racks and under the arch, just as Estella had said. Godolphin knelt beside the corpse and checked for a pulse. The body was already going cold. He stared down at the handle of the dagger protruding from her chest.

His dagger.

Godolphin knew that Bertie Littlefield kept rooms above the Quill and Parchment, an inn catering to the better sort of Brighton resident: merchants, shop owners, sea captains, the odd physician.

It was easy to slip past the publican and make his way up the carpeted stairs to the third floor. He turned left and strode to the last door on the left. It had taken but one penny for the little delivery boy who hung about the entrance to the inn to tell him the precise location of Bertie's quarters.

Once at the door, Godolphin's inclination was to shove a boot through it, but he decided on a more restrained entrance. With a hand on the knob and his shoulder against the door, he smashed against the wooden planks once, twice, and they yielded. He was inside.

Oddly, Bertie looked as though he was surprised to see him.

"What in blazes!" Bertie lurched to his feet, letting the book he'd been hunched over drop to the floor. "You can't just come smashing in here like a bally press gang!"

Job number one: procure the ledgers.

"You didn't actually think," Godolphin said, "that you could kill Violet Plympton, frame me for murder and get away with it, did you?" He stalked forward.

"You aren't going to weasel out of this one, old trout." Bertie maintained eye contact, but he edged sideways, toward the fireplace.

One glance told Godolphin that a dagger lay on the mantel. It glinted, as though recently sharpened and polished.

"I needn't attempt to weasel out of anything," Godolphin said. "You're trying to frame me. It won't work."

"You," Bertie sputtered, lunging for the dagger, "are going to die, you pain-in-the-arse nob." When he spun around, the dagger was pointed at Godolphin's belly.

"Unfortunately for you, you collect weapons." Casually, Godolphin bent and lifted a naval sword from the tea table. It didn't appear sharp, but it was heavy. "A dagger against a sword?"

Bertie seemed to have snapped. He came at Godolphin, his eyes wild and red rimmed. "You *will* die. Today, at my hand. Or at the end of a rope for the murder of that abominable hag. Either way, Estella will be mine. Seabrook will be mine." He stabbed and slashed the air.

"I can't imagine," Godolphin said, sidestepping the dagger, "what you mean." He backed into an end table, and it crashed to the floor. "Estella yours?"

"She was meant for me!" Bertie hurled himself, dagger raised, at Godolphin.

Godolphin made a neat sidestep, and Bertie hit the wall, sending a picture swinging on its hook.

Godolphin leapt over the tea table, crossing to the other side of the room. He'd seen another sword on a stand in the corner. "Here," he called. He tossed the sword to Bertie, who was already almost upon him. Bertie dropped the dagger and caught the sword. "Matching arms. It's fair, now. Come at me as you will."

Bertie smirked. "With immense pleasure."

They resumed their violent dance about the sitting room, destroying furniture, slashing savagely at one another. Godolphin did not want to harm Bertie. Every move he made was defensive. Bertie, on the other hand, seemed determined to draw blood. It was obvious he had practiced long and hard to handle his sword left-handed.

With a jerky move, Bertie sliced Godolphin's brow. It stung cruelly, and blood streamed into his right eye, clouding his vision, splattering on his cravat and jacket.

"Oh dear," Bertie mocked. He admired the blood on the blade of his sword. "Your face is no longer so perfect. Consider it a small return of the favor you did me." He assumed a thoughtful expression. "Of course, it's but a little scratch. Not as though it's your whole damned *arm*, is it?" He laughed, high-pitched, nearly hysterical. "Well, there's time yet."

Godolphin swiped the blood from his eye, his anger finally aroused. "See here, Littlefield. This has gone far enough—"

Abruptly, Bertie bent and gave the carpet that Godolphin stood on a violent yank. Godolphin lost his balance and fell heavily onto the settee behind him. The impact made him drop his sword.

"So much for fair play," Godolphin muttered.

Bertie loomed over him. His sword was raised high. "Life is simply not fair. And now your arm, Captain, is about to be severed from the rest of you." He brought his sword down with a brutal stroke, but Godolphin rolled to the side. Only the tip of Bertie's sword made contact with his shoulder. It cut through jacket and shirt, into flesh.

It burned like hell, but Godolphin knew the wound wasn't deep. Bertie lifted his sword a second time.

Godolphin raised his legs and kicked Bertie into a table five feet away. The crack of a snapping table leg punctured the air. Godolphin was on his feet in one second, Bertie in two.

"I want the ledgers, Littlefield." He snatched up his sword. "Then I'll go."

"Forget the bleeding ledgers. What about Estella?"

"What about her? She's not your concern."

"You don't want her and you know it, Godolphin. She's not your sort. A snip of a merchant's daughter, that's all. You want an aristocrat like yourself, with titles and land to bestow upon your godforsaken progeny."

"That's absurd."

"I'm feeling generous. I'll make you a deal. I will give you the ledgers." His eyes strayed to the floor beside the toppled side table. "In return, you give me Estella."

Godolphin followed his gaze. The ledgers were piled there, pages gaping. He looked back at Bertie. "You needn't have ransacked my entire home this morning just to get those. You could've guessed they'd be in the tower."

"Oh." Bertie made a maniacal snicker. "I was also looking for something else."

Godolphin frowned. "What?"

"Ask Estella."

"I don't know what you're speaking of." Godolphin's

head pounded, his arm was stiffening, and he felt blood trickling down beneath his jacket, into his palm. It made tiny plopping sounds as it dripped onto the carpet. He needed to bind his wounds. Quickly.

"She is mine," Bertie said. "She may reside with you, but she will be mine—"

"Stop this insane talk. Estella is my wife. You have no claim to her."

Job number two: make certain Littlefield never comes near Estella again.

"I have the right of natural law," Bertie babbled. "All the universe calls out for our union."

"You're mad."

Bertie blinked several times. "Don't ever say that again. I'm not mad. I'm *not*." He seemed paralyzed.

"Damned if you aren't." Godolphin threw his sword to the floor and stooped to pick up the ledgers.

Bertie just stood there, his hair matted, his face sweaty and streaked with blood.

As Godolphin walked into the hallway, the ruined door swung silently on its one remaining hinge.

"A judge from London is coming!" Bertie yelped after him. "In four days he will be here! None of the village constables is man enough to arrest you, but the London judge will order it!" Then, as though to himself, Bertie whispered, "She *will* be mine."

Before returning to the castle, Godolphin made one more stop in Brighton.

With his carriage waiting on the moonlit cobblestone street, he hurried up the flight of steps leading to the Hancocks' townhouse. All the windows were dark. He'd been correct in assuming that the Hancock servants had returned to the family's London residence.

At the front door, he stooped to place the ledgers on the porch. He winced as he did so; the gash in his shoulder was thudding dully, as if each beat of his heart squeezed out more blood. It was too dark to see, but his shirt and jacket were soaked through, and sticky. With his left hand, he fumbled in his pocket for the key.

Once inside, he stashed the ledgers in a cabinet in the shadowy front parlor. There was no time to waste looking for a better hiding place. He needed to get back to the castle to clean and dress his wounds, and, more importantly, he wanted to make certain Estella was safe.

"Who's there?" Estella whispered. She rolled onto her side, groping for a match. Then she froze, listening as her eyes tried to pierce the darkness of the bedchamber.

There it was again. Scuffling, clattering sounds inside the wardrobe.

Maggie, at the foot of the bed, awoke. She emitted a long, rumbling growl. In the silver light leaking through the windows, Estella could see the dog's ears pricked to attention.

The wardrobe doors had been tied tight with hair ribbons. But several powerful thrusts from inside loosened and ripped the ribbons.

When the wardrobe doors fell open, Maggie exploded in a torrent of barks, bounding off the bed and across the room.

"There's a good girl," Godolphin murmured, extending a hand down to Maggie. The barking ceased.

Estella struck the match. In the brief yellow flare, she saw Godolphin. She lit the wick, then dashed over to him.

"I couldn't sleep, I was so worried," she cried. "You've been gone since the afternoon, and—" She fell silent. He was wretched looking. His hair was plastered to his skull with sweat and blood, his clothes were torn. She noticed the oozing cut on his brow, the slash that penetrated the jacket sleeve, the dark stain on his right shoulder. The thick blood that covered his hand. "Oh my God! You're hurt."

Gingerly, he touched two fingers to the wound above

his eye, and then his shoulder. He winced. "Yes—I was actually wondering if you could help me. I've got a bit of a problem with my arm, you see—"

"Of course." With a shaking hand, Estella set the candlestick on the side table, took his hand. It was bare, icy. She led him to the sofa. "Sit," she whispered, shoving the pillows back.

As he lowered himself, she scanned his face, trying to keep her mounting panic at bay. There was so much blood. She felt utterly unable to handle this on her own.

"I'll send for the physician—"

"No." This was uttered with complete finality. "I want you to do it."

He leaned back on the pillows, a sound that was half moan, half sigh escaping his lips. "I'm sorry, darling, that I came through the wardrobe." One corner of his mouth twitched up. "You locked your bedchamber door."

"Not because of you," she whispered, brushing his damp hair back off his face, unbuttoning his jacket. "I just . . . oh dear, it's—who did this to you?" Bertie. She knew it was Bertie.

"The castle is open like a public house," he went on, ignoring her question. "Violet Plympton's laid out in the hall with a half dozen drunken mourners sharing a last tipple with her. No wonder you locked your door."

She was tugging at his jacket. "Sit up. We must remove your clothing."

"Impatient angel," he joked, even as he winced in pain. "First tell me how Timmy has been faring."

"As well as he could, I think. The Lovelys have taken him home with them for the night. They seem to have a way with him. But I must demand that you remove your jacket and shirt. Timmy will be fine." She gave his jacket sleeve a gentle tug.

He winced again.

"I'm so sorry," Estella murmured.

He stood and pulled off his jacket with his left hand.

His right hand appeared stiff. His shirtsleeve was dark with blood.

He removed his shirt. His wound gaped like a ghoul's mouth. The iron odor of blood filled the room, and Maggie whined.

"It's shallow," Godolphin said. "It only needs to be cleaned and bound."

Estella wrapped his shirt tightly around the wound to stop the flow of blood. Then she knelt before her husband, hands on his knees. "What should I do?"

"Really, I don't think it's as bad as it seems. Nor as bad as it could have been, my love. Bertie was intent on removing my arm completely."

"You *didn't* go after him . . . how could you?"

He ignored this remark. "The wound is already beginning to clot. Fetch a basin of clean water and some cloth." He smiled weakly. "But first, help me out of these clothes, will you?"

She had a thousand questions. The foremost being, what was he thinking, challenging Bertie after what had happened this morning? Bertie was clearly murderous and bent on Godolphin's destruction.

She held her tongue, went to pull off his boots. This took all her strength, but she finally managed it, and did away with his socks, too. His feet were freezing, so she rubbed them with her hands, then covered them with a blanket. Next, she crouched at the hearth to stoke the smoldering orange coals in the fireplace.

"What about my trousers?" he mumbled.

She peered over her shoulder. "Your . . . your trousers, sir?" So he wouldn't have a chance to see how flushed her cheeks were undoubtedly growing, she turned back to the fireplace, busying herself with placing wood on the coals. It was the first time she'd ever tended to the fire in her entire life. Remarkable that she knew how to do it so well just from idly watching the servants.

"Yes."

Was there a glint of humor in his ragged voice?

He was correct, of course. Every last stitch of his clothing ought to be removed.

He'd opened his eyes again, and she could have sworn they twinkled as she approached. Fumbling, she began to unbuckle his belt.

His eyes were shut again. Almost as though he were savoring the experience.

No. Of course not. He had to be in a hideous amount of pain. When she'd undone the buckle, she tugged gently. He tensed his belly as the belt slipped through the loops of his trousers.

That tensing brought his stomach muscles and his chest muscles into stark relief. Deep muscles, smooth, hard, and warm skin, with a dark cross-hatching of fine hair that led downward, beneath the waistband of his trousers, to—

"Are you quite all right?" he asked gently.

Drat. She'd been staring. Warmth spread over her face and neck. "Yes, I'm—I'm perfectly well. Now. Let us see about these trousers."

He leaned back against the pillows. With jittery fingers, she undid the top button. "Um," she said, hesitating.

"Go ahead," he told her. His voice had gone husky, and she felt his gaze burning into her.

"Yes. Yes, of course." Bracing herself, she unfastened the last three buttons. Then, scrunching her eyes closed, she tugged at his waistband. The trousers, and the underthings he wore beneath them, were adamant about staying.

"Um, they seem to be . . . stuck."

"You didn't pull hard enough."

She gave them another yank, looking past Godolphin's shoulder as she did so. They came down a little, she felt. They were bunched around his knees. And then she heard a peculiar wheezing sound.

Her eyes flew to Godolphin's face, terrified that he was having some sort of delirious fit from loss of blood.

No. He was laughing. *Laughing.*

"You're going to have to look," he was saying—or, rather, chuckling. "Otherwise, this could take an hour. Here—" he groped about behind him, producing a blue velvet pillow. This he placed across his hips. "There. It's safe now."

She looked. He was, well, decent. If reclining on a sofa with a bare chest, trousers round one's knees, and a boudoir pillow across one's middle qualified as decent.

"Thank you," she muttered. This whole experience was turning out too comical by half.

When she'd finally pulled his trousers off, she dragged the satin coverlet from her bed and tucked it all around him, up to his chest. She fiercely ignored his long, lean-muscled legs.

"I'll just clean your shoulder, first," she told him, "then your head. "It might—*Sir*, what in heaven are you doing?"

"Nothing," he whispered, clutching his left arm round her waist, pulling her so close she nearly toppled over on top of him. "If they had pretty little nurses like you in the navy instead of those moldy old physicians, I dare say we would've all pretended to have splinters and coughs every day. Napoleon probably would've won."

"You *must* lie still," she told him as she dabbed at his shoulder with a damp cloth.

Not because he was writhing in pain. Instead, the problem was that his hand kept creeping around and latching hold of her rump. It wasn't that his wounds didn't hurt like the dickens; her nearness was just too tempting. Besides which, her derriere felt deliciously lush and warm through her gown. "I'm just warming up my hand," he explained.

She gave her hips a hard wiggle in an attempt to loosen his grip. This only made him hold tighter still.

"I don't know why I allow you to even leave the castle," she said softly. "If this is the sort of thing you'll get up to, I ought to lock you in your bedchamber."

"Better still," he suggested, cringing slightly as the cloth skimmed over the middle of the gash, "lock me in *your* bedchamber. With you. We wouldn't have to come out ever again, if that's what you'd like."

She pressed her lips together, possibly trying to feign feminine indignation. But he could tell by the way her eyelashes drooped that she secretly liked his teasing.

This realization made any sort of physical pain easy to endure. She wanted to be with him. She wanted him to touch her.

When she'd rushed over to him with the candle, the expression on her face had nearly knocked the breath out of him. He hated to savor it, because she'd clearly been distressed. But that look—eyes wide, lips parted in a gasp—could only mean one thing.

Estella, his wife, cared about him.

"You ought," she said, "to lie down in the bed. You'll be more comfortable there. I won't . . . watch."

Godolphin grinned all the way to the bed. He was naked, but Estella studiously looked away.

She cleaned his shoulder wound and bound it with a clean strip of cloth she tore from one of her chemises.

"Lucky arm," he muttered. "Swathed in the beauteous Estella's bed attire."

She laughed. "You are too much."

Next she cleaned the slash on his forehead. "There," she whispered. In a fond gesture, heartbreaking in its tenderness, she swiped his damp hair back from his face again, and then dipped to kiss the end of his nose. "All clean. I know it must hurt awfully, but it shouldn't take too long to heal. It might leave a scar, though."

"Would you—" Why in hell was his voice breaking like a boy's? "Would you mind much? If I had a scar, I mean."

"Of course not, silly." She placed the cloth on the table, and then knelt down beside the bed so they were face to face. "It'd be dashing, actually. I am acquainted with a gentleman who has a scar across his cheek, and all the ladies are rather mad about him."

Irrational jealousy, hot and thick as boiling mud, sloshed over him. "Were *you* mad about him?" he grumbled, turning his head to the side to see her better.

"No," she laughed softly. "He married my cousin Henriette." She peered closely at him. "Are you jealous?"

With a sniff, he rolled his head back, stared at the shadowy ceiling. "Certainly not." It was true. Knowing that the scarred swain in question was safely married off had dispelled his jealousy. His head swam. He gave himself over to delicious sleep.

Chapter Thirteen

The Beast's Abduction

"Why does Bertie want to implicate you in a murder?"

"Good morning to you, too." Godolphin cracked one eye.

Estella, lying in the bed alongside him, head propped in one hand, studied him. She'd been watching him sleep, and he'd looked younger than when awake, and more vulnerable. The cut on his forehead was a tender scab now. "How are you feeling?"

He laughed and sat up against the pillows. "Which is a rather less pressing question than why Bertie wishes to kill me."

"Of course not." She brushed the hair from his eyes. "But I was thinking. I mean, I know he's not quite . . ."

"Not quite right in the head?"

"Yes."

"I don't know what happened to him. We've been friends since childhood, and even after his accident—"

Estella sat up. He was finally going to tell her.

"—we remained friends."

"Well, why wouldn't you?"

"The accident was . . ." Godolphin's eyes looked far away. "Never mind. It's not relevant."

"But I—"

He shushed her with a tender kiss. Then he frowned. "The truth, I think, is that I was wrong about Bertie all these years, and that is disturbing. To realize how wrong I was, I mean."

Estella held her tongue. She knew how difficult it must be for Godolphin to admit he was wrong. He was so proud.

"I think," Godolphin went on, "that he kept his deranged mind hidden, to an extent, and any odd behavior I suppose I simply wrote off as harmless eccentricity."

"You still haven't told me why he'd want to implicate you for murder."

Godolphin sighed. "I'm not certain. It's either that he wanted to kill Violet Plympton, and I was the most convenient scapegoat at hand, or else he killed her for the sole purpose of turning the villagers against me. Or *more* against me, I ought to say."

Estella took a deep breath. "Why are the villagers turned against you in the first place? What have you done?"

Subtly, he turned away from her. Avoiding eye contact.

"You haven't even *been* here," Estella pressed, "so why would they dislike you so—"

"That is precisely why," Godolphin cut her off. "Because I abandoned my duties as earl."

"That alone doesn't seem enough reason to—"

"Let's not speak of this anymore."

Estella closed her mouth. She knew there was something he wasn't telling her, but it was clear he wasn't going to reveal the whole truth just yet.

"May I look at your shoulder?" she asked.

"Please."

Delicately, she unwound the strip of cloth from his shoulder. He had to sit up in order for her to do this, but as soon as she'd removed it, he relaxed against the pillows again.

The cloth was rusty with dried blood, but his wound, a slash about four inches long, had already formed a scab.

"Doesn't look too terrible," Godolphin said.

"No swelling around it, either. I was worried about that."

"Bertie must keep his weapons clean," Godolphin remarked in a wry tone.

"Does it hurt?"

He shook his head. "It's only a scratch. A clean sword, perhaps, but not a very sharp one. And I dodged it just in time."

"The brute."

"For the life of me, I can't understand what he'd want to kill Violet Plympton for. They're utterly unconnected, as far as I've learned. Langlois, her gentleman friend, works for Bertie, but so do half the men in the village."

Estella's gut twisted with guilt. She thought of the necklace. That was the connection between Bertie and Violet.

"If you knew Bertie had a grudge against you," Estella began carefully, "and you knew he was mentally infirm, and dangerous, why did you go to see him last night?"

The muscles beneath Godolphin's eyes flexed.

Her heart sank. He'd gone to get the ledgers.

She leapt from the bed. "You got them, didn't you?"

"Darling, please. Haven't we bickered about those blasted ledgers enough?" He extended an arm, coaxing her back to bed.

"No! We haven't! And you speak as though the ledgers were merely some impediment to an otherwise blissful marriage, when in fact they are the very reason you married me in the first place!"

He sat up, and swung his legs over the side of the bed.

Estella kept her gaze high, for he was completely unclothed.

Slowly, he dragged his gaze down her figure. She was still in her nightgown, and she felt naked. "Actually, the ledgers weren't the only reason I married you." He bent, picked up his trousers, and shoved his legs into them. "Although, when you behave in this fashion, the reasons I *did* marry you become more and more blurry."

Wearing only his trousers, he stalked out of the room.

Another rude exit.

Estella's entire frame shook with rage as Godolphin left. Well, she refused to wring her hands over the beastly ways of her ill-gotten husband.

Because, when he'd violently pulled his trousers on, something had fallen out of a pocket, and landed silently on the carpet.

She knelt to retrieve it. A key. An oddly *familiar* key. She held it up, turning it in the thin morning light.

It was the key to her parents' Brighton house.

"That bastard," she spat, scrambling to her feet. She was about to go to her dressing table and lock it up, but she froze.

If Godolphin had gotten the ledgers from Bertie last night, and he had this particular key in his pocket, that would mean that he'd hidden the ledgers in the Brighton house.

Purposefully, now, she strode to her dressing table. First, she removed her gold wedding band and dropped it on the tabletop. It spun in circles before coming to rest by a scent bottle. She did not belong to that deceitful beast.

Then she slid open the second drawer on the right and pulled out a wooden box. Her fingers still trembling, she lifted the lid and gazed down at the silver, ivory, and gold pistol she'd received as a wedding gift.

"Why," Godolphin grumbled to Estella later that day, "can't we speak of whatever it is you wish to speak of *inside* the castle?"

Estella didn't answer for several seconds, but set out across the lawns that sloped to the formal gardens. Godolphin strode beside her. She sneaked a sidelong glance.

He was hatless, his dark hair swept back from his forehead, hands shoved in trouser pockets.

The dusky sky was like plum velvet, and a brisk wind had kicked up. She held the high collar of her pelisse at her neck to keep away the chill. But she felt cold inside. Godolphin had betrayed her by taking and hiding Papa's ledgers, and so soon after she'd decided to trust him, too. That had been a mistake. She set her lips.

"Because I don't want anyone to overhear our conversation," she finally said. They walked around the mossy fountain. The stone fish seemed to stare.

"I'm certain we could've found a private spot. It is a castle, after all, not a cottage."

"Indeed," Estella snapped before she could control herself, "your pretend staff is quite small. But you've been accused of . . ." She swallowed, tasting sour worry. "You've been accused of killing Mrs. Plympton. You cannot trust anyone. Not even your own servants. They go into the village, speak to the townsfolk."

Godolphin stopped suddenly, the gravel under his feet scattering. "This should do. It's far enough."

They were at the edge of the overgrown rose garden. There weren't any tall trees around, so he was technically correct.

Except Estella wasn't actually planning on having a conversation with him. At least, not yet. "Let's go farther," she said, holding her reticule handles tight.

He didn't budge.

She looked up into his face. He looked stubborn, and tired, too.

No. She would not allow herself to feel sorry for him.

"This is fine," he said. "It's growing dark. We needn't go into the wood. I've some things I need to do."

He had to come with her, or she'd never get those ledgers. Her first impulse was to complain, and act angry, but she remembered Madame Pettibonne's advice. Praise. Pet Names. Petting.

She placed a hand on his elbow. "Godolphin," she said, as sweetly as she could manage considering her feelings of betrayal and frustration. "Darling. I'm so appreciative that you're indulging me by coming outside to talk." She glanced over her shoulder. "But I'd really like to speak where no one can see us from the castle."

"I don't think anyone would think it amiss that a man is speaking to his own wife." His tone had softened.

"Let's just go a little way along the path that runs beside the drive." She laced her arm through his.

Amazingly, he walked with her.

She'd have to marvel at Madame Pettibonne's infinite genius some other time.

They walked through the rose garden, then turned onto a shadowy path. This snaked through the trees that lined the long drive approaching the castle. Godolphin held her arm snugly in his, and again she felt a pang of guilt. She was being manipulative. Indeed, she was being a trickster.

But Papa's future hung in the balance. Despite everything, Godolphin still intended to put him in prison. She'd managed to forget that fact in the aftermath of Violet Plympton's death. But it was up to her to save Papa.

So, when she sighted the hulking shape of the carriage through the foliage, she was resolute. She stopped, drawing her arm from Godolphin's. "Here is fine."

It was dark under the trees, but his face registered surprise. "Next to the drive? It's even less private than in the garden."

He hadn't noticed the carriage. Yet. She loosened the drawstring of her reticule, then quickly threw her arms around Godolphin in a hug.

"What's this?" he exclaimed, half laughing.

More guilt seared her. Ignoring it, she dug out the contraption she'd made from two of Maggie's old leather collars, a sort of handcuff device that could be tightened by pulling one end. She dropped her reticule. Then she pulled his hands clumsily behind his back, and managed to slip them through the collars and pull the leather strap tight.

"What in hell?" he snarled, the residue of laughter still lingering in his tone. "What're you playing at?"

She crouched and snatched up her reticule from the ground. Her heart was pumping painfully, and her fingers were fluttery as she dug inside the bag again.

"You don't honestly think you can restrain me," he said. He gave his arms three powerful jerks. The collars held fast. "For one thing, I could simply walk away. And what in God's name—"

He stopped. She had the silver pistol pointed at his chest, flintlock cocked.

"Estella," he said, soothingly now. He met her eye, no fear evident. He looked surprised, mostly, and confused. "You could have a beastly accident with that thing, darling."

"Don't call me that," she whispered, voice wobbling. Furiously, she blinked the tears from her eyes. "Turn round and go out onto the drive."

He just stood there.

She steadied the pistol with her other hand.

He turned.

Out in the lane, it was lighter, and the white gravel glowed in the fading light. She saw his shoulders tense when he spotted the carriage.

"I take it we're going for an evening drive, then?" he tossed over his shoulder.

"Get in."

He stopped beside the carriage.

"Get in," she repeated.

In a maddeningly relaxed, fluid motion, he turned to face her. "My dear, sweet, beautiful, angelic wife. Oh, and did I mention innocent? I cannot work the door handle of a carriage when my hands have been cinched tight with little girls' hair ribbons."

"They're *not* hair ribbons." She couldn't bear to tell him that he was restrained with cast-off foxhound collars. It was too ridiculous. "Don't you dare say anything to the driver." She gave him what she hoped was a menacing scowl.

He grinned back, white teeth flashing in the twilight.

Keeping the pistol trained on him, she flung open the carriage door.

He managed to slip inside, gracefully, for heaven's sake! She got in across from him, shut the door, and rapped on the ceiling.

"It seems you were correct," Godolphin said wryly, as the carriage jerked forward. "I can't trust anyone, if the driver in my employ is willing to participate in my kidnapping." He settled back on the leather cushions. Even though his arms were pressed behind him, he did this easily. "Mind you, I was uncertain about him when I hired him. Had a glint of the mercenary in the eye."

"I had to pay him."

"Ah. So my suspicions were correct. Is everyone in this cursed county so easy to pay off? First the villagers, now my servants—"

"Don't forget," Estella retorted, "that they were willing to play-act for *you*."

"Yes. But I am their employer. I don't suppose I could pay *you* off?"

Estella gritted her teeth.

Heavy silence fell on them. The carriage curtains were drawn, and it was almost pitch-black inside. Estella ran nervous fingers over the side of the pistol. It was cold, sickeningly cold. There was no way she could ever use a gun on anyone, let alone Godolphin. She'd never even liked to think about the poor pheasants the men hunted at Mama and Papa's country house.

She sat up straight. If she didn't bluff her way through this kidnapping somehow, she'd never get the ledgers. If that meant having Godolphin think she would use the pistol, then so be it.

"Off to Brighton, are we?" Godolphin said easily, as the carriage reached the end of the drive and turned left. "To pay a call on Sir and Lady Shipton, perhaps? Imagine the looks on their faces when you bring your husband to their doorstep bound like a Christmas goose."

"You know that's not where we're going."

"Do I?"

"You know what I want."

At this, he chuckled. A very naughty, suggestive chuckle.

Estella felt her ears begin to burn. "Must you misconstrue everything to mean—"

"You want the ledgers."

Her mouth snapped shut. Momentarily, anyway. "Of course, I want the ledgers. I cannot believe that you took them from the warehouse in the first place."

"All's fair in love and war."

"Then this is war?"

He paused for several moments. The carriage swayed gently from side to side, the horses' hoofbeats muted. Estella's pulse throbbed in her ears.

"The only alternative is love," he finally said.

Her belly twisted. "Then war it is."

Estella had never been in love, and had scarcely even considered it. But now, of all times and places, with a pistol pointed at her husband, she remembered her cousin Henriette telling her about love. Henriette at the time had been falling in love with the man she would marry. She'd said that, when the right person came along, you just knew.

Estella knew something about Godolphin. She knew that he'd never murder someone, and beyond that, she believed he was a good person. His intentions regarding Papa, she suddenly realized, were simply misguided. Yes, he had manipulated her, manipulated the situation they found themselves in. However, she was in no position to judge. She'd been just as bad.

She knew she felt fierce and brave and beautiful in his company. She knew he was wise, methodical, but very, very wild. And she knew, even just then, staring at his broad-shouldered silhouette in the darkened carriage, that she wanted to be close to him. Press her body alongside his, feel his heat, smell his skin. But could those things be love?

One thing was certain: With the ledgers so close she could almost taste victory, now was not the time to be contemplating such things. She held the pistol handle tightly.

"How," Godolphin said after several minutes of silence, "did you learn that I'd put the ledgers in the Brighton house?"

He heard Estella sniff.

"I'd have rather thought," she replied tartly, "that you would've ceased to underestimate me by now."

"On the contrary, I've completely given up on underestimating you. You've shown yourself to be exceptionally resourceful. For example, where did you get that gun? For that matter, how did you learn how to aim it at a man's heart with such enthusiasm?"

"The gun is mine. Don't suppose I would hesitate to use it."

"Oh," he chuckled, "I won't."

Godolphin shifted to make his bound arms more comfortable. The position, luckily, did not hurt his shoulder wound.

"I saw the key, the key to the Brighton house. It fell from your pocket." Estella's voice had crept up in pitch. She sounded accusing. "And I knew you'd gone to see Bertie last night."

"Flattering."

"What?"

"Your assumption that I'd gotten the ledgers from Bertie."

"Well, of *course* you did."

It took a moment for this to sink in. He felt the oddest flush of pride that she had such faith in him. Odd, he supposed, because she was at present kidnapping him. He doubted she'd shoot him. He knew he could maneuver the carriage door handle quickly enough with his feet, and he could jump out onto the starlit road in an instant. However, he wasn't certain she wouldn't shoot. He didn't care to find out.

Nor did he care to speculate on what sort of state his marriage would be in if she shot him.

They didn't speak again until the carriage rolled to a stop in front of Hancock's darkened townhouse.

"Out," Estella said.

Godolphin saw the silver flash of the pistol's muzzle. "I don't think my feet are quite dexterous enough to work the door handle," he lied.

Huffing, Estella opened the door and they both got out. She seemed to have made prior arrangements with the driver, because he instantly drove away. The crash of the ocean was audible, studded with the fading clip-clop of the horses' hooves. Salty wind blew strands of hair across Estella's eyes. She seemed to be hesitating.

"Shall we go in?" Godolphin suggested in a gallant tone.

That did it. Her eyebrows shot down in a frown. She gestured with the pistol. "Go up the steps to the front door."

He gave her a courtly half bow. "Madam." He started up the steps, she behind him.

All the way to the front door, he was grinning.

In the instant that she'd tossed him that petulant scowl, all of her stubbornness shining through, he'd been overcome with a new feeling. It was half lust—he recognized that part. The other half was an intense, affectionate admiration. He'd already begun to suspect that he'd been wrong about her. She wasn't a spoiled princess. Well, not entirely. She was actually the most determined, passionate, and loyal woman he'd met in his entire life.

She unlocked the door. Inside, she said, "Go up the stairs."

"Are you so certain the ledgers are up there?"

"Have you forgotten that your hands are tied, dear husband, and that I have a pistol aimed in your direction?"

It was dim in the entryway, but the gun gleamed wickedly. "No, actually, I haven't." He marched up the stairs.

She herded him down the corridor, and through the third door on the right.

The bedchamber—for Godolphin saw a four-poster bed—was bathed in silver-blue starshine. It smelled vaguely of dried flowers and dust, and beneath that, of honeysuckle soap.

Estella's old bedchamber.

"To the chair," she directed, gesturing with the pistol.

He sauntered to the chair across the dim room, and settled himself in it. "Oh—" He stood. "—You'll want my arms behind the chair back, won't you? So you can tie me up?" His groin flickered faintly to life.

Estella didn't reply, but when he'd repositioned himself so he was seated, with his bound arms slung behind the low chair back, she set to work. From her reticule, she drew a length of some sort of rope, and tied his wrists to the arms of the chair. Then she crouched, and bound his ankles to the front legs of the chair.

The pistol, Godolphin noted, had been placed on the carpet. He breathed an inward sigh of relief. He'd been worried that she'd fire it accidentally.

"Quite an endless Pandora's box of a reticule you have there," he remarked in a friendly tone. "Have you any other toys stashed inside?"

She stood, wiping her palms. "I might. If you're good, I won't have to use them."

"Perhaps I'll be inspired to be bad, so that you *will* have to use them."

"I cannot understand why you aren't taking this seriously. You are now my prisoner."

"I *am* taking it seriously." Quite frankly, he was beginning to enjoy it.

She moved across the room and lit three tapers on a squat candelabra. Then she returned to stand in front of him. The yellow flames swayed in some draft, and they lit her face a delicate gold. "Now," she said, "tell me where you've hidden the ledgers. I know they're in this house somewhere."

Godolphin considered. He didn't want her to have the ledgers. They were the only concrete proof he had to bring her father down. She could destroy them the minute she got hold of them, and then he'd be back at square one. However, at this moment, Bertie was a far more pressing problem that Hancock. And Estella looked quite prepared to keep Godolphin tied up indefinitely. Despite all his resources, he doubted he could manage to extricate himself from the ropes that bound him. If he was trapped here, God only knew what Bertie would get up to in the meantime.

Godolphin concluded that he'd have to tell Estella where the ledgers were. He stared up at her. She looked so lovely in the candlelight, and so wild. A foreign feeling of surrender took him. Not a surrender of spirit, but a more fleeting, erotic surrender. He smiled.

She glared. "What is it that you find amusing?"

"That I ever thought for a second that I'd be able to tame you. I was wrong about you. Very, very wrong."

Momentarily, her features softened. But she seemed to remember herself, and she set her chin again. "Where are the ledgers? I am prepared to wait a very long time until you tell me."

"I don't doubt it."

"I have ways to make you talk."

His manhood began to stiffen. He shifted as much as he could in the chair. "You have more ways to make me talk than you know, my dear."

Again, a flicker of confusion in her eyes. In an attempt to hide it, she moved away to place the candelabra on a table near the fireplace. Then, because the room was stuffy, she removed her pelisse and draped it over another chair. She wore a simple gown of some pale, diaphanous material. Her hair was unbound, cascading over her shoulders and down her back. When she came near and bent to retrieve the pistol, he caught a glimpse of the little shadow between her breasts.

"Beautiful," he murmured.

She froze, then straightened slowly. Their gazes snagged together.

Godolphin ached to grab her, kiss her, shred away that gauzy gown, haul her over his shoulder to the bed. But he could not move. It was contrary, and puzzling, but this only made his member throb in earnest. His breathing became shallow.

"You cannot breathe?" she asked.

"A bit stuffy in here."

"If I open a window, the candles will go out, and I haven't got a lamp."

"There would be one downstairs."

"Oh no. I'm not leaving you alone in here. That's why I'm not simply searching the house."

He laughed. "I'm not a wizard, for heaven's sake. I couldn't release myself. Even if I wanted to."

Her pale eyebrows shot up. "Even if you wanted to?" Her eyes skimmed down him. She eyed his chest, which was rising and falling.

"You could've come here and searched the house without the bother of kidnapping me, you know."

"But what if the ledgers really aren't here? It's only a hunch." She looked at his chest again, as though fascinated.

"Do you like what you see?" he asked.

She only bit her lip. Then her eyes fell lower. They widened visibly when she saw the unmistakable bulge in his lap. Her eyes shot back to his.

He gave her a lascivious grin. "You see? You *do* have ways to make me talk." He intended this as an invitation, but he couldn't ignore the rasp of need in his own voice. It was torture, not being able to grab her.

Slowly, she placed the pistol back on the carpet. Then she moved so she stood over him.

Because he sat in a low lady's chair, his eyes were exactly level with her breasts. They were small, true, but formed perfectly, round and firm. She was breathing quickly, too, he noticed. The lace edging on her bodice looked ideal for shredding.

She reached out, touched a fingertip to his cheek.

His eyes fell shut. This first contact brought some small relief. But only for a second. Then he was launched onto an even higher plane of raging need.

"Where," she said, taking her finger away, "are the ledgers?"

Groaning, he opened his eyes. "I," he said, "will never talk."

She began to unbutton his shirt.

The deft motions of her fingers stirred him. He watched her face as she undid the final button. Her features were sweet in concentration, and her eyelids were drooped with unmistakable desire. He felt so helpless with her bending over him thus. And he relished every second of it.

He gasped as she laid one palm flat against his bare chest. Her skin was a little damp because of the stuffiness in the air. She dragged it downward, over his pectoral muscles, across the bumps of his rib cage, onto the exquisitely sensitive plane of his belly. "Where are they?" she whispered hotly in his ear.

"*Never,*" he muttered on a sigh.

Her palm stroked lower, to the waistband of his trousers. It stopped.

"Tell me where."

He clamped his teeth, sure he was on the verge of exploding then and there, like an inexperienced youth.

Her fingers wiggled beneath the waistband.

"Oh God," he moaned.

She drew her fingers away, straightened.

"God, Estella, you're torturing me." He meant every syllable, with all his starving, need-drenched heart. "Touch me. *I want you.*"

"Where are they?" Her cheeks were aflame, her eyes sparkling.

She wanted him, too. He was certain. "In the front parlor, downstairs. In a cabinet."

Her smile was one of delighted victory.

"Now that I've told you," he said, "you can untie me." He had to have her. *Now.*

"Certainly not."

"You've got your pistol. You could get away."

"You were in the navy. I rather think I wouldn't."

Instinctively, he tugged his bound wrists. "If you don't touch me again, I'll perish. You wouldn't want the death of your husband on your conscience, now would you?"

Estella's mind refused to work. She now knew where the ledgers were—supposedly. She had what she'd set out to get. So why couldn't she move?

Well, it was simple, really. She couldn't move because she felt overheated, saturated with longing. Her whole body vibrated, her veins thudded, and in her center, between her thighs, she was aching.

He wanted her, too. Her husband, who had already Ravished her before. So why shouldn't she pause to Ravish him, before she went on her way?

"Why not?" he said softly, echoing her thoughts.

"Why not what?" Instinctively, she played naive.

"I can see it in your eyes. I've only seen them with that particular gleam on one previous occasion. Besides which, your hands are trembling."

She looked down at her hands. He was right. What was the matter with her?

"Touch me," he instructed. "You needn't untie me just yet, if you're worried that I'll get to the ledgers before you. Which, by the way, I would."

"Arrogant," she muttered. But she reached for his trousers, unbuttoning them.

"I'm faster than you," he muttered on a delicious exhale. The proximity of her fingers was . . . perfect. "I'm larger, stronger—"

"You are the most arrogant gentleman I've ever met." She let the lowest button pop free. She set to work on the smaller buttons of his underclothes, kneeling to do so.

"You didn't," he managed as her fingers brushed his manhood through the thin linen, "allow me to finish. I was going to say that, although I'm faster, larger . . . oh God—"

She'd run an experimental finger down the length of his now free shaft.

"—and stronger than you—"

"And arrogant." She tried stroking with two fingers. "Don't forget arrogant." Her touch was delicate, feminine, and he found himself arching his hips forward, urging her to press harder, stroke faster.

"—but," he said, "you are far more clever than I."

Surprised, she stopped stroking him, and gazed up in amazement.

"But, of course," he groaned through clenched teeth, "you needn't stop. Unless you'd care to kiss me."

"I will," she said. Her voice was low, almost breathless. "I'll kiss you for your compliment." She stood slowly, unfolding her slender length like a serpent from a basket.

"Not because you *want* to kiss me?"

She leaned forward and braced herself with her hands on his shoulders. "Of course not," she whispered in his ear.

Her kiss was assured this time. She was a woman awakened, sure of her desirability, and sure of what she wanted.

Godolphin's last thought, before he handed his mind over to ecstasy, was *Thank God it's me she wants, because that effectively makes me the luckiest devil in the world.*

Her taste was just this side of familiar, her lips silky. He wanted more and more, deeper, but because he was bound, he was helpless to control these things. Estella alone chose how deep the kiss was, and when he became too savage, she'd merely pull away, leaving him gasping. After a few minutes, however, she was stirred to a frenzy, swept along with him, and she didn't pull back again, but released small shuddering groans that vibrated against Godolphin's teeth.

He spoke against her moist, open lips. "Pull up your skirts."

Her breath hitched.

"Pull them up, darling, and allow me inside you. Now. Before it's too late."

"Surely it can't be too late," she said with a soft laugh, kissing him between words. "We've only just started. Unless—" She drew back, keeping her hands on his shoulders, so she could look at him. "Unless there is something about being my prisoner that sends you to the verge so easily?"

"I am," he said evenly, "your servant. Now pull up your skirts."

She laughed, and obeyed. The sight of her shining eyes, the burnished curls tumbling over one shoulder, and the flash of her teeth as she laughed, was the most erotic thing Godolphin had seen. Ever. Court beauties, tropical seductresses, perfectly formed actresses, the most celebrated Parisian courtesans, hell, even the exquisite Turkish princess he'd once been presented to . . . They all faded away to pale shadows. Here, before him, was the most natural, lovely creature he'd ever been near. And she was *his.*

She'd hitched her skirts high enough to expose her sweet round knees. The candlelight bounced off them.

He was flexing his arms, pulling against his tied wrists. His manhood stood stiffly before him. He wanted to pillage, and she was taking so bloody long to get her skirts up.

Holding her skirts just above the knees, she tipped her head to one side. "Are you quite all right?"

"For God's *sake.*"

She grinned. "Did I ever mention you are impatient, as well as arrogant?" She said this fondly.

"My dear wife, if you will kindly raise your skirts approximately twelve more inches, step two feet forward, and then lower yourself another twelve or so inches, I'd be only too delighted to listen to you list every last one of my deficiencies of character."

"You are *not,*" she said wickedly, glancing at his lap, "deficient." She finally bunched her skirts up around her hips. She wore short pantalettes, but they were, as was usual, split in the middle seam. Godolphin couldn't see anything, but it didn't seem to matter.

She took one step forward, positioning herself above his shaft. She released her skirts and they tumbled around his lap, spilling over the arms of the chair. She braced herself again on his shoulders.

And sank.

Oh dear Lord. Godolphin threw his head back on the chair, slammed his eyes shut. All his attention was riveted to the sensations buried beneath her skirts. The tip of his manhood was pressed past the crispness of her pantalettes, and he felt heat, and heavenly damp.

He wanted to clutch her waist, drive her down. But he couldn't. He moaned.

She wiggled, and his crest was positioned at her scorching-wet entrance. She sank lower.

He could only press his face into her neck, could only raise his hips a few inches to meet her fluid motions, but it was enough, enough, beautifully enough. He shuddered up into her, and she, gasping, clutched the back of his head with one hand. Her fingers were rigid—he couldn't see her face—and then as she cried out, her fingers went limp, cradling the back of his neck.

Wordlessly, Estella unwrapped her arms from Godolphin's neck. She rose, pulling her own body, with its still-tight embrace, from his. When she stepped back, her skirts fell back down around her legs. Except for a residual ache, and the dampness clinging to her underclothes, she was just as before.

Almost.

Because she longed to unbind Godolphin, to feel his arms tight around her, to lie with him in her old bed, to have him inside her again. But she couldn't.

He looked a little dazed. "Going so soon?"

She busied herself with knotting her hair at the nape of her neck.

"Of course." His eyes went flinty. "The ledgers."

After scooping up the pistol, she set off toward the door.

"Aren't you going to untie me?" he called after her.

Her throat was seizing with tears, and she couldn't respond.

Chapter Fourteen

The Revenge of the Necklace

Rage seared Godolphin's veins. He'd been convinced she'd untie him once their lovemaking was over.

He listened to her footsteps recede down the corridor, then down the stairs. Faint creaks, and a bang or two, were audible.

It seemed she intended to leave him there. To add insult to injury, with his trousers unbuttoned, gaping wide.

The front door slammed.

His belly sank, and then rage bubbled up, hotter than ever. Never one to remain helpless—unless, of course, it suited him—he scanned the room. If there was something sharp, he could bump the chair over, and perhaps manage to saw his wrists free. It would take patience, but he'd gotten himself out of stickier situations than this.

Then an awful thought occurred to him: what if Bertie found him here?

A creaking sound emanated from downstairs. He held his breath, strained his ears. A few seconds later, he heard a clatter of feet on the stairs.

Light feet. Estella, not Bertie.

He masked both his relief and his rage when she entered the room. "Good of you to come back. Did you forget something? Besides your lover, that is."

She blinked. "I . . ." She came closer, and stooped to pick up her abandoned reticule. "I'm going to cut the ropes," she said, "but you mustn't follow me for five minutes. Or else—" She waved the pistol.

He released an incredulous chuckle. "You wouldn't Ravish me and then shoot me. At least, not in such quick succession. Am I not allowed some sort of grace period?"

She set her lips, and crouched behind his chair. "Those ledgers are mine. I'll do anything to make certain they remain in my possession."

"You put them in the carriage, which is now waiting for you?" He asked this already knowing the answer.

No reply. He felt her begin to saw at the leather straps that bound his wrists.

"I knew," he said over his shoulder, "that you had more toys in that reticule of yours. What're you using now? A miniature scimitar?"

She paused in her sawing to wave the knife.

"Where did you—"

"Gardener's shed."

As soon as she'd finished with the bonds at both his wrists and his ankles, she snatched up the pistol. "Now, mind you, don't leave for five minutes." She walked backward, pointing the pistol at his legs.

At least she was no longer pointing it at his heart. Ah, love.

"I wouldn't," he said, "dare disobey my wife."

He didn't move from the chair until he heard her carriage clop away.

Estella had to climb on top of a chair in order to hide the ledgers on the canopy of her bed. Once she did this, she was able to sleep, but only a little. She was half-conscious of every sound, listening for Godolphin. But of course, he didn't come to her.

In the morning, she decided to review Madame Petti-bonne's manual. Perhaps there was some nugget of information that might help appease a recently kidnapped husband. She went to her dressing table to fetch the book.

Her wedding ring was gone!

It had been beside a jar of complexion cream, she was certain. But still, she checked all around the floor, in the drawers, in her jewelry boxes. Nothing. Godolphin had stolen keys from her, and he'd stolen the ledgers, but why would he want to steal her ring?

She shook her head. First, she needed a pot of tea.

She scooped up Madame Pettibonne's book and set off for the breakfast room.

"Your Ladyship," Teeters wheezed at Estella's shoulder.

She froze in the middle of the corridor, turned. As she did so, she clutched the manual close to her chest. "Yes?" Drat. The horrible little man had made her jump.

He eyed her as if she were a waif caught pinching bread. "May I . . . I must have a word with you. It's urgent. Could you come to the library?"

Estella glanced around. The corridor, lined with massive gilt-framed mirrors and threadbare tapestries, was empty. She lifted an eyebrow. "What are you doing about so early, Teeters?"

He pulled his shoulders back, as though offended. "I'm always awake, Your Ladyship. I do not lead a life of leisure and frivolous amusements."

She sniffed. "What did you want to speak to me about?"

His eyes darted, as though checking for spies. "Have you seen His Lordship? He's been missing since yesterday evening, and—"

"He's fine."

"Forgive me if I seem rude, Your Ladyship, but how would you know whether he is fine or not?"

Perhaps it was because she hadn't slept more than twenty minutes last night, or perhaps it was that Teeters had finally stepped over the boundary between veiled digs and sheer rudeness. Either way, Estella had reached her limit. She cocked her chin so she could look coldly down her nose at him. "I think," she pronounced, "that I've had quite enough of your sly remarks, Teeters. I am not a stupid child who is oblivious to your insults, or to the arrogant way you look at me. It would become you to remember that you are, in the end, merely a servant."

"A *servant?*" he spluttered, gripping his lapels for support.

"Precisely. Now, if you'd excuse me, I've things to do." Victorious, she sailed down the corridor.

She hadn't reached the top of the stairs when Teeters called after her.

"Your *Ladyship*," his voice dripped with sarcastic reverence, "you've dropped something."

For the second time, she froze, her belly seizing with panic. She'd forgotten about the book. It must have slipped from her fingers when she'd picked up her skirts. Summoning all her will, she turned to face him.

Sauntering down the corridor, he held Madame Petti-bonne's manual as if it were a soiled dishrag. "Your prayer book."

Estella swallowed. "Um, yes. Thank you." She walked briskly toward him. But before she reached him, he'd opened it.

His eyes bulged. After he flipped another page, his pudgy jaw went slack. Then he met her gaze, snapping the book shut. "It is so heartening to know you're a devout young lady. So few are these days. I do hope the vicar's silly little wife can match your enthusiasm for prayer."

Estella snatched the book from his hand.

"My French is only passable," he continued, shrugging as he turned to leave. "And I'm afraid the study of the Bible was never my favorite diversion." He broke into a slippery grin, and a tiny muscle beneath one eye twitched. "Yet I don't recall poodles jumping through flaming hoops in the Latin version."

* * *

When Godolphin heard Estella leave her bedchamber, he waited a few minutes, and then entered by way of the wardrobe.

He scanned the room. Dressing table, trunk, two chests of drawers, a writing table, the bed and bedside table, two chairs and the settee. He dragged the cushions from the chairs and settee. Nothing. He flipped up the lid of the trunk, but it was empty. He pawed through the chests of drawers, and the wardrobe. Clothing, clothing, more clothing.

She must have hidden the ledgers elsewhere.

Ah. His roving eyes rested on the window seat. It had shelves beneath it, stuffed with books. But the ledgers, with their plain black spines, were not among them. Nevertheless, he crossed to the shelf and crouched before it. The ledgers could be *behind* the books. He pulled books from the shelves, three at a time.

Then he saw it. Not a book, but a small, decorated wooden box. As he pulled it out, he recalled something Bertie had said. When asked why he'd ransacked the entire castle, he'd replied, *I was looking for something else.* And, *Ask Estella.*

Godolphin opened the box.

Inside was a velvet pouch, the sort used to store costly pieces of jewelry. He frowned. He'd never seen Estella wearing any jewelry, except her wedding ring and the silver chain with the key.

He undid the pouch's drawstring and poured a necklace into his palm. It was gold, with huge square emeralds that would have satisfied the taste of the most extravagant queen.

"I am delighted to see you have returned safely from your ordeal of last night."

Godolphin turned to see Estella in the doorway. Her skin was ashen, and she clutched her prayer book to her chest.

"Still more secrets." He stood, closing his fingers around the necklace. "Your father has been kind to you. Though even a man as wealthy as he would have difficulty acquiring a necklace like this through legal means."

"You imply he obtained it illegally?"

They stared each other in the eye, neither moving nor blinking. "Yes," he answered.

She gave a humorless little laugh. "But of course. How could I forget? Papa is a smuggler. No doubt he and Mama are at this moment ransacking the Caribbean for more loot."

"Well then, my pretty princess—for indeed, only a princess could possess such a necklace—if your father did not give you this piece, then who did?" He held it up, and the emeralds sparkled richly.

"No one." She swallowed. "I've just always had it."

"Ah. Just like the key your wear round your neck."

Abruptly, she crossed the room and placed her prayer book in a drawer of the nightstand. When she looked at him again, her features were tight. "I suppose it would be silly, at this juncture, anyway, for me to be outraged that you've ransacked my bedchamber, and are now quizzing me about its contents?"

He sauntered to the settee, plumped the pillows, and sat. "Yes, it would." He dangled the necklace, swinging it slowly. "Why don't you put it on for me?"

"No!"

"Come. I'll clasp it for you."

"Stop it. I don't—I *hate* that necklace. That's why you've never seen it before." She stood near the bed, arms crossed defensively.

"How," he demanded, "did you acquire it?"

"It's not mine . . . it's just . . . oh, never mind. You would never understand."

"Try."

"Someone gave it to me."

Bertie Littlefield. Why in blazes had Bertie given his wife such a luxurious gift? Pounding fury blindsided him. "Why do you need to hide it then, if it is legally yours?"

"Legally? Don't speak to me as though I were a thief! I—"

He sprang to his feet. "Where did you get this necklace?" He paced toward her.

She held her ground, but she seemed to shrink, and his anger dissolved a little. He wanted to hold her, tell her it didn't matter where the bloody thing came from, that she was all that mattered. But he was seized with the need to force her to admit Bertie had given it to her. "Well?"

She breathed in, out. "Littlefield."

Even though he'd already known this, her admission made him sick. "Why did he give it to you? Why did you accept it?"

"I told him I didn't want it, but he refused to take it with him when he left." She cupped her upper arms with shaking hands. "I hid it because I didn't know what else to do with it."

"You couldn't have simply given it back?"

"No. I—it was Violet Plympton's."

"Violet Plympton's?"

"I think he'd taken it from her. Stolen it, perhaps, or taken it as a payment or bribe. But she wanted it back. That's why she was in the castle when she . . ." Her voice trailed off in misery.

"Why did you not tell me of this at the time, when she was discovered?"

"I was afraid."

"Of me?"

A pause. "Yes. Of your anger."

Guilt pressed down on him, but before he could decide whether to forgive or not, he noticed something. His belly constricted.

She wasn't wearing her wedding ring.

"Where is your ring?" He could hear how weary he sounded.

Her eyes widened, two lavender pools of misery. "I don't know," she whispered. "It's gone."

His jaw went rigid. "I'm tired of the lies, Estella." He pressed the cold necklace into her hand and left.

The weight of the necklace made Estella's stomach churn. She dropped it on the carpet, and the gold chain clinked, as though mocking her.

She *wouldn't* cry. She had been wrong, perhaps, keeping it hidden from her husband. But he wasn't even a real husband. Not exactly. He was her enemy. Except . . .

He was also her friend. She'd run to him after she'd discovered Violet. She'd made love with him, kissed him, she'd taken care of him when he was hurt.

She moved to her dressing table, drew out a quill and a slip of paper from one of the drawers. Godolphin had left the table a jumble.

A tear slipped out. Despite everything, she wanted Godolphin to trust her and respect her.

She dashed out a note to Bertie, inviting him to call. She'd give the necklace back.

After sending the note off with the footman, she remembered the first rehearsal for the Michaelmas pantomime. It was in full swing by the time she arrived in the ballroom.

"Now then." Pansy clapped her hands sharply. "Everyone who has been assigned the part of a blackberry bush, stand to the left of the harpsichord."

A clutch of six children straggled over in silence. They seemed, Estella noticed from her vantage point on a chair in the middle of the castle ballroom, overawed. One small boy of about five, who sported some sort of pinkish, sticky-looking stain around his mouth, gazed up at the vaulted ceiling with bugging eyes. An older girl, wearing a coarse brown smock, toyed with the hem of her skirt, bewildered.

Estella wondered if they knew Violet Plympton had so recently been laid out here.

"All right, please pay attention," Pansy instructed. "Clouds over there—and Jemima, pray remember, dear, that the sun would not suck her thumb, would she?"

Mothers from the village huddled in corners and against walls, so ill at ease that at first they could not bring themselves to sit on the chairs arranged for them. Estella made her way from one small clutch of mothers to the next, trying to be friendly and gracious, inviting them to sit.

" 'Tis kind of ye, Yer Ladyship," one said shyly. "Me old man said 'twere nothin' but trouble to come 'ere, but I told 'im otherwise. Th' earl is a good man, for all that, and so 'is lady must also be."

Her companion, a pink-cheeked young woman with a babe in arms, nodded in solemn agreement. " 'Tis true some menfolk're angry at th' earl, but 'tis truly the *old* earl they have complaints against, and he's dead."

"The old earl?" quizzed Estella. All these endless hints about Godolphin's father, and no one would ever tell her outright what he'd done.

"Aye, His Lordship's father. He was an odd one, was he, and nothin' short of—"

The other mother interrupted. "Hold yer tongue, Beth. Th' young countess don't need to hear gossip about 'er dead family."

Frustrated, but unwilling to press the issue, Estella excused herself.

From a chair near the small stage that had been erected, she watched the pantomime. It was simple enough, outlining the exploits of St. George as, sword in hand, he rescued the princess and cast the evil dragon from the heavens. The fallen dragon ended up in a blackberry thicket, at which point the blackberry bushes themselves burst into a charming song about how one should not eat blackberries after Michaelmas, and that it was best, in fact, to stick to nuts and seeds.

The only problems, aside from the off-key singing and tentative dancing, were that the sun, who was supposed to beam brightly in the heavens (the heavens being a small dais raised two feet off the floor), had a tendency to suck her thumb; the dragon was a toddler in diapers, who kept scampering away instead of remaining lodged in the blackberry brambles; and St. George himself, a boy of ten with knock-knees and curly red hair, appeared terrified of his wooden sword.

Just as St. George was stumbling through his rhyming monologue, Estella noticed Timmy craning his neck around the doorway that led to the main corridor. He held a scone in one hand, but now, the scone seemed utterly forgotten. He was watching the proceedings of the rehearsal with the most heart-wrenching expression of longing on his freckled face. Estella looked away, feeling almost intrusive to have caught him watching.

She sighed.

"Oh dear." Pansy slumped into the chair beside Estella. The clouds, the sun, and the princess warbled along in their song about summer being over and winter starting. "It *isn't* going to be the best Michaelmas pantomime Seabrook has ever had, is it?"

"It's . . ." Estella glanced back over to the doorway. Timmy was gone. "The children are delightful. And you still have time. This is only the first rehearsal here at the castle. Perhaps, once the children are more comfortable . . ." Then she noticed Simkin loitering beneath one of the arched windows. He wore a harried expression, as if he was mortified at what all those little feet were doing to the parquet floor. "Just a moment," she told Pansy.

Simkin, of course, could hardly say no to the mistress of the castle.

"Play the harpsichord in a . . . pantomime?" He lurched over the last word, as if it were distasteful, quite possibly foreign.

Estella bobbed her head, flashing the butler her most entreating smile. "I'd appreciate it awfully. I suspect the children would sing a little more in tune if they had you to help them."

Simkin straightened, heeding the call of duty. Flicking imaginary lint off the lapels of his livery jacket, he marched, albeit arthritically, to the harpsichord bench.

The singing died away, and all the children gaped at Simkin as if he were a relic in a curiosity shop.

Simkin, utterly composed, removed his pristine gloves, rubbed his knobby old hands together briskly a few times, then played a major chord, adding an impressive flourish in the upper octave. "Now, children," he said. "From the beginning again."

"Thank you," Pansy whispered, as Estella sat down next to her.

Estella gave her friend a grin. "I've just had another idea, actually. I'll be back in a tick."

"A children's pantomime?" Mr. Pepys cocked his head to one side, considering. "I'm really up to my elbows here. The silk for the walls should arrive this afternoon, and the chandelier is clean and ready to be hung back up." He gestured broadly around the breakfast room. Three workmen were in the process of painting the woodwork a clean eggshell color. The whole room smelled of paint.

"*Please* say you will," Estella begged. "Think of it as another part of the job."

Pepys leaned elegantly on one hip. "You know, I always did want to go on the stage, but my father forbade it, as fathers are wont to do. This just might be the next best thing." He smiled, his eyes lighting up. "Ah—I've already thought of a marvelous idea for the sun. We can use gold lame for her gown, and a great papier-mâché sunburst round her face—"

"Good." Estella was already dashing out the door. "You have my permission to start as soon as you'd like."

Chapter Fifteen

The Prankster Unmasked

"I can't tell you how happy I am with the pantomime. Thank you so much for all of your generosity." Pansy Lovely studied Estella. "But are you quite all right?"

Once the children and their mothers had left the castle, Estella and Pansy had gone to the countess's parlor for refreshment. Pansy, especially, was famished, and thoroughly elated by the quick turnaround in the fortunes of her pantomime brought about by Simkin and Pepys.

"You look," Pansy said, "well, not *bad*, of course, and that would be a rotten thing for me to say—but you seem pale. And worried. Yes, that's it."

Estella clasped her hands in her lap, studied the low table before her. A crystal carafe of orangeade had been laid out, along with two glasses and a china plate of ginger biscuits. Madame Pettibonne's manual sat on the pristine tablecloth next to the refreshments. The white leather cover took on a subtle sheen in the shifting light from the fire.

"Despite," Estella said at last, "the, um, peculiar way we were betrothed, I've grown . . . well, I've grown fond of Godolphin." Oh dear. Soon she would disintegrate into a puddle of sentimental mush. She sat up straighter. "And in spite of everything, beast or no, I want my marriage to work."

"Then we should get to work."

Both sets of eyes fell upon Madame Pettibonne's book.

Pansy glanced at Estella and smiled. "Now, tell me. How is your hound responding to Step Two?"

"Not well," Estella admitted. "I have a confession to make. I bungled Step Two so badly, I was forced to rush on to Step Three as an emergency measure. I do hope you don't mind."

"Of course not. But how could you ever bungle Little Endearments? Edwin responded instantly, and he even agreed to sit in during a pantomime rehearsal and give suggestions to the children. I usually can't tear him away from his study long enough for him to take regular meals, he frets so about his sermons."

"The endearments worked at first," Estella sighed. "Just like Step One worked at first. But I ruined it by accidentally calling him duckie—"

"Duckie?"

"—and poppet."

Politely, Pansy attempted to conceal her smile.

"I know, I know," Estella grumbled. "Ridiculous. But they just came out. He was growing suspicious, even asking me what I was up to, so I jumped to the Petting Technique. Which worked."

"Did it? That's good news, then. Although dear Edwin is not quite ready for that. He's skittish. Yet," Pansy added in a brighter tone, "I am ever so grateful for Madame Pettibonne's advice. Now I know that skittishness is normal hound behavior."

"Yes. Normal." Estella tried to sound convinced. Godolphin had not seemed skittish in the least when he had Ravished her in the warehouse. Or when *she'd* Ravished *him* in her parents' house.

"I think I'm ready to advance to Step Four." She reached for Madame Pettibonne's book, opened it to the page she'd marked with a bit of the pink ribbon her husband had shoved at her just days earlier. The ribbon served as a reminder of just how undomesticated her beast was. She cleared her throat, then translated aloud:

" 'Four. Food Rewards. As a last resort, the Lady Handler must add food to her arsenal, for to win a hound's heart she may first have to win his stomach. Dear Reader, do not be downcast. I am well aware that Lady Handlers often have distinct ideas of pleasurable pastimes that do not involve labors in the kitchen. And though I do not generally recommend the use of culinary tidbits as a reward for obedience and pleasant behavior, when applied, it has never been known to fail.' "

"Are you quite certain?" Pansy's mouth formed a circle. "Madame Pettibonne said you must proceed with caution, and use Food Rewards only as a last resort."

"I am certain. I haven't a choice. Would you meet me tomorrow at the village bun shop, and bring a copy of a cake receipt with you? I haven't got any."

Pansy arched one delicate brow. "Of course. I'll bring my grandmama's honey cake receipt."

After Pansy left, Estella remained in the countess's parlor. She looked at the necklace in its velvet-lined case. She'd be glad to be rid of it, even though this meant having to see Bertie.

Her eyes shot to the clock on the writing desk. Ten minutes till three. Bertie wasn't due for several more minutes.

With a sick fascination curling in her belly, Estella took the necklace out of the box. It was heavy, and the filigree clinked softly. She carried it to the mirror. She hesitated. But her feminine love for jewelry got the better of her, and she put it around her neck, fastening the clasp.

The weight of it was almost strangling, and it somehow possessed the power to make her look years older. Instead of lighting her complexion as gemstones ought to, the emeralds made her skin sallow, and faint dark circles appeared under her eyes.

She reached up behind her neck with both hands to undo the clasp. A flash of motion in the mirror caught her eye.

Her pulse set off at a gallop.

"It's splendid on you," Bertie said, coming through the doorway. "I'm so glad to see you've decided to wear it. But alas, I do need it back. Where did you hide it, by the way? I searched everywhere."

Unable to move, Estella stared at Bertie through the mirror.

"You're early," she stammered after she'd found her voice. She fumbled with the clasp, but she was so jittery that she couldn't manage it. Why hadn't a servant announced his arrival?

"I let myself in," he said, answering her unspoken question. "Allow me." He moved toward her.

She spun around, backed up against the mirror. She felt the cold glass through her gown. "I don't want—you needn't help me. I was simply trying it on, and I—"

"I *did* want you to have it." Bertie said, stopping a few paces from her. "You're the only woman I've ever met with sufficient beauty not to be overpowered by such a gorgeous piece. Unfortunately, I need it back."

"I know you do." Estella lifted her chin in challenge. "Which is why you ransacked my home—"

"Your home?" He snickered.

"Yes, you ransacked my home in an attempt to find it." She drew a big breath. "You found the ledgers, but didn't find the necklace, and that's why you killed Violet Plympton. You thought she'd found it before you did, because she was in the castle searching for it, too, and you murdered her to get it."

Something tormented and dark transformed Bertie's features. "I didn't kill that slattern. Godolphin did."

Although it took all the courage she had in her body,

Estella met his eye. "*You* killed her. And for a mere *thing*, too. It's disgusting. A person's life is worth infinitely more than even the costliest *thing*."

He blinked, as though she'd spoken gibberish. "When you are my wife—"

"Your wife?" She felt dizzy, and pressed her palms against the mirror.

"You *will* be my wife. You'll see. In your heart of hearts, that is what you desire."

She was speechless.

"And, when you're my wife, I shall buy you all the jewelry you desire. But right now, I urgently need that necklace." He took a stride closer.

"Don't you come near me!"

He stopped. His one fist clenched and unclenched.

Estella tried to control her breathing, which had grown too quick, too shallow. All she wanted to do was take the necklace and hurl it at him. She hated it, almost as much as she hated him. But he was so very desperate for the necklace. Which could only mean that he needed it to accomplish whatever cruel goal he had set for himself.

If she gave him the necklace, she suddenly realized, she'd be helping him.

"Why do you want it?" she asked. Her eyes darted past him, to the open door. How was she going to get past him?

"You needn't fret your pretty head about such things." He took another step forward, slowly, like a man trying not to startle a wild bird. "But it is, in the end, for you. All that I do is for you, my little Estella."

"Bertie." She tasted bile as she said this.

His eyebrows lifted at her intimate use of his given name.

"Bertie, if I am ever to be your wife, then you'll have to understand that I am clever, and I *like* to fret my pretty head about all sorts of things."

He was breathing heavily. "So you admit that you wish to be mine?"

Her very bones felt ill. "Perhaps." She didn't allow herself to look past him again to the door. "But I am a proper young lady, and I must insist on a proper proposal of marriage."

He ran the tip of his tongue over cracked lips. "I had already asked your father—"

"Not my father. Me."

"Ah, yes. Of course. I had every intention of . . ."

Raising her eyebrows, she pointedly stared at the carpet in front of her.

"Now," he said. "Yes, now, of course now. There might not be time later." Awkwardly, he knelt before her on one knee.

She fought the urge to shrink farther away from him. He was so close she could smell his acrid sweat.

"Miss Hancock," he said, gazing up at her. "Estella."

"I would hope that the gentleman I accepted a proposal of marriage from would make his suit humbly," she said crisply.

He looked confused for a moment, then caught her meaning and looked down at her feet. "Estella," he began again.

She leapt around him and ran for the door.

Bertie's eyes were squeezed shut. She would be his.

But he heard the patter of feet, felt a swish of displaced air. His eyes flew open. She was fleeing.

"Damn you," he snarled, and struggled to his feet.

She was already out the door. He chased after her, not knowing whether he wanted to catch her or the necklace. And whether, after he caught her, he wanted to beat her or embrace her.

Perhaps both. The thought made his groin tingle.

He reached the main entrance foyer. It appeared to be empty, but he couldn't hear footsteps from any of the many corridors that led off it, and she wasn't on the grand staircase. Six huge marble pillars supported the three-story-high ceiling, pillars more than wide enough to conceal his soon-to-be bride.

"I know you're in here," he called, his shrill words bouncing off the walls and ceiling. "Come out. Don't be childish. My patience is wearing thin."

Silently, he slunk to the first pillar on his left, and peeked around it. She wasn't there, and from this vantage point he could see that she wasn't around the second pillar, either. He crept toward the third.

A clatter of boot heels erupted, multiplied so many times by the vaulted space that he couldn't tell from which direction it came. Then he saw her streak past him, just an arm's length away, and throw herself on the massive front door.

She pulled on the handle, dragging with all her weight, but it was stuck.

He rushed toward her, and he heard her whimper. It was the most erotic sound he'd ever heard. He grabbed at her wildly, catching only a fistful of sleeve.

"Get away, you monster!" She tore away from him, the emeralds glittering at her throat. Her sleeve ripped, and she was across the foyer, leaving him with nothing but a shred of her gown in his fingers.

Bertie saw crimson, and as he set off after her, he was vaguely aware of the spittle foaming at the corners of his lips. Enough presence of mind remained for him to tuck the precious shred of cloth in his pocket. He might have use for it later.

She'd dashed down one of the corridors flanking the staircase, and as he followed, he saw that there were no doors leading off of it. No matter. His blurred vision was fixed to the fluttering skirts and kicking heels of the woman running away from him.

When he caught her, he'd have no choice but to cover her writhing body with his. Oh, he'd get the necklace. But he was aroused now, and he wasn't going to leave her without satisfaction.

And if Godolphin came upon them in such a situation, so much the better. Estella would be forever marked as Bertie's.

The long corridor funneled out into another lofty space, which Bertie dimly recognized as the Great Hall, part of the ancient castle.

The huge, empty space had windows on either side, a cavernous fireplace on one end, and on the other end, three doors. The middle one, he knew, led to the tower stairs, and the third to the cellars.

She was trying the middle door, her motions frantic. It appeared to be locked.

Panting like a dog, he ran as fast as he could to the door on the left, gaining it just as she reached for the door's handle. He slammed against it with all his might, this time pinning her arm beneath him.

She looked directly into his eyes. Then she screamed.

"Shut the hell up," he hissed.

"Help me! Somebody help me!"

"It would seem, my love, that none of the earl's thespian servants are willing to assist you." He lurched forward, lips gaping open, trying to cover her screaming mouth with his.

She scrunched up her face, rearing away, but her arm was still pinned beneath him.

"Bastard!" She kicked him in the shins.

Bertie winced in pain, instinctively doubling forward. She was no longer trapped beneath him, and she pulled away. He recovered quickly, and circled around, cornering her in front of the third door.

The cellar door.

She backed up, her eyes crazed. "I'll give you the necklace," she whispered.

His groin pounded. "Oh, but I don't want the necklace anymore."

Her features twisted. She dodged to the left, and he leapt in front of her. Next, she made a feint to the right, but he blocked her path. The entire time he was advancing toward her, and after a final, pitiful attempt on her part to dart by him, he pinned her to the door.

"Why are you doing this?" she asked, stumbling over a sob.

"I love you."

She shook her head. "This is not love—"

He moved close enough to place his one hand on the door planks beside her shoulder. "I shall show you what real love is, my Estella."

She kicked his shins again, but this time he felt no pain. He took a shuddering inhalation of her luscious honey-suckle scent, dipping his head close to the creamy curve of her neck. He kissed it.

This drew another delicious whimper from her throat.

He pressed his pelvis hard against her. He moaned.

But she took a wide-stretched hand and pushed it into his face, digging with fingernails, and jabbing one eye till he yelped. She shoved him back, and he was temporarily blinded.

When he could see again, the third door was open, and she'd disappeared.

Enough light slanted down the stairwell that Estella could see. She couldn't move very quickly, though, because the steps were slippery with moss. She placed a hand against the wall to brace herself, only to pull it away in disgust. It was slimy and cold.

She managed to reach the twist in the stairs just before Bertie's shadow blocked the light.

Mustn't panic. Mustn't panic. There is a way out, through the caves, onto the beach.

"You're behaving like a child again, Estella." His voice was deadened in the close space.

Estella picked her way down and down, her progress slowing as the light faded. Her heartbeat reverberated through her skull and her own breath sounded distant. Dripping water punctuated these sounds. Now and then an icy drop fell onto her head, like the tap of death.

She couldn't hear Bertie, but she knew he was behind

her. She picked her way down the blackened steps, feeling each one, gaining a foothold, before shifting her weight—

"Foolish little girl."

Her heart wallowed in her mouth. He was so close.

She plunged forward without checking her foothold. Then she was falling down, down, into inkiness, for what seemed like a long time, but which could have only been a second.

She pitched, hands outstretched, onto the floor. The wind was knocked from her, but she hadn't fallen far.

"You're trapping yourself," Bertie called, "in the dungeon."

A scream lay just beneath her ribs, unable to budge. Ahead there was light, blessed light. She staggered forward, blinking. The light came from sconces on the stone walls.

She ran.

They were in the wine cellar, with rows and rows of wooden barrels on racks, four barrels high, and more racks of bottled wine. She ran down an aisle. Sticky, invisible webs caught on her face, her throat, but she plunged forward. Bertie's footsteps were brisk behind her.

At the end of the aisle, she skidded to a stop, then careened to the right. Her stop was so sudden, she heard Bertie smash into something and curse.

She ran the length of the cellar, dully counting eight rows of barrels, to a low arched doorway. There was more light beyond. Perhaps there was someone down here. She was too breathless to call out, and could only run forward.

On the other side of the doorway was an empty room the size of a small stable yard. No sconces burned there. She ran toward the light coming through one of several arching doorways that ringed the chamber.

Over her footsteps and Bertie's, and her own panting, she heard a sound coming from the direction of the light.

Hope flared, and she tried to speed up, just as Bertie's hand grabbed her shoulder.

"You're quick," Bertie wheezed in her ear.

His grip made her do a half spin, and stumble. She pitched face first to the cold stone floor, and he fell on top of her, never releasing his grip. Her cheekbone met the floor. Pain seared through her face, and down her spine. This was nothing compared to the disgusting weight of Bertie's body on top of her, and his moist breath at her neck.

She strained her head up. "Help," she called out toward the lighted doorway. "Help."

"No one is there." Bertie's hand was at the back of her neck, grabbing her hair till it made her neck arch back at an awkward angle. Then he released it, and her face nearly crashed to the floor again. He was fumbling with sweat-slick fingers at the necklace.

"Take it," she said, battling a sob.

He'd undone the clasp, and then he ripped the necklace free. The edges of the filigree chain snagged on her skin, making her cry out. He was pushing his pelvis hard into her back—

Her mind went blessedly clear.

The breathing sounds became distant, and she could think. And her single thought was, *I will not allow him to win.*

With all her remaining strength, she pushed up with her hands.

Bertie responded by making himself heavier on top of her. "I do like spirit," he hissed. "It makes things ever so much more interesting."

Her arms wobbled under their combined weight. Suddenly, she fell forward, and in the fragment of a moment before Bertie landed heavily on top of her, she twisted sideways. There was a crack as his face hit the floor. He wailed, the sound oddly muffled, and his body went limp enough for her to wriggle out from beneath him, and struggle to her feet. She pitched to the side, dizzy, and thought she might vomit.

He grabbed her ankle.

She stomped on his arm with her free foot. He loosened his grip momentarily, and she ran toward the light, toward where she'd heard that sound.

There was a long corridor, fading to blackness, through the doorway, but just to the left the light was bright, coming through an open door. She stopped in the doorway. And stared.

"Teeters!" she yelled.

Teeters, hunched at a desk in the corner of a little stone cubbyhole. Light bounced off his spectacles, concealing his eyes.

"Why didn't you help me?" She heard moans, dragging footsteps advancing behind her. Bertie was coming.

Calmly, Teeters removed his spectacles and began polishing them on his cuff. "I was not aware, Your Ladyship, that the duties of your husband's personal secretary extended to assisting you, especially during my off hours."

Estella's jaw went slack. "Are you *mad?*" Her eyes flew wildly around the cubbyhole. "What're you doing down here?" The little room was nearly bare, save for the chair and desk Teeters sat at.

On the desk was a clay pot, with streaks of dried black paint running down the sides—

Black paint. Godolphin's vandalized portrait.

—and a serpentine heap of pink ribbons.

Godolphin's horse.

Estella narrowed her eyes. "You. *You* played those pranks on him!"

Teeters was expressionless. He replaced his spectacles on his nose. Subtly, he covered something on the desk with his arm.

Estella leapt forward and snatched a piece of paper from under his arm. Something metallic clattered on the floor. It glinted. Her wedding band. She crouched to retrieve it, still clutching the piece of paper.

Teeters's expression remained blank. His eyes flicked over Estella's shoulder. She stood.

"I see you've found a friend," Bertie said.

Estella shrank against the door frame, made a half turn. Blood flowed freely from Bertie's nose.

Again, she ran, grasping her ring and the piece of paper. She ran past Bertie, back through the wine cellar, and stumbled up the mossy stairs and through the Great Hall, even though she heard no one in pursuit.

She saw no servants, no one, and the castle seemed so dark and huge and evil that she had to get out.

She burst out the front door, stumbled down the steps, onto the drive. The sky was glowing blue, the sea air was fresh, but these things did not diminish her panic.

She could take a horse into Brighton. Go to Lady Penelope and—

A black horse was trotting toward her, up the white gravel drive. She watched, fear draining, as Godolphin came into focus, framed by the sapphire sky and the red-orange leaves on either side of the drive.

He pulled back the reins as he drew close, and the horse came to a stop. "Estella," he said, curious laughter in his voice.

She lacked the energy to speak. She just stared up at him, clutching the paper hard against her chest.

"Oh my God!" He leapt from the horse and held her close.

Chapter Sixteen

Working Breeds

Godolphin didn't know what had happened to Estella. What had caused the blooming beginnings of a bruise on her cheekbone? How had her clothing become ripped and wrinkled and stained with flecks of blood? Soon enough he would learn, and he felt as though he could kill whoever had harmed her. But first, he knew he needed to hold her. Her eyes were so dull, and the life seemed bleached out of her skin. She needed him.

He held her against his chest, encompassing her small body with his arms, swaying slightly. Her face was buried in the crook of his shoulder, and she began to sob silently.

He kissed her hair and rocked her like a mother would a child, and this didn't seem strange, although he'd never behaved in such a fashion before. Like so many things with Estella, he was learning.

She pulled her face away, looked up at him with red-rimmed eyes. "It's not safe here."

"I'll keep you safe."

"Can we go away? Go to Brighton? Or to London?"

"I've been accused of murder. If I leave my home, it'll only make me appear guilty. We need to stick it out here, carry on as usual, until this is all sorted out. Then we'll leave. We'll go anywhere you like."

Her face crumpled. "But Bertie—"

His fists balled against her back. "I knew it. Did he . . . are you all right?"

She nodded.

He touched featherlight fingertips to her bruised cheekbone. She winced. "He hit you?"

"I fell. He pulled me down, and—" She glanced over her shoulder at the looming castle. "Can't we go somewhere? He'll be coming out."

"I'll deal with him." A cool wash of murderous intent bathed Godolphin. He could kill Bertie, and gladly.

"No." Estella clutched his arm. "That's what he wants. If you try to hurt him, then you'll really look like a criminal, and it'll be that much more difficult to be proven innocent of Violet's death."

She was right. "The orangerie," he said, taking her hand and guiding her toward the side gardens. "They won't look there, and we can decide what to do."

"Teeters?" Godolphin bolted from the stone bench he'd been sitting on, and paced back and forth along the row of potted lemon trees. "*Teeters?* Why the hell would he do that to you?"

Estella remained on the bench, fingering the piece of paper she'd taken from Teeters. He'd been in the midst of crafting another prank when she'd found him. The picture depicted a stick person hanging from a scaffold, and around the person's neck was a pencil tracing of Estella's wedding band. He'd probably been planning to affix the ring to the page to look like a noose.

"Teeters," Godolphin said, "has been in my employ for seven years." He kept staring at her left hand, at her wedding ring, which she'd slipped back on her finger. Staring at it with the oddest expression. It almost looked like . . . relief.

"Perhaps he simply hates me. Or he didn't want his life to change so much."

Godolphin cocked his head. "Or he was jealous."

Estella frowned. "Why would he be jealous?" Why, indeed? Teeters, of all people, had to know what a sham their marriage was. Then understanding hit her: Teeters had been trying to turn Godolphin against her because he hadn't wanted the sham marriage to become something more.

She studied Godolphin as he paced a bit more, then sat beside her on the bench. He kissed her cheek, looking distracted, just like a real husband would.

"What will you do?" she asked him softly.

"First, I'm going to discharge Teeters. Then I've got to find a way to restrain Bertie, although that's tricky, since I've nothing to charge him with."

"Nothing? He killed Violet Plympton! He tried to—" Estella hated the frantic edge in her voice.

Godolphin wrapped a comforting arm round her shoulders. "I know, darling. But we need proof, something tangible. The law loves what it can see and feel with its own eyes and hands."

"We could charge him with trying to usurp Papa's business. All those crates in the warehouse are empty. They're an obvious sham."

"That would invite scrutiny of your father's business by the authorities."

"Papa could endure any scrutiny." For the thousandth time, she wanted to confront Godolphin about The South China Company, and his suspicions of Papa. But she held her tongue.

Godolphin kissed her cheek again. "You're willing to risk it?"

"There is no risk." Estella set her lips. "Bertie must be arrested."

*   *   *

Godolphin took Estella up to her bedchamber, and rang for a servant to bring her hot water to bathe, and to bring Maggie up from the kitchens, where the dog had apparently been helping Cook dispose of table scraps. He applied a salve to Estella's bruised cheekbone, and loaded her pistol.

"If either Bertie or Teeters enters this chamber," he told her, "you must shoot. Neither, I think, are in the mood to allow you any more free rein. Aim for the heart, and don't shoot till he is nearly upon you. These little pocket pistols have almost no range."

She nodded gravely, and he saw that her shoulders shook.

His search of the cellars yielded nothing. Teeters had even taken the evidence of his pranks that Estella had described. When Godolphin checked Teeters's bedchamber in the farthest wing of the castle, all his personal belongings were gone. The secretary had fled.

"They've both gone," he told Estella when he returned to her. She was staring into the fire, stroking Maggie, who was lolling across her lap. The still-cocked pistol lay a few feet away. "It looks as though Teeters isn't planning on a return."

"I'm sorry." Estella's eyes glimmered with tears.

He sat beside her, stroked her cheek. "Sorry for what?"

"I don't know. Making everything so complicated."

She *had* made everything complicated, but not in the way that she thought. The tenderness and protectiveness that were flooding Godolphin's soul were what made things so complicated.

"We'll carry on as though everything is normal," he said. "You'll go into the village tomorrow—"

Estella gasped. "What? Bertie might be—"

"I'll have him arrested tomorrow for swindling your father. You'll go and be friendly with the village folk. We need them on our side. Above all, we cannot hunker down in isolation, and we cannot be afraid."

They slept close, Godolphin only dozing, lying with his wife's body wrapped in his guarding arms.

"Do you know, I think I'll just walk to the bun shop." Estella gave the coachman, perched on the dumpy castle carriage in the front drive, an apologetic smile. "The weather is so fine. I'm sorry to have troubled you."

The coachman inclined his head. "Not at all, Your Ladyship." He flicked his whip, and it wiggled like an eel against the clean blue sky. With a crunch of gravel under the wheels and a few snorts from the horses, the carriage rolled around the drive and behind the castle.

Yes. She retied her bonnet ribbons more firmly under her chin. She wouldn't take the carriage out of fear of Bertie. She was too stubborn for that. Reminding herself to move regally, she descended the broad front steps of Castle Seabrook and set off across the lawns.

The day was sunny, but the moist wind whipping up over the sea cliff had a bite to it. She was thankful for the high, mink-trimmed collar on her pelisse, for her sturdy leather gloves. Her high collar concealed the chafing on her neck from when Bertie had yanked on the necklace yesterday, too. As for the bruise on her cheek, well, if anyone asked about it, she'd have to lie.

Picking up her pace, she skirted the ivy-covered walls of the kitchen garden. She stopped in her tracks, just as she was about to round the farthest corner.

She'd heard some kind of . . . scream.

Pressing her body close to the wall, she listened. Dead ivy leaves snagged on the fur cuffs of her pelisse. The wind shook the tree boughs with a gusty whisper. A seagull screeched.

"Take that!" a voice yelled.

Estella's heart pounded.

"And that! And that! I'll kill you I will! Kill you with my sword, you horrible heathen beast!"

Why were there no cries of protest? And why did the

murderous voice sound so . . . childish? She peeked around the corner.

Timmy, wearing woolen trousers patched at the knees, his mucky, two-sizes-too-small boots, and a knitted jacket of pumpkin-colored wool, leapt, slashing the air with a stick. He landed gracefully, then held his sword aloft. "And *stay* out of the heavens, you horrid dragon! We don't stand for the likes of you up here!" He made one last stab at the air.

Tears pricked at Estella's eyelids. Silently, she pulled her head back around the wall.

Poor Timmy wanted to play St. George with all of his boyish heart. As he'd flayed the imaginary dragon with his stick sword, his freckled face had been pink, his eyes aglow in a way she hadn't seen before.

Creeping away (she'd just have to take another route to the forest path), she set her chin. Things would work out for Timmy. She would see that they did.

"That is terribly sweet, the poor lost lamb." Pansy's eyes misted as she listened to Estella recount what she'd seen. "And I do know what you mean about feeling protective of Timmy. Why, any lady with at least one maternal bone in her body would."

"Do you think," Estella began slowly, as they strolled arm in arm across the village green, "that there is a way he could be included in the pantomime? Not as St. George," she hurried on, "of course. I know that role is taken. But perhaps as one of the clouds, or a blackberry bramble?"

Pansy smiled. "I am most certain that we shall find a role for Timmy. Here we are. Let's go into the bun shop. It is high time you tried one of Mrs. Hadley's cream buns. And," she winked cheekily, "she can be counted on to serve up heaps of gossip along with them."

Inside the shop, it was warm and bright, and it smelled of sweet cream, baking cakes, and anise. There was a small table at one of the bow windows. However, the shop appeared to be empty.

"Come on." Pansy led the way to the table, then perched herself on one of the dainty chairs. "Mrs. Hadley is probably in the kitchen. She'll be out in a moment."

"You seem to be an expert on bakery shop etiquette," Estella said. It was an effort to seem carefree after her horrible encounter with Bertie yesterday.

"Oh," Pansy smiled, untying her bonnet ribbons, "I am. This is the nicest spot in the entire village. Besides which, as the vicar's wife, I must be seen in public, make myself available to the villagers."

Estella sat. As distracting as it was to banter with Pansy, there were grave matters to discuss. Like the villagers. And Godolphin. And the necklace. She chewed her lip. How could she begin?

Belatedly, she realized that Pansy was regarding her bruised cheek with something akin to horror. "Complexion powder can work miracles by candlelight, I am told, but in broad daylight it hides little. What happened to your face and neck, Estella? Surely Godolphin—"

"No! He would never harm me."

"Then who?"

"All right. I shall tell you from the beginning. Did you ever—" she lowered her voice, eyes flitting to the door behind the counter. Someone could be heard humming faintly. "Did you ever see Mrs. Plympton wearing a necklace made of emeralds and diamonds?"

Pansy lifted her eyebrows. "That thing? Oh course I saw it—but wasn't it paste? An awful gaudy thing." She sniffed. "She was fond of telling everyone that her gentleman friend had given it to her as a gift. No one believed it to be real."

"Oh, it was real," Estella said. She told Pansy all about Bertie and the necklace, and how he had chased her, and what Violet had said to her that day in the wood.

"So that," Pansy said, "is why Violet was in the castle the day she died. She was looking for her necklace."

"Yes. I think so."

"And then Littlefield caught her?"

"I believe so. He must have attacked her with Godolphin's dagger, which he'd stolen from the tower, and left her for dead."

"Then promptly accused the earl of the murder to anyone who would listen." Pansy shook her head wonderingly. "This makes no sense at all," she murmured. She focused her eyes hard on Estella. "Why would he want to get rid of the earl? What are you leaving out?"

"He—" Estella gulped back her disgust. "He wants me for his wife."

Pansy's hand flew to cover her open mouth. "He can't have said such a thing."

"He did."

"Good afternoon, ladies!" a voice chirped.

Estella and Pansy both jumped and froze, like two bandits caught in a searchlight.

Pansy recovered first. "Good afternoon, Mrs. Hadley. We've just come in for some tea and cream buns."

"Oh ho, getting nippy outside, then, is it?" Mrs. Hadley grinned. "I know, 'cause when it was warm, ye were always askin' fer cream buns and lemonade." Her eyes fell on Estella, and she squeaked. "It's the countess!" She bobbed a curtsy. "Do forgive me, Yer Ladyship. I didn't recognize ye—ye look so much *smaller* up close."

Wonderful. Instead of giving a gracious nod, Estella blushed furiously. "It's a pleasure to make your acquaintance, Mrs. Hadley. I've heard wonderful things about your cream buns." *That* had come out sounding rather funny.

"I'll jest get you some, then," Mrs. Hadley exclaimed. "Raisin cakes, too. And of course, nice hot tea." She bustled into the back and out of sight.

"Your bruise," Pansy said sadly. She gently tapped her own cheekbone. "Do you think you ought to be walking about alone?"

Estella set her chin. "I won't allow Littlefield to terror-

ize me, and besides, Godolphin is going to have him arrested for trespassing—"

Mrs. Hadley returned, bearing a tray piled high with a
teapot, cups, and plates mounded with sweets. "Here you
are, Ladyship. Some nice hot tea will bring the roses back
to yer cheeks. If ye don't mind me sayin' it, ye look in
need of refreshment. What?" Mrs. Hadley gave Pansy a
half-jovial, half-reprimanding glance. "Ye tellin' her about
the ghost in the cemetery?"

Pansy forced a chuckle. "I was actually telling her that
by the time you're through with us, we'll have to be rolled
home in wheelbarrows."

"That's what I like to hear!" Mrs. Hadley placed four
plates on the table, then pointed to them in turn. "Cream
buns—Mrs. Lovely's favorite—lemon shortbread, chocolate biscuits, raisin cakes. And," she poured from the
teapot, "steamin' China tea." She curtsied, and was about
to retreat when she spun back around. "Yer Ladyship, and
I hope ye don't take offense at me being too forward, but
I jest wanted to tell ye that most of us women here in th'
village are pleased as punch that the earl has got hisself a
bride. Jest what we been needin', that's what we women-
folk all say." She curtsied again, and left.

"It has occurred to me," Pansy told Estella, "that we
must cancel the pantomime. With so many problems be-
leaguering you and the earl, how can we go on as though
nothing is wrong?"

"Oh no. We *must* go on. We must act as though nothing
is wrong."

The bells on the door jingled, and two women entered
the shop. Mrs. Hadley reappeared from the kitchen and
greeted her customers. "Will it be a loaf and six scones, as
usual, Margaret?"

"Aye. And a dozen tea cakes, too, dear."

Over the crinkle of brown wrapping paper, the women
gossiped.

"Ah, Betty," the second woman said, addressing Mrs. Hadley. "You missed a ruckus down at the courthouse not half an hour past."

"Indeed?" Mrs. Hadley cast a nervous glance Estella's way.

"Sure if the earl didn't order his constables to go after Littlefield, but the constables refused."

"Heavens! Might they do such a thing?"

Estella felt as though her limbs had turned to aspic. "I must go home, Pansy." Abruptly she stood and pushed her chair away. "Now."

"Shall I accompany you?"

"No, thank you. I will be fine." At least, she hoped so.

"Don't forget the honey cake receipt," Pansy said, digging in her reticule. "Here it is." She held it out.

Estella took it, folded it carefully and placed it into her own reticule. "Good afternoon, Pansy."

From Madame Pettibonne's
Treatise on Canine Behavior, Prepared Especially for the
Lady Handler

Hunters. Generally handsome, quick-witted and gregarious, this likable athlete is bound to turn the head of many a Lady Handler. If you possess one of these beasts, do not be surprised by his lack of loyalty. To the hunting dog, all of life is sport, every lady a potential mistress. I can reassure you only by saying he will come home eventually.

Many Lady Handlers ask me, "Might I retrain a Hunter to be loyal without breaking his spirit?" My answer is "Not likely!" In his prime, this happy, affectionate creature, so highly prized for his keen sense of fun, physical agility, and ability to retrieve whatever his mistress throws, cannot limit himself to a single lady. However, there are three solutions for the Lady Handler who, despite herself, cannot resist a Hunter:

1. Should you acquire a Hunter and find his playful na-

ture more than you bargained for, the first solution is to do absolutely nothing. Simply wait till time takes its inevitable toll and the Hunter has cavorted until he can cavort no longer. Alas, this may prove too painful for many ladies. They must tearfully part with their pet and begin anew.

2. If, Dear Reader, you cannot resist a Hunter and are willing to wait until he has matured, a second option is to acquire a less trying sort of dog with whom to bide your time until your Hunter returns to you. Should you accomplish this to your satisfaction, I send my heartfelt congratulations.

3. The third option is to purchase a retired Hunter. He will still have his handsome countenance (with perhaps a little dignified graying about the muzzle), his athletic drive, his charming personality, his wit. But now matured into a true gentleman, he will be faithful to his final mistress. Yet I must warn you, Dear Lady Reader, that to take this action is to guarantee that you will be utterly absorbed by this beast for many, many years. A word of caution: Do NOT acquire a retired Hunter if you wish to hone your handling expertise on more than one or two canines.

Estella rubbed her eyes. It did not sound as though Godolphin was a Hunter. She studied the tinted illustration. It depicted a handsome dog with silky, golden-brown fur posed nobly on a purple chair. Five beautiful ladies, all outfitted in décolleté gowns, French-heeled slippers, and white curly wigs, surrounded him.

No. Estella thumbed the corner of the page, flipped it. Godolphin barely had the patience for one lady, let alone several.

The Working Breeds. There is a sort of dog whose greatest urge in life is to serve others. This beast finds it difficult to derive much pleasure from daily existence. Life is a burden to be borne, a puzzle to be solved, a challenge to be survived. Though he will lay down his life for his mistress, he may seem to take little enjoyment from her presence. He has bigger problems to tackle, greater obstacles to confront.

Workers are generally large, strong, intelligent, courageous, and exceedingly handsome. However, they have little interest in the niceties of life, and will wander about with a matted coat or bleeding wound, hardly aware of the social codes they trample beneath their muddy paws. If the Lady Handler attempts to improve his appearance (and any Lady of Fashion would find it impossible not to), the Worker will growl even as he submits.

As troublesome as a Worker is, there is hardly a Lady Handler who will leave this dog to his own devices. Indeed, ladies clamor to train him. Why? Because, Dear Reader, utterly misguided as this type of beast is, he offers the most thrilling, potentially satisfying challenge of all the breeds.

Simultaneously, due to his fierce independence, and willful, domineering nature (indeed, many a Worker has been known to nip at the heels of his mistress as if she were cattle to be herded), ownership of him can be frustrating, even frightening. Workers have been known to duel to the death for the sake of honor, or in the process of protecting their mistresses.

This authoress, Dear Lady, does NOT recommend that a novice handler attempt to train a Worker. A favorable outcome simply cannot be guaranteed.

The black typescript covering the thick, well-thumbed pages blurred before Estella's eyes. She didn't know if she should feel relieved at having found so accurate description of Godolphin, or disheartened by Madame Pettibonne's grim warning. Estella was an utter novice, unless one took into consideration the various spotty, earnest young peers she'd waltzed with and teased during her single season in the ton. The likes of the hapless young Lord Spencer Buckleworth were mice in comparison with the masterful beast she'd unwittingly married.

She heaved a deep breath, pushed a stray ringlet from her eyes, and read on.

> *If, however, the Reader through no fault of her own discovers herself in the possession of a Worker, here are some hints which might help bring him to heel:*
>
> *1. Treat him as your adversary: He will never (unlike Toy Breeds and Hounds) undergo training willingly.*

Estella indulged in a smug little smile. She'd certainly managed to treat Godolphin as her adversary. Purely by instinct, too. Step One? Check.

> *2. A Worker MUST be rewarded continually for any behavior, be it voluntary or accidental, that his mistress finds agreeable.*
>
> *3. Above all else, a Worker values loyalty, trust and truthfulness. A Worker is a keen observer. Should he perceive even the slightest sign of disloyalty, untrustworthiness or untruthfulness in his mistress, he will surely slip free from his leash.*
>
> *4. Edible Rewards are rarely an appropriate prize for this type of dog. He prefers, above all else, petting: a scratch behind the ear, a stroke of the whiskers, a pat on the flank. The variations are as endless as they are effective. Petting will work wonders for soothing the Worker's moody disposition, and gradually tame him—as much as he is able to be tamed.*

"Crikey," Estella muttered. She reread the entire Working Breeds section, this time carefully noting and underlining with pencil. Now that she knew what sort of dog Godolphin was, she wasn't about to let any useful information go unnoticed.

For example, Madame Pettibonne wrote that edible rewards were "rarely" the thing for a worker. By definition, that meant that once in a while, at least, they *did* produce good results. Although Godolphin was of late far less beastly than he had been, there was still the matter of The South China Company, and his designs on Papa, that needed to be mended.

Anyway, it was too late. She'd already sent the note.

"Coffee, Your Lordship," Simkin said, bowing before placing the silver tray on Godolphin's desk in his tower study. This utterance would have been characteristically discreet, if it hadn't been for the way Simkin was puffing and wheezing.

Godolphin looked up from cleaning up the mess Bertie had made when he'd ransacked the study. "Good Lord, Simkin, are you quite all right?" he asked, alarmed at the way the butler's curled white wig was askew. "You oughtn't to have climbed all those stairs."

Simkin withdrew a handkerchief from his cuff and pressed it to his reddened forehead. "Pray do not worry, Your Lordship. Contrary to what one may surmise based on the way I hobble about, a spot of exercise is good for a gentleman of my advanced years."

Godolphin nodded slowly, unconvinced. He couldn't imagine life without Simkin. And he didn't want to have to. "Please, sit a moment before going back down. Catch your breath."

Simkin pulled his chin back into his ruffled collar, appalled. "Servants, Your Lordship, do not sit with earls."

"True, true," Godolphin sighed. He didn't know what had gotten into him. All these old customs and rules and tedious traditions suddenly felt so stifling. He wondered if Estella could be to blame.

Simkin poured coffee into the cup in a long, fragrant brown stream.

"Thank you," Godolphin murmured. "Next time, send one of the boys to climb the stairs with that heavy tray."

"Perhaps I would have this time, Your Lordship. However, I was entrusted by Her Ladyship with a missive to deliver to you."

Coughing, Godolphin forced himself to swallow a scalding sip of coffee. She was always up to something.

Simkin produced a folded note, sealed with a drop of red wax. "She said no one else must see it, Your Lordship." He placed it neatly on the desk beside the coffee tray.

Both men stared down at the note as if it were about to grow legs and scuttle away.

"By the way," Godolphin said, "I must apologize for the countess. She oughtn't to have forced you to play the harpsichord in the children's pantomime."

"Quite all right, Your Lordship."

Godolphin's eyes focused hard. He was certain Simkin had actually smiled a little. As though he *enjoyed* accompanying off-key village tykes.

"Will that be all, Your Lordship?"

"Yes." Godolphin frowned. The imp was casting her treacherously charming spell on the entire household.

Simkin bowed, and then melted away.

Godolphin tore open the note.

He hadn't seen her handwriting since that very first note she'd sent him, on that faraway day in Brighton. It was disconcerting how unfamiliar her handwriting was: neat, rounded, unmistakably feminine.

> *G—*
> *Meet me in the kitchens at five o'clock. I'll have a surprise waiting for you. —E*

Chapter Seventeen

The Proper Administration of Edible Rewards

"That is correct," Estella repeated to Cook. "We won't be having dinner tonight. In fact, wouldn't it be nice if you and all the kitchen staff took the evening off?"

Cook, a tall, narrow woman with a pigeon's breast and a carrot nose, peered at Estella as though she were crackers. "With all due respect, Your Ladyship, the evening meal is always prepared for His Lordship."

Estella laughed, still breathless from her journey to the kitchens. "That can't be so," she said, smiling. "What about when his Lordship was paying visits to Brighton this summer?"

"Ah, Your Ladyship, even then we cooked a meal every night, for we did not know when the master would return."

"No?" Estella twitched her eyebrows together. Godolphin was the most responsible gentleman she'd ever met. It wasn't like him not to inform his household staff, pretend or otherwise, of his plans.

Cook wiped her work-reddened hands on her apron. "He always said he'd be in Brighton but a few hours. But then he always stayed and stayed." She presented Estella with a curtsy. "I must say, Your Ladyship, an evening off would be most welcome to me and my girls. Thank you."

"Good, then." Estella looked about the kitchen. Arching stone vaults divided the various sections. A cavernous hearth, with black iron pots and skillets hanging on hooks, dominated one end. A long, salt-scrubbed plank table stretched across the center of the room, circled by wooden chairs. Bundles of onions and drying herbs dangled from the ceiling. One of the sections seemed to be a china closet, with blue painted cabinets filled with dishes. Another, judging by the burlap sacks and wooden barrels along the walls, was some kind of storeroom. "Where is the oven?"

Cook, who'd been happily untying her apron, froze. "Oh dear me, Your Ladyship. Were you planning on doin' some bakin', then?"

Estella tilted her chin up a notch. "Yes. I love baking." It was only a partial lie, really. As soon as she'd baked the honey cake and had tamed Godolphin via his stomach, she *would* love baking.

"I see." Cook didn't seem convinced. Nevertheless, she showed Estella across the flagstone floor, to the oven. It was huge, set in the wall, and coals smoldered in the bottom. "To take things in and out," she explained, "use these boards."

It looked simple enough. Estella gave a confident nod. "Brilliant," she said. "Now remember, no one is to come into the kitchen until tomorrow."

The note, already a little dog-eared from several reviews, was clutched in Godolphin's fist as he entered the kitchens at ten minutes after five o'clock.

At first glance, the cavernous chamber appeared to be empty. Annoyance made his neck tight, his eyes hot. The imp probably had another hide-and-seek game planned, like that night in the orangerie. If not an outright kidnapping. He stood still at the bottom of the stone staircase for a minute. Faint acrid smoke nipped his nostrils, but still he saw no one.

He wouldn't stand for it. Not this time. Wadding the note in one fist (it made a rather satisfying crunch), he swung around to head back up the stairs.

He stopped when he heard an indistinct *drat* behind him.

Striding forward so he could peer around one of the stone arches, his eyes widened in alarm.

There she was, his slight little bride, wearing an apron smudged all over with some brown mucky substance, trying to open the iron door of the oven. It seemed to have stuck, and she was tugging it to no avail.

"Shall I assist you?" he asked.

She jumped, then turned to face him. Her curls were utterly out of control, clouding around her face in unruly ringlets. Nonetheless, she beamed. "Godolphin. You've come. Is it five o'clock already?" She rubbed her forearm across her brow, leaving a trail of flour. "No, you needn't help. It's all under control."

It didn't *smell* like it was all under control. Unless she was making peaches flambé.

"Please, sit down." She gestured to the long kitchen table. It was covered with earthenware bowls, a sack of flour that had tipped over and spilt half of its contents across the tabletop, several brown eggshells, sticky-looking wooden spoons, and what appeared to be a clay pot of honey.

Godolphin lifted an eyebrow. "Sit down where?" The whole thing smacked of Estella's trademark frivolity. And, as always, her motives were as clear as bog water.

Still, his chest expanded with patience. Even affection. Maybe she was trying to thank him for his generosity in allowing her to keep the ledgers. That, of course, was only a temporary arrangement, until he'd figured out precisely where she'd hidden them.

She bustled over, pulling out a chair at the far end. "Here." Quickly, she brushed away a snowdrift of flour.

"Are aprons au courant these days?"

"Oh." She looked down her front. "I suppose they might be. All it would take would be a few of the more respected ladies of fashion to turn up at the opera wearing them."

Godolphin sat. "Would they be far too large and covered in honey?"

She pursed her lips in mock arrogance. *"Mais oui."*

"Perhaps," Godolphin added, noticing the black smoke billowing out of the cracks around the oven door, "you should check whatever it is you're making."

With a stifled squeal, Estella dashed to the oven, nearly tripping on her outsized apron, and with all the weight of her body, dragged the door open. A cloud of smoke worthy of a battlefield puffed out. Coughing and waving her hand before her face, Estella bravely stood before the oven. When the smoke had subsided, she pulled the pan from the oven on a long wooden plank, carried it over to the table, and set it before Godolphin.

He wasn't sure what his reaction was supposed to be. What rested on the plank was a round, cast-iron cake pan, and inside this was a hard looking substance that had splotches on the top as black as the pan itself. He cleared his throat, searching for a way to formulate the pressing question without hurting her feelings.

Luckily, she noted his confusion. "Honey cake," she chirped. But he heard the tremor behind her cheeriness. "Pansy gave me the receipt. I've never . . . this is just my first attempt. I hope to improve, and . . ."

Good Lord. She wasn't going to weep, was she? "It looks delicious. And as I said earlier, I love honey cake." He eyed it. The cake appeared to be deflating into a little rock. He swallowed. "Perhaps a cup of tea would go nicely."

At last, her expression brightened a little. "I've already

thought of that." Placing a cup before him, she poured tea from a clay pot. He watched her hands, distracted. They were bare, and a few flecks of cake batter stuck to the backs. But God, they were still lovely hands, soft-looking as peach satin, the nails pale rose and tapered. Although she was jittery, and her hands shook a little as she poured, the innate, noble grace of her movements shone through.

They were, he mused, the hands of a born countess.

And, by the look of the tea, which was barely tinged with amber, a countess who'd never made tea before.

Reaching out, he pushed out the chair that was on the diagonal from his and gestured for her to sit. With a weak smile—why was she so nervous?—she perched on the very edge, watching him with that bright periwinkle gaze.

Again, he stared down at the so-called honey cake.

The terrible truth stared him straight in the eye. He was going to have to eat it.

"It really does look revolting, doesn't it?" Estella said. She examined the honey cake as if it were a fossil in a museum. "The receipt called for more eggs than I could find. And I feared I wouldn't be able to tell bicarbonate of soda from rat poison, so I opted to leave it out entirely. Unfortunately, that seems to have been an essential ingredient." She lifted her eyes to Godolphin's and sighed. "You needn't eat it. In fact, it would probably be best if you didn't. I imagine such a thing could give one a belly-ache."

"Nonsense," Godolphin announced heartily. "Pass me a knife and fork, madam, and I will eat your culinary creation with relish."

Her eyes, glowing in the last light slanting through the kitchen windows, opened still wider. Without a word, she handed him a knife and fork, then watched, fascinated, as he began to eat.

When held upside down, the honey cake adamantly refused to dislodge from the pan. So he proceeded to poke through the top with a fork. It had the consistency of a boot sole. He lifted the first bite to his lips.

With the same iron resolve a man summons from the depths of his soul when preparing for the hangman's noose, he chewed and swallowed. It was very gummy, very sweet, yet filled with pockets of dry flour and little crunchy bits. Possibly eggshell. He lunged for his tea to force it down, tried not to grimace at the scalding, weak sip.

Estella had leaned forward watching, as though mesmerized. When he took up his fork for another bite, she burst out laughing. "You are brave. I must admit, I am honored that you pretend to enjoy the awful thing."

He forced down a second bite. "If your intention is to master the art of cookery, madam, it would not serve you well to have your husband turn up his nose at your virgin attempt."

She was staring at his cheek, and he wondered if she would comment again about his neglecting to shave. It seemed that more and more, he was too weary to bother.

Instead, she reached out one of those lovely bare hands and brushed his cheek. Her palm was like a flower petal; his groin stirred to life. "A crumb," she whispered. She met his gaze briefly, and then her eyes flicked away. The light was failing. The only illumination now came from the radiating orange embers in the fireplace. But he would have sworn that her eyes had betrayed shyness, coupled with a secret longing.

"And you," he replied, his voice so strained with desire that it barely made a sound, "have what appears to be honey on yours. Not to mention flour, and something near your eyebrow that could very well be cinnamon."

He watched as she swallowed, the skin of her neck shifting slowly.

"It would probably be most efficient," he went on, "if we did away with this honey cake, and I simply ate *you* instead."

Her eyes were cast down to the tabletop again, lashes shadowing over the curves of her cheeks. *"Sir,"* she breathed. By now, he knew she'd meant to formulate a retort dripping with maidenly outrage. But she couldn't quite manage it.

Though the ancient fear of rejection taunted in the back of his mind, the need of his body was a clamoring, begging, pulsing scream. Reminding himself of her status as a woman who'd only recently lost her maidenhood, however, he would go slowly. So, as he rose from the chair, pushing himself up with fists clenched with control, she was not startled. Her eyes were wrenched away from the tabletop, but her body remained still. He prowled slowly toward her, allowing her ample time to get away.

She stayed. By the time he'd moved the few feet to her side, his desire was raging white-hot, making it an effort of excruciating proportions to reach out just one arm, take her hand, and pull her to her feet.

What seemed like a decade, but was perhaps just two seconds, throbbed by. He kept her hand in his, trying valiantly not to squeeze too hard, and she looked up at him with an open gaze of wonder.

And surrender.

If she would have him here and now, at his bidding, he decided in a need-drenched rush, then she would be *fully* his. Fully tamed. Wasn't that all he wanted?

Her face was illuminated on one side by the golden light of the fire. The other side was was hidden in shadow.

"Estella." His intended whisper came out as a raw groan, and the stillness was broken. He dipped his neck, touched his lips to hers. "I see," he muttered, pulling back and licking his lips, "that you sampled the honey."

She shrugged, the corners of her lips twitching upward. "I couldn't resist." Then, in a gesture that nearly ripped his heart from his chest with its innocent simplicity, she coiled her arms about his neck, tugged his face close to her own, and kissed him.

The kitchen was gone, every care forgotten, pushed far away into a different, lower sphere. All that remained was her warm mouth, her cinnamon-scented cheeks, her body, soft and small pressing up against his chest, and, distantly, the persistent glowing heat of the fireplace. When she wiggled her moist honeyed tongue between his lips, he was done for.

He swiveled her around by her shoulders, pressing her against the edge of the kitchen table. Bowls clanked behind her, so with an impatient arm he swiped them aside. A metal spoon clattered to the stone floor. Estella jumped. They both cocked their heads to watch as the sack of flour overturned and poured in a billowing white stream to the floor.

"I want you," he told her, schooling the barbaric urgency in his voice. "But I don't think," he added, fumbling with the tie at the back of her apron, "I want you in this apron."

She blinked. "No?" Her voice was far away. Her arms hung obediently at her sides.

"No," he replied. "It reminds me of Cook." At last, he'd undone the knot, and he stripped the apron off, tossing it aside. Beneath she wore a simple gown of pale green. He eyed the neckline, where her chest was obscured by sheer white modesty panels. The gown would have to go, too. But he didn't have the patience to bother with it at this precise moment.

Wrapping his hands round her waist, he lifted her easily, set her so her bottom was on the table. God, she was so slight. It must be the fire in her eyes, her sparkling liveliness, that made her presence so intense.

Her arms were still wound around his shoulders, and now they clutched at him for balance, her feet wiggling in space.

He snagged her gaze with his and held it fast. With one hand he steadied her at the small of her back. With the other, he gripped the hem of her skirts (why did she wear so many blasted petticoats?), and shoved them upward.

This wasn't going to be like the last time. His hands

were free, he could touch whatever he liked, whenever he wished.

Her skirts rustled crisply, bunching around her upper thighs. He could not shove them as far as he'd like; her bottom anchored the last few tantalizing inches firmly to the table top.

"Oh dear," she gasped as her thighs instinctively clamped together.

Still, he could not help noticing how she clutched her hands still tighter into his shoulders. So hard, in fact, he felt the nip of her fingernails through his shirt.

An idea, almost shameful in its very deliciousness, hovered over him. That they didn't *have* to be an earl and countess, bound by duty, married by mistake, entrenched in tradition. If only for this moment, they could be lovers like all the other lovers through history. He was the footman, say, and she the luscious scullery maid. This notion, so refreshing, so freeing, spilled molten heat down his legs, coiled like the core of a volcano in his belly.

He gazed down, still clasping the hem of her skirts. He couldn't let go. How he longed to shred them away like a beast. "At last," he muttered, "I am allowed to see your more intimate perfections once again. It has been far, far too long."

Her sweetly rounded knees trembled.

Her calves were skimmed in cream-colored silk stockings, just sheer enough for him to make out the gleam of her skin beneath. One of her silver-blue satin slippers had fallen to the floor. Peering down through the shadow his own body cast, he thought he detected her toes curling inside the stocking. However, his attention was pulled upward, along beautifully turned calves, lingering once more on her knees, still clamped and quivering a bit, up to the rounded firmness of her thighs.

With one very careful finger, he reached down, tucking it under the snug ruched satin of her garter and allowing it to linger there. It was nearly impossible to decide whether the skin or the satin was smoother. But, he decided, the skin, being warm and alive, was infinitely preferable.

Hooking his finger, he wriggled the garter down a bit, revealing the faint pink dents the garter had made. These he caressed with a fingertip, in a swirling pattern, until he heard her gulp.

"You like that," he said, more of a comment than a question.

Her only response was a shuddering inhalation.

Then he traced a slow, deliberate line over the top of one thigh.

For a moment, it seemed her knees relaxed a bit. Indeed, glancing into her face, he saw that her lips were moistened, parted slightly. She sucked in another quick, sharp inhalation as his fingertip ran beneath the bunched-up skirts. It was hot under there. His hand, wedged between burning soft flesh and the crumpled cotton of her petticoats, was restless.

"Estella," he pleaded in a rough hiss, pushing his lips against her ear. Her hair smelled faintly of smoke and cinnamon. It tickled his eyelids. "Open for me."

Her breath had quickened against his chest, fingers digging still harder into his shoulders.

"Open," he repeated, more forcefully this time.

With a quivering sigh, her hips swiveled open. With a soft thud, the other slipper fell to the floor. His finger, having been poised so unbearably long in the hot crevice between her thighs, swam upstream to what was, at least at that moment, in that honeyed, rustling heat and ember-glowing dimness, the very center of the world.

"Oh God," he rasped. In that silky secret spot, she was damp.

He tore his hand away, fumbled with his belt and trouser buttons, yanked them down.

"Godolphin?" she squeaked. Her eyes were riveted to

his shaft, engorged and eager, thrusting forward and up. Demanding.

"I will try," he responded gruffly, spreading her knees with insistent palms, "to go more slowly than you did the last time." He bent his neck to kiss her again, to heat her blood, to make her open to him willingly.

As they ate of each other, honey-sweetened lips and tongues working themselves into a hot and frenzied primitive dance, she opened her knees wide, gripped the edge of the table, leaned back, shut her eyes.

Positioning his tip at the impossibly hot and heated entrance to her center, he pushed. But only a little. Her eyes flew wide, and she gasped. He slid deeper. Her gasp was louder this time. Her knuckles, wrapped around the edge of the table, had gone white.

He waited as long as he could bear. Then, spanning her waist with his hands, he thrust himself home with a groan.

She cried out in pleasure. She squeezed her eyes shut, held his shoulders as though he were the only anchor in a treacherous sea.

And that somehow made him want to fly. She trusted him. This wasn't about a woman performing her wifely duty. She wanted him close, held on to him. Trusted him.

So then, at least for this fragile moment, he was not alone in the world. He was part of her. Part of Estella. His wife.

And she was so wet, so warm, so sweet, and as he rocked his hips in an accelerating tempo, moving inexorably along the tide, in, out, in, out, he obeyed every law of the sea, every law of the moon and stars. He found inside this woman, like no woman before, the very essence of life and nature.

She'd found the tempo, too, reaching around to cup his back, to pull him still deeper inside. When she pressed her face into his chest, moaning, he felt the wet heat of her breath through the thin linen.

It was too much. He thought of her pleasure, yes, but there wasn't enough time. Greedy from more than a week of marriage with barely enough contact with the woman he craved, he could not wait.

He worked faster within her slippery heat, he buried his face in her hair, then spilled himself, shuddering, overflowing, deep inside her.

"I ought to apologize."

With great effort, Estella dragged one eyelid open. Her lumpy bed had never felt so comfortable and warm, and it seemed as if it had been ages since she'd had such a blissfully blank mind. Godolphin lay next to her, she saw blearily, head propped in one hand. She struggled upright on the puffy feather mattress.

"Apologize?" she mumbled sleepily. "What time is it?"

"Just before nine."

"In the *morning?*"

"Evening. You've been asleep."

It took her several moments to remember how they'd ended up in bed together in the first place. Then it came back in a rush that made her cheeks go hot. Her botched attempt at the Food Rewards Technique . . . or *had* it been botched, exactly? The honey cake.

Ravishment.

And then their secretive, laughing, hand-in-hand flight from the kitchen to her bedchamber.

Oh dear.

She burrowed back down in the bed, peered up at him over the edge of the sheet. "Why would you need to apologize?"

He wasn't beneath the covers, she noted. And, though he reclined on his side, he was fully clothed. Except— she peeked down to the foot of the bed—his large feet were bare.

Reaching out, he gently brushed a tangle of hair off her

forehead. "I was too impatient. I didn't wait for you to . . . it might've been nicer for you."   •

What on earth was he rambling on about? "I . . . um. Godolphin." She forced herself to look into his face. It was shadowy in the bedchamber, but someone had lit a fire at the far end of the room. His eyes were blue-black, glittering like gemstones. She was sure she detected a tinge of worry in them. "I did like it." Her ears were scorching. She had to look away.

"You did?"

"Did it seem as though I didn't?" she huffed. She had made what was, in her view at least, quite a wanton display on the kitchen table.

A hint of a smile danced on his lips. "Yes, I suppose you did. But, my darling"—he leaned closer, so close that the tip of his nose brushed hers—"there is more to Ravishment than that. You at least know that much from our . . ."

"Past episodes?"

"Mmm. It will take us several years just to cover the basics." His arm had worked its way under her neck. His grin was, in short, lascivious. "And the rest of our lives to perfect them."

She squeezed her eyes shut.

"Is there something wrong?"

"No. Yes. It's just that I was . . . remembering something."

"The note."

Drat. There was no way a moment could be more mortifying than this. She took a deep breath. "Yes."

"The one you sent me in Brighton." Humor glinted around the edges of his words.

Her eyes flew open, and she glared. "It's not funny."

"Yes, it is."

Again, she hoisted herself up against the squashy pillows, crossed her arms across her chest. She was still wearing her afternoon gown. It was disgracefully wrinkled. "I didn't know what it—Ravishment—meant," she muttered. "Otherwise I would never—"

"I know." He kissed her forehead. "Blame your mama." He brushed his lips across the arc of her eyebrow. "Or perhaps your nanny." He kissed her cheek. "Or was it your governess who shirked her duty?" He pulled his neck back a little, regarding her with mock earnestness.

She'd never seen him with his hair completely untied before. The deep brown locks, glossy in the firelight, just brushed the top of his collar. The loose tendrils made him look so wild. Like an ancient warrior who'd just ripped off his helmet.

"For my part, however," he went on, "I'd like to personally thank each one of those negligent ladies."

Estella frowned. "Why?" It was extremely distracting, the way his big body was hovering over her. The way she could hear the thump of his heart, see each bit of stubble on his chin.

The way something as hard as a rock—admittedly, she *did* have an inkling of what it was—was pressing into the top of her thigh.

"Because"—he lowered himself farther, so his taut, flat belly pressed against hers—"their negligence has allowed *me* the pleasure of teaching you exactly what Ravishment means. Consider what happened in the warehouse and your parents' house and the kitchens the first in a long series of lessons." His voice had dropped, low as a secret oath.

She had no choice but to nod. But she frowned as she did so, because it did not seem at all as though Godolphin had been tamed by the Food Rewards Technique. Instead, she felt as though *she* was the one being brought to heel.

He rolled off of her, and she felt chilled without him covering her. A sensation akin to anger curled in her chest; he couldn't just leave her all alone like that.

But he was nudging her onto her side, so her back was to him. Her body was as pliable as modeling clay. Under his wide palms, her limbs *had* to yield.

The first glimmer of arousal was a quicksilver flash between her thighs.

"I have always thought," he said in her ear, "that the base of a woman's neck was her most desirable asset."

She stared at the mounds of white linens and pillows before her, unseeing. All her attention was instead riveted on the sensation of his hands behind her. They deliberately pried open the top three buttons at the back of her gown.

"In the Far East," he went on, his breath skimming over her cheek, "the courtesans wear gowns especially designed to reveal this very spot."

The gown was gaping on top. Cold air swirled with the heat of his voice. Brushing her hair upward with one stroke, he kissed her there. "It is at once vulnerable and erotic. Somehow unattainable, for the woman herself cannot see that part of her own body. Yet at the same time, it is the source of all her strength and pride. How you especially, Estella, are able to hold your chin so high."

She held her breath as he fingered the silver chain around her neck. He said nothing, but only kissed the top of her spine again.

There were a series of tugs. Several more buttons were freed. More fumbling ensued, and then cool air rushed along the length of her spine.

"Um," she said.

"It's just your stays, darling. They couldn't be comfortable to sleep in."

"Indeed, I do not sleep in them. However, when in the company of gentlemen, I prefer to keep them intact." Her arguments seemed futile, considering she had no intention of moving from this languorous position on her side.

Anyway, he didn't pause for a second. There was a tiny whooshing sound as he whipped the laces from their eyes.

"I am not a gentleman," he retorted mildly. "I am your husband. Everyone knows that a husband deserves to see his wife fully unclothed at least once in his life."

"You already have," she gasped, as the gown and loosened stays were tugged down past her hips, leaving her torso and bottom utterly bare.

"No," he murmured. "Only the bottom half. Now I can see the top."

His fingertip, warm and probing, ran down the groove of her spine, bumping over the vertebrae, along the dip of her lower back, stopping just inside the cleft of her bottom.

"I have to make an amendment," he announced, circling his palm over her buttock.

"Indeed," she mumbled. Her eyes had fallen shut. There was nothing but the seductive rumble of his voice, the smooth warmth of his skin against hers, the delicious surrender of her entire backside laid bare for her Ravisher.

"Yes. While the base of your neck is succulent in its way, and I was altogether smitten with your knees when I saw them dangling over the kitchen table, I am wondering now if, perhaps, your loveliest asset is in truth your lower back." With the back of his hand he stroked the dips next to the base of her spine. "You've the sweetest golden fuzz there. Just like a peach. And two matching dimples at the back of your hips."

She wasn't certain if his intention was to torment her, but tormenting her he was. Because, though it felt awfully good to have him speaking like that in her ear, and touching her, she craved his touch elsewhere. Lower. Instinctively, she arched her back.

"And when you do *that*," he went on in a hushed, scolding tone, "I've no option but to conclude that this rump of yours is the pinnacle of earthly delights."

He grabbed her buttock, kneading it till she trembled. Then he wasn't touching her anymore, but fumbling about behind her. The feather mattress bobbed, and there was a soft swishing thud as something hit the floor.

When he touched her again, it was with his whole naked body pressed against her back. He was warm, taut with well-used muscles, and she felt the tickle of his chest hair between her shoulder blades. He buried his face in her hair, positioned himself at her entrance, squeezed himself snugly inside.

"Oh," she gasped.

"I was completely wrong on all counts," he whispered against her neck. "*This* is your perfection beyond all perfections." He began to thrust, burying one big arm under her neck, and reaching over her with the other to touch the spot that had been begging to be touched all along.

Their hips rocking gently, pressing deeper and harder into the feather mattress, he rubbed her in a circular motion. She didn't know which felt best—the way he filled her and completed her inside, or the hot spirals of blooming fuchsia heat building between her thighs, under his delving fingertips.

At some point all sensations melded into one, and as his thrusts deepened, his fingers pushed her off a high cliff into the sky. As he shuddered himself to completion inside her, she drifted down through the clouds, relaxed back into his sheltering chest, and slept again.

Godolphin waited until Estella's breathing became deep and regular. Then, moving slowly, he disentangled himself from her and rose from the bed. Standing over her, he watched her. In sleep, all of the little devil in her face was wiped away. All that remained was the angel.

His heart lurched. After all that she'd done, and all that he'd done to her, all the lies, the manipulations, the sneakiness and stealing of keys and ledgers . . . After all of that, he still felt incredible tenderness for her. And beyond that, something else. Something that felt so big, so important and overwhelming, that he dared not think about it.

Once he was certain she would not wake, he pulled on his trousers.

He'd never been in love. It was laughable even to think it. Estella had an erotic hold over him, that was all.

That's not all, a tiny voice whispered in the back of his mind.

He shushed it. This wasn't the time. Her white leather prayer book sat on her dressing table, in plain view. A stealthy trip across the carpet, however, confirmed that it was locked tight.

Moving slowly, he bent over the bed. He reached for Estella's neck.

With a sigh, she rolled onto her back.

He pulled away, froze. He waited several beats to ensure she was still sound asleep. Then he leaned over her again.

It would have been easier if she'd stayed on her side. The clasp of the delicate silver chain had been in plain view. Now, it was behind her.

Delicately, he pulled the chain, swiveling it around her neck two inches.

In her sleep, she made an inelegant sniffing sound.

He smiled. Even that was somehow endearing. He pulled on the chain again, and the clasp came into view—

Just as her round periwinkle eyes popped open.

"Godolphin?" she said, her voice thick with sleep, but her eyes questioning. "What're you doing?"

It occurred to him to drop the chain, to kiss her, to deny any wrongdoing. But there had been enough lies between them already. He was itching with curiosity to see inside that book of hers. He held the clasp gingerly and stared straight down into her eyes. "I," he stated softly, "am removing the chain from around your neck."

Chapter Eighteen

The Ledgers Decoded

Estella struggled upright in the bed, and for fear of hurting her, he dropped the chain.

"You can't—it's for my private book," she said. "My prayer book."

"I have reason to believe it isn't a prayer book at all."

Her lips parted. She was breathing heavily.

"And now"—he leaned over her once again—"I am going to remove this key from your neck."

She didn't jump out of the bed. She didn't try to wriggle out of his reach. Instead, she sat perfectly still, eyes averted, and allowed him to remove the key on its silver chain.

Something like shame rippled through him as he stalked across the room to the dressing table and the book. But he was a proud enough man to also gloat a little at his victory.

She'd allowed him to remove the chain, meek as a lamb. Which could only mean one thing: The imp was fully tamed.

He picked up the book.

"Godolphin," she called, the softest of wails.

He fit the key into the lock.

"Godolphin, please don't think poorly of me. It's—
Lady Temple—"

He pried the book's covers apart.

"She gave it to me. As a wedding gift. It's just a—"

"What in the blazes?" Godolphin said under his
breath. It wasn't a prayer book at all, but what appeared
to be a French dog training manual. His ribs stopped
clenching. "For Maggie," he said, relieved. He gazed
back at Estella. She looked very small, her bare shoulders
pale, the bedclothes clutched to her chest. "I am sorry,
darling. For some reason I thought . . ." He shook his
head with a laugh. "I don't even want to tell you what I
thought." Idly, he flipped through the pages. "Why do
you bother locking it up and carrying the key about with
you everywhere? It's not as though Maggie can read and
realize what sort of clever tricks you're employing to
train her."

Silence from the direction of the bed.

He glanced up. A look of utter horror had transfixed
Estella's features.

He looked back down at the book.

What in hell *was* it? He flipped to the preface, noted
the etching of one Madame Pettibonne, Lady Handler
and Dog Trainer extraordinaire. She of the high wig and
exceptionally low, bountiful bodice. He thumbed, reck-
lessly, through page after page.

Estella said nothing.

Canine Personality Traits, Hound Behavior, Training
the Toy Breeds—with a canine in a royal blue jacket who
looked remarkably like the decorator Pepys.

Then he flipped to the chapter on the Working Breeds.
The heading Working Breeds was starred with pencil, and
someone had jotted *Godolphin!* beneath. The following
chapter was heavily underlined, asterisked, circled, and
annotated.

Pain stabbed at his temple, his lungs felt sore. He
could barely bring himself to look at her. "I recognize

your handwriting from the notes you've sent me," he ground out.

"It's not what you—"

"Not what I think?" His voice was shaking. "Yes, I believe it is."

"It's not so bad—I—"

"Silence." He did not yell. Instead, his voice had dropped to a low snarl. "Do not leave until I finish reading this."

Mute, she nodded. She looked as though she was about to cry.

Fine.

He slumped down on the dressing table stool, and began to read.

> *From Madame Pettibonne's*
> *Treatise on Canine Behavior, Prepared Especially for the*
> *Lady Handler.*
> *An Urgent Word of Caution.*
> *Dear Lady Reader, please take heed in what I am about to relay, for it will save you much time and heartache. There are some dogs who cannot be trained!*
>
> *I am certain that my more astute students have already suspected this, whether from observing the Toy Breed who cannot be housebroken, the Terrier who nips at small children and chews the draperies, or the Working Breed who coldly ignores his mistress. These beasts are beyond redemption, and simply not worth the bother.*
>
> *"How," you may query, "may I determine if my pet is one of these hopeless cases?" What follows is a series of questions to aid you in this heart-wrenching decision.*
>
> *1. Has his training been in progress for two or more weeks, with no sign of improved behavior?*
>
> *2. Does his behavior give the outward appearance of improvement, only to relapse more than once per week?*
>
> *Or, more frighteningly, is he aware of your efforts, yet still angry and stubborn?*
>
> *1. Does he routinely rebel against your training efforts?*

2. Does he scoff at and make light of your training efforts?

3. Does he publicly flaunt his refusal to comply with your training efforts?

Alas, should the answer be affirmative to more than one of these questions, it is advisable to set your canine free and replace him with a tamer sort of creature.

He couldn't read any more. It made him ill, and purple splotches fogged his vision. His head ached, every inch of his skull pulsing with rage. There was disappointment, too, somewhere deep inside. That was like a small cowering animal, soft and hurt. The anger was easier to manage, his self-righteous fury almost delicious in its intensity.

"I have known," Godolphin said, slamming the manual shut, "husbands and wives who have chosen to live apart—"

Estella sucked in a painful breath. She'd never seen her husband so near the verge of losing control.

"—and it's really not as uncommon as you'd think. Unfortunately, now that we've shared a bed, an annulment is out of the question. That is, unless you're willing to lie." He rubbed a palm across his jaw, in that gesture which had become so dear.

"*Annulment?* You would speak of annulment again? Now?"

Coolly, he turned to eye her up and down. As though appraising a criminal in his court.

She was shrinking.

"I do realize," he said, "you've proven yourself quite willing and capable of lying, as long as it suits your purposes."

"That's not true." Quickly, she wound a sheet around her naked body and stepped out of the bed. She rushed across the room, hugging the sheet around her like a toga, but halted several paces from him. There was an impenetrable barrier around him. Invisible, yet harder than a fortress. "I admit, I may have misled you about the contents of the book, but I never told an outright lie. I simply didn't correct you when you assumed it was a prayer book." She swallowed, tongue dry.

"Then the option of not using the book at *all* didn't occur to you?"

"What was I supposed to do? Hand it over for your approval? Besides, Lady Temple said that I oughtn't show the book to anyone, so—"

"Lady Temple." He laughed, a soft, dangerous laugh, shaking his head. "Lady Temple gave you that preposterous book." Deliberately, he placed the book on the dressing table. He rose, so he was towering over her.

Her voice chose at that instant to stop working entirely.

"Just when we gentlemen think it's safe, that we've figured out all your tricks, you women come up with another one."

"You're being too *serious*," she pleaded, recovering her speech. "It was just a lark between Pansy and me. I didn't think it would work—and it didn't, did it?"

"That's beside the point. And the *vicar's wife* was in on this?" He snorted.

"No, it's not beside the point. If you'd suddenly become some sort of groveling slave, consenting to my every whim, perhaps you'd have grounds to be angry. But since you're just as undomesticated as ever—"

"Undomesticated?"

"Well, yes." She gulped. "I didn't want to break your spirit. I just wanted to create a marriage that was tolerable. I wanted you to be less ill-tempered. I wanted a husband who trusted me. One whom I could trust, who wasn't trying to frame my own father for a crime he didn't commit." Tears sprang up behind her eyelids. "A husband who loved me." Checking herself, she wiped her eyes on the sheet. "To tell the truth, the only behavior I wanted to change was your rude entrances and exits." She tried out a weak smile. It felt too beseeching, though, and she let it drop away.

Unmoved by her stab at a smile, he appeared even more furious. Looming, heavy, silent.

"And," she stumbled on, "Madame Pettibonne's manual seemed to offer a solution."

"I wanted a marriage that was tolerable, too," he cut in sharply. "A wife who'd allow me to sleep by her side, who didn't"—he stalked closer—"treat me as her adversary."

"Is there not a bond between husband and wife—between us—that might transcend all this nonsense? For I have trusted you with my body." She tried to swallow away the salty-sour taste of tears. When she spoke again, her voice was uneven. "I trusted you with my maidenhood. With my *heart*. I believed, if only for moments here and there, that you trusted me."

He turned halfway, staring out the windows, at the nighttime sea. In the weak starlight, his face looked ten years older. And so very far away. "None of that means anything." He shoved his hands in his pockets.

She was certain they'd been shaking.

"People are willing to say anything in the afterglow of lovemaking." His voice was almost brutal now. "It's only—"

"That's not true!" The passion had come back, like a jolt of pure life. She wouldn't allow him to discount what they had shared. "I cannot speak for you, but I felt something real. I *feel* something real. Right now."

For a fleeting moment, the muscles in his jaw tensed, as if she'd struck a nerve. Then his features settled back into distant coolness.

Desperation hit her, making her pulse surge forward. She moved close to the window, next to him. He could still stare out into the night, but she'd be in his peripheral vision. She wouldn't let him disregard her completely, blot her out as if none of this had ever happened.

There was nothing left for her without him. This reality was as stark as the black night.

Her old life was over. There could never be any other man for her.

"Please listen!" she pleaded.

Snatching up the book, he made for the door. "Do think about whether you'd like to lie in order to obtain an annulment. It'd probably be for the best."

"Think about what you're saying! An annulment at this point is impossible—"

He ignored her, kept walking.

Stunned, Estella watched his retreating back. His bare shoulders were rigid. When he passed by the bed, he snatched up his shirt and shrugged it on, still holding the book.

She felt as if she'd been slapped. "I'll give you the ledgers if you give me the book back," she blurted out. It was a gamble, but she knew that, whatever was in those ledgers, Papa was innocent.

He stopped, turned slowly.

Relief washed over her, and her fists relaxed. He was going to be reasonable.

But when he turned, his expression was as disdainful as ever. Perhaps even more so. "You'll say anything, won't you? I should've realized you were the most manipulative little chit to ever emerge from the ton when you tried to trick me on the beach in Brighton. I got the better of you then, but now I rather wish I hadn't."

The bedchamber walls and ceiling, it seemed, were moving in. Soon they'd crush her under all that plaster and paint and upholstery. And she'd be glad. Because nothing could hurt more than this.

"As I was saying before," he continued, "if you won't lie to obtain an annulment—which seems hard to believe, since lies flow from you like air—we'll have to settle for one of those fashionable arrangements where the husband lives in one place and the wife in another. I'll stay at Marblegate House, perhaps, or even here. I know you hate the castle, and you'd be happier if I set you up with a townhouse in Mayfair. Or even a villa abroad, if that's what you'd like. Fitting for a spoiled princess like you, don't you think? A sort of wedding trip you could take all by yourself. Escape the inevitable scandal and gossip. After the coming Season is over, everyone will be bored with us, anyway."

She couldn't look at him anymore. She wanted to dash away. But her bare feet felt as if they were glued to the floor, and all she could do was stare at the carpet near his feet. She couldn't believe she'd once thought the pattern was pretty. It resembled a seething mass of worms and flies. Her eyelids drooped shut. Her mind went numb.

"I suppose I'm one of those dogs who simply isn't worth the bother," he snarled. "At least, that's what your French slattern-slash-authoress would say. Now, if you'll kindly excuse me, I'm going to make one of those rude exits you tried so diligently to train out of me."

He was pulling away, and she felt smaller and smaller, and so alone. In one instant, she realized how foolish she'd been to try to use the manual on a man like Godolphin. A man whom she liked and respected. And more.

"I love you," she said sadly, mostly to herself. She didn't think he'd hear.

He froze, one hand on the doorknob. Slowly, he turned. His eyes glowed strangely, and his expression was unreadable. "What did you say?"

She swallowed. There was no sense being cagey about it. She did love him, and though he clearly didn't feel the same, it felt wonderful to say it out loud. How long had this feeling been there?

She took a deep breath. "I love you, Godolphin. I don't want an annulment. I'm sorry about the book. I—I made a mistake. It was foolish and childish, and I'd do anything to take it back. You must believe me when I say I meant no harm."

His hand fell away from the doorknob. He was walking toward her. His feet were still bare, and he wore trousers, but his shirt was unbuttoned, billowing a little to either side to expose his hard brown torso.

Estella was rooted to the spot. She still clutched the rumpled bed sheet around her, but it had slipped down on one shoulder.

He stopped abruptly, three paces away. His bruise-colored eyes crackled, and his lips curved slightly up. "Come to me," he said in an undertone.

She tilted her head. "Come?"

"Prove that you love me. That you're tame."

She loved him—she knew it. But she was too proud, and far, far from being tame. She tossed him a half smile, hoping that her sudden desire for him wasn't too obvious. "*You* come."

He chuckled softly. "And prove that this blasted book has gotten the better of me?" He looked down at Madame Pettibonne's manual in his hand, and then flung it off to the side. It landed with a crash somewhere across the room. "I've come this far. You come the rest of the way."

"But I told you that I love you, and you said nothing of the kind."

"Then let's meet in the middle." He pointed to a spot in the carpet between them. "Then we'll both be tamed."

"Or both of us"—Estella stepped one pace forward—"just as undomesticated as ever."

He closed the distance between them with a single stride, and dragged her to his chest. The bedsheet slithered to the floor, but she didn't care. She was naked, pressed against the warm chest of her husband, the man she loved. Nothing else was even real.

He tilted her chin up, stared down into her eyes. His own gaze was sparkling, and she'd never seen him look so happy. "I love you," was all he said. He kissed her.

All the jarring desire was there, even more intense than the previous times they'd kissed. There was something else there now, too. Something sweeter, something that felt new and old at once, as though it was going to last forever.

Forever? No, it couldn't. Not when their entire marriage was based on lies.

She pulled away, something hardening under her ribs. "Let's destroy the ledgers and the book. We can burn them."

He blinked, his arms around her, stroking her back. "A sign of good faith, do you mean?"

"Yes. And of trust."

His eyes were hazy for a moment, thoughtful.

Her stomach sank. He was thinking about Papa, and his plans to—

"All right. Where are the ledgers?"

She grinned. "I'll get them."

Godolphin watched with unmasked interest as Estella, utterly unclothed, retrieved the ledgers. She had to drag a large armchair to the bedside, and then climb on top of it in order to reach over the tapestry canopy. The ledgers were already a little dusty.

Once down from the chair, Estella twined the sheet around her again, then brought the ledgers to the hearth and Godolphin.

He crouched to stoke the fire. "Did you look at the ledgers?" he asked in a careful voice.

"I glanced at them. It would take a great deal of study to make heads or tails of them, I'm afraid."

He glanced up at her, over his shoulder. "They're encrypted?"

"Yes. Just like your Marblegate House records. You and Papa are alike in that way. . . . Do you mean to say that you don't know what's in them? After all of that?"

He looked almost sheepish. "I was told by the man who sold the Brighton warehouse to your father—"

"Milton."

"Yes. He informed me, just before he left for good, that your father kept incriminating records. When I discovered Bertie was looking for ledgers, too, I was sure Milton had been telling the truth. Would you allow me to look at them? Before we destroy them?"

Her throat tightened.

"Not if you don't want to. I'm only curious. I've been chasing after the blasted things for so long, and now we're going to burn them."

"You won't try to hold anything in them against Papa?"

"I couldn't even if I wanted to. I'd need the actual ledgers in any court . . . in any situation."

"I can't believe you would think of taking Papa to court and—" She took a huge breath. "I know about The South China Company. That it's yours, and how you and Papa have been in neck-and-neck competition for years. Is that why you wanted to frame Papa? For the sake of your business?" She'd finally said it, but now she was afraid to hear the answer.

His face was open with surprise. "My business never had anything to do with this."

She stared. It truly seemed as though . . . as though he meant it. The relief she felt was like fresh air.

"Please." He wrapped a hand around her bare ankle. "Let's speak of this some other time."

She swallowed. "All right." She sat down on the little sofa facing the fire. "Let's look at these ledgers."

He glanced at her, surprised, but placed the coal rake on its hook and came to sit beside her.

Estella opened the ledger marked *I*.

The records began with the year 1799.

"That's the year you were born, isn't it?" Godolphin said.

Estella nodded. Then she frowned. "And the first entry is . . . my birthday."

"So it is."

They both stared at the long columns, filled with black ink. The first column had dates, then a space filled with abbreviated words, and then two columns of pound amounts. The first seemed to be the amount paid for whatever was in the second column, and the last a running tally of expenses.

Estella flipped page after page, with mounting confusion. They were all filled with the same sorts of columns. "I don't think these have anything to do with Papa's business."

Godolphin had opened the ledger marked *II*. "More of the same in here. What's this?" He pointed to a line, sounding as though he was about to laugh.

Estella stared down at the page. *Wlsh. Pny.,   1.* "Welsh . . . pony? One Welsh pony?" Then she started laughing. "Dated April 17, 1807. Strawberry! That's a record of my pony Strawberry's purchase!"

Godolphin flopped his head on the sofa back, laughing, too. "These ledgers are full of your personal expenses, darling. Or rather, all that your Papa spent on you through your life."

Estella whipped through page after page, scanned column after column. She couldn't believe that so much money had been spent on her during her short life. Godolphin had been right; in some ways she really was a spoiled princess.

"Five *pounds* on what appears to be honeysuckle soap," Godolphin chuckled. "And here—in the year 1816, a single visit to your modiste came to twelve pounds six pence."

"Oh, stop." Estella jabbed him with an elbow. "It's not unusual for a girl of my position in London. That might've been my presentation gown, besides."

"But why did your father keep such scrupulous track of all of this?"

"He keeps scrupulous track of absolutely everything. It's just his habit. What I don't understand is, why were these particular ledgers locked up in that safe in the warehouse?"

Godolphin didn't answer, but scooped up the ledger marked *III*.

"Perhaps," Estella went on, "they were intended as a decoy? Did he know you were looking for them?"

"I don't know how he could have. I learned about the

ledgers from Milton, remember. But it rather looks like Milton duped me." He frowned. "I did have to pay him for the information—perhaps he only wanted to make a bit of extra blunt, and he saw I was eager for information."

"What did Milton say they contained?"

"He was rather cryptic. Information to do with smuggling, he said, worth its weight in gold. And then when I realized that Bertie wanted them so badly . . ."

Their eyes locked. "Bertie," Estella mouthed. "Milton must have told Bertie about these ledgers, too. He tricked him."

Godolphin tipped his head, thoughtful. "Perhaps Bertie paid him for the information, like I did."

"It doesn't make sense. Papa isn't a smuggler, and Bertie knows that."

Godolphin flipped through the third ledger. "No matter what your father's intentions were, you are one expensive little creature." He clucked his tongue like a disapproving schoolmaster.

Estella stared into the fire. "I admit, I feel a little ashamed. I don't know if I've ever really thought about how expensive my style of living has been."

Godolphin gave her a squeeze. "It's all right. You're a sweet, good person."

"You've told me on at least one occasion that I'm spoiled—"

"That was before I really knew you." He kissed her forehead. "And you are a lovely princess who deserves the best of everything." He grinned. "I might have to sell off one or two of my country houses to keep you in shoes"—he placed a fingertip on a line in the ledger for a Bond Street shoemaker's bill—"but I'm perfectly willing to do so."

"Stop teasing."

"Sorry. I happen to love the way it makes your cheeks go all pink." He flipped to the last filled page of ledger

III. "I wonder if the expense log carries all the way to your wedding day."

They both studied the final page.

Estella's belly twisted. The final entry read, in clear, non-abbreviated English: *Silver, Ivory, and Gold Berezka pistol, One. Wedding gift to Estella from Papa.*

"That was the gun you used to kidnap me with," Godolphin remarked wryly.

"I never knew whom it was from. I thought Bertie, even, or Lady Temple, or . . . I don't know who else. I never suspected Papa. And why?"

"Why indeed. Perhaps to give you something to protect yourself from your new husband."

Estella gave her head a vigorous shake. "Papa would've never consented to our marriage if he thought I'd require a *pistol* after the nuptials, Godolphin. No. He knew someone could be a threat, but he wasn't thinking about you."

Again, their eyes met over the open ledger. Orange firelight wavered between them.

"Bertie," Estella finally said. "Papa knew about Bertie, and he trusted me—trusted you, too, no doubt, to set things right." She watched the licking flames in the grate. "Shall we burn them? And the . . . the other book?"

Tenderly, he kissed her ear. "We needn't. But no more deceit, Estella. No more lies, no more secrets, and, for God's sake, no more training me to be a lady's lap dog. We've got to work together to make certain Bertie doesn't destroy the village, and whatever else he has planned."

Solemn, Estella nodded. "Yes."

Chapter Nineteen

In the Caves

From Madame Pettibonne's
Treatise on Canine Behavior, Prepared Especially for the
Lady Handler.
Varying Personalities of the Domesticated Breeds.

Terriers. This sort of beast is suitable only for a certain sort of lady. She must be robust, patient, and levelheaded in order to endure a relationship with this scrappy creature.

Terriers tend to be small, possessing short, bandy legs and a great deal of fur all over the body. (Although, quelle horreur, I have had the occasion to meet more than one Terrier who had fur everywhere except on the top of his head!) Terriers adore tidbits. Alas, they are prone to obesity, so these must be administered sparingly. They are generally not considered handsome, but under their dowdy exteriors lurks the cunning of foxes. Many an otherwise fine little beast, however, is blighted by a rash of defects and bad habits loathsome enough to make even the most stouthearted Lady Handler think twice before adopting a Terrier as a pet.

What follows is a list of common Terrier foibles, along with suggestions regarding how to mend (or at least modify) them:

1. *Sneakiness. Cursed with an intelligence that surpasses their modest size, maladjusted Terriers are frustrated with their lot in life and will stoop to any means to achieve what other more comely creatures gain easily. Like canine magpies, Terriers are also prone to stealing small, shiny objects from their mistress's chambers. The Lady Handler must keep a close eye on such a naughty little beast.*

2. *Snapping. Terriers are given to nipping when agitated. This can be an awkward habit, for even in his most intimate moments with his mistress, the overly excited Terrier may snap, harming the lady. In my youth, I struck upon the notion to amuse myself with a Terrier while my Hunter was frolicking in the boulevards and at the opera house. I paid the price, Dear Lady Reader, for when my Terrier found out, he nipped me. To this day, I am obliged to wear a beauty patch to cover the scar.*

3. *Aggressiveness with Other Dogs. The Terrier is rarely enamored of other dogs, and indeed would appear at times to be desirous of a brawl. The affable Hunters rarely can be distracted from their various games to fight; likewise, the Working Breeds can only be goaded into a growl. The Toy Breeds will respond to the Terriers' insults, though, and nasty brawls may ensue. NEVER keep a Toy and a Terrier in the same house; the flying fur and yips are ungodly.*

It must be mentioned that, above all else, there are certain of this breed that can never be trained. Unlike other breeds who merely abandon an unwanted mistress, these nasty little gentlemen will take their revenge. So, my dear Lady Handler, be forewarned: A TERRIER WILL TURN ON YOU!

"Look around you!" Bertie cried to the crowd of men ringing his table at The Wicked Mermaid, Village Seabrook's tumbledown public house. "The earl has abandoned you for years, leaving you without even a schoolmaster for your young ones! Now he's gone and murdered, in cold blood, one of your own! Why? Because he thinks he can get away scot-free because he's a blue blood!"

A resentful murmur rose from the crowd. Their rough faces shone with too much ale.

Bertie resisted a satisfied smirk. It was necessary that he act like one of them, so he ordered another pint, then raised it with his one arm, mainly to draw attention to the fact that he had but one.

"What happened t' yer nose, Littlefield?" a stringy-haired fisherman asked.

Perfect. "The earl did this to me." For emphasis, he touched a finger to his broken nose, which was in a plaster.

The crowd gasped, cursing Godolphin's hide.

"What about yer arm?" another man called.

"Again, the earl. He never did apologize." Bertie shrugged. "Of course, a man like that would never consider that he should. After all, he was captain while I was but a junior officer."

There were more mutters and curses directed at the earl. Bertie seized the moment, slamming his tankard on the table. "We cannot allow a parasite like Godolphin to continue to run this village into the ground! He must be stopped! He's holding his wife captive, a poor young thing he took to wed by force—"

More astounded murmurs.

"That's not so!" A high, feminine voice pierced through the men's grumbling. All heads turned to a red-cheeked young woman standing in the door of the pub, a baby slung on her hip.

Trust a biddy with a slobbering infant to throw a wrench in his plans. "You assert," Bertie said coldly, "that the earl has made this village a fine place to live and raise your children?"

The men grunted.

"No," the woman said. "Seabrook's a miserable place, but it in't because of th' earl! The countess is a charming young lady, and I happen t' know she loves 'er husband."

Bertie steepled his fingers. "What, pray tell, does this have to do with the earl's heartless ruination of Seabrook?"

"Th' ruin of this village is due to the fact that for the past three years you"—she prodded a finger in Bertie's direction—"have been payin' our menfolk t' smuggle instead of workin' th' fishin' boats and tillin' th' fields. Th' smugglin's brought in bad folk from out on th' Channel, and made our menfolk lazy."

The crowd of men barked and sneered in protest, and turned their backs on the woman.

Bertie smiled. "Who's with me to drive the earl out? My assistant beside me here will take your names and furnish you with advance payment."

The men jostled to the table's edge.

Teeters, a fastidious sneer on his lips, wrote their names neatly in a ledger.

Estella stared down at the note that the messenger boy had delivered. She struggled to read it a third time, because her hands were shaking.

My Dear Estella, it said in a hasty scrawl, *Please exercise the utmost caution today, for the ladies of the village have informed me that Bertram Littlefield has assembled a group of village men, and they intend to go to the castle to confront His Lordship, some say even to depose him. Do take care, and remember that Edwin and I welcome both you and your husband at the vicarage at any time of day or night. Your friend, Pansy Lovely.*

The note floated silently to the floor. "Godolphin," Estella croaked, walking blindly from the parlor. Then, more loudly, *"Godolphin."*

Godolphin knew something was wrong as soon as he reached Castle Seabrook's gate.

"Whoa, girl," he murmured to the chestnut mare he'd ridden into Brighton. The horse ignored him, eager to get back to her stable. He reined her in harder, and she pranced to a stop.

The old iron gate gaped open. It was customarily kept shut, although never locked. Now, one half of the gate was crooked. Someone, or rather, several strong men, had broken the hinges.

He dug his heels into the mare's sides and turned back onto the road.

Estella raced up to the tower study first, but Godolphin wasn't there. Next she tried his bedchamber, and even hers, but she couldn't find him anywhere. She tore about the castle, her thoughts a frantic muddle, looking for him, Maggie following with her ears slicked back. Every room was empty.

No servant could be found, either, nor was there any sign of Pepys and his workmen. She even went down to the kitchens. No one was there. On the big wooden table, a mound of fresh vegetables sat half-chopped. At the fire, a copper kettle sputtered; it had been left unattended and the water had boiled off.

It was clear that the servants had fled, and on the spur of the moment. Someone must've warned them of Bertie's plans. Why had no one warned *her*?

She ran back up the stairs, now and then calling Godolphin's name.

No answer. She was alone in the castle.

She couldn't hitch a carriage herself, let alone drive it. She thought she could figure out how to saddle a horse, though, and Maggie could run alongside. So she ran through the dining room and down the long corridor to the front door.

Halfway down the corridor, she froze in her tracks. Someone was pounding on the door.

Maggie began to growl.

She heard the hinges of the front door creak open, then the angry shouts of men.

She knew she ought to have run the other way. But the sheer gall of Bertie coming to her home like that made her angry. Head held high, she marched to the entrance foyer.

She expected to see Bertie and a crowd of men, but instead she saw the stooped, liveried form of Simkin standing at the door.

"His Lordship is not at home at present," Simkin said in a loud, dignified tone to whomever was outside.

"Balls and blatherskite!" someone shouted.

"He's never a' home!" cried another. "That's exactly th' problem!"

Someone shoved the door, and Simkin stumbled, but held fast to the door handle. "I will," he said, "tell him that you've come calling, and I'm certain he'd be delighted to accept visitors at his convenience."

This was met with roars and jeers, and more futile shoves of the door.

Maggie barked.

Simkin turned his head. "Your Ladyship," he whispered, "it would be best if you went at once to a far chamber and bolted the door—"

"But where's Godolphin?"

"He went to Brighton on an errand. I expect he'll be back shortly."

"He'll have to come down the drive, and they'll see him!"

"Not necessarily," said a deep, smooth voice just beside her.

She spun. "Godolphin!"

He took her hand. "I came by way of the beach, through a side entrance."

Estella's relief was replaced by fear. "All those men—"

"How many?" Godolphin called to Simkin.

"Thirty or thereabouts, Your Lordship."

"I'm going to take Estella where it's safe."

Simkin strained to keep the door from flying open as someone shoved it from the other side. "Very good, Your Lordship. I know precisely where you mean."

Godolphin pulled on Estella's hand. "Let's go." He turned her around, and began striding down the corridor, but he stopped. "Simkin," he called over his shoulder, "if you have a mind to be *someone else's* butler for a spell, I think it would be a fine idea."

"Very good, Your Lordship," Simkin said.

Godolphin held Estella's hand tightly, and they ran.

Godolphin would have liked to confront Bertie and his militia face-on, like a gentleman. However, his foremost concern was keeping Estella safe.

He led her through the Great Hall, to the cellar door.

Estella balked. "Down there? Bertie knows about the—"

"He doesn't know all of the caves." Then, "Wait here." Godolphin dashed to one of the side tables and lit a candelabra, shoving the box of matches in his breast pocket.

Distant shouts echoed from the foyer. Bertie and his men were inside.

Godolphin led Estella into the dank stairwell. After closing the door behind them, they took the steps slowly. Godolphin kept hold of Estella's hand, and Maggie picked her way down in front of them, slipping here and there on the damp stone.

At the bottom, Godolphin led Estella through the wine cellar and outer rooms, and he noted how she clutched his hand harder when they passed through one huge, empty chamber.

"It was here?" he whispered.

"Yes."

He led her through chamber after chamber, down passageway after passageway, in twists and turns that would have seemed mazelike to someone else. To him, it was as familiar as the upper part of the castle. The air grew more and more stale, and the massive weight of the castle above was almost palpable.

Presently, they came to a small door, almost square, made of rusted iron. It was hinged directly on a wall of bedrock.

"Through there?" Estella asked, clearly reluctant.

"It's better on the other side. Trust me. There's fresh air." He passed her the candelabra. He drew a key ring from his pocket, fitted one of several keys into the lock, and shoved the door open. The hinges screeched, but a blast of cool, briny air burst through, along with faint natural light.

Maggie went through first, nose twitching. Godolphin went next, and after passing him the candelabra, Estella followed.

"These are the sea caves," Godolphin said. He locked the door behind them. "I believe you saw them from the beach one day, didn't you?"

She nodded, looking about. The walls and ceiling were all curving, wet rock, and tidal pools were scattered about the uneven floor. A zigzag of daylight glowed from the narrow mouth. Ocean wind gusted through and swirled about, instantly extinguishing the candles. Enough natural light remained to see by.

"This is just one of the caves," Godolphin said, leading the way along the back. "It's likely that Bertie knows about this one."

"Then why are we—"

"He doesn't know about *all* of them. Follow me."

He led her to another iron door like the first. He unlocked it, and the three of them passed through into a similar cave, locking the door behind them. They repeated this three times, stumbling in the half-light over uneven rock and around glimmering tide pools.

"Here we are." Godolphin stopped before a rock slab that was as high as Maggie's back.

Estella looked about. "Here?" She glanced anxiously at the mouth of the cave.

"Help me push." After placing the candelabra on the floor of the cave, he began rocking the slab back and forth to gain momentum. Estella bent beside him, pushing hard.

An irrelevant thought flickered through his mind: No spoiled princess ever shoved a rock with such determination, wearing slippers soaked by brine. But Estella wasn't a spoiled princess. At least, not anymore.

They'd gained enough momentum, and a final heave sent the rock toppling and rolling a few feet before it stopped.

Behind it was yet another iron door.

Estella was eager to hide, and she trusted Godolphin wholeheartedly. But the idea of hiding in a cramped, dark, airless space made her uneasy. She didn't speak, but followed Godolphin and Maggie. She had to crouch to get through the iron door, and the sense of confinement made her belly curdle.

There was light on the other side. She sighed her relief. The source of light was several patchy holes in the high rock ceiling, reminding her of the skylights in London art galleries. Fresh air swirled through these, too. The cave was smaller than the others, about the size of her parlor, but the ceiling was so lofty it didn't feel cramped at all.

Godolphin slammed the door shut, and straightened. "Obviously we can't move the rock to cover the door. We'll just have to hope that since Bertie has never seen this particular door before, he won't notice it if he comes looking now."

Estella moved to a large barrel beneath one of the skylights. It was full of water.

"That's good to drink," Godolphin said. "Rainwater."

Grateful, Estella filled the tin dipper that was hooked over the side of the barrel, and drank deeply. Then she poured some more water into a bowl-shaped indentation in the rock floor for Maggie.

Godolphin was busy in a low-ceilinged corner. Estella watched as he dragged a pile of woolen blankets into the middle of the cave and spread them out. "Join me, my love." He grinned.

For the first time in what felt like hours, Estella breathed a real, satisfying breath, and smiled, too.

Before she could reach Godolphin's side, though, she heard a loud splash. She swung to see Maggie paddling inside a deep rock pool that appeared to be . . . *steaming*.

"Natural hot springs," Godolphin said. "Quite good for the constitution." He met her gaze, and his own eyes sparkled. "We'll have to try them."

Maggie got out of the water and shook, spraying Estella. This was perfect timing, because Godolphin's comment had sent Estella's cheeks burning. "Naturally." She swallowed.

"Come," Godolphin said. He was sprawled like a sheik on the blankets, patting the space beside him.

Estella glared. "I hope you are instructing Maggie, not me."

He smiled. "Naturally."

It was good to simply sit still for a while, side by side on the blanket. The cave felt safe, and to be with Godolphin *always* felt safe. She lay on her back, hands behind her head, and stared up through the holes in the ceiling, watching streaks of clouds waft through a blue sky. An odd, silent peace fell on them. Maggie was curled up on a corner of the blanket, and Godolphin was on his side, head propped on a hand. He seemed ever-wary, as though he were listening, guarding.

"Why are there blankets here?" she asked, sitting up.

Godolphin studied her face. "I brought them down here. I suspected we might have to hide. There is some food, too, and gas lamps. We oughtn't to use those unless we have to, though, because the light would be visible from the sea and the beach. Those holes on the ceiling open out onto the side of the cliffs, under a portion of the cliff path."

"I thought we were in the most remote of spots."

"We are. One would have to be an Alpine climber—or a monkey—to scale down from the path to these openings. They're not visible from the path, either. They're not accessible at all from the beach. An outcropping drops straight down into the sea."

"Why are there all those iron doors?"

"These caves were used by smugglers for years. They unloaded cargo brought in from the Channel—from France, mainly—at high tide, using rowboats. They'd store it here, and send it out little by little. The doors were to protect the booty."

"Booty?"

"Guns, bootleg brandy. Of course, now the villagers all have a piece of the smuggling trade, so it isn't kept secret any longer. They have no use for the caves, since they can bring smuggled goods onshore freely through the fishing hamlet."

Estella chewed her lip. "Didn't you live here at the castle as a boy? For years and years?"

Slowly, he sat up.

"Didn't," Estella went on, "your parents know about the caves and the smuggling?"

Godolphin massaged the heel of a hand into his forehead.

Estella held her breath.

Finally, he dropped his hand and gazed into her eyes. "Estella. Haven't you guessed it by now? My own father was a smuggler."

The shame that Godolphin had carried for half a lifetime was so familiar, but admitting it to Estella seemed worse than anything. For the first time in his life, he found it difficult to meet a woman's eyes.

But when he did, there was no judgment there, no scorn, not even pity. Only a wide-eyed, sweet confusion.

She touched his shoulder. "How terrible for you," was all she whispered.

Godolphin squeezed his eyes shut. What did it matter if he told her everything? He was well aware that his married days were dwindling to a precious few. As soon as Bertie had been taken care of, there was nothing, nothing at all, to hold them together. Their marriage vows had been false. Every last pretense their marriage had been founded on was a lie. Well, the lie would soon be over. As much as he wanted to keep her by his side forever, he knew he'd have to set her free.

"I didn't," he finally said, "learn of my father's smuggling until I was seventeen years of age, just after he had died. But it had been going on my entire life, just down here, under cover of darkness, and I'd never guessed." He heard his own voice go flat. "I'd grown up admiring my father, even revering him, and the news of his death was difficult enough. The news that he was a smuggler shattered me. I left home soon after that, went up to Oxford. I swore I'd never set foot in Castle Seabrook again. After he died, my mother moved to London. She lived there until she died six years ago."

Estella was silent, her expression grave.

"I did come back, though, didn't I?" He raked the hair from his eyes. "How I loathed this place, the mockery it made of the Godolphin name. It took me more than a decade, but I returned."

Silence. A few plovers flew over the skylights, peeping shrilly. Maggie got up and settled herself below the skylights to watch the sky.

"Why did you return?" Estella asked softly.

"Because it took a disaster in Village Seabrook to knock some sense into me, make me remember my inherited duties, my obligation to my people."

"Disaster?"

"Edwin Lovely sent word to me at Marblegate House, as soon as he was appointed vicar here." He paused and caught her eye. "I am so sorry. About the deception regarding the castle."

She looked down, studied the blanket.

"Reverend Lovely wrote," he went on, "that the village had been destroyed by smuggling, and asked me to come back and set things right. The farmers don't farm, Estella. The fishermen don't fish, the local government is corrupt, paid off by smugglers. All because they've been working for a smuggler, content to obtain easy money by turning a blind eye, or delivering booty instead of making an honest living."

"A smuggler." Estella's features hardened slightly. "You believed this smuggler was *Papa.*"

He waited. His throat was tight, and the horrible reality of what he'd done, tricking a hapless young woman into marriage for the suspected sins of her father, slugged him like a prizefighter's blow. "I'm sorry, Estella," he managed. "Really and truly sorry. I was wrong about your father. All the things that I thought pointed to him, because of the links of his business to the village, were actually pointing straight to Bertie."

Her face was a mask of pain. Her eyes dropped, and she toyed with a loose thread in the blanket. "Which is why"— she swallowed—"which is why you married me."

No more lies. "Yes."

She continued to play with the thread, twisting it in slim fingers until it snapped. "I wonder why Papa didn't stop Bertie. How could he have not known what was going on?"

"I've been wondering the same thing myself. Your father gave you that pistol, remember, so he must've suspected something was afoot, perhaps only recently—"

"—but he had to leave for America. Then why didn't he tell *you* about Bertie?"

Godolphin sighed. "Perhaps he wasn't totally convinced of anything, including how deserving *I* was of trust. After all, my own father was a smuggler. I am certain your father knew at least that."

Suddenly, Estella rose so she was sitting on her heels. She wrapped her arms around him. "Just because your father did that," she whispered against his neck, "doesn't mean *you* are bad. You're good, Godolphin, and you've been trying so hard to help the village, and you've exposed Bertie, and everything's going to be fixed." Then she pressed her face harder into his neck, squeezed his shoulders tighter, and mumbled something indistinct.

He pulled away in order to see her face. "What was that?"

Her eyes were shining with . . . tears. "Nothing." She tried to laugh it off, swiping a rolling drop from her cheek.

They sat quite still, kneeling like nomads on the woolen blanket, facing each other with hands clasped. Maggie sighed in her sleep. Afternoon sun slanted through the skylights, putting Estella half in golden light, half in shadow. The light picked out flaxen threads in her hair, made her periwinkle irises glow as though lit from within.

Loss gripped Godolphin. He wanted to keep her here forever, and the realization that he couldn't, and that she'd be gone from him soon, shredded him inside. He leaned forward to kiss her, and it was a kiss of desperation, of bone-deep longing, a kiss to memorize her feel, her taste, forever.

Her response was sweet, but hungry. Though his eyes were closed, he felt how she rose on her knees, how she gently grabbed fistfuls of his hair, how she kissed him with what seemed like a desperation to match his own.

Of course not. She'll be glad to get away. What I did is unforgivable.

A new kind of lust gripped him. He understood that this was the last time he would ever have her. A voracious beast unfurled from his soul, made him knead her shoulders, her arms, made him press his palms over the swell of her breasts, down her sides, up to her neck, and force her mouth ever deeper against his.

She was taking off his jacket, tossing it aside, caressing his chest with hot hands, unbuttoning his shirt.

"Touch me," he muttered against her neck. "I adore your touch." He reached up to pull the pins from her hair.

Her only response was to open his shirt, reach under the fabric, and rake her fingernails slowly, lightly, down his chest.

His lips parted, his eyelids were heavy. Her beauty was too much to absorb, and the colors and textures of her— coppery-gold curls, lily-petal skin, the flashing violet-blue of her eyes—blurred together.

He heard his own shallow breath.

As though she alone could give him the air he needed to survive, he dragged her close and kissed her desperately. He had to *absorb* her somehow, to possess her to such a degree that it would be enough to last him the rest of his life. He must. Because this was the last time.

So he kissed her more roughly than he intended, but she did not seem to notice or mind. Her breath had grown ragged, too, and her cheeks burned against his.

She peeled away his shirt, and the slippery cool of the air made his back rigid. Then her hot little hands were on his back, stroking the ridges of muscle on either side of his spine, palming the planes of his back, digging beneath his belt.

"Godolphin." She pulled away from the kiss, speaking against his lips.

He inhaled deeply of her breath, which smelled sweet and clean and alive.

"Godolphin," she said again, now leaning to kiss his collarbones. "I need you."

She sounded choked up, but he couldn't see her eyes.

"I need you," she repeated. Softly, she touched his belly. Reflexively, the muscles clenched under her fingertips. She looked up. Her eyes were round.

"Darling." He undid the top button of her gown. "As luck would have it, I need you, too."

She laughed a little, but her eyes remained sad.

He undid the next button, and the next, never looking away from her eyes. Why did she look as though she were going to cry?

"Will you . . ." She cleared her throat, and her gaze darted past him.

He parted the back of her bodice, drew it down to her waist. "Will I what?"

"Will you Ravish me?" she said, the words an embarrassed tumble.

"That"—he drew her arms from her sleeves—"was my general plan."

"Oh, well," she blurted out, "I just thought that, because we are hiding, and we need to be wary, that perhaps we wouldn't and I just . . ." Her cheeks were crimson.

"First," he said softly, "your nanny and your governess and heaven knows who else told you that you needn't— or mustn't—enjoy Ravishment, were wrong. Second, stand up."

At last, her eyes shot back to meet his. Their roundness betrayed her confusion.

"Stand up, so I can take this confounded garment from your body."

With a laugh, she obeyed, and he peeled it off, along with her chemise and petticoats. She stood before him on the blanket, a slim siren. When she moved to kneel back down beside him, he grabbed her hips.

She gasped, but remained standing.

He inched his fingers around the tender flesh of her hips until they cupped her buttocks, then drew her to him, so the downy apex of her thighs was before his mouth. He leaned forward to taste her, and she moaned, shuddering, and braced herself against his shoulders.

He tasted again, kissed, licked, until her knees shook and her fingernails nipped into his shoulders. Then he stopped, kissed her sloping belly, and drew her down to the blanket.

Her eyes were hazy, her skin flushed, her limbs jittery. Leaning over her, he eased her onto her back, cradling the back of her head with his hand as he did so. Then he stood to remove his trousers. He gazed down at her, delicious and prone on the blanket, the last beams of late afternoon sun illuminating the golden down on her skin. His ribs clenched with anguish and loss at the very same moment that his manhood grew so rigid that it ached.

He knelt over her, trying to remember the sight of her, the sweet anticipation, the look of innocence and need on her features. But then that desperate beast unfurled itself again, and he couldn't think. *This is the last time. Take her now. Now or never.*

"Turn over," he commanded.

Her eyes flared, lips parted.

"Turn," he repeated, forcing gentleness into his tone. He cupped her hip, softly pressed.

She turned, stretching long like a reed over the coarse blanket. He lowered himself atop her, taking care not to crush her, resting most of his weight in his hands. He positioned himself at her entrance and, for the last time in his life, slid home.

Estella clamped her eyes tight as Godolphin—her almost husband—entered her body, filled her. To her surprise, tears leaked out and dripped onto the blanket. Not from pain, but from sorrow. He'd finally told her the whole truth. He hadn't married her for love, or even friendship. Their marriage was founded on lies, and it could not continue.

She blinked, and tried to concentrate on memorizing the feel of him, for it would be the last time. The feeling of fullness, the pressure of his hot, smooth skin against her back, his weight, the sound of his exhale just beside her ear.

Remember. His achingly slow, fluid strokes, his kisses on her side-turned face.

Remember. How it was to feel possessed by him, to be needed by him. And to need him, too.

His thrusts grew deeper, and she gasped, clawing at the blanket, grabbing fistfuls of the coarse wool that felt so foreign, compared to the silky heat of his body.

She jumped as his hand burrowed beneath her hips to touch her center, and he caressed her there, spiraling and stroking, until she could scarcely think at all. She smelled the mineral tang of the cave rock, and the fading light made the air like watercolors. She thought she tasted him in her mouth, and the rush of his breath and her breath twined with the muted crash of the ocean outside. Her pleasure mounted, vivid, beautiful, just as his thrusts quickened, and she felt as though she understood. She was part of the universe, but she needed Godolphin to feel that. And she understood the animal possession in the way he took her. It made exquisite sense.

She began to moan. His fingers quickened, his hips bucking.

Her eyes slammed shut.

"Estella," he breathed, a sound made jagged by his thrusts. "Estella."

Remember.

She cried out as the tide overtook her, and a second later he called out her name for the last time, a plaintive, primal cry.

He sank over her, cradling her, possessing her even as the pleasure washed back out to sea. They dozed until the pomegranate glow of sunset seeped through the skylights.

Chapter Twenty

Oracle of Pranks

"Yer Lordship!" a child's voice squeaked.

Estella bolted upright, yanking the blanket close around her naked body. Her pulse throbbed at her throat.

"Lordship!"

Maggie barked at the skylights. Then she wagged her tail violently.

Godolphin covered his lap with another blanket, and gazed upward. "Timmy?" he called.

"Aye, sir. I climbed down from the path."

Estella made out Timmy's round head, peering down through one of the skylights. The red sky behind him made his face difficult to see.

"Simkin sent me," Timmy said. "He bade me tell you that Littlefield has taken up residence in the castle—"

"Indeed," Godolphin growled. He scrambled to his feet, clutching the blanket around his waist, and strode directly under Timmy. "I thought he might."

"'E wants to be earl, is the thing. An' Simkin is playin' along, bein' his butler, like you told 'im to."

Godolphin scratched his head. "I wanted Simkin to avoid a struggle for his own safety, not—"

"Master Simkin has a plan," Timmy said. "'E says you

oughta stay down here till sunrise, an' then he'll send me with another message. So don't come up, Yer Lordship. Simkin said you'd want to."

"You were going to leave me down here?" Estella said.

Godolphin glanced over his shoulder. "You'd be perfectly safe. But . . ." Then, to Timmy, "You're certain Simkin has everything under control?"

"Aye. Sit tight, an' I'll be back at sunrise." Timmy disappeared.

Godolphin returned to Estella's side, frowning.

"You did," Estella said, "say it would take a monkey to get to this cave from up there. But you weren't really going to leave me?"

"I can't very well sit about here like a coward while another man is taking over my home."

"But Timmy said we ought to stay! Simkin has a plan, and he knows what's going on. We don't."

Godolphin paced back and forth in front of her, looking no less formidable for his bare chest and the blanket draped around his hips. He looked, actually, like some sort of Roman general, and Estella wanted to smile.

She got up and went to the low overhang where Godolphin had gotten the blankets. She rummaged around in a wooden crate and found a loaf of bread wrapped in cloth, cheese in another cloth, and some apples. There was a clean knife in the bottom of the crate. She brought all this back to the blankets.

"Here," she said. She held out a slice of apple to Godolphin, who was still pacing. He looked at her, and then the apple, as though he didn't recognize any of it.

"We need to eat," she said. "You can't think right if you don't eat." She waved the apple slice.

He took it, and finally sat down beside her. They made a picnic of the food, washing it down with dippers full of cold rainwater, tossing the crusts to Maggie. The sunset was nearly gone. The sky was purple-black, and Estella had to stop cutting food with the knife when it got too dark.

They let Maggie out into the outer cave for a few minutes, and Godolphin and Estella took turns going into the dim outer cave to relieve themselves. Estella's impulse was to be embarrassed, but this was secondary to her physical need. And Godolphin laughed about it, setting her at ease.

Back inside, he said, "I'd never have thought it of you, Estella, but I dare say you'd survive in the wilderness if you needed to."

She couldn't make out his expression, but she thought she heard admiration in his tone. He stepped close, so she was shrouded in his shadow, and he tugged the blanket she held around her. It dropped to the floor. She shivered.

"Let's go in the hot spring," he said softly. "I'll light one candle—that won't be visible from outside."

The hot springs were deliciously warm, smelling faintly of sulfur, but more strongly of good, clean minerals. The light of the single candle bounced off the cloudy surface of the water, off Godolphin's bare, rounded shoulders, off the bumpy sloped walls of the cave. Seats had been crafted with flat rocks around the periphery, and Godolphin moved close to Estella's side and bathed her with a soft sea sponge.

"I need to make something very clear," Godolphin said in low tones after a few minutes. He moved wet tendrils of hair from her neck.

"Yes?" She was growing sleepy.

"As soon as this is all over, this . . . problem with Bertie, I mean, I fully intend to release you from your wedding vows."

From Madame Pettibonne's
Treatise of Canine Behavior, Prepared Especially for the
Lady Handler
As you may well have deduced, my Dear Lady Handler,
there are as many sorts of Old Dogs as there are gems upon
a czarina's breast. Some are given to slobbering and drool-

ing, some must lap only mash, and some poor dodderers fancy themselves young pups, still in the blush of youth. There are those with the rheum, others with the gout. One ancient one is given to lying upon the hearth rug and snoring night and day, whilst another prefers the foot of his mistress's bed, where he scrutinizes life with hurt expressions and dour remarks. None of these, my friend, are of any interest to the Lady Handler.

There is only one sort of Old Dog we shall consider. Our Old Dog may merely be sporting his first grey whiskers or well into antiquity. It matters not. These are the gallant old beasts who have made it through life with their wits unaffected and their joie de vivre intact. They are the knowing elders whose sage advice and noble deportment make them indispensable guides for beasts younger than themselves. Be he a Hound, Hunter, Terrier, Toy, or Worker, a fine Old Dog is worth his weight in gold.

"Another bottle of brandy, Simkin," Bertie commanded. "No more of that cheap rot." He hurled the rubbishy dog training book to the carpet. He'd found it in Estella's bedchamber, but he'd yet to find the ledgers. "I know there's good French stuff down in the cellar, and you'd do well to serve it to your new master."

Simkin, his droopy old face blank as a cow's, bowed slightly.

The bow sent shivers down Bertie's spine. He could get accustomed to this.

"Very well, sir," Simkin intoned.

"Very well *Your Lordship!*" Bertie yelled. He sat up on the pillows of what had been, until quite recently, Godolphin's kingly bed. "*Your Lordship!*"

Simkin bowed again. "Very well, Your Lordship." He evaporated in that perfect butler's way he had.

After he'd left, Bertie flopped back on the pillows. Simkin was the most refined of butlers, and he'd like to be able to keep him, as was fitting for an earl. But the fellow was going to have to be a good deal more reverent or he'd be in the ditch, and without a penny of severance pay, either.

Bertie gazed about the palatial chamber with satisfaction. His plan had gone off without a hitch. So far. The village men were at their posts about the castle and grounds, keeping watch for Godolphin and Estella's return. The two couldn't have gone far, and he knew they'd be back because Godolphin's ridiculous medieval instincts wouldn't allow him to flee like a coward. Bertie snickered, reaching for the silver cheroot case he'd found in the tower. His original plan of taking over Hancock's business paled in comparison with this. As soon as he'd got hold of those three ledgers and the precious information they contained, he wouldn't only be king of England's most lucrative smuggling enterprise. He'd be an earl, too, and the husband of that flighty twit Estella.

Bertie selected a cheroot from the case, gave it a long sniff. It really was a pity that he was going to have to kill Godolphin, if only because it'd make Estella weepy and untractable for a spell. But she'd come around, eventually. Even if he had to beat it into her.

He struck a match, relaxed on the luxurious brocade pillows, crossed his ankles, and took the first puff of his victory cheroot.

In the hot springs, Estella felt cold. Godolphin's words screamed through her head. *I fully intend to release you from your wedding vows.*

"I cannot," he went on, "possibly insist that you honor wedding vows that were predicated on deceit. What I did is unforgivable. I know this, and I'm very sorry, but I can't possibly keep you as my wife."

She inched along the ledge of rocks, creating distance between them. She fought the sting of tears, the sobs that were unfurling in her chest.

His expression was empty, blurred by the steam that

rose around them as the night air grew chilly. "As I suggested before, we can try for an annulment. You are no longer a maiden, but it's unlikely that you are with child, and as long as you're willing to . . ." The muscles around his eyes flexed. "I suppose you'll have to tell one more lie to your new husband, which you will undoubtedly have, and soon. Yes. The sooner the better."

She felt blank, tissue thin, like the steam. She wanted to drift away, too, out of her body, her mind, away from this unbearable pain. But wasn't he voicing what she'd been thinking herself? She gulped. "Of course. One more lie. Out of necessity."

"If you like, you needn't marry, in which case I'm perfectly willing to support you, keep you in the lifestyle you're accustomed to—"

She cut him off. "Papa will take care of me."

A pause. "Yes. Of course he will."

"Well then." Estella climbed from the hot springs, vaguely shy at her nudity, but too pained to really care much. She began drying herself with one of the blankets. "Now that that's all sorted out—and I am relieved that we're of one mind on this topic—we can rest easy."

He was staring at her. She had the oddest impression that he was growing smaller, as though she were racing away in a carriage. She blinked, surprised at the tears that came out. Thankful for the darkness, she wiped them away, and went to get dressed.

They didn't speak again. They slept side by side, beneath a heap of blankets, with Maggie curled at their feet. They didn't touch.

As sunrise leaked through the skylights, she dreamt that Godolphin's big arm was wrapped around her. When she woke, however, his arm wasn't there.

"Yer Ladyship," Timmy said, breathless as he peered down through the skylight. "I think it might be time fer one last prank."

Godolphin glanced at Estella. Her eyes were still sweetly puffy from sleep, her clothes rumpled from the night on the hard cave floor. They'd barely spoken since waking. He was beginning to realize that he'd hurt her terribly last night when he'd suggested ending their marriage. If that idea hurt her, then perhaps . . .

"What do you mean, another prank?" Estella asked Timmy.

"Well, Master Simkin says Littlefield keeps askin' and askin' fer some ledgers—"

Estella's eyes shot to Godolphin's.

"—and he seems t' need them badly to finish his takeover."

"Takeover?" Godolphin echoed.

"Aye. Of th' village, th' castle, and Her Ladyship's pa's business. Master Simkin told me this. Littlefield told him."

Godolphin managed a bitter smile. He wasn't at all surprised that Simkin had managed to insinuate himself into Bertie's confidences so quickly. The man had a way of seeming almost invisible, which probably gave Bertie the impression that he was trustworthy.

"Where," Godolphin said to Estella in low tones, "did you put the ledgers?"

"Back on the canopy of my bed."

"But," Timmy called, "Master Simkin don't know where th' ledgers are, an' I don't neither. And Mr. Pepys—"

"Pepys?" Estella said. "What's he doing about?"

"He came to work on th' decoratin'," Timmy explained, "but I met him in th' stables, an' I told him about Littlefield, and he's ever so worried about you, Yer Ladyship. I didn't tell him where ye were. I jes said you're all right. He went back t' Brighton, but he said he's not goin' back t' London till he's certain you're fine."

Estella nodded. "You told him that Bertie wants the ledgers?"

"Aye, and he and Master Simkin thought ye might be able to bait Littlefield with 'em, like."

Godolphin had already thought of this. The problem was the thirty-odd men prowling about the castle. He was an able warrior, but he wasn't a fool. He knew those men would be armed.

"What about the men?" Estella asked, as though reading his thoughts. "Are they still there?"

Timmy nodded. "They don't pay me any mind. They think I'm on their side, see, 'cause of me ma bein' a villager and all." His face crumpled a little, but quickly smoothed out again. "Yer Ladyship, I think ye could play a prank on the men, make 'em go away. Then His Lordship could deal with Littlefield." His eyes glowed.

Estella tipped her head, thinking. "A prank?"

"Th' ladies in th' village all say you're awfully good at pranks!"

"Mr. Pepys might be willing to help?"

A vigorous nod.

"And you've spoken to the ladies of the village?"

"Oh yes, they've all been comin' t' the vicarage since last night, talkin' to Mrs. Lovely about what's to be done."

Godolphin watched as Estella paced to a boulder, sat down, propped her chin in her hand, and began to think. Her brows were furrowed, her eyes bright as she stared at the rocky floor.

Yet again, he wondered at his own stupidity when he'd supposed she was a silly flibbertigibbet whom he could control. She was too clever, too stubborn, too full of life.

If they had been able to stay together as man and wife, he wouldn't have wanted to tame her, anyway. He loved her just the way she was.

Something inside of him expanded at this realization. But instantly, it shrank, and his insides felt cold and hard. It was a realization made too late. She wanted to get out of the marriage.

"I've got it," Estella said crisply, rising from the boulder.

Godolphin and Timmy both watched her expectantly, as though she were the oracle of pranks.

"Pepys," she said, pacing, "has a penchant for the the-atrical. In fact, he once confided to me that he'd always dreamt of being on the stage. Now, suppose he dressed up like the London judge who's expected in two day's time, come early?"

Godolphin forced himself not to laugh. "Pepys. Isn't he a bit . . . foppish for the role?"

Estella gave him a stern glance. "He may be a fop in or-dinary life, but if he is a good actor, then he can manage. Besides, who is to say a judge cannot also be a fop? In any case, he'll arrest all the men—"

"How?" Godolphin asked. "With no backup?"

"Then he'll threaten to arrest them. They're working for Bertie for money, Godolphin. Their loyalty can't be very strong. They're not going to resist arrest from a king's advocate!"

Godolphin sighed. "Isn't this a bit harebrained?"

"Absolutely not. The best pranks are also the most spec-tacular, walking a razor's edge between lunacy and utter perfection. Besides, can you think of anything better?"

His mind was a blank.

"I thought so," she said tartly. She met his eye, and de-spite her businesslike tone, he saw the sadness there. "I ask you to trust me one last time, Godolphin. *One last time.*"

He knew what she meant. Every fiber in his body re-belled at the great loss he was going to have to bear. He was adrift in the clear blue-lavender of her gaze, and it was an effort to rip his eyes away. "I trust you."

"Go, Timmy," Estella said. "Tell Pepys, Simkin, Mrs. Lovely. Then come inform us when it's going to happen."

From Madame Pettibonne's
Treatise on Canine Behavior, Prepared Especially for the
Lady Handler

The Toy Breeds. Tiny, tremulous, fastidious, given to adorning themselves in diamond collars and silk tail rib-bons, the Toy Breeds make charming companions. As

such, these creatures make the ideal pet for the elderly Lady
Handler: She may enjoy stylish friendship and lavish at-
tention with no more demands on her than a new bauble
or satin vest every few weeks or so.

    Costly as they are, these tiny dogs bring untold pleasure
to their mistresses, and nearly every fine noblewoman, once
she is of a certain age, indulges in a Toy or two. I myself
possess two thimble caniches, Beau and Bartolomieu, the
finest little dandies in all of Paris!

It was four hours before Timmy returned. Estella felt as
though she would go mad, waiting in the cave all that
while. Godolphin and she hadn't spoken, out of a mutual
understanding. They would sort this out, go their separate ways. There was nothing more to discuss.

Except, he'd sat in a corner, under a sunbeam from the
skylight, lost in thought. Estella had been sitting dully on
the blankets, and now and then she'd glance up and catch
him staring at her. Then his eyes would turn away.

He was probably thinking how wonderful it would be to
be free of her.

So it was a relief when Timmy returned to tell them that
Pepys, dressed as a sort of vicious-looking judge-pirate,
with huge, loaded pistols strapped to his hips, a dagger in
his boot, an eye patch, and a black curly wig, had arrived
at the castle. Bertie's hired men had feared the simmering threat of violence in the judge, although Timmy confided that a few men had said he was foppish, prompting
Pepys to fire a round of shot at the ceiling in the foyer of
the castle.

"The ceiling?" Godolphin cringed.

"He's a decorator," Estella reminded him. "He'll redo it
beautifully."

Despite himself, Godolphin had to laugh.

"What happened next?" Estella asked Timmy.

"Well, I told Mrs. Lovely about th' plan, see, an' she told
the village ladies who've been worried about all this, and

worried about Her Ladyship. An' they told Pepys what their husbands looked like, and some things about them they'd not want a judge to know, like when Mr. Parsby sold some gypsies a lame horse, or that Charlie Higgins poaches on Lord Piltonshire's estate down the road." Timmy took a huge breath and continued. "So, when Mr. Pepys went to say he was goin' to arrest th' men, he also mentioned some o' these little crimes, see, an' they were really worried!" He grinned. "That was Mrs. Lovely's idea. She's a first-rate prankster, too, 'twould seem."

Estella avoided looking at Godolphin, because she knew he was thinking about Madame Pettibonne's manual.

"Mr. Pepys also told some o' th' men, th' ones who hadn't any little crimes to be reminded of, of what an awful state their wives 'n kids would be in if they went t' jail. Well, it didn't take him fifteen minutes t' clear th' lot of them out."

"What about Littlefield?" Godolphin asked.

Timmy scrunched his little face. "He's still in th' castle. But 'e's alone. Tearin' th' place apart, lookin' fer those ledgers. He hid when Mr. Pepys came, see."

Godolphin's jaw was tight. "It's time for me to go up," he told Estella.

"For *us* to go up," she corrected.

"I'm not putting you in that madman's path, Estella."

"Well, I am not staying here."

"You shall."

"You can't keep me down here against my will!"

They both seemed to remember that Timmy was still there.

"Timmy," Godolphin said levelly, never taking his eyes from Estella, "you may go now. Go back to the vicarage and stay there, do you understand?"

"Yes," Timmy squeaked, and he was gone.

"I'm coming," Estella repeated. "Our marriage is all but annulled now, and I am my own mistress."

She watched as he swallowed hard.

"I've got to catch Bertie, restrain him. I don't need your help."

"No?" Estella raised her chin in challenge. "Do you really think Bertie will just walk into your hands like that?"

"Yes. Because he wants to kill me, so he'll have to at least get close enough to do it."

That did it. Estella moved to the iron door that led to the outer caves. "I'm coming."

"Estella, be reasonable."

She swung around. "I'm not going to loaf about down here like some bleeding damsel in distress—"

His brows lifted at her base language.

"—while you're all by yourself seeing if Bertie can manage to polish you off!"

"He'll hurt you, too."

"He wants to *marry* me, for heaven's sake, so he wouldn't ever hurt me that badly. Listen. I'll get the ledgers, and bait him with them, and you can catch him then."

"This is madness—"

"My last plan worked perfectly."

"True enough."

"Because you trusted me."

"You said that was the last time."

She bit her lower lip. "Second to last time, then. This is the last time. Now let's go."

Bertie stepped down from the chair he'd stood on to reach over the canopy of Estella's bed. He glanced at the neatly made up blankets and pillows. He'd have dearly loved to bury his face there, sniff her essence, find a stray gold-red hair, perhaps lie atop the linens for a spell and pleasure himself. But he didn't have time.

Because, at long last, he had the three ledgers again. He cradled them in his left arm like a baby and rushed for the door.

Gloating mingled with pulsing rage. He'd heard the gunshots earlier, and had hidden upstairs, watching at a window overlooking the front drive. One by one he'd seen his militia leave. Teeters might still be loyal, but he was holed up in The Wicked Mermaid.

Bertie had counted the leaving men with mounting panic. They'd been paid with real silver, and they needed him, needed the smuggling business. They hated Godolphin, so why were they abandoning him?

He got his answer when he saw a man with black curly hair, what appeared to be an eye patch, and several comically large pistols, leave after the last man.

At first he'd thought it was the London judge. But he recognized the man's foppish gait. It had been the decorator he'd seen about the castle days ago, now dressed in a preposterous disguise.

"If they're that bloody stupid," Bertie muttered to himself as he descended the stairs with the ledgers, "then I can do without their help." Now that he had the ledgers, all he had to do was disappear. With the precious information they contained, he could set up shop as smuggling lord anywhere in England. He was through with Seabrook. Let the cowards starve.

At the bottom of the stairs, he looked left and right. Someone was trying the front door. He slunk off to the right. He'd have to leave through the cellars and the caves. Stopping in the dining room, he took a small lamp from a sideboard and lit it.

He'd descended just three steps when he saw wavering light coming from below. The slimy stone walls shone. He froze, clutching the ledgers to his chest so violently that he nearly knocked himself off balance. He heard voices.

Godolphin. *Estella.*

Again, he teetered on the stairs, this time dizzy with anger. Because of the tight twist in the stairs, they couldn't see him. He turned to leave, perspiration trickling into his eyes.

"May I be of any assistance, Your Lordship?" Simkin asked from above, blocking the doorway to the Great Hall.

He held a blunderbuss, aimed straight at Bertie's heart.

Bertie was trapped. His sweaty hand had gone too slippery, and he fought to keep hold of the lamp, but it slipped from his fingers, crashing and splintering down the stairs. The flame sizzled out on the damp moss.

Barking. Did that cursed foxhound ever shut up?

Breathing hard, Bertie sensed Simkin's eyes boring down on his back, and he knew the blunderbuss was still aimed at him. A second later, Godolphin appeared around the twist in the stairs below.

"You've got the ledgers," Godolphin said. "Congratulations."

Oh, that wasn't *all* he had. Bertie also had a pistol hidden under his jacket. The problem was, having only one arm, he couldn't get to it without releasing the ledgers.

"Have you looked at them?" Godolphin asked.

"Of course," Bertie bluffed. "Of course I looked at them."

"And what do they contain?"

"Do you mean to say that you haven't looked at them?"

"My wife hid them from me, as well."

His wife. *His* wife? Bertie pressed his right shoulder stump against the wall to keep his balance. Moisture seeped through his sleeve. "Must you gloat?" He panted in and out through his nostrils. "You always gloat and flaunt!"

"I'm sorry, Bertie," Godolphin said softly. "That day in the Caribbean was the worst day of my life."

"Of *your* life?" Something about the echo in the stairwell made his words sound shrill, hysterical. "Why? Did your hair get mussed by all the shooting?"

The high-pitched keening started in his head.

Godolphin unclamped his jaw. "I've carried guilt and responsibility about with me every day since. I wish it had been I who'd lost an arm—"

Bertie sneered.

"—and sometimes I wish I had died, instead of Ben and Joseph and Pierre. I'm responsible."

"You *are!*" Bertie shrieked. His foot slipped a little on the stair, but he regained his balance. "We should've left that ship alone! It looked like a bloody ship of death! Pirates! Even I could see that when it was miles off! Tattered sails, all those mismatched cannons and—"

"Smugglers, Bertie. Slavers. It was our duty to catch them. That's why the navy had sent us there."

"But not *then!* Not when we hadn't adequate backup! We should've waited! But no, you said they'd get away—"

"They attacked us," Godolphin said in low tones, "remember? They hunted us down."

"Only because you waffled for a half hour trying to decide whether or not to go after them. Precious time wasted! Do you know how many times I've lain awake at night and wondered what might've been if you'd made the right decision, and we'd gotten away? I'd have *two* arms, I could've had a normal life, perhaps a woman might've fallen in love with me!"

"I've lain awake, too, Bertie, but I know it's not the same. I'm sorry."

Bertie stared down at him, now panting through his mouth. *Kill him. It'll feel so good, it's the only way to have a bit of relief. So what if the butler shoots me in the back? At least Godolphin will be dead, too.*

"You can have the ledgers," Godolphin told him. "You can go."

"What? And allow me set up a smuggling operation elsewhere, only to have you come and shut me down again?"

Confusion flickered across Godolphin's brow. "What do you—what's in the ledgers?"

"Every contact I'll ever need, that's what! Names, addresses, code words, for every arms and bootleg supplier on the Continent, every Russian jewel thief, every tomb

raider in Egypt and Persia, and every receiver in England!
Every inn that sells smuggled spirits, every collector who
buys stolen antiquities, every person who doesn't fancy
paying tariffs on his rifles or opium! Hundreds upon hundreds of contacts, three times more than I'd ever need!
Milton!" He laughed. "Milton! He was a master! The king
of smugglers! Richer than Midas! I made a deal with
him—he'd leave the ledgers in the warehouse if I convinced Hancock to pay that ridiculous price for the place.
Hancock agreed, but the wretch Milton forgot to give the
ledgers to me, and Hancock locked them up. Didn't even
know what they were! The fool!"

"Milton duped you, Bertie," Godolphin said. "There is
nothing in those ledgers except financial records belong-
ing to Hancock. Milton made a false promise to squeeze a
little extra profit in the sale of the warehouse."

Bertie choked on a gasp. This was too, too much,
Godolphin spewing outright lies as though he, Bertie,
would believe them. That was just it. Godolphin had
never treated him as an equal. Under the guise of nobil-
ity, compassion, friendship, was a profound, infuriating
snobbery.

Bertie stood there, fighting for his balance on the stair.
Everything drifted up, out of his chest, until all that remained was a molten core of hatred for Godolphin.

The ledgers were forgotten, they slipped from his fingers, tumbled down the stairs, pages fluttering.

Slowly, Bertie reached under his jacket for his pistol.

"Easy, Bertie," Godolphin said. He sounded so far away,
his voice buried beneath a rushing sound that was perhaps the sea. Buried under that piercing wail in his skull.

The snick of the butler's blunderbuss being cocked
pierced through these sounds. It barely registered.

Bertie's pistol was out, in his hand, but damn it, his
hand was shaking. He had a certain way of cocking the
hammer with his thumb, but it kept slipping. Hot in here.

Sweaty, which was odd, really, because the damp from the wall seeping through his jacket was so cold, so cold.

There. Hammer cocked.

Godolphin, raising his hand, as if to say stop. Bossy ass. Why didn't he duck behind the twist in the stairs and save himself? Oh, yes, because he's too *noble*. Can't be a coward, can we? Can't turn round and get away from the slave ship and save ourselves! Can't duck behind a wall instead of taking lead shot in the forehead!

Bertie aimed.

There was an ear-cracking explosion, and a shattering ricochet off the wall above Bertie's head. He started and had just enough time to glance down at his pistol in puzzlement, for the hammer was still cocked. As he lost his footing on the stair and staggered and groped forward into space, falling toward Godolphin, he realized that it had been the butler's gun that had gone off. Just before he slammed into Godolphin, the bastard stepped round the twist in the stair, and then the stone wall hurtled at Bertie, the pebbly texture of each stone rushing into precise focus. There was an impact of more force than he'd ever felt, and a cracking deep inside. And blackness.

At long last, the wailing in his head was gone.

Chapter Twenty-one

Forever Untamed

"Bravo!" Estella called, applauding the blackberry brambles' song. The villagers in attendance clapped and cheered loudly, making up for the small size of the audience. All the mothers were there, of course, but there weren't very many men. They were, Estella supposed, too ashamed to show their faces just yet. It would take some time.

The beaming children bowed, holding hands, and scampered off the dais. Pansy was visible through the curtains, herding the next troupe of pantomime performers onstage.

"Mrs. Lovely," Godolphin said in Estella's ear, "has the organizational skills of a military field commander."

Estella nodded. It was awkward, sitting with Godolphin like a proper earl and countess, when she knew she'd be leaving tomorrow for London. She'd stay with Lady Temple until the annulment was finalized, and until Mama and Papa returned from America. She hadn't discussed this with Godolphin. They'd avoided each other since Bertie's death two days ago, and mealtimes had been nearly silent, ponderous with unspoken words.

Her heart was heavy, now. She wanted to savor being by

Godolphin's side, because she knew it was the last time. At the same time, she *didn't* want to savor it, just because that might make it hurt all the more when they parted for good.

"I've something I want to show you," Godolphin told her during the intermission.

Estella furrowed her brow. "What is it?"

"Come."

She scowled.

"Or, rather, may I have the honor of your company?"

Why did he look so . . . nervous? He *never* looked nervous.

He led her through the villagers milling in the ballroom, and out onto the rear terrace that overlooked the sea.

"Oh my heavens," Estella breathed. "It's beautiful."

Every single star was out, handfuls of diamonds strewn across a black satin sheet of sky. Below, the sea rippled darkly. The crash of the surf was muted, but she felt its vibrations under her slippers.

Suddenly, though, the universe seemed too big, too frightening. She felt tiny and so, so alone. She drew her shawl close.

"I will always," Godolphin murmured, "think of you when I see the stars."

Estella continued to stare up, unable to look at him. She felt as though she were balanced on a delicate precipice, and she was afraid even to breathe.

"Which means," he went on, "that I'll either have to avoid looking at the night sky ever again, for fear of the pain it will bring, the memories . . ." His voice had drifted into gruffness. "The loss. My foolish mistakes." He stopped.

She kept her eyes fixed on the brightest star, one that hovered low on the dark horizon like a beacon of hope. Salty wind twined around them. "Or?" she finally said. She could barely hear her own voice.

"Or I could make you my wife. For real this time. Then I wouldn't suffer."

She felt blank inside, wiped clean, unable to think.

"Then," he said, "I'd be complete, I'd feel at home, with my friend, my lover. My wife."

The blankness rushed away, replaced by an enormous sob. Still, she couldn't tear her eyes from that low-slung star.

Then his arms were around her, solid, guarding, tender. Her face was tipped up to his, and when she looked into his eyes, all she could see was the same pure glimmer as starlight.

And the largest, silliest, cheek-cracking smile was stretched across her face.

"Will you do me the great honor," he said, "of being my wife?" He knelt before her, clasping both of her hands in his. "Marry me, Estella."

She was laughing, but tears were streaming down her cheeks, and all she could do for a moment was hang on to his warm fingers with all her might. *"Yes,"* she whispered, her nose sounding stuffy. She laughed. "Yes, Godolphin. I love you, I really do—but we are already wed."

He rose, pulling her close by her hands, kissing her hairline, her cheeks. "It wasn't done properly. For the wrong reasons. I swear on my life, though, that the second I laid eyes on you last summer in Brighton, I recognized something in you. That night, it was some dinner or musicale—I can't remember what, because everything was dimmer than you—I meant to stay only a moment to see an old friend, but *you* were there, and I stayed and stayed, and came back again the next day. And the next. I was drawn to you. To *you.* Your energy, your smile, your beauty, yes, even that spark of naughtiness that I hope never goes away. Even on our wedding night, when I was half-sick from the terrible thing I'd done, I still went to your bedchamber, madly hoping that I could just touch you for a moment. I was drawn to you like that, and that is completely separate from all the wrong reasons we were wed. But I've found the right reasons, Estella. I love you, and I want to start again. Just for the two of us. Here. Now."

She gazed up into his face. Though his features were shadowy, she knew them, loved them, so well, that it didn't matter. They would be forever imprinted in her mind.

"I marry thee, Estella," he said.

Her own voice was choked with tears, but she managed, "I marry thee, Godolphin. Truly."

He tipped his head to kiss her. When their mouths joined, it was as though their whole bodies merged, and the enormous dark universe around them became a warm blanket, no longer frightening and bleak. In his kiss, she was home, just as he'd said. He made her safe, and at the same time he made that vivid desire flame up.

"We mustn't," he said presently, pulling away, "be rude to our guests. The second act will start soon, with Timmy's appearance, and I don't want to delay it." He cupped her cheek with his palm.

She swayed into his touch. She always would. "Delay? Why not?" she asked.

"Because then it'll be that much longer I'll have to wait to take my new bride to my bed."

She laughed, wiping the last of her tears away. "Ravishment on the mind again?"

He grinned down at her through the darkness. "Naturally. Come, Countess." He proffered his arm. "Let us go in."

"*You* come!" Playfully, she proffered her own arm.

It was his turn to laugh. "I am certain," he said slowly, "there is some center boundary between us. On the count of three, we'll step toward each other, and then both of us shall be tamed."

"Or both of us shall remain forever untamed."

"Ah. I do like the sound of that. One."

"Two."

"Three."

They stepped toward each other, linked arms, and walked back into the light of the castle together.

Epilogue

From Madame Pettibonne's
Treatise on Canine Behavior,
Prepared Especially for the Lady Handler
Afterword

So, Dear Lady Reader, I leave you with a final word of advice: Treat your darling beast well, and he will return your love, admiration, and respect tenfold. For the true secret to happiness (and even longevity, though some do claim that ingesting curdled goat's milk stored in the belly of a yak will have much the same effect) is to give both love and respect most generously, and to graciously accept the same. And if this adulation is properly dished out upon a silver platter, and lapped up by the handsomest dog in all of Paris, well, so much the better!

And so, adieu, Lady Handler. I bid you many warm and frolicsome good nights.

Connie Mason

Highland Warrior

She is far too shapely to be a seasoned warrior, but she is just as deadly. As she engages him on the battlefield, Ross knows her for a MacKay, longtime enemies of his clan. Soon this flame-haired virago will be his wife, given to him by her father in a desperate effort to end generations of feuding. Of all her family, Gillian MacKay is the least willing to make peace. Her fiery temper challenges Ross's mastery while her lush body taunts his masculinity. Both politics and pride demand that he tame her, but he will do it his way—with a scorching seduction that will sweep away her defenses and win her heart.

CONNIE MASON

TO TEMPT A ROGUE

Kitty O'Shay has been living outside the law for years. Dressed as a boy, she joined the notorious Barton gang, robbing banks and stealing horses with no one the wiser of her true identity. Except their newest member: Ryan Delaney. He is the only one who sees through her charade.

Ryan has infiltrated the Barton gang, hoping to find some information on a dying man's missing illegitimate daughter. Little does Ryan know he'll find her *within* the group. Stealing Kitty away is easy; controlling his desire for the maddening vixen is not. Ryan thought his biggest problem would be convincing Kitty to visit the father she'd never known—until he realized he was in danger of losing his heart to the beauty.